ALSO BY FREDRIK NATH,
AVAILABLE FROM FINGERPRESS.CO.UK

The Cyclist—*World War II Series, part I*

Farewell Bergerac—*World War II Series, part II*

Francesca Pascal—*World War II Series, part III*

Galdir—A Slave's Tale—*Barbarian Warlord Saga, volume I*

ABOUT THE AUTHOR

Fredrik Nath is a full-time neurosurgeon based in the northeast of England. In his time, he has run twenty consecutive Great North Run half-marathons, trekked to 6000m in Nepal, and crossed the highest mountain pass in the world.

He began writing, like John Buchan, "because he ran out of penny-novels to read and felt he should write his own." Fred loves a good story, which is why he writes.

Catch Fred online at:

www.frednath.com

GALDIR REBEL OF THE NORTH

Fredrik Nath

FINGERPRESS LTD
LONDON

Galdir – Rebel of the North

ISBN (pbk): 978-1-908824-18-9

Published by Fingerpress Ltd

Production Editor: Matt Stephens
Production Manager: Michelle Stephens
Copy Editor: Madeleine Horobin
Editorial Assistant: Artica Ham

www.fingerpress.co.uk

To

Matt and Michelle
'Best in the Business'

Acknowledgement:
I would like to acknowledge the kind help and superb editing skill of Madeleine Horobin whose patience and skill have been of enormous value.

—Fredrik Nath

GALDIR

REBEL OF THE NORTH

BOOK I: THE WALL

CHAPTER 1

"Pleasure in the job puts perfection in the work"

— Marcus Aurelius

We rode north in the usual downpour behind two centuries of grumbling Roman legionaries. I could smell sweat and leather from them as their iron-studded sandals clicked and clattered on the slippery grey stones beneath their feet. They always marched in step too—an irritating trait for a cavalryman like me who had to follow behind. They were obsessed with keeping damned well to time, unlike my own warriors at home. My men had never complained like this lot, they had been true warriors; undisciplined it is true, but all heart when it came to fighting and dying for their Warlord—and die they did.

Chilly drops of rainwater meandered down the back of my neck as I rode and I realised with resignation I would have to oil my chain mail yet again in the evening. The shower came as no surprise, for it had rained every day since I Galdir, Warlord of the Franks, had come to this cold, wet country, three months before.

Galdir was not always my name you know, but what does a name matter anyway? It is only a label like "slave", like "Warlord", like "Auxiliary Cavalry Commander". It is the man inside who really matters, and in my case I was struggling to be anything I valued or esteemed, for I could never

3

now return home. In those days, my bitterness was as boundless and deep as the seas I had crossed to be there in Britannia. The Sarmatians too were far from their homes, north of the Roman wall, and I knew they felt the same as I did. What warriors in our place would not?

I had been the leader of the Franks, a small confederation of tribes now living in that part of Gaul where the Eburones used to live. Now I was only the displaced leader of a defeated people and far from home. My almost daily prayers and sacrifices to Wuotan, the Allfather, gave me little respite from the pain I was suffering deep inside. Defeat is hard for anyone. Perhaps I should have prayed to Loge the fire God and trickster instead, for I sometimes think he is the one who really moves my destiny.

It was the memories galling me. I rode and they kept coming into my head. I recalled a hayloft, for example, in the Dacian town of Lovosice, and a girl called Medana with long brown hair. I remembered how I had resented our betrothal. The king's niece, she had been as unwilling to wed me as I was to engage in the nuptials myself. The memory of her tears and the two gentle nights we had spent next to each other on the straw, created pangs of nostalgia. Memories of those sweet nights seemed to prod at my heart like a spear.

Through the curtain of sloping rain, the distant, rolling green hills were unwelcoming and seemed cold and bleak. A couple of magpies rose, startled by the sound of our approach, and disappeared into the morning haze layering in the still vales like steam on a boiling cauldron. I regarded those birds with envy: at least they could fly away.

There were only a hundred Sarmatians riding with me that day. We had left the other four hundred and fifty behind in Vindolanda with Lazygis, because our Tribune

4

decided greater numbers were unnecessary. Lazygis was my friend and a Sarmatian king in his own right. The Tribune might have been right, but who was he to tell me about fighting and war bands? I who had been Warlord, leading an army of forty thousand?

One of the two centuries was a group of Batavians; they were Germanic and auxiliaries like us. The others were Tungrians. Our Prefect was in command and we bore a vexillium with us, which the Romans regard very highly. It is a triangular flag, which represents part of a legion; the Romans call a war band like that a vexillation. In our present circumstances, I thought it was bordering on ridiculous to carry such an emblem. There were less than three hundred of us. It was as if our Tribune wanted to show we mattered. I knew though, we did not matter to the Romans; they only tolerated us, as we had to tolerate them.

Our orders were to locate a supposed rebellious village or tuath and burn it to the ground to discourage others from joining in a general revolt. They meant they would kill everyone. It was the usual way for the Romans to try to keep order on their borders, and nowhere more so than here, north of the wall they had built sixty years before, in the time of the Emperor Hadrianus. There were occasions when they ordered us to kill any Briton we saw north of the wall with no questions asked or explanations required. They never held a court-martial for a dead Briton. The locals were of no importance in the Roman scheme of things.

By noon, we were approaching a gully slashed out of the ground between two hills. The slopes were wooded and dark with a slight mist whispering and wavering at the tree line. My people call such mists 'the dance of the elves', for some say they can see the elves holding hands and dancing,

5

shrouded in the watery wisps of grey. Fanciful perhaps, but I clung to the Gods and legends of my homeland, for there was precious little else left for me to hang on to in those days, so far from home.

The rain had attenuated slightly, and it was now only drizzling; the air was windless and still. In the bottom of the gully was a small stream trickling and giggling merrily as we approached, but it made the going difficult for the infantry since the many rocks and boulders made it hard for them to maintain formation. I rode ahead to the front.

'Flavius Cerialis,' I said, 'can I have a word?'

Cerialis was the Legionary Prefect and that means he should have been back in Vindolanda, making use of the fact he was the highest-ranking officer in the entire Second Legion below Tribune. I thought he was there because he enjoyed this kind of work. He was a tough, ugly brute of a man who had fought his way to the top and his stubbly face looked up at me with a scowl. At first I had wondered if he always scowled, but I had seen him with the other members of the centurionate and he never scowled when he talked and joked with them. He was short of stature but built like a bull, broad, muscular and fearsome. His brown skin, hooked nose and black curly hair showed he was a real Roman. He had a scar on his left cheek, a relic of a former battle on the wall in the north, which the Romans had lost to the Caledonii and others, some twenty years before.

'What do you want Galdir?' he said.

'I just think this would be a good place for an ambush. Would you like my men to split up and sweep the hills either side, before the centuries enter the gully?'

'Yes, I think it would be a good idea. I thought the gully would be a good place for an ambush too. We will have to go through though. The Votadini village is on the other side of that hill.'

'You'll wait?'

'No, we'll continue, but I will depend on you and your men to rout any Brittunculi you come across.'

He grinned then for once, and I remained impassive for I never liked the disparaging nickname the Romans seemed to use for the Britons even to their faces.

He led the men forward and I and Panador, my second in command, each took half the men to scour the woods on either side.

We entered the wood spread out in a flat formation to cover as much ground as we could. We might come across a group of Selgovae or Votadini warriors any time and I wanted to be sure to find them before our infantry were too far into the defile. Our sweep was uneventful at first, and as the two centuries passed into the gully I was well aware they were particularly vulnerable if the Britons attacked from the misty wood. It all depended on whether or not we discovered an enemy before they attacked our men.

As we approached the trees I had mental pictures of riding before my own host of Franks. There had been more than forty thousand of us. I could see the final battle, my men attacking, vastly outnumbered by five Roman Legions arriving fresh to the battlefield. We had already defeated Licinius Piso and his army following a long siege. My mind often flashed back in that way since the defeat. The visions impinged on my dreams as well as my waking moments as if they were imprinted and I had to relive them in atonement for my failure. It had changed me too. My mood was low and I was seldom like the young man I had been in my twenties. No future you see.

Faces came to mind: friends, laughing and drinking. I pictured my warm and cheerful hall, buzzing with merriment and feasting. Was it now silent? Was it perhaps slumbering in the expectant deprivation of its Warlord like some hibernating bruin? I pictured Stator, who had known my father. He had been a fierce warrior in his own right and steadfast in his loyalty to me and to Frankia. He fell in that last battle. Losing men like him made my defeat even harder to bear. I saw the old face of Eudes, a king of my nation, and remembered how he had led a small band of re-grouped men against a wall of Roman shields and how he fell, sword in hand, as they hewed him. At least he will feast with Wuotan in the Allfather's long halls and will be there to welcome me when my turn comes as I hope it will one day.

The Votadini attacked before we made contact with them in the wood, so maybe Cerialis should have waited after all. The attackers were not like the Germans I was accustomed to march with at home. I was used to fighting with tall blonde warriors who looked and dressed like me. If there is one thing you learn in Germany it is to wrap up warm, for cold weather makes it difficult to move fast unless you spend time warming up. We have a saying at home: there is no bad weather only bad clothing.

The Britons fought wearing leggings or braccae as they called them, no armour and no clothing on the upper parts of their bodies. Some of them were completely naked, but I think they had battle-fury or some potion to keep them warm. They had blue dye streaked in different patterns across the exposed skin, even their faces. I wondered often at that time whether it was tattooing such as we did at home or whether it was war paint. They were wild, fierce people who, despite their lack of armour, moved fast and fought ferociously. The Romans called them Nudis, another disparaging nickname they used to make the locals feel diminished. They were an arrogant people the Romans.

There must have been about five or six hundred Votadini warriors; for them, it was a large war band. They had hidden in the woods and when they saw us riding through to search for them, they decided the game was up and they would have to attack. Cerialis reformed the men so the centuries were next to each other and they turned, so each was facing outwards towards the attacking foe. I had never seen a military manoeuvre accomplished so fast, and it took place before the first of the Nudis reached the wall of shields.

They attacked as the usual mass of fighting, screaming, jostling warriors they always became. The Romans kept formation, as Panador and I formed up our cavalry, either side of the stream running through the bottom of the gully.

Our assailants were not big men, though they were bigger than Romans. Some of them were huge but most came to shoulder height on me although I am a tall man. Mostly they were dark-haired but about one third of them had red hair. Red hair is unusual amongst my people, the Franks, and a little more common in the Chatti tribe at home, but there seemed to be more than the fair share among these half-naked warriors. They whooped and screamed in a fearsome way but the Romans had trained so as to ignore such things and they fought in strict silence. I always thought the quietness in their ranks was more daunting than war shouts, and if the Romans won a battle or skirmish it made their opposition look foolish; the legionaries knew it too.

The Romans maintained a wall of shields and began to push forward. The Votadini outnumbered them hopelessly

9

but, as is often the case, battle combat is a matter of technique rather than staunch warrior skills. There are times when the Romans fought battles with tiny numbers but defeated huge numbers of my people, and I had learned long ago that without strategy an army is a rabble and no more. I felt sorry for the Britons. I knew what they did not and I knew they would run in the end. It was a waste of men, for although they were brave they had not given enough thought to their plans. It was easy to see how the Romans had entered this land and walked right through it, the only limitations for them being their supply lines.

The Votadini had squashed together so tightly they could not swing their battle-axes and heavy swords. Each of them fought as an individual, seeking glory. The legionaries' gladii therefore made quick work of the front ranks. They had a particular technique with the short swords. They pushed with their shields and stabbed with their gladii and the opposition could do little apart from stand and die. They were falling in droves before the legionaries.

We started at a walk. Our speed gradually increased and we loosed a flight of arrows before we drew our long cavalry swords. We were on the attackers' flanks so they were using their shields in front of them, which made our volley particularly effective. When we hit the tribesmen we were cantering and the force of the impact was horrific. The mass of fighting and pushing barbarians shuddered as we rode into them. We were slashing to left and right, killing. Their lack of armour made us doubly effective. Although they fought back hard, they were no match for our horses who had kirtles of chain mail. My horse Valknir kicked and bit, as only a good warhorse could. I remember feeling proud of him. The Britons of course folded before our onslaught.

Even the warriors on the opposite side of us howled and ran. We rode among them. We slashed with our swords and felled any of them who dared to stand. It was a slaughter and it did nothing for pride or honour.

I found it hard to feel any enthusiasm for the fight because the Votadini stood little chance against heavy cavalry and they seemed to be the only ones who were in ignorance of that. I looked down at the stream. Its waters ran red now with the blood of the attackers. Once the escaping men had reached the tree line we left them to run. There was no point in taking our horses into the forest.

It was an odd little skirmish, mainly because it had been so short. The whole battle lasted thirty minutes from the time we entered the woods but at least a hundred of the attackers lay dead. We had only sustained light casualties, ten men dead and four wounded—none of them seriously.

I looked down at a naked Briton, his face obscured by blood where a sword had struck him. He lay still, his twisted body stiffening in the cold rain. I thought we had much in common, this dead warrior and me. We were both defeated killers, but the difference was that Rome had all but enslaved me. He had died defending his homeland. There had been times when I wished I too had gone that way but it was not to be. I could ill afford to show my true feelings to these rulers of the modern world. If I rebelled, they would kill all my own people. What choice had I?

Marcus Aurelius had said it himself: *'Kill for me or the Franks will vanish from the world forever.'*

I wanted to fight the Romans, not the Britons. I remember thinking, 'If only there were some way in which I could fight on their side'. My own people were far away and I had loyalties to the Sarmatians who would never change their allegiance for they had sworn an oath. We Germans take oaths seriously and I too had sworn, but it rankled. I also felt sorry for these blue-painted warriors. They fought so hard but they so were vulnerable even if the Romans had not had heavy cavalry. I thought someone ought to straighten them out; show them the way. Fighting legionaries requires discipline and the poor Brittunculi seemed to have none.

The Romans piled their dead near the stream and decided to burn the bodies on the way back. I knew this was because Cerialis thought there might be other bodies to burn. The centuries marched on.

We too rode on afterwards. I looked at the landscape around me and the similarity to my own German lands saddened me. The dense pine forest of home and the endless hills and mountains where we had made our strongholds forced themselves into my mind. All in Roman hands and rotting like the Britons' corpses, without men, without leaders and above all, without a future. With no Warlord to lead them, the Franks did not exist and I knew it.

An hour later, we came to the Votadini village. It was a round conglomeration of huts with thatched mud and wicker walls built around a central square. There could only have been about twenty families living there and I suspected the inhabitants had appealed to local chieftains to help, which was why the defenders who had attacked us earlier numbered as many as they did.

A palisade of sorts enclosed the village. It was the height of a tall man and not of sufficient size to have a wall walk from which to defend it. There was a throng of people at the gate, and looking at them I felt this was ridiculous. Half were women. The other half consisted of boys and old men.

'You know, Panador,' I said, 'there can be no honour in

fighting with such people.'

He looked at me sideways and grinned.

He said, 'What do you expect from Romans, they make us look civilised.'

I was glad he spoke in the common German tongue for none of the Romans would understand.

'I don't want to be part of this.'

'No, we can hang back, while our brave Roman comrades proceed to storm the place.'

Simple rustic gates blocked the entrance to the village and we watched as the legionaries pulled them down. Once inside, they began to kill anyone who moved, with no discrimination.

They call us Germans barbarians because some of the tribes indulge in torture. This is surely no worse than decapitating small children in front of their mothers, raping the women and then slitting their throats like these men were doing. The Romans say they are civilised, but I saw no hint of it that day. In disgust, I rode through the village and left by the already opened gate at the north end.

I was twenty yards from the tree line when I heard the scream. It sounded like a child.

CHAPTER II

I entered a small clearing opening off the edge of the forest. There were four of our men in the glade. On my left was a kneeling legionary, undoing his under-cloth beneath his tunic. The other three stood around in a semicircle and laughed. The object of their mirth was a girl. She could hardly have been more than ten or twelve years old and they had stripped her, ripping her clothes into rags left lying in a forlorn and meaningless heap beside her. She lay on the cold wet grass, her back against the knarled, green roots of a pine tree, regarding her captors with a look of abject horror. She whimpered as only a child in extremis can do.

She had red hair and her small white, nascent breasts heaved up and down rapidly as she whimpered in her panic. There was the faintest trace of red pubic hair she tried to cover with her hand and her other arm lay across her chest. The legionary who had discarded his under-cloth was kneeling and trying to force her legs apart and she screamed again, trying to fight him off.

I have a temper. I am not proud to be afflicted with that loss of control, but in battle, when released, it is fearsome and stands me in good stead. I also have a deep anger within me, expressed when I see something I regard as dishonoura-

14

ble.

The scene was almost familiar and the similarity to another occasion when I had to act did not escape me. I had seen a man attempting rape on a child before and had reacted. It had changed me, changed my life and destiny and thrust me onto a path from which I had never diverted. That girl had been Roman, her attacker had been Roman too and it had taken much to bring me to action and to kill, for I had been the man's slave at the time. Many things had happened since then but they had not blunted my temper. They say one becomes inured to such brutalities as rape, but not so in my case. Like all my people I have a sense of honour, and in particular raping children offends it. I knew why, for I had analysed it in my head many times. Roman soldiers had brutally killed my mother and it was the violation, its seeds rooted deep within me, giving me the rage—a rage sufficient to forget my surroundings and forget who I was. The crime I now witnessed drove me before it, thrusting me into violent action.

So that was why I dismounted with the speed of a diving hawk. I kicked the legionary full in the face. It was a forceful kick. It bruised my shin and dented my greave, but it was adequate to the task. It pitched him sideways and he did not get up.

'Hey, what the...' the snarling legionary nearest to me said. The expression on his face told me what he was thinking.

'Bloody Sarmatian, what do you think you're doing interfering? I'll kill you, you bastard,' one of the others said.

The third man was silent, and I thought he was the dangerous one. He had drawn his gladius. It is a fact, when a serious man wants to kill you he does not waste time talking about it.

'Have you no honour? What kind of men are you? Do you not see this is only a child?' I said, watching the third man out of the corner of my eye. He was sidling around to my right. The girl lay cradled in the arms of the tree roots, crying and trying to cover herself up now with the rags lying at her side. I stepped back. I drew my sword.

The Legionary to my right lunged at me as soon as he thought I was within range of his short weapon. I parried from right to left and with the same stroke, followed through in an upward movement. I stepped forward and as my blade rose in the air, I caught him a nasty blow on the chin with my sword hilt. I am a big strong man. He collapsed like a tent in a storm.

The other two had now drawn their weapons. They were approaching fast. They reached me together. They stabbed at me. I stepped back but caught my foot on a tree root. I staggered backwards. The one to my left saw his opportunity. He ran at me and lunged with his blade. Despite being unbalanced, I turned sideways. The weapon glided past me. I turned full circle to the right. My sword arm was out-stretched. It was not as forceful a blow as I am capable of, but I drew the blade in, two handed, as it contacted his neck. A sword is, after all, a cutting instrument not just a cudgel. If I had used more force it would have taken his head. As it was, it half did the job and he fell twitching and exsanguinating at my feet. His companion backed away. I could ill afford for him to escape and tell his fellows what I had done. I approached and he turned and ran.

I dropped my sword and leapt to Valknir, removing my bow. I am a good shot but I knew he was well ahead of me. I strung the bow fast. I nocked an arrow, calm and unhurried;

I drew the string. There was a soft twang as I released the missile. The bowstring was a little damp but it was not a long shot. I saw my missile fly straight to the mark. I could feel it was true as soon as I fired. The Roman fell halfway between the forest and the palisade. There was a lot of hate concentrated into the tip of my arrow. I confess I enjoyed the feeling as it sped to its target. I was aware then I would have killed a hundred of those Romans if I had been able. I recognised the feeling from before too. I ran to the man's side and extracted the arrow. It would have been obvious to whom it belonged. I left him where he lay and re-entered the clearing.

The girl lay still, propped against the damp, green moss of the tree roots, perhaps shocked. She buried her face in her rags. One of the legionaries was stirring. I could not afford for him to give evidence against me any more than I could his comrades. I knelt with my knee in his back and putting both hands under his chin I leaned back. There was a loud crack and I knew it was over. The last soldier was still unconscious. I swung my sword. I knew he would never testify against me unless of course some clever military surgeon could sew his head back onto his neck. I picked up the head by the hair and threw it ten yards away into the bushes. The Britons took heads you see, and his friends would probably not find it.

I removed the cloak from the man with the broken neck and held it out to the girl. She looked up, pupils widely dilated, like a terrified doe ready for the hunter's knife, but she remained immobile. I reached down and spread the cloak over her shivering little frame. She began whimpering pitifully. She was only a child.

I heard the noise of approaching men from the direction

17

of the palisade. They were laughing and calling out.

'Galba?' one voice shouted.

'Junius, you bastard where've you got to?' another said. Then there was silence as they discovered the body where I had felled it with the arrow.

I wrapped her in the cloak as fast as I could, picked her up and ran through the forest until I had moved perhaps two hundred yards into the thickest part of it. I tore my cloak on a gorse bush and almost knocked myself out banging my head on a tree branch, but I had her clasped firmly to me. The girl was limp in my arms and I wondered whether the soldiers had done her some physical damage too. There was certainly no blood staining the cloak. I found a clearing, stopped and listened. There were no sounds of pursuit. I could hear a blackbird high above me laughing, uncaring.

I put the girl down and kneeling beside her, stroked her brow. I smiled and said in the German common tongue, 'Don't worry you're safe now. I will not harm you.'

Pondering my next move I knew I could hardly leave her there. Anything could happen to her and I had to get back or they would miss me. I wasted precious moments wondering whether, if I left, one of her own people would find her, but I could not leave. I stood for a few minutes in a quandary.

I remained there, contemplating my options in the oppressive silence of the forest. Nothing stirred; I waited. What I thought might occur to me I have no idea, but I stayed where I was. All at once sounds of movement around the clearing startled me. Twigs broke, bushes rustled. With eye-blinking speed, about twenty blue-painted men emerged from different directions. Before I could draw my sword I had five spears prodding my ribs. I looked at my assailants. I realised they looked like the Nudis we had defeated at the stream.

'I saved her from the Romans,' I said in German.

A big, hairy, redheaded man approached; he seemed to be their leader for they gave way before him.

'You not Roman,' he said in my own tongue and pushed me roughly in the chest.

I stepped backwards, a spear-point pricking my shoulder blade, and said, 'You speak my language?'

'Yes.'

'She was attacked, I helped her. Ask her.'

He looked down at the girl. A frowning tempest showed on his bearded face, but she was silent, eyes shut. The big man raised a battle-axe above his head, his intentions clear. I thought the end had come.

Then the girl said something I did not understand. I looked down at her face; tears the size of lakes ran down her cheeks.

The big man lowered his axe in silence, a slow movement, his thoughts written all over his red-bearded face. He looked at me with curious eyes. They were blue and hard, looking out from a freckled countenance. I could feel my heart thumping beneath my vibrating ribs as if it wanted to escape, as he struck his broad chest with a closed fist.

'Oengus,' he said, 'my child. You go. Next time, I kill you.'

Such was my introduction to the Votadini; it was one I never forgot.

When I reached the clearing, there were legionaries all over it. They were dragging the bodies of their comrades away.

'What happened?' said Cerialis.

19

'About six or seven men. I gave chase but they got away.'

'You chased six men?'

'Maybe it was stupid, but I saw what they did to our noble comrades and I was angry.'

He looked at me, frowning. Then he smiled and slapped me hard on the back.

'There's more to you than meets the eye, Sarmatian.'

He was right. The slap on the back did not hurt for I was wearing chain mail. Besides, I had hidden my secret well and I am no Sarmatian either.

CHAPTER III

"Short is the joy that guilty pleasure brings"
—Euripides

When we first arrived in Britannia I met a man in a tavern in Lindum on the way north. He was a miller and we drank beer with him until late that night in the earth-floored tavern with the leaky roof.

'It's always wet in Britannia, except when it snows,' he laughed and said, 'even in the snow, it's damp.'

Neither Lazygis nor I could see the funny side of it since we had been unable to dry out at any time since we had arrived from Gaul. No amount of oil seemed to stop the rust appearing on our weapons and when you live in a leaky leather tent you never dry out.

It was spring now I supposed, but one could hardly tell from the weather, for it was cold and the evenings were still dark. I had been a slave in Rome, then a hanger-on in my uncle's court among the Franks. I succeeded him and we moved the entire Frankish nation across the Rhine where we had formed the new land of Frankia. Establishing that place as our own had been my hope of a bright new future for the Franks. The Gods willed it otherwise and they left me with the legacy of that foundered hope.

Our Legate, Marcus Licinius Piso, had sent for us. We crossed the field in which we had encamped, neither of us expecting the meeting to be pleasurable. I was always re-

21

lieved Piso never made the connection between my escape from Rome and his father's death, but how could he? He could never have known that Sextus, the escaped slave and Galdir the Warlord could be the same person. There was an odd satisfaction in the knowledge. I knew something he did not and it made a fool of him in my eyes. Even better, I had slept with his wife.

We may have been damp and cold but we were in good spirits for we had been lucky in our hunting the day before. Lazygis had killed four pheasants with his bow and I had taken down a boar with a heavy spear. We had feasted most of the night away, drinking vinegary wine and beer and eating wild boar, a meat so succulent I can recall the flavour even now.

The military road ran behind the wall throughout its entire length, hard and flat underfoot. Two oystercatchers flew up in front of us, though what they were doing so far from the sea I could not envisage. I could smell food cooking as we walked up the slope leading to the General's quarters. It nauseated me, for we had over-indulged somewhat the night before and I have always been intolerant of beer. The rain had eased to a faint drizzle, but the morning sky was a uniform grey above us and the smell of the food became attenuated by the damp odour of my cloak, greased as it was with goose-fat to keep out the water.

'Wonder what he wants us for,' I said.

'Nothing nice, of that we can be certain,' Lazygis said.

'Probably just another mission, to kill more of these poor Britons. I often wish I could fight on their side.'

'You would be breaking your oath. Do you not fear your Gods?'

'Of course I do, but there are times when they would

forgive, especially when it means fighting the Romans who don't believe in the same Gods as I do anyway.'

'Galdir, an oath is an oath. You swore on your Gods, not theirs.'

I was silent for a moment for I had no arguments to mount.

'Piso has never given us orders in person before. This might mean bad news,' I said.

'Is it the first time you have spoken to him since the battle?'

'Yes but he's looked at me.'

'Well looks can't kill. Anyway, we have the Emperor's protection.'

'It won't stop him from exacting revenge in some way.'

'Maybe not,' Lazygis said.

We did not speak again until we mounted the steps of the Praetorium where Piso had his command post. It was an extension of the largest mile-castle where they had built a wide courtyard at the gates. At the opposite end from the wall there was a large single-storey building next to a granary, big enough for it to have several rooms. There was a guardhouse on the other side from the granary and an orderly stood outside when we approached.

'You the Sarmatians?'

I did not bother to correct him, so I said, 'Yes.'

'You're late. The General was expecting you half an hour ago.'

'We only received the message then.'

'Well, all the same, he's been waiting. Mind your tongues when you see him and be respectful even if you can't be civilised.'

I felt like striking him, but controlled it because we were

all on the same side and I knew he could not help his ignorance and rudeness.

The steps led up to a corridor with several doors into
rooms whose contents I could only guess. The orderly led us
into the second one on the left where there was a desk and a
brazier burning red and hot. The room had a stuffy, damp
smell. Behind the desk, facing away from us was the General. He was sitting looking out of a window with a grey
linen drape partially obscuring the view beyond the open
shutters. He had his feet up on a chair, warming them by the
brazier and he did not look round at first.

Eventually he stood and turned to look at us. From the
expression he bore we could have been two unusual fish in a
tank. That he had no respect was written all over his face.
Even though I had beaten the four Legions he had commanded, he still looked down on me and I knew it.

He was a man in his mid-thirties, which had always surprised me, for his brother Lucius had been seven when I had
escaped Rome some twelve years before. I assumed he was
born of a different mother, but the face was that of his
father. He was lean and handsome with dark-brown, curly
hair and a beak of a nose like an eagle. His sunburn had
faded since coming here and he bore a sour expression as if
the bitterness of his defeat was beginning to gnaw at him, as
I wanted it to. He had voiced his irritation with Marcus
Aurelius' decision to spare my life and those of the Franks.
The Emperor expressed his too—he sent Piso to the north of
the most barbaric province in his domain, but perhaps that
was only the way I read it. The mind often sees what it
wants, in particular when the facts are unknown to us.

'You're late,' he said, lips tight.

'Noble General, we came as soon as we received your

summons,' Lazygis said.

'You're late nonetheless. Remain standing,' he said; he sat down and pushed the chair back so he could look up at us without straining.

Neither Lazygis nor I spoke. There was nothing to say. He studied our faces and I wondered if he was also uncertain what to say to us. I knew if I drew my blade I could cut his throat in the same movement and it gave me satisfaction—childish, as it might seem. He remained like that for a few minutes, staring at our faces. I stared right back at him. I was not afraid. He was trying to intimidate us and I was not about to cooperate. I felt I knew more than he did about the important things in his life, his wife, his father.

He said, 'I need you both to take some despatches to Cataractonium in the south. It is a matter of a two-day ride. The despatches are important, which is why I am sending you two. You both speak Latin unlike most of your rabble.'

'Yes sir,' I said.

It was as if hearing my voice was a trigger. He frowned and I could see thunder on the horizon of his glare. He curled his lip when he spoke and I knew then I should have remained silent, although I suspect he would have said what he wanted whether I spoke or not. He was that sort of man.

'Don't use that tone of voice with me. You two are little people now. You command nothing but a gang of mounted Scythians and you are only alive because of the infinite mercy of the Emperor. If I had been granted my wish, you would both be hanging from crosses on some hill in Gaul.'

'Sarmatians sir, not Scythians,' I said.

'What?'

'Our men are Sarmatians, they are quite different.'

'You filthy barbarians, you all look the same to me. You

25

think you are in a position to teach me? Another word out of you and I will have you put in chains.'

'I only...'

'Enough. You will pick up the despatches in the morning and take them to the General's quarters in Cataractonium. Now get out, you filth.'

I smiled at him. I had nothing to lose. He hated me but I should have known better than to goad him. He had the power and I was a nothing to him or to anyone else for that matter, but I still had pride. It had never died and I did not want him to think he could demoralise me further. Anyway, I had slept with his wife.

'What are you grinning at you barbarian ape?'

'I was being polite. Is there a problem?'

'Problem? Problem? Yes there is a fucking problem—you. You are the fucking problem. By Jupiter Optimus Maximus, I could have you crucified and if you cheek me again I will do it—written contract with Marcus Aurelius or not. Do you understand me?'

'Only too well sir,' I said, serious now. Our eyes met for one instant. There was enough emotion in that glance to light a fire.

'One of your people killed my father. You waged war against Rome. I will never stop. Never stop, do you hear? You even took my wife prisoner and held her hostage. Do you think you won't be made to pay? Well, you will pay and I will be the one to make sure it happens.'

'May I go now sir?' I said. Lazygis glanced sidelong at me. It was fleeting, but I read the warning.

'Get out,' he said, his voice controlled and even.

We turned around and left the building, then stopped outside. I noticed my heart was beating fast and I realised with pride I had kept control, despite my rising tension. It was not like my old self. My temper usually gets the better of me. Keeping an even temper had been my way of showing Piso I would not yield to his bullying, or at least I would not fold. I would bend in the wind of his hatred and not fracture like some rigid fool.

'What did you goad him like that for?' Lazygis said.

'He irritates me. I defeated him.'

'Didn't stop the fresh Romans from wiping out your men. He was on the victorious side and he knows it. If you annoy him enough I have no doubt he can crucify you for insubordination,' Lazygis said, his Sarmatian accent stronger than before. I thought perhaps he had been as emotional as me and it explained his silence.

'I wish the Britons would unite under a great leader and wipe them all out. For the price of a good meal I'd do it myself.'

'Do you know what sedition is? Keep your voice down.'

'All right, all right. I'll watch what I say. Back to the camp?'

The Roman wall has good defensible forts at one-mile intervals with two towers between each. Their problem was the wall's defence depended mainly on locals, conscripted into the Roman army and a few cohorts of auxiliaries like us. One cohort even had 'Tungra' attached to its name making it obvious most of them were from Germania Superior. You would never have known it though: they spoke Latin all the time. They were neither Romans nor Germans now; they had no pride in their heritage. I knew I could never become like them, I still had my pride and sense of identity.

Lazygis had reacted to defeat differently from me. He had responded to the annihilation of his nation, his friends and family, by developing a death wish. When he fought, it was without care—without defending himself. He could ride into a mob of Britons slashing from side to side with his spear or sword, killing many, and he always escaped unscathed. I envied him that in many respects. His life had been so shattered he felt little. He at least still had his countrymen around him. I had no one. The Romans had destroyed my own cavalry to a man and what remained of my infantry, they sent far away, leaderless and hopeless. For a man like me, making me ride with despatches, however important they may have been to the Romans, was ignominious. Piso was exacting his revenge, and although I hated him, his feelings for us were the main driving force of our very existence here in this strange land. He was determined to make us miserable in every respect, as indeed he could, for he had power of life or death in this part of Britannia. Though despite his efforts, he had not entirely succeeded in crushing our spirit. Lazygis had a sense of humour like mine. We often laughed together in our bitterness. We often laughed at the Romans too, and their very rigidity which made them so well suited to our humour.

That night, we sat in a tavern in Vindolanda drinking beer. There was no decent wine to be had in this establishment but I was certain the Romans would have some. They seldom went without any kind of creature comforts. Some of the legionaries even had socks sent from home.

'I keep thinking about that last battle, Galdir,' Lazygis said.

'Me too. I wish I had known what we were up against.'

'No, that wasn't what I meant. I keep thinking about who survived and who didn't.'

'What do you mean?'

'Well, we were six hundred Sarmatians. All of us were riding to our deaths and believe me we looked forward to it. Only fifty of my men fell and the rest are with us now. Of your army of forty thousand only half remained alive and they are now fighting in some eastern war.'

'Your point?'

'Ma moves in strange ways,' he said referring to the chief Sarmatian deity and looking thoughtful. 'It should have been us who died and we didn't.'

'Eudes died, so did Stator even Chilperic. Every one of our leaders apart from me went to Valhalla to feast with Wuotan. All it has left behind is my abhorrence of everything Roman.'

'All things?'

'Yes.'

'What about that woman?' he said.

'Woman?'

'Yes that Roman woman you made such passionate love to when we were in the hills?' He was teasing me.

'After I gave her back to Piso she must have remained in the Roman camp. He doesn't know I made love to her. If he did, he really would have me crucified. She was his wife after all.'

'She in Rome now?'

'No, he brought her with him.'

Lazygis smiled a knowing smile.

'So maybe you will see her?'

'No. I saw her in Eburacum—that time when we had to escort Piso there. I know she saw me.'

'What happened?'

'She looked me in the eyes and I looked at her. She smiled.'

I was silent for a moment then said, 'I wanted her. You have no idea how much I wanted her. There is of course no way I could ever have a moment alone with her now.'

'Pity.'

'Yes, she is a beautiful creature. I... I was fond of her even if she was Roman.'

'I know,' he said drinking a long draught from his ale horn.

I nudged my companion and smiled, 'When we made love, she scratched my back with her nails. She actually drew blood. It was delicious. I have never known anyone like her. What do you think of a woman who would do that?'

'I could scratch your back with my sword if you like.'

'Hardly the same thing.'

We laughed and the humour was a release for we were both down and unhappy. We drank more beer. It made me maudlin and flatulent and I went to bed early, leaving Lazygis talking to a group of Selgovae traders.

My head hit my cloak folded over my boots, and I tried to sleep. Recurring thoughts of what I had been through in the last years kept prodding me and in the end I sat up, sleep elusive.

Living at Vindolanda was dull. I had come to Britannia expecting to be in wars, fighting for my new Roman masters. What did I find? I was on garrison duty and there were no barbarian armies to fight. I am a sort of barbarian myself of course, but my master in Rome, had made me have an education. He did it, not out of kindness but for a bet. He learned that one cannot entirely trust education as a means of subduing a barbarian's natural sense of honour. It was the last thing he ever learned. I still smiled at the thought.

The education I had received made me feel different

from the Sarmatians. Their writing was crude compared to Greek or Latin and only one or two of them could use even their own runic script. We Franks have our own runes but they are nothing like the symbols the Sarmatians put onto their embroidered badges and cut into their blades.

I had fought in battles with hundreds of thousands of men who had struggled, killed and died with honour. To be here for the rest of my days in a tiny group of sad Sarmatians was pushing me close to despair. I muttered a prayer to Wuotan and wished it could all have been different, but the Gods do as they wish, not as we pray.

CHAPTER IV

"Waste not fresh tears over old griefs"
—Euripides

Lazygis had a thin, black, droopy moustache and black braided hair. His almond shaped eyes slanted a little, for the Sarmatians are of eastern descent. His dark eyes were sharp and clear and he had the best horse-archer skills I had ever seen. Although I am a fair shot with a composite bow even on horseback I could never come close to his accuracy. He was a wonderful horseman too. His whole life was devoted to caring for his horses and when it came to breaking in a wild horse, he had techniques I had never seen before. It takes a certain kind of man to be one with a horse. My mentor Cornelius, who taught me to fight was one such. He could talk to a horse in a way which could persuade it to fly, well almost.

We rode hard in the rain to Cataractonium and delivered the despatches. They gave us more to take back and we rested there for only one night. In all it was a four-day trip and it was the only time either of us had been away from the cavalry under our command.

The sun was shining for the first time in recorded history as far as I could see when we returned but we did not dawdle. We stopped first at our Tribune's quarters. His name was Appius Claudius Pulcher. Piso had put him in charge of us as liaison officer. He was friendly but barely competent. Only a young man, he had no experience of fighting at all.

We knocked on the door. The wooden hut was much the same as all the others the Romans built in their permanent camps. There was one storey, and a short corridor separated two rooms, one for sleeping and the other for working. Appius bade us enter and we walked in smartly, helmets in our hands. He sat at a table and looked up when we entered.

'Galdir. Lazygis. How good to see you both.'

A nervous smile flitted across his lips, as if he was ill at ease. He was only in his twenties, a tall angular boy. He had dark brown curly hair and a clean-shaven face, which made him appear even younger than his years. Nature had thus been a little unkind to him, because when trying to order the likes of us around it put him at a distinct disadvantage; we were after all, seasoned veteran fighting men in our thirties.

'We have despatches,' Lazygis said, placing the brown leather cylinder on the table.

'Well before I read them, I need to tell you about some changes since you two left.'

'Changes?' I said.

'Yes, the Legate has decided to redistribute the heavy cavalry so as to increase the spread of protection to the wall.'

Lazygis said, 'What do you mean by spread?'

'Well,' the Tribune said looking down at the desk, 'it's like this. General Piso decided the discipline among your men was not what he considered adequate and he thought they might pose a threat if they all stuck together. Five hundred and fifty heavy cavalry is a big force.'

'We were divided into two Ala by the Governor. Any smaller groups would make them ineffective as a fighting force. The power of heavy cavalry is lost if you have too few,' I said.

'Well all the same, the General decided some of your men might be better employed as infantry.'

'Infantry!' Lazygis exploded. The despatches jumped as his fist struck the table. Pulcher, startled, threw himself back and almost cockled over in his chair.

'You can't do this,' I said in alarm. 'They are Sarmatian horse archers. They would be no use as infantry. No one else can do the things they do on a horse.'

'Well they will have to do it on foot now. Sorry. We had a request for two hundred and fifty horses from the commander of the equites and the Legate decided to give them yours. Look, I'm sorry; there is nothing I can do about it.'

'What about the other three hundred?' Lazygis said.

I recognised the cold edge to his voice and I thought I would somehow need to prevent him from killing this imbecile.

'Well, the Legate felt dividing them each into turmae would be the best thing to do. A turma is about thirty men so there are ten of them now. One is based at each fort as far as we could divide them up, going west from here.'

'But most of them can't speak Latin. There were only four others apart from me who speak any foreign language and those four only spoke the common German tongue. How will anyone ever command them? It's ridiculous,' Lazygis said.

'So that's why the General sent us to Cataractonium is it?' I said, 'He wanted to make sure we didn't cause a problem.'

Pulcher lowered his voice. He looked miserable. 'Look I'm really sorry. There was nothing I could do. I'm just a very junior officer and although I know you're right I can't argue with Legate Piso if he's made up his mind. If you must know, I haven't come out of this very well either. They've sent me to Eburacum to play nursemaid to a bunch of Numidian horsemen who don't speak any Latin at all.'

'I will appeal to the Governor,' Lazygis said.

'Won't help. You would have to go all the way to Londinium and I have strict instructions to confine you both to base here on the wall. I'm sorry but I have my orders and I have to follow them. I'm only a soldier you know.'

'You realise,' I said, 'your General has just disbanded the best fighting force he had in this army? Separated in small groups they won't be effective and worse, they can't be commanded because they won't understand the orders. You have to do something.'

'What? I can't disobey a direct order. I don't understand why he's done this, but like I said, there's nothing I can do.'

'You could take a message to the Governor.'

'Me? I can't go behind my Legate's back. I would be court martialed.'

'You could send a despatch.'

'And say what? My Legate has gone mad?'

'Well it would be a start. No, I want you to send it for us but just make sure it gets there. That's all.'

'You want me to write it for you?'

'No I'll write it,' I said.

'You can write?'

'Yes,' I said, feeling impatient.

'Well I suppose it won't do any harm to try. Here, you can use my table.'

I began to write on the bleached papyrus. Someone had used it before and had removed the old ink by soaking it in vinegar or urine.

'Hey, that's Greek isn't it?' Appius said.

35

'Yes.' I was having difficulty remembering the word for 'unwise' so I wrote 'foolish' instead.

'I didn't realise you could write Greek,' he said.

Lazygis was staring at the ceiling. I knew he was wondering whether to use his sword or his knife.

'You didn't ask,' I said. I was not in the mood for pleasantries.

'Well, I didn't expect...'

'Here,' I said, handing him the document. He read it through and picked up the despatch container from Cataractonium. He emptied out the despatches we had brought and placed my letter into it and left the room.

'Lazygis, you can't kill him.'

'Why? Even their famous Julius Caesar was known to kill the messenger on occasion.'

'What?'

'Forget it,' he said, 'I won't kill anyone, but my men will feel I have let them down. They will feel betrayed after all we have been through, to end up here and then split up into little groups. The ones who they want to use as infantry will be suicidal.'

'I know, I explained that in the letter to the Governor.'

Pulcher returned. He walked smartly in, with a smile on his foolish face. I wanted to hit him. I think it was then I realised I was on the wrong side. If I could leave and join the warring Briton tribes fighting these arrogant Romans, I would have. What stopped me was my oath. A promise made to my Gods. The Gods punish oath-breakers, but what if the oath is against their wishes? The thought disappeared as quickly as it had come—daydreams are like that.

'Well, I've sent your message by despatch rider and it should only take about a week. I made sure he would give it to the Governor personally and it is marked urgent.'

'Don't you want to read the message from the Tribune in Cataractonium?'

'Oh, yes. I was so emotional about all this I clean forgot.'

He picked up the despatch. He read silently, moving his lips like a woman spooning food into an infant's mouth. He lowered the document and stared straight ahead.

'Jupiter Optimus Maximus,' he said to no one in particular, 'I have to get this to the Legate at once.'

He pushed past me and all but ran out of the door.

'Wonder what that was all about,' Lazygis said.

CHAPTER V

"Put more trust in nobility of character than in an oath"
—Solon

Even the sunshine failed to raise our spirits as we left the Tribune's hut. My heavy sandals were clogged with mud and I was still damp, but the best way to dry my cloak seemed to be to wear it. Dejected and disappointed we took ourselves to the area where our men had been camped and it was, of course, empty. A wide field of cold, trampled stodgy clay was all that remained. I looked at my companion, he was as depressed as I was and neither of us knew what to do next. We had no orders and no men to lead. It was exactly where Piso wanted us.

I walked across the field, stepping past the horse dung. The dung made me feel even sadder, as if it were some melancholy remnant of a beautiful thing. It was too, in a way. The Sarmatians I had brought with me were the last remnant of their migration. The entire nation, driven west by even fiercer foes in the east, had crossed into Pannonia and when Marcus Aurelius defeated them he annihilated most of the soldiers, women and children indiscriminately. Lazygis had fled with a thousand men but they were not even a tithe of the army to which they had belonged. It seemed to me the only remains of a once great and proud people was a pile of horse manure on a field in Britannia and it made me wonder if all nations end like that.

'What are we supposed to do now?'

'No idea, we seem to be as much use on our own as a cart with no horse.'

'Speaking of horses, the Sarmatian horses won't be of any use to the equites. They won't respond to their commands and they aren't used to Roman saddles. It will be worse than if they never sent us here,' Lazygis said.

'I know; that's what I told the Governor in my letter. The fact I wrote it in Greek was designed to make sure it was only read by an officer and I hope it will be the Governor himself.'

'Do you think the message will get through?'

'I suppose even Pulcher could be trusted to send a message.'

'Don't count on it. He's an imbecile.'

'What do we do now?' I said.

'No idea. Two armed Sarmatians are of no use on their own if we are attacked.'

'No, but we can ride with the Roman cavalry.' I said. We were silent then. We had killed a pheasant on the road home and Lazygis set about roasting it.

I felt as if my whole life had stalled. It was hopeless—as if I had risen to power among my people for no reason at all. There was nothing of any substance left in my life, nothing to which I could look forward. I came to realise that losing a battle and surviving afterwards was a warrior's worst outcome. You never really recover. The defeat stays with you like some festering mental ulcer, never healing. Even my Gods had deserted me and my dreams were always full of unhappy events.

*

Lazygis and I stood side by side on the wall. To our left was the tower of the mile castle at Arbeia. The sun was shining which despite all that had happened, raised my spirits as nothing else could. We looked out across the vallum below. It fell away into the fosse, a deep ditch, dug out on the northern side.

'Look,' I said, pointing to a rabbit sitting on the edge of the vallum below. He seemed not to mind all the military activity on the opposite side of the wall, munching quietly on some grass, and I was tempted to shoot him for our midday meal, which the Romans call 'prandium'. The Romans have a special name for every meal, which is good for them, but if you don't know the names in the Legion, you don't get fed. No wonder the only Latin names the Sarmatians spoke were to do with meal-times.

I was stringing my bow when Lazygis said, 'Leave him, poor fellow. He has not much peace left. I think this place will be awash with blood soon enough.'

'Aren't you hungry?' I said.

'Well we've just had the weekly corn ration. We can hunt a little after we've eaten. I just like the look of the rabbit. He seems at peace with the world.'

'I don't understand you. One minute you want to kill the Tribune, next minute, you baulk at killing a rabbit.'

We waited around all the next afternoon. No one spoke to us for Piso had not assigned us to any particular force. After lying down next to Valknir for two hours, lost in thought about the Roman woman I had no access to, I stood up. The whole life I endured on the wall was boring. There was nothing for a man to do. The more time I had to think, the more angry I became. I was getting desperate.

We walked to the cavalry Legate's quarters. He had a room in the Praetorium where the overall commander lived with his family and slaves. We knocked on the door and a slave opened it. He looked like a Votadini, with dark hair, small features and a drooping moustache.

The commander of the cavalry was a Tribune and he was unusually pleasant. His name was Clodius Super.

'Well, you two must be the remains of our Sarmatians,' he said with a broad smile.

'You think it's funny?' Lazygis said frowning.

'Funny?' he said. 'No, but I think it is bloody laughable. I asked him for more horses to be sent up from Eburacum, not stolen from your men you know. To have two ala of Sarmatian heavy cavalry and give half their horses away can only be described as risible.'

'At least we agree on something,' I said.

'What can I do for you? I must say I wish there were more than two of you,' he said.

'A little less than we do, don't you think?' Lazygis said.

'Yes, well...'

'We came to ask if we can ride with you and your men if there is a fight. We can't stay here after all,' Lazygis said.

'Of course you can. You are most welcome. Please sit down. Wine?' he said. Turning to the slave he said, 'Ciniod, wine for the barbarian commanders please.'

Ciniod bowed his head and left the room.

'He's a Votadini. If you treat them kindly, they do as you ask. If you try to be unpleasant to them they do nothing right. A fool is created not born you know. One of those things, don't you think?'

I had no idea what to say. Ciniod was a man like me. I

41

had been a slave in Rome as a child and it was the worst experience of my life. I had to endure forced boredom and still pay enough attention to respond immediately to a master's call. If I was tardy, I was whipped.

'I'm sure you're right,' I said.

Lazygis said nothing but studied our host closely.

'What?' Clodius Super said.

'I apologise, I have never met a polite Roman before, that's all.'

'You shouldn't insult your host. That's impolite in itself.'

'My friend does not mean to offend,' I said. 'He is a Sarmatian and takes to the treatment he has had from some of your colleagues, badly.'

'I understand. Some of the men don't quite understand who they are dealing with. I heard about you in particular.'

'Oh?' I said.

'Yes, I heard you defeated four legions under Piso and that was why he hates you so much.'

'Yes,' Lazygis said.

'No it isn't that. It's because his father was killed by a German and he hates us all for that,' I said.

The wine arrived. We drank a cup each.

'Beautiful wine, sir,' I said, 'it reminds me of a vintage from Surento I purchased in Dacia, many years ago, it had the same aroma of cherries.'

Lazygis looked at me in disgust. He could see I was showing off.

'Well I don't know about that,' Clodius Superior said, 'it's just wine to me.'

'Ah,' I said realising the stupidity of my posturing.

'Perhaps they will attack tomorrow,' Lazygis said.

'Yes, that seems to be the likely thing. It's getting late

now and will be dark soon. They don't often fight at night,' the Tribune said.

We talked some more about our circumstances and the fight at Sicambra and it was dark by the time we left.

It meant retiring to bed early again but we had ridden hard to get there and I think we were both tired.

'Galdir?' Lazygis said as I was dropping off.

'What?'

'Could you really taste cherries on that wine?'

'Yes of course,' I lied.

'Oh.'

'Why?'

'I just wondered. It tasted of grapes to me.'

'If it tasted of grapes it means the entire vinification process was wasted on you,' I said, a trace of indignation creeping into my voice.

'Yes, you are probably right,'

He went quiet, and seconds later was snoring. Left alone with my thoughts my mind drifted back to Livia who was my first love. She was the niece of the man who taught me to fight. Had she lived I would never have looked at another woman. A Roman brigand killed her and it was yet another reason for me to hate the Romans. She had not visited me in my dreams for months and I thought it strange I should think of her now, on the eve of a battle. Perhaps it was a warning. It is often strange how the mind plays tricks when tension descends.

CHAPTER VI

"If all men were just, there would be no need
for valour"
—Agesilaus II

Fire arrows are not what they seem. The arrow does not burn. It is the wick, tied around the shaft burning. The arrow remains as effective as if it was not aflame. My first waking thought was the camp was on fire. It was a ridiculous thought because there was only Lazygis sharing a tent with me, so when it caught fire my impression of a major fire were foolish. I awoke to the feeling of heat on my face and as my eyes opened, the brilliance of the flames dazzled me. I wonder sometimes how the damp leather could catch fire but it happened that way.

We both seemed to awaken at the same instant and rolled off our straw palettes. We crawled out of the burning tent and I had to dowse flames on Lazygis' back with my bare hands.

'I think they have started early,' Lazygis said, as he reached into the conflagration that was our tent, for his sword. I had left mine near the entrance too and was able to retrieve it but I lost my cloak and saddlebags.

For a few moments, we stood and looked at our burning tent as if it were some funeral pyre over which we should grieve. In one sense, I did grieve over the cloak for I was dressed in my chain mail and tunic and had no other clothes. All else had gone up in smoke.

I looked across the field in which we had camped. The roof of the left hand turret was on fire and so was the roof of one of the granaries. Fire arrows flew all around and we knew action would follow. Retribution from the Romans would be swift. We ran to our horses. I had to saddle Valknir in a hurry and he seemed displeased with the sudden rush, requiring him to stand still what with all the surrounding action. I patted his neck, and spoke low and slowly to him and he calmed. We put our feet in the stirrups almost simultaneously and rode towards where we could see the equites gathering. We sat still in the saddle then for there was no action from the Roman Garrison.

We had not long to wait. The arrows flew and most of them carried an incendiary wrapping of straw soaked in pitch. The roof of the right hand turret caught fire and they ordered out the cavalry to dispose of the archers.

The archway was narrow and as we were not part of the equites we had to tag on behind. It took precious minutes for us all to exit and the infantry followed us immediately. They were a whole cohort of five hundred men and as I rode out, I wondered how many we faced.

Not far from the gate was a crowd of archers. I could see no one else but knew quite well, there would be more. They numbered about five hundred men and continued to fire missiles over the wall. When they saw us they began to target us as well, but they were not concerted volleys; they seemed to have no discipline. We rode towards them and they began to run. A man on foot stands little chance against a mounted man especially if they have no armour and they only have bows. We rode among them dealing out death at will. I used my sword to good effect and swinging it alternately to left and right managed to kill a number of the bowmen. We pulled up short as soon as we reached the crest of the glacis. What I saw made me whistle. I looked out upon a sea of adversaries and I realised this was no ordinary rebellious attack. It was a full-scale uprising. There were thousands of men all with shields and spears. The equites turned, having despatched the archers and we withdrew to the side of our infantry. The Tungrians advanced undaunted. We had two turmae of cavalry and it meant there were only sixty or so mounted men.

What I would have given then for three hundred mounted Sarmatians. We could have routed them in one charge.

As it was, the Tungrians mounted the crest of the glacis and stopped, perhaps perturbed by the numbers they were facing. The delay was only for about a minute. They marched on. They were in typical staggered ranks and as soon as they came within range, they launched their pilae. These javelins were of different weights. The front rank had the heaviest and the rear ranks had lighter missiles. They launched them together and most landed in close proximity. Hundreds of the unarmoured enemy fell. The legionaries pressed on.

They began to fight in the way they always did and the front ranks of the rebels began to die. It came as no surprise that few Romans fell. They were heavily armed and armoured and they could certainly fight, whether they were honourable or not.

Our troop of equites rode out on our right flank. The idea was to hit the enemy once the Tungrians had engaged with them. We were only sixty or seventy men and only lightly armoured. I could not help thinking the Romans needed to update their saddles, for they had no stirrups and the chance of an equitus falling was high. We waited. The Votadini were falling back already and at that moment, we rode. There are psychological factors in battle, which can often give the smallest army confidence to attack and thus it was with us then.

We rode into the Votadini. It was a slaughter. We turned and backed off, resting our horses. The Tungrians fell back as well and formed up again, in two staggered lines of centuries on the earth wall of the glacis. The stupid Britons then thought they were retreating and they came on to attack again. Although almost a hundred of our infantry had fallen, our men stood still waiting for the enemy to charge.

We turned and reformed. We waited. A blown horse cannot charge, so we needed to preserve the strength of our mounts. The Votadini ignored us. They moved en masse towards the Tungrians and ran at them. It was foolish for them to attempt to take on the Romans in that way. The Tungrians just launched more pilae. The men at the front of the attackers fell. Some were screaming with horrible wounds and pilae sticking up from their writhing bodies. It interfered with the progress of the men behind who had to step over and around their comrades. Many tripped and the surging ranks behind trampled them underfoot. The Britons were still shouting their war cries despite their loss of forward momentum but the Tungrians, stony-faced, were silent.

Still we waited. The barbarians swung their weapons but so great was the crush, the front ranks had one opportunity to swing their battle-axes or swords and then they were pinioned against a wall of Roman shields bristling with Roman short-swords. Some of them tried to insinuate themselves between the centuries but the gap was soon filled by eager Tungrians in the centuries behind, who threw pilae and advanced enough to make it impossible for the attackers to get between the front ranks.

The crushing force of the assault made little difference to the Romans who stabbed at anything moving in front of them, their short swords easy to use in the press of men. Half an hour passed and the scene changed little. The front ranks of the barbarian army fell. The Romans replaced their front ranks with men from behind. The line surged and ebbed as battle lines always do but the Tungrians remained still. They had the high ground. The legionaries began to move forward then, stepping on the barbarians' bodies as the ranks of the Votadini began to dwindle and thin.

It occurred to me this was a repeat of the battle in which I had been involved on the raid days before. The Britons seemed inexperienced and undisciplined. I remembered how my own heavy troops in the Frankish army had been similar and how the Romans made it impossible for my men to use long weapons. There was still a plethora of war cries, but now mixed with men screaming in pain, begging for help. It was the sound of a progressing battle. The sounds change from aggressive shouts to an eventual chorus of dying men's screams.

It was then we charged. We hit their rear and left flank hard and I could see Clodius Super at the head of the wedge, spear in hand, meting out death and destruction from his horse. He had a grin on his face. It was a fixed grin; I knew it was not one of humour. He was enjoying the battle lust and I recognised how it felt. I had none. I had little enthusiasm for this fight and it struck me it must have been how all auxiliaries feel. They are, after all, fighting on foreign soil for a master who has vanquished their own people already. I would never have run away but I felt ambivalent about it all.

I half-wished the Tungrians would fall and get trodden underfoot.

When more than a third of their number had fallen, the enemy began to fall back. I think they realised they had no techniques that would avail them against the Romans whose discipline made them solid and unassailable by such ragged barbarian hordes.

Many ran towards a nearby wood and we chased them, reaching down with long swords and bitter spears. We were stabbing, slashing and cutting at the fleeing men. I skewered one man who had turned and aimed an axe blow at Valknir. I leaned to the side, low down in the saddle, almost hanging off the side with my sword arm straight out in front. The blade struck him in the midriff and pierced him through and through.

A stout leather thong attached my sword to my wrist, so it would not get lost. The blade stuck in the body of the dead man. I could not release it. Valknir, of course, continued cantering forward towards the wood. Had it not been for my stirrups, the weight would have dragged me from my saddle. I tugged and wrenched to get the body off my weapon, then had a choice; cut the cord or dismount. I reined in and dismounted, but the weight of the body attached to my weapon nearly dragged me to the ground.

I put my foot on the man's chest and pulled hard. The blade must have embedded itself in his spine for it seemed solidly wedged at first. It came away after repeated attempts. I turned to remount and something hit me on the head. There were colours spinning around me. The world rotated faster and faster. Then all went black. I cannot even now recall what happened afterwards.

When we have choices to make, it is no good looking

back and wishing we had decided to do something else, and I am a decisive man. Perhaps Loge the God of tricks and jokes was playing a prank on me as he had done before or perhaps it was just ill luck. I should have known better than to dismount in the middle of a battle.

CHAPTER VII

"Not even the gods fight against necessity"
—Plato

It was dawn when I awoke. I must have been a little confused for I thought at first I was on a boat. Everything seemed to move up and down. My head was thumping and I opened my eyes with difficulty. I was in a cart and it was daylight. I tried to sit up, but my hands were tied behind my back and a thong encircled my neck. The thong secured my feet, so if I tried to straighten out my legs I found myself choking. I lay still. The cart bounced and rolled and I began to feel nauseated. It was misty and I could not work out in which direction we were travelling. I wondered what had happened to Valknir.

I lay in the bottom of the cart for hours. I began to shiver with the cold. In the end, I called out. The cart stopped. A large rounded figure appeared from the front of the cart. He had a scar on the side of his face and his hair was black. He wore a leather jerkin and his long hair dangled onto the neckline. Even by my standards, he looked filthy. He looked at me, frowned and scratched his beard.

I asked for water. He raised his open right hand and struck me hard across the face. He did not speak, and as my head swam I realised there was no relief from the thirst or the discomfort of my bonds. I could hear him urinating against the front wheel of the cart. Presently, we started moving and the journey began again. I needed to urinate too and knew there was nothing for it in the end; with my bladder on the point of bursting, I wet myself. I was angry now. Even we Germans do not treat prisoners in this way. The Marcomanni torture their prisoners in the belief their captives' pain gives them power; it is a religious thing to them. The Franks of whom I was the Warlord never tortured, they only killed. I was in an agony of pain in the end, because I could not move or stretch my legs out. My knees were on fire and my neck ached as if it was in a vice. I expected this to end in torture. I had no way to fight or escape.

They had removed my chain mail and my tunic was insufficient to keep out the cold. My hands became numb and my feet felt like blocks of ice. It must have been hours but it seemed like days had passed when we stopped. I knew there was no chance of help or rescue, and began to feel real fear. I am not a fearful man by nature but it occurred to me I had never experienced this type of treatment. It reminded me of when brigands had captured Cornelius, the man who trained me in weapon skills. I remembered they had bound him in the same way. I remembered how they had tortured him and he remained silent waiting only for a chance of revenge. That experience taught me much, and as it came to mind I became determined to face what little time I had left in the same way as Cornelius.

The man who had hit me came around to the back of the cart and pulled me out onto the ground. It winded me, for it was an unpleasant fall since the man could not support my weight. He looked at me and must have realised he could not put me back into the cart, so he cut the leather thong keeping my legs flexed. I began to straighten out my legs but my knees were very painful and I realised I would have to do it slowly. I stretched.

The man waited with obvious impatience for me to recover and dragged me to my frozen feet. He took me to a tree and putting his foot behind me tripped me backwards. I fell heavily against the tree and he tied another thong around my throat and took a turn around the tree. At least this time I could move my legs but my fingers gained no relief from the pain and numbness.

It was still misty and I could only see we were in a clearing of a wooded area. It was almost dark and I watched as my captor lit a fire. He took a tiny board of dry wood and swivelled a pointed stick in a groove of the board. It became hot and ignited some dried grass. He blew on it and began building a fire. I was not close enough to benefit from it however and I licked my dry mouth desperate for some water.

The man began heating a pot of water on the fire and he added two turnips. He then unwrapped a round sausage-like object, which he also put into the pot. I licked my lips in anticipation. I had not eaten or drunk all day.

It seemed like an age until the man lifted out the turnips and mashed them with a pronged instrument. He lifted out the round sausage and cut into it. It was filled with a brown granular material. To my hungry senses, it smelled wonderful. He proceeded to eat. He did not look at me, not even a glance. When he had finished his meal he threw some leftovers into a bush and without giving me a glance arranged a blanket near the fire and was soon snoring, fast asleep. He had not fed me and he gave me no water. I had to wet myself again during the night and was then wet and cold, the drying urine chapping the skin of my legs.

I began to experience a mounting anger. I would never

have treated an animal in the way this man treated me. It was as if I was not even a piece of furniture. My head swam from the injury and from hunger and thirst. Sleep came, grudgingly and in fits and starts despite my situation.

The following morning, I awoke early and could see the burly man lying still by the embers of the fire. I was in a sorry state. I needed water at the least. When he awoke, he approached me and looked me in the face. He spat on the ground at my side and reached for a water-skin. He drank from it and then washed out his mouth. He held the water-skin to my mouth for a few moments and the water trickled slowly in. It spilled down my front and soaked my tunic but I did not care. I cared later, because it was still cold even in the daytime and being wet made it worse.

Still he did not speak, and I knew better than to try to converse with this man who starved me and gave me no more thought than one would a beast led to slaughter. He helped me into the wagon and tied me to the side of it. At least I could move my legs this time but there was no way to loosen my bonds and there was no opportunity to consider escape. I became more and more scared, terrified in fact.

The next three days passed in this fashion and still he did not feed me. He gave me a little water in the morning and apart from that, I had nothing from him. On the third day, the cartwheel broke and he needed to change it. He pulled me from the back of the cart and stood me up. My head was still swimming from fatigue and hunger but I managed to stand. Without untying me, he stood me with my back to the cart and indicated I was to hold it up. I pretended not to understand and he removed a whip from the front of the cart. He struck me with it on the shoulders. I realised it was futile to be uncooperative and I did as he ordered. The man changed the wheel without a second glance at me and we proceeded on our way. It was the worst journey I have ever experienced and it made me regard my captor with a burning hatred such as I have never felt for any living man; not since a brigand called Sartorius killed someone dear to me.

On the fourth day I could see buildings as the cart bobbed around on the uneven surface upon which we travelled. At that stage, even the one horse pulling the cart was better fed than I was.

I lifted my head from time to time, wondering where he had brought me. There were thatched roofs on mud and wicker houses and I could smell middens as we entered the conurbation. We stopped for a few moments at a wall six feet high; spikes pointing vertically into the air adorned its top to keep people from climbing in. We passed through and although I could not see very much I realised we were in a sizeable town, since we were travelling in a straight line for what seemed a long time after passing the gates of the wall, and the cart track seemed smooth.

Eventually we stopped and the man jumped from the cart. He went somewhere, possibly into a house, and I heard laughter. Two men came out and dragged me from the cart. They put an arm under each of mine and pulled me towards a building. One of them sniffed at me and said something in a language I did not understand and his companion laughed. It was a low-roofed building and inside there was a hearth with a smouldering peat fire from which the smoke, or at least some of it, went out though a hole in the thatch above.

They took me out of the building through a doorway at the other side and one of the men opened a gate. I looked around. There was a smell of pigs in the air and I could see a palisade of wooden stakes and a deep pit in the ground.

They pushed me into the pit almost breaking my ankle in the fall. It was a simple clay lined pit and the walls were smooth and hard from the cold weather. It stank of offal. I looked up and could see the sky for a few moments, until a wooden hatch eclipsed it as they placed it across the opening. I had never been imprisoned before and I realised it could be a long time before I saw daylight again. I was in despair.

I had always been a creature of daylight, loving the open air and the feel of the breeze on my face. Leaving Rome and escaping from slavery there opened a new world of freedom for me. To be imprisoned in this place in the dark, cold and damp represented more to me than simple physical deprivation. It was a mental stress such as I had never imagined I could suffer, let alone endure. I endeavoured to persevere in my belief I was not powerless. I was a Warlord and a leader of men. Above all, I thought to myself, even in that awful place I was still a warrior, and if physical hardship was what the Allfather had sent for me to endure, then I must bear it and I must survive. Frija my witch had said I would and I was not deaf to her prophesy.

A vision came to me then in my hunger and thirst. It was a vision so clear that I thought if I only reached out with a hand I could touch it. It was the face of the old witch Chlotsuintha who was Frija's predecessor. She had been an old woman who had loved me, despite my weakness for women, despite my inexperience of life and my mistakes. She looked up at me as she had often done and I could feel her presence come to me from the grave.

'Galdir, be strong,' she said.

'You always say that,' I said.

'This time, be strong for a little longer. You must go

home to lead your people. They will become a great nation and will rule all of Gaul and even lands beyond the seas, where black men roam and the sunshine is never broken all year round.'

I shook my head. I thought I must be going mad. I knew where I was and she was not there, but I listened to her and I spoke to her, and she seemed to respond. I cannot explain it. It could only have been a vision granted to me by Wuotan. She smiled and was gone.

What could I do? I had my hands bound behind my back and I was cold—bitter cold and hungry. My anger began to burn then. I came from a strong line of warriors; I would not end here. It could not be my destiny and perhaps it was what Chlotsuintha was telling me if indeed she was not simply a figment of my tortured mind.

I started by sitting on my hands and slipping my arms underneath me. I was able to bring my hands around my ankles and then in front of me. There was little light but a faint radiance peeped through the slats of the wooden cover. I examined the knots as best I could in that half-light and began chewing at the leather through dry swollen lips. It took time and my mouth was strangely clumsy for I bit my lip and tongue numerous times as if they were too large for my mouth and my rodent–like activities. It occurred to me too I was becoming like some rat, gnawing in a dark place away from the disturbance of human activity, alone with my task.

I cannot tell how long it took but I did unravel the thongs with my teeth. I had difficulty using my fingers for their circulation seemed stagnant and slow. I rubbed them, and crossing my arms, held them in my armpits. More time passed and I wondered if I was any better off than before but

I knew I had done something at least, and that small grain of comfort from being in control of my hands seemed to mean much to me. It was out of all proportion to my predicament but it is strange how when one is suffering even the tiniest encouragement can amount to something huge. As soon as my hands began to recognise their ability to move, I loosened my feet.

The space was perhaps four feet in diameter and round. The walls were smooth, for the clay had been flattened when wet, and now they were dry, cold and hard. They resisted any attempt from my fingers to impress them at all.

I searched the floor. It was equally smooth and I wondered what I could do to make a hand hold in the walls for I was determined to climb out. It was only a distance of four or five feet above my head but too far to jump and catch the edge of the pit. I needed a foothold and a handhold. My weakness forgotten, my hunger became a thing of the past. I needed my freedom.

CHAPTER VIII

"A man's character is his fate"
—Heraclitus

I felt my way around the floor again. This time I did it slowly, and having found a slight protuberance in one corner scratched away at the bare hard earth. I must have left fingernails there, for it was a painful procedure. After what seemed to me to be a long time I uncovered a rock. It was the size of my hand and it had a blunt point but it was useable.

Chipping away at the wall level with my waist, I began to smile. It would be typical of Loge, the trickster of the Gods for me to get to the top at the exact moment when my captors were coming for me. I tried to hurry, but within a few minutes, I became so breathless and exhausted I had to stop to rest. If they came for me, I could at least use the rock as a weapon. I laughed aloud once. Perhaps I was a little mad then; hunger and the unfamiliar sensation of fear were taking their toll.

I persevered. With the passage of time I had hollowed out a dent big enough for my foot, and next I began to fashion a handhold above shoulder level. I had no idea then I might not have the strength to pull myself up but it is amazing what reserves necessity can drag from starving limbs.

I stood , putting my foot on the foothold and my hand in the space I had created for it. I needed another foothold higher up and I spent more precious time in creating it. I climbed. It required more effort than I had imagined but perhaps it was because of the starvation.

At the top of the pit, I tried to lift the wooden cover. It did not budge. I almost cried tears of frustration. Had it all been in vain? Had they placed a heavy rock across the planks or perhaps it had a crosspiece bolting it shut?

I pushed first with one hand then another, then both, using my feet in the sides of the pit to give leverage. It began to move. First, it was a tiny crack then a gap big enough for me get my torso onto the edge of the pit. The weight of the cover coming down on my shoulders and back was considerable but I managed to crawl out beneath it and lay on my back with waves of exhaustion sweeping my tired brain and body. I had no time to rest and knew I needed to distance myself from that place as soon as I could walk. Even rising to my feet was an effort of superhuman proportions; I had spent what little reserves I had on climbing out of the pit.

A palisade the height of a man surrounded the area of the pit. There was a central post in the middle with a stanchion used for some purpose I could not understand, unless it was there to tie people to. I made for the side of the palisade away from the entrance and used a broken handcart to climb over. I dropped to the other side and squatting, took stock of my surroundings.

To my left was a green pasture with enclosures where they kept horses. I could see them grazing quietly. They were small, brown and white ponies, but they looked strong despite their small size. It is strange how one's priorities are driven by need. I needed a horse, I needed a weapon and I needed clothing. Above all, my aching, shivering body dictated I needed food. I had not eaten anything for more than four days and almost anything would have done. I envied the horses, they were feeding and I wished I could eat grass. Life would have been much simpler. Directly in front of me was a midden. In front of that was a row of the little mud houses and I could make out people walking back and forth beyond, as I looked through the gap between two of the dwellings.

I made my way around the midden to the back of the nearest house and stood for a moment leaning against the wall. I peered around the edge cautiously. There were carts and horses, men and women, passing along the street. I was clearly in a big town for there were many people.

It was almost dusk, and I realised I must have spent many hours in the pit. I wondered how soon they would go out to check on me but if they had not done so by now, it was my guess they would probably not do so until morning. Their exact intentions towards me remained a mystery and I should confess I did not much care. It would not have been wise to stay and find out, although I was tempted to go into the building and kill them all. The principal thing stopping me was that I felt so weak I doubted I could have killed a mouse. The little energy I had in reserve had been spent in escaping.

Crouching, I made my way across behind the row of buildings. I do not know what I was expecting to do. The chance of escape seemed slim but I had to try. A covered wagon had come to a halt at the end of one of the little alleyways and I could see it was almost empty. The man leading it was standing holding the traces, talking to some-one who had his back to me. I took a chance. I ran crouching and got into the wagon. There were some empty sacks and bales of hay, so I covered myself with the sacking, then as gently as I was able and trying not to rock the cart, slipped behind one of the hay-bales.

I wondered if they were taking the hay away or had brought it into the town. If it was the latter, I would be discovered. If it came to it, I would fight. I was weak but I would fight, since anything was better than the treatment I had received at the hands of these people, whoever they were.

At last, the driver laughed and slapped the other person audibly on the back and we set off. It was a less bumpy ride than the one in which I had entered the town and the sacking upon which I lay, and which covered me, kept me warm enough.

After I had lain like that for some minutes, we stopped. I realised we were back at the town wall and the cart was leaving. I estimated we were probably heading east and I wondered if the town where they had imprisoned me was Dalriada, the main town of the Scotti. I waited until we were well out of the town and sat up. I could see the man driving the cart from behind and wondered if I could overpower him. It was far from certain however; since I was feeling so weak, my limbs trembled when I moved them. The journey went on. By the evening, it became dark and the cart-driver stopped. Without looking back, he reached behind for a sack. I stayed where I was until I saw he had lit a fire. No doubt he was about to eat. Still I waited.

When I was satisfied he had prepared his food and the smell of its cooking wafted enticingly into the cart, I knew I had to act. I crept stealthily out of the wagon. The man had his back to me but I had no weapon. I looked around and found a rock the size of a man's foot. I crept slowly up behind, and although I am not proud of it, I struck the man a single blow on the back of his head. He lay still and I examined the contents of the cook-pot. It was a similar meal to the ones my first captor had eaten. I burned my fingers and mouth in my eagerness to eat. I ate all there was and not satisfied, began to look for more. There was a sack nearby, which contained some apples and some bread, but nothing more substantial. I ate greedily for hunger will do that to a man and I could feel my strength returning slightly. I tied up the cart-driver and sat for a while by the fire. I realised I stank and went to the cart to see if there were any clothes.

I rummaged in the cart under the seat-plank and all the time the sight of that pit and the post near it, kept coming to mind. It was not a simple memory: it was a vivid picture in my head. It kept flashing before my eyes and the feelings of loneliness and fear kept returning. I shook my head. I had to keep control or I would never get back to the wall.

There was another sack of food and a spare pair of leggings. I removed mine and bathed the skin of my legs with water before donning the leggings. They were not clean but they did not smell of urine. My thighs were painful for the blistered skin was red and sore where it had been exposed to the contents of my bladder for days.

Courtesy of the cart-driver, I now had a knife and I had his horse. It was dark and horses dislike being ridden in the dark, but I had no intention of waiting here to sleep. I felt the chance of someone else passing by and seeing the fire was real. Despite all my negative feelings about the Roman army I had supposed the right thing for me now was to return to the wall. An idea began to grow in my fevered mind however, for they thought I was dead or captured. I could not imagine Piso sending out search parties for me. It began to dawn on me that perhaps I did not need to return. I started to think it was possible this was my first opportunity to get away from the Romans since coming to Britannia. If they thought I was dead, they would hardly exact retribution on my people. If I went north, I had no idea what I would find. The Britons might take me in. They could use my knowledge, that was certain. Had I not seen them die in droves at the hands of the Roman legionaries? Whatever my plan, the first thing I had to do was escape and I turned my attention to the most urgent thing.

The man had unhitched his horse and I went to it and spoke to it in the low tones with which horses feel comfortable. I reached up, and stroked his mane. I scratched gently behind his ears, talking all the time. He shook his head in appreciation. The little horse seemed calm enough and I decided to try to ride him. I slipped a leg over his back and he responded by standing stock-still. I gently pulled on the bit. He remained standing where he was. I kicked him with my heels in a soft commanding way but he did not budge. I remembered Valknir and wondered if the horse was like him, and would only respond to one rider. The horse bucked suddenly, his hind legs kicking out, and his withers heaved me up in the air.

Dismounting, I looked at his feet and realised the knock on my head must have made me stupid, for he had been hobbled. The carter had tied his front legs together and no amount of talking or goading would have made him move. I untied his legs and he gave me a look of reproach worthy of a wife. I shook my head and exhaled close to his nostrils. He knew me then and he stayed still while I mounted. He obeyed me this time and I realised my haste was working against me. I needed to think a little more.

I dismounted again next to the cart-driver and cut his

bonds. I had done him a disservice and I had no intention of leaving him there, bound, for the wolves to find. He would have a long walk back but at least he could hide in the wagon until dawn.

Using some sacking for a cloak, we were off. The horse obeyed me well enough and we set off at a slow pace for he had been pulling the cart all day and I did not want him exhausted. I headed north first to get away from the cart track and then after a few hours, rested and headed east. It was my best hope of coming upon a village where I might steal a weapon and some more food. Despite the pain from my sore thighs, I rode all night, fearing pursuit and then entered a wood where I thought the horse could rest and I could conceal myself. I ate another of the sausage things. They contained barley but other than that, I could not identify the contents apart from to say it was some kind of meat stuffed into a caul and spiced with pepper.

By nightfall, I was beginning to feel a little more human. I decided to travel again and rode east. The loneliness and isolation of my predicament was the worst thing. I talked to the horse and I talked to myself. Perhaps the confinement had in the end, driven me mad. I knew I was at least three more days from where they had captured me and I would need more food. I dared not stop. The wall should have been visible but I could not see it from any rise when I stopped because it was dark. My determination was wavering and I was undecided whether to return to the Romans or go elsewhere. I delayed the choice as one often does when decisions are difficult. I would decide when I got back to the battle site where they captured me. Near dawn, I made a bad mistake.

The predawn light was beginning to illuminate my way

when my horse stumbled and threw me. I hit the ground but not hard for it was a grassy slope and we had been ascending. I got up and was aware to my horror the horse had thrown me because we had ridden into a camp. There had been no fire and I had seen nothing amiss until awakening men surrounded me, shouting in a language I could not understand. It sounded familiar and I caught one or two words sounding like German. One of those words was kill. I drew my knife. I gained my saddle-less horse and tried to ride but the place was full of half-naked men, some with swords and some with spears. They were all heading towards me in the half-light. I turned my mount around several times to prevent them from finding an easy target and rode back down the hill, knocking one man to the ground. It was getting progressively lighter and I could make out more and more of my attackers.

There was a copse back in the direction from which I had come. I made for that—a distance of perhaps a quarter of a mile. I was half-way there when the first rider attacked. I heard his mount before I heard his heavy breathing. I looked over my shoulder. I was lucky, for my timing was perfect.

He was almost upon me when I turned my horse fast and to the left. For a moment, we were next to each other and facing opposite directions. It was exactly what I had hoped. He raised his sword-arm and let loose a powerful downward blow. I reached up and caught his arm, for my reach is long and my height was an advantage. My knife went to his throat. He sat still for a moment and I said, 'Get off the fucking horse or fall from it dead.'

It may not have been an elegant speech, but it was adequate to the task. He not only understood my German, he obeyed me. I swung my left foot into his stirrup and holding the pommel of the saddle, turned and threw my right leg over the back. I rode then, knocking the owner over as I set off. It was a good horse, by which I mean he was fast and seemed to enjoy the gallop away from the camp. This time, when I glanced over my shoulder, I could see four more men rapidly gaining on me and I rode as hard as I could towards the copse.

My only weapon was a knife. I had no real chance and I knew it. I was determined they would not capture me alive. I did not want starvation and brutality to be the last thing the Allfather saw visited upon me in this life. I wanted to keep my honour. I wished I had a sword.

Once I had gained the copse, I slowed and turned with the bole of a tall aspen tree to my left. I had no shield but I felt it added a little security on my unarmed side.

The four riders came to a halt in front of me. At the front was a tall, fair-skinned young man with hair of wheaten colour, tied in braids like my own. He had a wispy yellow beard and I could not make out the colour of his eyes in the early dawn light.

'That's far enough,' I said in the common German tongue. I hardly expected them to understand Latin or Greek.

'German?' said the warrior.

'You speak my language?'

'Yes, we are a band of Cimbrian mercenaries,' the man said. 'We kill for money, although in your case we might do it free.'

'If you are from Germania what are you doing this side of the wall? All auxiliaries are in the south. You can't fool me with that one,' I said.

'We don't work for them. We work for whoever will pay

us. There is no money in killing you. You look German too. Why did you attack us?'

'I didn't attack you. Do I look so stupid I would attack a camp of armed men with only a fruit knife? I stumbled into your camp by mistake, you chased me.'

'If what you say is true there won't be any others then?' the rider said, looking around the wood.

'Maybe there are others. I think they will be here very soon,' I said. 'If I were you I would leave while you still can. My friends are powerful warriors.'

He said, 'You know, I don't think anyone else is coming.'

'You'll soon see. If I were you I would ride on.'

'You seem to have forgotten one thing,' said the warrior, 'you are still sitting on my comrade's horse. We want it back.'

'Well you can't have it back. He attacked me and I took it in a fair fight. He is lucky I didn't kill him as he deserved. If you wait for my friends you will soon see the right of it.'

'There is nothing to stop us taking the horse back and you might make a good slave for some farmer.'

'You have seen what I can do with only a knife. Do you think you will all survive to see the sunset? I promise you, before I go to Valhalla I will take at least one of you with me.'

The warrior was becoming restless and irritated. The first man joined them, and he was now riding my recently abandoned, absurd little pony. One of his comrades said something I did not hear. The four men I had talked to began laughing. They laughed so much they rocked in their saddles. I wondered if they were helpless enough with their humour that I might have a good chance of killing one or two of them even with only a knife. The rider of my late steed was scowling and he approached me slowly, sword in hand. I thought he had a mind to finish what he had started before I had unhorsed him.

I confess I found the situation funny too. The man looked ridiculous. His feet almost touched the ground, yet there he was, sword in hand, riding a child's steed. I began to smile. I knew death was coming but I wondered if perhaps I would die with a smile on my lips. He did look ridiculous.

The warrior I had spoken to said, 'Horsa, he is right. You lost your horse in a fair fight. You can hardly complain.'

'I'm not complaining Cimbrod, I'm killing,' said the discomfited Horsa. 'I'm going to kill him in a fair fight and then I will have my horse back. We can eat the pony.'

'Hardly a fair fight,' I said, 'I only have a fruit knife. You have a sword. If one of your friends lends me a sword, I will kill you and then have the use of your horse and your sword.'

Horsa rode forward. He swung his blade at me. I leaned back as far as I could, but the tip of the blade scored a line across my chest. Had I remained where I was, I am sure he would have killed me. As I leaned back I jumped from the saddle and ducked under the horse. I stood beside my pony. The rider had his feet almost on the ground astride the little horse, as I had too, before. It was of course an absurd mount from which to fight. Horsa swung his blade at me again. I was on his right between the two steeds. He had to raise his sword high in the air and backhand if he was to land a blow.

I stepped towards him fast. Inside his reach, I grabbed his sword-arm. I pulled, turning slightly to my right. He fell from the pony's back and I had him. I tried first to stamp on his neck but he fended my foot off with his arm. I stepped back with the tree behind me. I felt faint and was breathing hard, still tired from the long starvation of the previous days,

69

but the tree's firm and steady presence gave me enough support. Horsa was up in a moment. He stood glaring at me as if I was his worst enemy.

'Look, I only want the horse. It isn't worth dying for,' I said.

'No but it is worth killing for. You're a dead man.'

He swung the blade in a high arc at my head. He was slow and I could read his movements easily. He struck the tree hard and it must have reverberated all the way up his arm. I had sidestepped and stabbed the underside of his outstretched arm high up. It was a very fast movement and as I drew the blade out, I heard him yelp. I only had the knife, but it was a wicked little blade.

I stepped fast to the other side of the tree. A thought occurred to me, my choice of meeting these men in the wood was a good one. The tree had shielded me after all.

Horsa was now out of control. He made an animal grunt and held his blade in both hands. He ran around the bole of the tree, his blade raised high above his head. My murder was on his lips and in his mind. I stepped into him as he rounded the bole of the tree and used my left hand to stop him striking. I used my little blade to stab him in the midriff. Even though it was a short blade it must have done something, for he grunted. I stepped to the side and tripped him.

He fell forward and as he passed, my hand moved fast. I stabbed the knife into his throat. There was a gush of hot red spurting onto the ground. He writhed and began to shudder in that little dance of death we see so often on the battlefield, as he bled out. I took his sword; I was ready for his friends. I had a chance now; they had to advance toward the two unfettered steeds.

Nothing happened. I could hear them talking and presently they approached. None of them had drawn their blades.

'Well, are you waiting for me to kill you one at a time or all at once?' I said, all bluff.

'Why would we want to kill you? It was a fair fight before the Gods. Wuotan will be satisfied. I will give you an offer. You can have Horsa's things if you ride with us. You can obviously fight. What do you say?'

'Can I trust you?'

'Can we trust you?'

'It seems a good basis for an agreement. I swear upon Donar's hammer I will not fight any of you if you will swear also.'

'We swear. Follow us, we can return and burn Horsa later,' he said and turning his horse, he rode away towards the camp. The sun was shining and there were few clouds in the sky. I began to feel more optimistic. I wished I had not killed the man in the woods but he attacked me first. I felt I had no option. It was clear to me he would rather have died with honour and a sword in his hand than lived with the shame of me taking his horse, and I told myself that what had happened was therefore, for the best. Besides, had he lived he would have killed me at the first opportunity. It is the way of things. The Gods decide.

CHAPTER IX

"It takes a wise man to discover a wise man"
—Diogenes

There were eleven of them, a mixture of different Germanic people. Their chief was a Cimbri warrior. He came from a far off land to the east, across the sea, and his people were fierce warriors. He had six brothers with him. His name was Cimbrod which, in the Cimbrian tongue, meant raven. He was a tall man, of my height, with blonde hair and blue eyes. He tied his hair in two braids, one at either side of his head, and he had a scar on his right cheek.

He was a generous man but fierce and strong despite his youth. I saw him fight in battle once and he killed with a skill and bravery which was a privilege to watch. As is often the case with my people there was no discipline in the camp, and when they fought each man tried to outdo the other in equalling their older brother. The others in the group were Teutones. Their tribe lived to the south of the Cimbri. Both had become small nations, for Caius Marius, a great Roman General whom the Romans much revere, destroyed a mass-migration into Italia two hundred years before.

I followed them to their camp and dismounted. Lugius, one of the brothers, pointed me at the dead man's belongings and I examined what I had won. I had his horse which was a beautiful beast with a wide chest, but a little cow-hocked, which did not put me off. I thought about Valknir as I stroked my new horse's mane. I talked to him as I used to talk to Valknir, and wished I knew what had happened to him. He was the type of horse who would let no one but me ride him and I worried in case whoever found him would treat him badly if he refused. Horsa had some spare clothes and a leather jerkin, which he had not had time to put on before he rode after me in such haste. There was little else of value in his sorry pile of possessions. I thought it was a sad way to end a life and wondered if there was anything I could have done to prevent his death. That I had killed him with honour, there was no doubt, but it still made me thoughtful as I stood next to his horse looking at his gear.

Cimbrod approached me after they had burned their comrade's body. He said, 'You fight well. I have never seen a man with only a knife kill a man with a sword who is mounted on a horse.'

'I had a good teacher,' I said. 'A Roman gladiator taught me to fight. I can use most weapons. Anyway it was a pretty small horse.'

He smiled and said, 'How did you come to be here?'

I told him the tale of my capture and enslavement by the Scotti man and how I had escaped from the pit in Dalriada.

He regarded me with a strange look on his face. 'You escaped from a bear pit?'

'What do you mean, bear pit?'

'So you didn't know why they put you down there?'

He laughed. He called his brothers over and said something in a language I did not understand. They all began to laugh, and because I thought it was at my expense I began to scowl. I half drew the sword at my waist.

'No. Please, I'm sorry. It was just you didn't realise what they intended and you actually managed to get out,' Cimbrod said. 'You see, you will have caused a lot of anger. In your absence it will be turned on the man who took you there.'

'That gives me great satisfaction after the way he treated me.'

'The pit you escaped from is an entertainment the Scotti value greatly. They put a man in that pit with a wounded bear and then cast lots as to how long it will take for the bear to kill the man. The last man to place his bet wins.'

I said, 'Certain death then?'

'I saw a man who was nimble when we were in Dalriada, he side-stepped very fast and climbed up the bear until he stood on its shoulders. He grabbed the side of the pit to climb out.'

'He escaped?'

'Well no, the bear clawed his back to the bone and he fell back into the pit. The bear ate him. You are the first man to escape; admittedly there was no bear, but all the same...'

'So that was what the post was for?'

'Yes, well, they chain the bear to it, stab it with spears and then guide it into the pit. A man told me once the bear fell on top of the victim and killed him. Many bets were lost that night, I can tell you. I think you only had time to escape because they were looking for a bear to use. It's not easy to catch one you know, even though the Scotti are great hunters.'

'What will happen to my captor?'

'They'll use him instead. Can you imagine spending several days catching a bear and laying huge bets on his ability to end the fight quickly and then finding you lose everything because the victim has escaped? Once they have bet, the entertainment has to go on. Perhaps we should call you

Björn-runner. It would be fitting!'

'No, my name is Galdir. I am a warlord of the Franks and proud of my name. I did not always know it was mine you see.'

'If you like,' Cimbrod said.

'You men are a long way from home too.'

'Yes. At home, there is little to do apart from feasting and sitting around like old women. We wanted to do some fighting. We came across together on boats carrying iron ore.'

'How far is it?' I said in amazement.

'Twenty days hard rowing. We went southeast first and then crossed the Narrow Sea to the Briton coast, where we raided for a week. Then we came here. We tried to raid the Roman towns along the coast but they have many coastal forts and it became too dangerous. We saw some other raiders when we got to the lands of the Votadini and they showed us where to go. We sold our iron ore and bought horses, at a big hill-fort called Traprain to the north and east of here. We visited Dalriada and now we are going to the far north to fight for the Caledonii; they are always at war with someone.'

'I think I should be heading south to the wall, I have friends there and I swore an oath of service to Marcus Aurelius, the Roman Emperor. It would be a pleasure to go with you but it would dishonour me,' I said.

I more than half wished I could go with these tough young men. They looked like the kind of warriors I had stood shoulder to shoulder with, fighting the Romans in Frankia. They reminded me of home. There were no rules, no Roman discipline to follow, and most of all no one scorning me. It was as if I was at a crossroad. On the one hand going south to try to find Valknir and rejoin Lazygis or go north with these Germanic men. Going south, I knew was foolish. I felt bound by my oath yet there was nothing there for me and they thought I was dead anyway. They would not miss me, but Valknir? What would happen to him? I realised though that a man who sacrifices life's opportunities for his horse is a fool; horses do not live as long as men do and when they have gone, you still have your own life to live. That thought swayed me in the end.

'Well, I don't think that will happen.'

'What do you mean?' I said.

'Well, you killed Horsa. You owe us something. Do you have anything with which to pay us for the loss of a good fighter?'

'He didn't seem too good a fighter to me,' I said.

'Well he was one of us. I grew up with him. You owe me for his life. Until you pay me for the loss, honour dictates you must serve me until you can pay.'

'I have a sword now,' I said. 'If you want to make me stay it may cost you even more lives. It might be wise not to tempt me and find out how good I really am with a sword. I can kill you all, you know.'

'It is not that we will force you, although no man is likely to live through a fight when the odds are so heavily stacked against him. I have six brothers and these four others. It would be foolish to rely on your undoubted fighting skills. We don't want to fight for nothing anyway; I had hoped you had enough honour to recognise the debt.'

I looked at him. I felt almost indentured, trapped. He had treated me fairly and I recognised that. It was equally true I had no way to recompense him for the death of his comrade and I knew it was what I would have ruled if I had still been in my own country. If you take a man's life you have to pay, unless you kill him in battle. It was our German law you see. A man with honour does not desert the basis of his own culture.

'But you weren't kin were you? Surely the normal rules don't apply?' I said, but it was half-hearted and I knew deepest down he had the right of it, and anyway I recognised I had always wanted to go north. It was the only way I could finally fight the Romans.

'Like I said,' Cimbrod said, scratching the back of his head, 'we can't force you. I thought maybe you might enjoy it instead of being on the wrong side.'

'Don't get me wrong, I hate the Romans.'

'They think you're dead anyway. They may even have heard you were destined for the bear pit. Who knows?'

I thought for a few moments. There was surely no harm in riding north just until I could pay them for the inconvenience of losing their comrade. I still wished I could look for Valknir. It was on my mind. I knew Lazygis could look after himself and I was not concerned about him. He had a death wish anyway. The Romans killed his family, and now he had to tolerate the ignominy of being what he considered a slave to them and their army. He waited for death, but as so often happens to a warrior seeking death, it becomes elusive. The more he fought and rode into an enemy the longer the Gods seemed to protect him.

'I had a horse when I was captured. He was special. Is there any way I could go and look for him?'

'Galdir, we have to head north. You will never find us. Will you come? We have to meet the others by a lake in the north within a few days.' He tapped his sword hilt with his index finger showing his impatience.

'Others?' I said.

'Yes, there were forty of us when we set off. We had two ships. Each carried the iron ore as ballast.'

'Ballast? What's that?' I said.

'It is a heavy weight in the bottom of the boat adding stability. Don't you know anything?'

'I do know I hate boats and sea-water. I've only ever been aboard one proper ship and it was coming here from Gaul. I was sick all the time.'

'We are a seafaring people. Each of us can sail and row anywhere we choose. It is strange to talk to someone who looks so like us but has no knowledge of the sea.'

'Who are the other men you are meeting? All Cimbrians?'

'No, we collected some Teutones from south of us and there were a few Marcomanni who had escaped the slaughter when the Roman Emperor defeated their people. You should hear some of their stories. The Romans really are violent people, despite what they say.'

'Believe me I know. I lived in Rome for eighteen years.'

'Really? You must tell us about it later. Now we ride.'

Cimbrod mounted his horse. It was a beautiful roan mare. He called her Stigund, which means "spear path" in the common tongue. I had not named my horse. I felt it would be a breach of faith between Valknir and me. I missed him.

We rode north for several hours and stopped to hunt. We lit a fire and roasted a stag that Adelmar, Cimbrod's youngest brother had shot. The Cimbri only used bows for hunting, and although most of them fought from horseback with spears, they could all use swords well enough. Their swords tended to be shorter than the usual Germanic blade and it may have been that which had made them so successful at fighting the Romans when half their nation migrated into southern lands a couple of hundred years before. They were one of the few Germanic nations the Romans still respected.

Adelmar had no beard. He was younger than the rest and I thought he was not much more than a youth. He looked the most like Cimbrod of the seven brothers. I liked him; he had a ready smile and tolerated any hardship without complaint. He was tall and slim and when I later saw him fight he whipped his sword around him using his long arms to great advantage.

We travelled north for four days. The change in the scenery was dramatic. The flat green lands north of the wall, were soon replaced by tall hills, green slopes and pine forest reminding me of home. I had not been so far north before, but there were still Roman roads and they were easy to ride upon, long straight and flat. We spoke little when we rode, but at mealtimes I came to know my companions better. I felt somehow closer to them than to the Sarmatians who were from a country far away in the north and east that the Romans referred to as Scythia. In typical Roman fashion they lumped all the people north of the Black Sea together, as if their different tribes and divisions were of no importance. My Roman education had not had the effect upon me my master had hoped. It had taught me to hate Rome even more and it had given me much knowledge with which to fight them successfully.

The Cimbri entertained me with tales of their land and their heroes. They were pleasant, humorous people with whom I had much in common. I was glad to be with companions who shared my Gods. There was no difference between us in that respect and we all recognised it. On the fourth day we stopped at a small lake beneath a steep hill. It had pine forest on its slopes and we lit a fire beside the lake to cook the game we had hunted. I borrowed a bow and impressed my companions with my ability. I had, after all, been taught by Sarmatian horse-archers more recently, but my early lessons had been from my first love, Livia. I thought of her then as I loosed an arrow at a hare. She could hit a moving hare at forty yards and that had been only one small thing I remembered of her. I often saw her in my dreams in the following years, but not recently.

We had sword practice in the evenings when we waited for our food to cook. They began to respect me, for apart from Cimbrod, they realised my sword skills were far beyond their own. Cimbrod had an exceptional talent for anticipation. Inexperienced though he was, he had amazing speed; I could see he was a natural swordfighter.

'Cimbrod,' I said, 'you did not realise your danger when you allowed me to have a sword.'

'No, Galdir, I can see that. You said you could kill us all when we surrounded you on horseback. I see now you were not boasting. Who taught you to fight?'

'I was a slave in Rome and escaped. The man who helped me was a retired gladiator called Cornelius Nepos, I never knew his first name.'

'Sounds like a vegetable to me. Nepos. Pass the boiled Nepos would you?' Cimbrod said, laughing. He laughed so much he had to support himself with his hands on his knees or he would have fallen over. I smiled; he and his brothers were young men, all seven of them. Although they were almost ten years younger than I was, I enjoyed their youth after the awful seriousness of the Roman Legion.

I endured his amusement for almost a minute then I

pushed him over as I walked past and he just lay on the damp turf, convulsed with laughter. Shaking my head I walked back to the fire. The nights should have been getting warmer, but the further north we rode the colder they became. I was aware the landscape was changing as I looked around me. This place was wilder and we seldom saw habitations or people. I put it down to a healthy caution on the part of the locals. We were twelve heavily armed men on tall horses. Few people would risk exposing themselves to us.

On the fifth day, we came to an earthwork wall. There were brick forts at intervals but more frequent than the Roman wall I had been guarding. I realised this was what was left of the wall the Romans had lost, twenty years before. There were no signs of habitation and I wondered where the fighters who had overrun it had gone. They had not stayed to enjoy the proceeds of their efforts, but who could blame them? Only a deserted earthwork remained, enshrouded by mist. It had a ghostly quality as if some wandering spirits traversed it from time to time and kept men away.

We did not stay there long since none of us liked the place and one of the men, called Marcomir, said he thought there were evil spirits there. We rode on instead to a more hilly area to the north, and found ourselves on the shore of a huge lake the following day. It was miles long and we could see the far shore was clothed in thick green forest right up to the waterline. It was much longer in a north-south direction than it was wide, but it was a beautiful place and one remaining in my mind for many years. On the west side, was a track and we followed it for half a mile before we made camp, threading our way between tall trees and boulders strewn in our way as if some great giant fighting with Donar in the sky above, had thrown it down across our path.

'Tell me Cimbrod, what kind of people live here?' I asked.

'I don't know exactly. We are south of the Caledonii and north of the Selgovae. I don't see anyone around to ask either.'

'Where do we meet your men?'

'At the north end of this lake. It was the only landmark I knew we couldn't miss, which was why I picked it.'

'Have you been to the Caledonii to find out if they want you?'

'No. My father has been here in the past and he told me what to do. He still has dealings with the Votadini.' He smiled and called to one of his brothers. I had trouble telling them apart for they all looked similar. His name was Henge-ist.

'He wants to know how we approach the Caledonii,' he said.

The Cimbri warrior grinned. They seemed to grin and laugh a lot these Cimbri, but I did not mind: it was better than all the grey, long faces I had become used to in Vindolanda.

'Carefully,' he said.

My comrades found this very funny and I began to wonder if their whole expedition was all a big joke. Perhaps they could not fight; they seemed so youthful and foolish. It made me realise I was no longer as young as I had been when I escaped from Rome. It had all changed me. I was almost thirty years old but I had been in many battles and killed many times. It had hardened me. Everyone who had loved me on the way had died or been killed. The only survivor among my own people, was Frija. Small, dark Frija, with her black hair and her deep blue eyes. Chlotsuintha the old witch had raised her from the age of ten and taught her to be a witch. She could tell the future when she dreamed, but she had other qualities too. Her eyes were knowing and sage. They looked through you somehow, and she could read a man, know his thoughts too. I wished she were there with me to help and guide me. A Warlord with no witch to help him is nothing.

I slept badly, having nightmares about wolves and battles and a tall white clothed man with a white beard. He pointed his staff at me and I felt fear as if there was a danger coming but I could not recognise what it was.

CHAPTER X

"Happy is he who dares courageously to defend what he loves"
—Ovid

It was still dark when I awoke. I heard a noise. For a few moments I could not identify what it was. Then I knew. A twig broke off to my left, and I was up, sword in hand and shouting. I cannot recall what I said but it was enough of a warning and loud enough too to awaken my Cimbri friends.

A man rushed out of the thicket. He went straight for me with a long-handled axe. He swung it around his head so it gained momentum. He brought it down diagonally. I stepped back and he missed. I killed him then. His right arm had passed me. He almost stood sideways on to me. It was an easy stroke with the short blade. I stabbed his throat. I stepped back as others approached. They carried similar arms, running towards me and screaming. It was a war cry such as my men at home would use in battle.

I was aware of my Cimbri friends standing back to back, with shields in their hands and swords drawn. The two who attacked me came on. The first buried his axe in Cimbrod's shield. My friend had to let go. He stabbed with his sword. The shield caught him as the attacker swung it on the end of his axe. I was tired of this now. I stepped round my fallen friend and stabbed once fast with the sword. The attacker screamed. He fell to one knee. I turned to face two more attackers. Both swung at me with simultaneous overhead blows. I stepped into the one on my left and stabbed him in the midriff before he could bring his axe down. He fell back with a look of surprise on his face, writhing in agony. The third man landed his axe but it struck a tree stump when I sidestepped. For one instant he stood there. He was leaning forward. He had both hands on his axe. His dying comrade lay at his feet. Blood shone black in the half-light on the ground.

In that instant, I had him. I do not know why, but I did not kill him. I should have, and it was a foolish thing. I had killed the other three, but was unwilling to do more unless I had to. Swinging the sword forwards and past him in an upwards stroke, I caught the man on the chin with my elbow. The elbow is the hardest part of a man: it is solid bone. I put all my weight behind it and twisted as I hit him. I heard a crack and guessed I had fractured something, probably his jaw.

He slumped back. I stepped over him to help the others. They were fighting hard and were as outnumbered as I had been. I came to Hengeist's aid first. The man he fought had raised a war axe and was about to land a blow when I stabbed into his neck from the side. I twisted the blade. He dropped the axe. He tried to scream. All that came was blood. I saw his right arm go limp as he fell. I moved fast between the attackers. I stabbed, cut and killed. I was their worst nightmare.

Hengeist joined me. We proceeded to slay the remaining seven or eight attackers. Soon all lay dead.

'Where is Cimbrod?' asked one of his brothers, I think it was Adelmar or it could have been Boior. Like me, he was breathing hard.

'He fell over there,' I said, indicating where he and I had been fighting.

We walked fast to the young warrior and his brother knelt by his side. 'He's breathing anyway,' he said.

'Of course he's breathing. It didn't look too bad an injury. Mind you, you can't always tell with a head wound. I think it was the shield striking him. He should be all right.'

We carried him over to the embers of the fire and Adelmar put a folded cloak under his brother's head. We waited and then, as he was still unconscious, we decided to clear the camp. Boior sat with his brother while we piled the bodies at the far end of the clearing. The one I had hit was beginning to stir. We tied him up tight and dragged him across to his friends. The attackers had no possessions worth taking and I thought it meant they were brigands. It would be a shame if they belonged to the tribe we wanted to work for.

Cimbrod started to move, and as he came to we sat by the fire which had been nursed back to life, like the Cimbrian warrior next to it. Hengeist had a cut on the shoulder but his brothers and the two Teutones were unscathed. We had done well for we had been outnumbered two to one and none of us had died.

'What happened?' Cimbrod said.

'You decided to head-butt your own shield, but it was attached to an axe at the time,' Adelmar said, smiling in the flickering flame light.

'By Donar, it feels as if I did,' Cimbrod raised his hand to the side of his head, where a bump the size of a duck egg had grown.

'All dead?' he said.

'No,' I said, 'there's one of them tied up over there. Maybe we should question him.'

'I'll question him alright,' he said and got slowly to his feet. He was a little unsteady but managed to walk to the spot where the survivor lay. He looked down at the hapless captive and I could see he wanted revenge.

I said, 'I don't think he is a Caledonii warrior, I think they would not have behaved so dishonourably, attacking us at night.'

'Perhaps. I have no idea what they think honour is. Maybe we should keep him alive. When we see the Caledonii they can question him. My father said they have ways to entertain prisoners even he did not like to talk about.'

'I don't like torture,' I said.

'What?' said Cimbrod.

'I don't like torture; my people see it as dishonourable. I never allowed it in Sicambra.'

'What's a Sicambra?'

'It's the name of my capital city. If you start that vegetable nonsense, I'll give you another lump like the one you have already, and people will think you're growing horns!'

'I only asked,' said Cimbrod with a smile. 'How do you mean "capital city"?'

'I told you I am a Warlord at home. I ruled the Frankish nation.'

'A real king?'

'Yes, a real king, but much more than that. I commanded all my people, not only an individual tribe.'

The boy regarded me in a different way after that. I think he had realised all of a sudden who I was. To be Warlord among my people was important and it was more than he had anticipated.

'I didn't realise,' he said.

'Well you wouldn't would you? You found me with a torn tunic and a sack for a cloak, riding what I can only describe as a child's pony. Anyway, we are a defeated people and Rome has annexed my home, so there is an end of it. There is nothing I can do now unless I remove every Roman between here and the southern ports where there are ships which can carry me across the sea to Gaul.'

'You saved my life, Galdir,' he said.

'And next time you will save mine and we will become battle-kin, sword-brothers. Our people describe it as a brotherhood. When each of you saves the other's life in battle, neither of you owes the other anything, but you are like brothers. I had such a friend once.'

'Really?'

'Yes , we fought in many battles against the Romans. He was a Dacian.'

'Was he killed?'

'No, he went home to Dacia to claim his birthright and become king of the Dacians in Lovosice. He will have become an ally of Rome by now, for the Romans were fighting the Marcomanni who had captured his city. He could only rule with Rome's complicity.'

'Too complicated for me,' said Cimbrod. 'But you really are a king?'

'Look I just told you. Do you think I would lie?'

'So does that mean you and I are sword brothers? You would have died if we had left you?'

'No; it only counts in battle. Right now, you owe me a life.'

'Oh.'

'Come on, this is not the real world. Rules do not apply here. I am a displaced king and you are my friend. There is nothing more than that.'

'I can't let you lead us.'

'No I understand that. I have not earned it and I do not want it. I am glad to ride with you until I have paid the weregeld for your dead companion, Horsa. When that is done we owe each other nothing.'

'But I owe you a life?'

'Cimbrod, there may be many chances to repay it before we are done. Don't worry about your honour.'

He smiled and I realised he held me in more respect than I deserved. It was true. I was nothing but a displaced king of a defeated people, who wanted to return home. Now the Romans thought I was dead I had a chance of doing that, but I had to find a way south without being caught and I had no way to do it. I decided the Gods would show me the way in their time and not mine.

We set guards and they honoured me for saving their leader's life by allowing me to sleep. These were only young men and although they were fearsome in battle, I thought they were still wet behind the ears. Their respect flattered me I suppose. I knew I had to earn that respect in times to come but for the moment, I enjoyed the respite from Roman denigration which I had almost learned to expect from people. I hated the Romans still. I would have been happy to fight them, even though my honour pricked me over the oath I had sworn to Marcus Aurelius.

The next morning we rode to the north end of the lake. We took our prisoner tied on the little pony I had stolen from the carter. I had scorned that horse but he was stronger than I had realised. He took the burden of the captive without any visible complaint and seemed unabashed by the weight, or the speed at which we travelled. I missed Valknir still. I knew I would never see him again and it burdened my heart, for he and I had been together since long before I had killed my uncle to become warlord of the Franks.

The prisoner kept repeating his name.

'Philip,' he kept murmuring. I wondered if the knock on his head had addled his wits but it was all we could get out of him, through his broken jaw.

'Philip,' he said.

'Will you shut your prisoner up my Lord? He is going to drive me mad if he continues like this,' Cimbrod said.

'If you call me Lord again you will drive me mad too,' I said.

'All right but at least gag him or something.'

In the end, we did just that. He kept murmuring despite the cloth in his mouth so we strung the little pony to a spare mount at our rear and managed to get a little peace from the endless 'philiping' as we moved north.

CHAPTER XI

"Courage conquers all things"

—Ovid

When we met up with the rest of the Cimbrian warriors, it was early afternoon. The cold sun was shining and the smell of the damp grass rose to my nostrils evoking as always memories of home. They had camped on a hill, which seemed sensible, for there was no knowing whether approaching men would be friend or foe.

Cimbrod greeted the leader of the contingent warmly and I noticed most of them were his age. There were one or two Marcomanni, a few Chatti and one Frank. I had never seen him before, but he said his name was Drogo. I knew from the name he was one of my people. When I had declared myself to him, he smiled.

He said, 'Many of our people thought you were dead. The Romans came and they have all but enslaved our people. My heart soars to see you free and strong. Will you lead our people now to freedom?'

He had a strange accent for a Frank; I found it hard to place. I thought perhaps he had spoken so much of the common tongue he was forgetting his origins.

'I wish it were possible. I will return one day but now I have to stay here, for I owe a debt to these men and I must repay it for honour's sake. Will you come home with me?'

'Lord, I will follow you where ever you go. It is a great

honour to even speak to the Warlord.'

'Do not humble yourself too much before one who has lost in battle to the Romans. Some would say having lost the battle at Sicambra that I am not worthy to lead.'

'Never, Lord. Our entire nation knows what happened. The Romans killed most of our warriors and I only escaped north by luck. They took all of my comrades prisoner. I heard afterwards they were sent to the east to fight for the Emperor.'

'Drogo, if they had not obeyed, the entire nation would have been slaughtered. They live their lives now with Roman masters but by doing so they keep our people at home alive. It is a noble way to serve their homeland.'

A slap on my back brought me back to reality.

'Well Galdir, have you found a kinsman?'

'Cimbrod, you see here a true Frank. He is only young as are most of your men but this one knows me and is my man, whether he rides with a pack of Cimbri youths or not.'

Drogo smiled as if he knew the truth of it.

'I am honoured to be considered a servant to my warlord,' he said.

'No, Drogo, you are no servant, you are my comrade,' I said and the smile on the boy's face said enough.

'Well at least you have someone who speaks your native tongue,' said Cimbrod.

'Yes, at least that,' I said.

We spent the rest of the afternoon resting after the long ride north, and in the evening Cimbrod held a council. It was clear the other mercenaries held Cimbrod in high esteem. I was unsure why, for many of them were older. When I asked, they told me it was because he was the son of the King of the Cimbrians. I realised there might be more to the lad than met the eye.

The little council progressed the way such meetings always did. Each man had his say and their speeches were long and tedious. They praised each other, reciting their brave deeds since last they had met. They talked of bravery to come. They made me sleepy.

We decided to ride north in the end, to where one of the men had seen a tall tower, which we thought might be a town or city. Adelmar thought it would only take a few hours, but they had talked so much that the day was wearing on and nothing was going to happen until the next morning. We camped on the hill and Hengeist and I went hunting.

He was a good shot with a bow although he seemed a little hasty. His arrows tended to land in front of their mark when he fired at a moving target. I taught him a trick Lazygis had shown me for sighting with the bow, and he was well pleased with that. He took a huge stag in the forest. It was a fine beast with massive antlers and it needed both our horses to drag it back to the camp. The antlers kept snagging in bushes and in the end, we had to cut them off. Hengeist was loath to leave them so he carried them. He was a strong man.

At the camp, we roasted the whole stag over a massive fire. No one worried about the fact anyone could see it for miles for we felt strong and unassailable. We were all warriors and we knew we could fight any number of the local men.

With full bellies we sat around the fire swapping stories of great battles we had heard about and in my case, in which I had been involved. I soon understood that these young men whom I was sure could fight were not talking from experience. They realised in their turn I was experienced, and as the evening wore on I found I was the one telling tales of my life and they were the ones listening. I looked at their young faces and could see the wonder expressed in them. I could feel how they wished they had been there at Aquileia as I explained how we had defeated the Romans. I told them tales of the Greek heroes, which I had learned in Rome. I told them tales of Leonidas, and the three hundred Spartans who gave their lives to defend their country and ultimately, saved democracy.

I grew tired in the end and wanted to go to bed. They pestered me for more; I described how my entire nation had migrated across the Rhenus and settled in the land of the Eburones and how we had made a life in that green and pleasant land.

'My friends, it is late,' I said. 'I will tell you how I came to be here to-morrow night. We have many nights on the road.'

'Galdir is right,' said Adelmar, 'let's save a little of our stories for tomorrow. It is like a feast, eat too much tonight and tomorrow we will not be well enough for the next one.'

He raised a laugh from his comrades and we all went to our bedding. I was settling down and putting my head on my folded cloak when I was aware of someone approaching. The figure stood above me.

'Sire, may I speak?'

It was Drogo.

'Of course' I said.

'Will you teach me to use a sword as you do? I heard from my cousins there was no one in all of Germania who could wield a sword as you do.'

'You have heard a lot of silly rumours Drogo. I can fight; the man who taught me was a gladiator in the Roman arenas. He taught me much. Perhaps I might consider passing on what he taught me.'

I reached forward fast and grabbing the young man's ankle pulled with the speed of a cat. He fell over backwards cursing.

I said, 'One of the first things he taught me was to be always on my guard.'

He looked at me and although he was scowling at first, his expression changed. He was young. He laughed with me for a moment and said, 'Lord I will always guard your back. I know greatness when I see it.'

'Drogo,I am no great man. I am the Warlord of a defeated people and I deserve no praise for my position. I tell you this, it has been prophesied I will return, and return I shall, but only the Gods know how that home-coming will be.'

'I am sure,' he said, 'it will be a noble and glorious moment.'

'Drogo, I keep telling you, I am not a Warlord now. I am only the man who was your leader. You have too much respect for me. Let us be friends instead. It will be easier to ride together if we are friends. I do not want you to be subservient, only loyal.'

'My loyalty is always yours. You are all our nation has.'

'Good, don't serve me, share with me.'

'It is as you wish.'

*

I awoke before my companions. I did not understand why, but I slept little in those days. I was haunted. Haunted by my broken oath to Marcus Aurelius, and by all I had lost in the years before. I looked out on a beautiful landscape. To the north were rolling hills, green and pleasant with the mist in the valleys seeming to hold up those hills in a spectral elevation of one of nature's best creations. I loved the place. It was cold and I imagined it could be grim in winter, but the beauty of the Caledonian lands still impressed even me, despite all I had been through.

There was an eagle soaring high above and I questioned what he might have made of the gathered sleepers. I watched as he flew high above me and wondered what it would be like to fly in the sky. To be unfettered and unashamed in that freedom and see the earth below teeming with its warriors and huntsmen, yet soaring above them with no concern greater than where the next prey might be lurking. I wished I could be like him, free and flying away, but I knew if the Gods wanted me to be like that they would have engineered it long ago.

What design of the Norns was I playing in? They had brought me from slavery in Rome to greatness among my own people, but let me throw it all away, making wrong decisions and wasting the God's gift of an army of men who had believed in me and trusted my ability to command them. I felt shame ; I had let them down. I had no way of negotiating when the Romans came, but I should have sued for peace much earlier instead of fighting them. I had laboured under the foolish belief I could bring my enemies to their knees.

It had been a hard lesson. I learned that the Roman's Gods are strong and they had taken their chosen people to the peak of military prowess far beyond the abilities of my poor Germans. Perhaps it was no use fighting them. They were like a scar. I would have to tolerate them for the rest of my life.

Drogo interrupted me. He had wakened early too and approached me as soon as he realised I was awake.

'Lord Galdir,' he said, 'Should I make something for you to eat?'

'What?' I said.

'Some food?'

'Look, Drogo, I don't need a servant. I need a friend. If you can't free yourself from that then we have nothing between us.'

'I am sorry, Lord.'

'And stop calling me Lord. It irritates me. I am a lord of nothing now. I have a name and you know it well. Use it. And stop apologising.'

'Yes Lor... Galdir.'

We both smiled at that, and went to find some food together. We ate some leftover venison and bread, and it seemed to me this was an attractive life in many ways; yet I needed to return. It stabbed me and goaded me, but I had no way to achieve my goal. I put all such thoughts out of my head and decided to go with what the fates had brought me. Anything was better than a bear mauling me in that Scotti pit.

CHAPTER XII

"Rule your mind or it will rule you"
—Horace

We rode early to look for an employer. Cimbrod had the idea that all we needed to do was to find a major city and offer our services to the king. He was sure they would not pass up the opportunity to have men like us on their side.

'Do they have proper cities?'

'Well they must have' he said.

'Why? All I've seen are a few groups of houses and farms. There don't seem to be any stone buildings anywhere.'

'There was that tower Adelmar sighted.'

'Yes, where is it?'

'He isn't sure, he said it was near the coast but we've ridden inland so maybe we've missed it.'

'Cimbrod, you don't seem very organised. You're supposed to be our leader.'

'Maybe you should lead? You're a warlord after all and I'm just a Cimbri chief's son.'

'No, I don't want to lead. As a leader, you have responsibility for the men. I have none. I am content for once to follow you, my friend.'

'If you say so. I'm going to tell them to move west and head for the coast, then maybe we will hit Adelmar's tower.'

It seemed a good plan, so I said nothing more and we rode hard, hoping to make the coastal area before nightfall.

By midday we had not seen anything apart from the odd deserted homestead. They were mud-built thatched houses and we saw cattle but no human presence. I was not surprised at the absence of people, for who would want to be at home to a band of forty fierce –looking warriors?

In the end, we came to a tower exactly as Adelmar had described. It was an odd building. At the wide base, there was an entrance and the stone-built sides rose to an apex. It was almost pyramidal in shape and reminded me of a siege tower made of stone, but at intervals, there were wooden platforms where men could stand and fire arrows. It rose many feet into the air and perhaps thirty tall men standing on each other's shoulders could have reached the top. That someone had made it for defence was obvious, but whom it was constructed to defend and what aggressors it was intended to keep at bay, remained a mystery to me.

We stopped short of the entrance and Cimbrod and I rode forward to the gate. It was a stout oak door and looked as if it the makers intended to keep out an army.

I dismounted and thumped on the door with my fist. There was no answer. Puzzled, I stood back and looked up at the platform above. There was no one there. I would have assumed there was no one home but thought they would not have been able to keep the door shut unless someone was inside.

'Hey, is there anyone there?' I shouted, but as I did not know their language, it was probably a waste of time.

A stony silence greeted me and I continued to stare at the sheer face of the tower. All remained silent. I looked around. To one side was a fenced area with a horse and next to it a small cart. There was no sign of life and the quiet became oppressive as we stood waiting for something to happen. I walked back to my horse and muttered to Cimbrod that there was no one home.

Cimbrod jerked at the reins of his horse with a suddenness that surprised me.

'Galdir,' he said, 'they're firing arrows.'

I looked back and sure enough, an arrow all but skewered me. It pierced the hem of my tunic between my legs and passed through without touching me. An inch or two higher and I fear to think what the consequences would have been.

We rode to what we thought was a safe distance. No one emerged from the stone-built tower and we sat there, out of range wondering what to do. It seemed an inauspicious start to my career as a mercenary.

'Damned difficult to make contact with these folk,' said Cimbrod.

'Perhaps we need different tactics,' I suggested.

'What do you suggest,' Cimbrod said, scratching at something under his arm.

Looking around, I could see we were downhill from the odd-looking tower. It was unassailable without siege equipment and we seemed to be at stalemate. The occupants were unwilling to communicate or emerge and we did not know their language.

Dismounting, I removed the leather jerkin and unslung my sword. I walked slowly towards the tower. I had my hands above my head and hoped it was clear I meant no harm. I stood below the tower and shouted I came in peace, in the German common tongue. I did not expect them to understand but I thought my voice would make them pay attention to me.

Minutes passed. My arms began to grow tired and then a boy came out onto one of the platforms above. He was no bigger than a ten-year-old at home, but I assumed he was probably older. The locals would not be as big as Germans. He was dressed in a simple grey tunic and he carried a bow in his hand. He had a quiver of arrows on his shoulder. He nocked an arrow in defiance and aimed at me. I was well within range.

I held my hands up further and called to him. His bow wavered and he lowered it. He seemed to have understood. He shouted something to me I could not understand. He pointed to the west. I tried to indicate he should come down but he smiled and shook his head.

'Tell him we come in peace,' I heard Cimbrod shout behind me.

I turned and said, 'I think he knows that. Maybe he's alone. Would you let us in if you were him?'

'No, but I don't know what we're supposed to do. We can't stand here all night, can we?'

Walking back to my horse, I looked up at Cimbrod, who was frowning, and said quietly, 'You are supposed to be the leader. If you don't make some decisions soon the men will wonder who their chief is.'

'Yes, you're right.' He turned to the group. 'Men, we make camp here. This boy is obviously alone. We need to wait for his parents or at least the rest of the people to come back.'

It was decided that in the early spring afternoon we would simply sit and wait. I shook my head and led my horse away. We camped on a hill and waited. Nothing happened. We hunted and found food. It was a long wait. Night fell and still there was only a boy in a tower and no indigenous people. I heard the men muttering that they wondered what we were doing here.

I filled in the time by telling them the story of the siege at Sicambra and the valiant defence of the town put up by my Franks. I described the last ride of the Sarmatians when Marcus Aurelius arrived with fresh legions after we had defeated the first Roman army and how it had felt to ride with them.

They were silent when I had finished. I looked at their faces. They were spellbound as I am sure I might have been had I had their youth. At the age of thirty, I had begun to feel like some old war-horse, battle-torn and tired. Each face I looked at sitting around the flickering fire reminded me of good times at home, listening to stories of heroes and battles long since disappeared.

There was a chill wind blowing around my ankles as I stood there and the overcast sky made that hilltop feel bleak and dark. Reliving the tale of the fall of my little kingdom had made me emotional and I walked to the edge of the camp to look out across the dark vale. Visibility was poor but I still caught a flash of light far below us. It was faint and far off but I knew I was not mistaken. Someone was approaching. Whoever it was, they were either blind to our presence or not afraid. If they were unafraid there would be many. I roused the camp and we organised the men, prepared for an attack. Each man stood by his horse and we were all armed and ready.

I scratched my horse behind the ears and talked to her soothingly and she stood still and calm. A mare is often the best of horses for they are more compliant. A stallion is better in battle but I was not expecting a fight, our purpose here was to make a peaceful entry into the country.

'Galdir?' it was Drogo.

'Yes?'

'Will there be a battle?'

'I hope not. We are hoping to join them aren't we? Where's Cimbrod?'

'I'm here,' he said, behind me.

'It seems to me we don't really want to look too battle ready. They may think we are raiders, not penniless soldiers looking for employment.'

'What do you suggest?'

'We could ride away as soon as they approach. If we don't offer battle perhaps they will understand.'

'I'm not running away from a pack of Caledonii. What do you take us for?'

'Cimbrod, my friend, I'm not suggesting we run away, we just stay out of range of their arrows and spears and try to look peaceful. The trouble is none of us speaks their language.'

'Well I speak a few words but it is a different kind of language to any of the German dialects.'

'Are there no common words?'

'A few I think, but I'm no expert.'

'Why didn't you bring an interpreter with you?'

'We did. You killed him. He spoke quite passable Britannic. He was raised here for some of his life before his father brought him to Cimbria.'

'What? Horsa was the only one who could communicate with these people?'

'Afraid so. You had to kill him.'

'This gets worse and worse. Maybe one of them speaks German. They must have traders.'

'Most of the trade is with the Romans and with the Gaels across the sea.'

'I speak Latin, Greek and a bit of Dacian. There's some

chance I suppose.'

We set about lighting fires all around us so we would have warning of anyone approaching. We piled them high and waited.

When they arrived it became obvious they had come in strength. At first there seemed only to be about twenty men who stood near one of the fires. We began to relax. We had nothing to fear from so few men. We laughed and teased one another for being old women. Drogo slapped me on the back.

Our relief did not last long. As if they had rehearsed it, the Caledonii all lit their torches at once. The whole area in front of us was lit up in a semicircle. They stood at the edge of our now well-lit camp and we realised they were perhaps two hundred strong. They were shadowy warriors, their front ranks illuminated but casting a ghostly shadow, flickering and fluttering in the wavy firelight. They were silent and threatening. I could make out they all had round wooden shields, some covered in shiny leather and others bare wood. Each man carried a spear with a round, metal shod tip. Some had horned helmets but few had chain mail. They looked fearsome and strong and the main difference between them and the Votadini, whom I had fought before, was that few of them were naked warriors. I thought it meant they would be more likely to be organised. I should have known better.

Presently, a big warrior walked into the light. He had a full beard and a tangled shock of red hair. He carried a sword and shield. His leggings were not unlike the ones we wear in German lands but they bore a pattern with squares of different colours, not stripes like ours. His tunic was also brightly coloured but the light was not good enough to pick up details, although I noticed he wore a torc about his neck and his helmet had points at the crown like little horns.

He beat on his shield and shouted in a strange language. He strutted up and down and looked fierce. It was a challenge. He wanted to fight so much I could almost smell his eagerness.

'What do we do now?' Cimbrod said. 'Do I kill him?'

'No, if you accept his challenge and kill him they will attack. Let me go and talk to him,' I said.

'You don't speak their language.'

'No, but there are other ways to communicate you know.'

'All right, as you wish. You killed Horsa after all.'

I took off my sword and belt. I had no armour and being unarmed, thought my intentions could not possibly be misinterpreted. I approached with slow deliberate steps, holding my hands out at my sides, hoping he would not rush me and try to kill me with the huge sword he carried. I stopped ten feet from him. I smiled and held up my right hand.

The Caledonian warrior turned to me and looked me up and down with an expression of scorn. He turned to his people and said something. There was scattered laughter and I could imagine the sort of comment he must have made. I was unperturbed. I did not want to fight; I had to find a way to communicate. I squatted and gestured him to do the same. He cocked his head to one side and looked. He did not move towards me, which I interpreted as a sign he did not want to kill me. It was a mistake.

He looked at me again and charged as fast as he could with his sword raised above his head. It was a problem for me as I was squatting. It is hard to duck or dodge from that position. The sword descended. I moved fast. I put out my right hand and swivelled on it. The blow missed me and struck the ground. I turned, still squatting. I swiped his left leg with my outstretched foot.

His sword buried itself in the turf. His left knee gave way. He ended kneeling. I stood, fast as a bubble bursting and kicked. My left foot struck him in the face hard. He was a big man, not as big as I was, but he must have been tough. He did not go down; he merely shook his head to clear it. In that second, I stamped on his sword. It broke. It must have been made of poor steel. I backed away.

His head cleared. He stood up. He looked at the broken sword and he roared. He ran at me. He should have kept his temper. I remember Cornelius, the old gladiator who taught me, saying, 'Never, never, never get angry. Cold steel is better than burning parchment.'

I don't know quite what he meant, but I understood the underlying principle. Anger makes you rash, stupid and unprepared. The warrior swung the remains of his weapon two handed at my head. I leaned back and as it passed my face, I leaned forward again. I head-butted him. Not once, twice. He staggered back. I tripped him as he backed away. His broken nose made tears in his eyes. I took advantage of his loss of vision. I picked up his broken sword and held it to his throat. There was a gasp from the surrounding warriors.

I knew then they would either attack or kill us all, or they would talk. It had been a gamble.

CHAPTER XIII

"Choose a subject equal to your abilities; think carefully what your shoulders may refuse, and what they are capable of bearing"
—Horace

'You're quite good at communicating,' said Cimbrod smiling as he approached.

'Yes, you should see me negotiate,' I said.

I backed away to let the big red-haired warrior recover enough to get up. His comrades still kept their distance, but I hoped it was clear we had not come to fight. Any fool could see they had started it.

I think Wuotan did something then. Perhaps he had watched and enjoyed the fight for he took pity on me. I had retrieved my weapons and the Caledonii's warrior was staggering back to his people when a girl came out of the crowd of men. She bore a torch and wore a simple, clean tunic and a brightly coloured, hooded cloak fastened at her left shoulder by a shiny silver pin. Her feet were bare but she walked proudly as if she was not poor. I could see a light silver torc at her neck. She had long black hair tied in a single plait and a pretty, friendly face with eyes seeming to smile. She must have been a similar age to Cimbrod.

'Do any of you speak Latin?' she said.

Her voice wavered a little as she spoke and I could hear she was scared.

'Yes, I do,' I said.

I smiled to reassure her.

'My Lord sent me to find out your intentions,' she said.

'What Lord?'

'The Ri of the Caledonii. He is a king in his own right. He is over there. He wants to talk but did not know whether you were slavers from Rome or not.'

'Slavers?'

'Yes, they come here from time to time and we hide in the brochs.'

'What are brochs?'

She said, 'The big tower is called thus.'

'You speak good Latin,' I said, 'you are not from here then?'

'No my parents were Gallic traders. They both died of a fever when we came here. The Lord Nechtan took me in and clothed and fed me from the age of ten.'

'They were kind to you then?'

'Yes, they are good people. They hate the Romans but have to trade with them so they found my language-skills useful. My name is Ancamma. My parents named me after our Goddess of water because we came from over the sea.'

I said, 'Well Ancamma, I am Galdir, a German lord. This is Cimbrod, son of a King of Cimbria and these are his men. We have come to fight for the Lord Nechtan if he wants us. We only want to be paid and we will all fight for him.'

'If you wait there, I will go back and speak to him. These are war-like people and it might be wise if you do not provoke them.'

'It would be equally wise for them not to provoke us, we are not men of peace either,' I said.

'What did she say?' said Cimbrod, 'A very beautiful girl

like that would make a good Queen at home.'

'We haven't fought a battle yet and you're already talking of marriage. You have to do a bit of fighting sometime if you want to be paid as a mercenary.'

'Yes, well, yes you're right. She's very pretty though. Perhaps I can earn her hand.'

We stood and waited. Presently, a big black-haired warrior came out of the crowd of men. Four others accompanied him. One of them carried a stool and he put it down for the big man to sit upon.

Ancamma approached, 'This is Lord Nechtan. He wants to speak to you.'

Cimbrod and I approached and sat cross-legged on the damp ground before the Ri. Ancamma translated, I spoke and translated to Cimbrod as we went along. It made conversation hard but it worked well enough.

'I am Lord of this land for as far north and south as you can see,' he said. 'Why have you come to frighten my people?'

'We are sorry if our intentions were not clear. We have come to offer our services. Even far away across the sea we hear how great a King there is in Caledonia and these men have travelled here to serve you as soldiers and do your bidding. We will fight anyone you wish, all we ask is for payment in gold.'

The Ri looked at me. He had a thick red woollen cloak and a green tunic, but I saw he wore chain mail beneath the cloak. Around his neck, there were four golden torcs and a chain of silver. His belt had gold adornments too and I could see the pommel of his massive broadsword had a huge pearl in it. He had no helmet and his long black hair hung wild about his shoulders. He made me think of a raven, big, black and wise.

His dark eyes shone in the torchlight as he answered me. He smiled as he spoke and I was surprised to see he had near perfect teeth, which of course is a rarity anywhere in the modern world.

Ancamma turned to me and said, 'My lord Nechtan says you may stay. In the morning, he will discuss terms. He was impressed with your fighting skills and looks forward to you all fighting on his side if indeed you can all fight like that.'

Cimbrod was smiling at Ancamma. Every time she opened her mouth, he smiled at her. I knew only too well what was going on. I also have a weakness for women but he was even worse. She never took her eyes from my face when she was speaking which made me uncomfortable. My heart was elsewhere at that time and I have never been a philanderer.

Hengeist pushed our bound prisoner towards us. The man stumbled to his knees before the Ri. He kept repeating his name.

'Philip,' he said, across his swollen lips and fractured face.

The Ri for his part stepped back with a look of horror on his face and glared at me. It was as if we had insulted him.

'Philip,' the stupid man kept saying.

The Caledonian leader continued to step back and called in a loud voice over his shoulder. I wondered if we had betrayed him in some way.

Out of the surrounding darkness, I could hear a bell. The faint tinkling seemed incongruous in the dark of this Caledonian night. A figure approached. He walked with an odd shuffling gait, two short steps with the left and one long step with the right. His hair and brown beard were tangled and his clothes tattered. In his hand he carried a bill-hook such as Egyptians fight with, but the inner surface was smooth. It was similar to a sickle with which one cuts corn.

Ancamma said, 'Step back. This is serious magic.'

'What?' I said.

'The man you brought is a seer and was thrown out of this tuath years ago. I recognised him and so does the Ri. He is a fillid and makes evil predictions and curses.'

'A what?' I felt stupid.

'A fillid. One who predicts what will happen. If they dream and tell the future it can come true. The only way to rid the tuath of an evil fillid is to throw him out or kill him. Only a Druid or another fillid can kill him.'

'I thought his name was Philip.'

'Philip? There is no such name. Look away or you may be affected by the evil.'

Despite her warning, I could not take my eyes from the scene unfolding before us. The newcomer began to chant. The bound prisoner began to whimper. He fell to the ground and his whole body began to convulse, eyes staring, limbs jerking. It was indeed powerful magic.

With the speed of a blinking eye, the wild-haired man swung his billhook. It took off the prisoner's head in one movement. Blood spurted onto the grass as the head flew away, rolling on the turf. It seemed to me then that in the light of the torches, a brown mist appeared from the neck of the bleeding corpse. I know not if it was an illusion or the effect of suggestion working on our senses, but Cimbrod later told me he saw the same. The brown mist hovered for a moment then dissolved in a sudden gust of wind that appeared from nowhere and was gone.

The wild-looking man, scythe in hand turned and humming, walked away with a normal gait, his steps seemingly lighter than when he approached.

'Why did you bring this man here? Did you not know he was evil? Could you not feel it?' Ancamma said.

'No, we thought he was just a brigand. We brought him as an offering.'

'We don't eat people you know,' she said, smiling at last.

Nechtan approached and he was smiling his perfect smile. I remained uncertain whether it was a smile representing danger to us or simple relief to him. His perfect dentition was irritating.

We gestured to the king to enter the camp, but he declined. They left the body where it had fallen. No one paid it any attention as if it was a vessel, now quenched and empty, to be discarded and ignored. He left Ancamma and two of his men with us in the hope that she could teach us some of the language, but I knew there was little chance of that tonight.

The defeated warrior stood at the edge of the firelight and shouted. He was in a rage over something. Whatever he had said I recognised Ancamma's name.

She turned and said something with venom. He shook his fist and stormed away. There was something happening here I did not understand. We were hampered in our communications by the lack of language and I realised that Cimbrod and I had to learn to converse in the Caledonian tongue. I knew I could do it in the end, but I was worried for Cimbrod. The only part of the language that Cimbrod would have wanted to learn would not be suitable for polite conversation in any case.

'Cimbrod,' I said, 'however much you want that girl, leave her alone.'

'Why? She's beautiful.'

'Yes, but we need her and we don't need any entanglements. You know nothing about this place. Getting into trouble over women is the last thing a leader should do. Try to be patient.'

The word 'leader', seemed to do the trick. He looked down at the ground and spoke little for the rest of the evening. Every time he looked up, he was unable to take his eyes from the girl. We sat at one of the fires and she told us about the Caledonii and the wars that they were fighting against the other local tribes.

'Many of the people here have come from the south, they shelter among us from the Romans,' she said.

'Our only worry is that we can't speak the language. We haven't met anyone since we came. They all seem to run away.'

'That is because they are afraid you might be Roman slavers. There are brochs all over our coast where the people can take shelter. They are strong structures.'

'What did she say?' Cimbrod said.

'Just about the people here,' I said.

'Ask her if she's married,' Cimbrod said.

'Shut up,' I said.

Cimbrod frowned and began sulking.

'Who was the warrior I fought with?'

Ancamma said, 'His name is Drosten. He thinks he is one of the best fighters in the tribe. He wants to marry me.'

'He's too old for you isn't he?'

'They take young wives here,' she said, 'I wish I could leave.'

She looked up at me with plaintive eyes and I could sense Cimbrod next to me shifting slightly. I had no intention of allowing this girl to come between Cimbrod and me so I

113

said, 'We are here to fight for the Ri. We are not here to find women. If you are promised to Drosten then that is how it must be.'

She looked at the ground. Between her and Cimbrod, it promised to be a miserable time, and after she had left to go back whence she had come, Cimbrod said nothing. I knew he found the situation frustrating, but I found the fact that the boy had only just laid eyes on Ancamma reassuring because I thought that we might not see her again. I should have known about that too. A woman arousing lust is like a small fire that spreads through all the forest. It is unstoppable, but one of nature's most wonderful creations.

CHAPTER XIV

"Mistakes are their own instructors"
—Horace

The morning was cold. It did not rain and one has to accept cold is better than wet and cold. I awoke early, as was my habit. It was misty around the hill where we had made camp and the cinders of last night's fire glowed a sorrowful parting as I retied my sandals. I still had the same leggings I had taken from the carter and they needed changing, so I was glad we had the opportunity to mix with the Caledonii, for there was much I wanted to obtain. Horsa's clothes were too small for me and were restrictive.

Birds were calling somewhere in the mist but they were unfamiliar. Everything smelled damp and I took some of the moist wood and piled it onto the remains of the fire in the hope it would catch, but of course it did not.

I walked around the camp to keep warm. My footsteps were silent in the dew-laden grass and I found myself thinking about the events of the previous night. Cimbrod was sulking when we had settled to sleep. He wanted the girl and I had hoped it would not become an obsession. She seemed to have an interest in me and that made things complicated and possibly dangerous.

Thoughts of Lucia intruded. Her fierce aggressive lovemaking, her sense of humour and above all the defiance against anything that might stand in her way, made her twice

115

as attractive to me, though I cannot now say why. I had only had a short time with her so it was perhaps unreasonable, even foolish to think about her so much, but all through the Roman siege in Sicambra she had been there, hidden in the recesses of my mind.

At the far edge of our camp, I saw a figure sitting with his back to me. It was Cimbrod. He had clearly awoken early too and he was sitting on a stone looking into the mist.

'The fog in this place never seems to let up in the early morning, my friend,' I said.

He turned and looked over his shoulder at me. 'No. We have sea mists at home moving in to the forests at night and retreating back to sea in the day. My grandmother used to call it the elves' dance.'

'Yes we have some similar tales in Frankia. Could you not sleep?'

'No. You know what I was thinking?'

'No. It isn't like you to think, is it?'

'Stop it, I'm serious.'

'Yes, I think I do know what is going in your mind. It is part of the burden of your responsibility as leader, not to threaten our employment for the sake of your own desire, my friend.'

'How did you know?'

'I am not a sensitive man apart from reading horses, but I can read a man's eyes. Yours were full of desire as soon as you saw that girl. I remember those feelings myself.'

'She couldn't take her eyes off you.'

'Don't worry. I'm not free to play around with girls just because they look at me. We are nearly sword-brothers and women must not interfere in that bond.'

'You are a strange man. At home, men kill each other in

quarrels over women. Perhaps we Cimbri allow our hearts to guide us more than our heads; my father often says so.'

'He is a wise man. I first fell in love with a girl from Gaul. Her name was Livia. She could run, hunt and shoot a bow with the accuracy of Frij himself.'

'Where is she now?'

My face must have clouded over, for he frowned and went quiet.

'She died. She meant much to me. She visits me in dreams sometimes. She warns me of danger. There is a spirit world all around us. From it, there come glimpses of what is to come. I had a witch, an old woman who used to have dreams. They were portents and warnings and she was very powerful like that.'

'Where is she now? Let me guess, she's dead too.'

'It seems sometimes as if everyone in my life whom I love dies. Maybe that should be a warning to you. Don't become too close a friend to me.'

'I can look after myself. But this girl is seriously on my mind.'

'She's promised to Drosten of the recently broken nose. No doubt you could kill him, but it would have to be an honourable fight. And don't do it until we have been paid. Hear me?'

'I hear you.'

I slapped him on the back. I could not help myself. I was becoming very fond of this Cimbri lad; he was too much like me.

When we had eaten and washed, we packed up our belongings and waited. Ancamma came. A boy riding a pony like the one I had stolen from the carter accompanied her. She smiled at me as she rode up the hill. Her brown hair hung free and it spread out behind her as she rode. She was a beautiful girl but that only evoked a sense of danger in me. I was clearly not myself in those days, but my youth felt as if it had departed a thousand years before.

'Greetings Galdir,' she said.

'Greetings indeed.'

Cimbrod said, 'Your presence brightens the morning. Tell her.'

'No,' I said, still smiling.

'Please. You said we are brothers.'

'What did he say?' said Ancamma.

'He says,' I said with my eyes turned skywards, 'you brighten up his morning.'

I could not keep the boredom out of my voice.

'Oh.' she said. 'We are going to the Ri's tuath. That is a family group who live together. There are no big towns or cities. All the Tuaths communicate and can gather as an army very quickly by lighting beacons if their need is great. Otherwise they meet at markets and special days when they celebrate their Gods.'

'Who is the boy? I think he shot arrows at us when we first arrived.'

'Yes, he thought you were Roman slavers.'

I showed her the hole in my tunic.

'Even if we were, there was no necessity for this.'

Ancamma laughed. 'He is usually a better shot than that. He is Taran's son. Taran is one of our great warriors and hunters. We left the boy behind when we travelled to the market gathering. He kept you away, did he not?'

'Yes, you could say that.' I smiled to the boy but he looked me in the eye with a stony glance and I could see he was proud. He probably felt he had won our last encounter.

Ancamma led us away to the east and it took almost an hour for us to arrive at the Tuath. There was a stockade around the low buildings where several families must have lived. We mounted the summit of a hill and I could make out the road running down to the gates of a small community settlement: the tuath. There was a palisade and I could make out twenty or so buildings.

We rode down that path, forty mounted warriors, each with peaceful intentions but I only had to look at my comrades' faces to read the tension they felt. They were prepared for anything; they did not know the language and they had no trust after the fight the night before. Adelmar had wondered if perhaps it might be an ambush. He warned us all to be on guard and not drink more than was expected in hospitality. I had new respect for the young Cimbrian. He seemed wiser and older than his years for he had voiced what had been at the back of my own mind.

The gates were open and there were no guards apart from a boy the same age as the lad who rode with us. We passed a smithy close to the wall. I could see steam rising from a vat and heard the hiss of quenching metal. Next to it, a building stood that smelled like a cheese house. We passed its door and I could see the stacked cheeses, round yellow bullets all around the room and in the middle a great churn where they made it.

There were pens around the outside of the compound and I could make out goats and sheep, the cattle being far up the hillside grazing even as early in the year as this. Ancamma told me the market they had attended the day before was a festival celebrated locally called Imbolc. It was a celebration of the ewes coming into milk. She explained how there had been a great feast and fines and tuaths from all around had gathered for the annual festivities. She called the smaller family groups within a tuath a fine. My head buzzed in the end with all the strange names but still she kept on passing information to us and I translated to the others all the time. Translating is no fun. One has no time to savour the content. It is like drinking wine too quickly, all in the mouth at once and nothing on the nose to think about and then it has gone, leaving no finish on the palate either.

I passed a woodworking building where I could see men making curved slats of wood.

'What are they doing, Ancamma?' I said.

'Why, they are making timbers for boats. The Caledonii are great wood-workers and make fine boats they use for trade with the Gaels across the sea.'

'Which sea?'

She laughed then and it was a sound like silver bells. I had not met a girl with such liveliness and humour for a long time and I found I liked this Gallic trader's daughter.

She said, 'Don't you know anything? To the west is a great sea and across it there is another country where the Gaels live. They are a rough wild people even by Caledonii standards. They raid and trade in equal proportion.'

'Is that why the brochs are built?'

'No. The Caledonii can handle them without running away. Even though the Gaels have fierce warriors, my people can fight them without much difficulty. You may not realise it, but half of the battles consist of the warriors lining up and shouting insults at each other. Then one champion on each side has a fight and takes the other's head and they all go home again. You men are a strange folk I think.'

'Is that what happened last night? We won the fight?'

'Yes, it is the same as if you had defeated the whole army.'

'You don't resent me defeating your betrothed?'

'He isn't my betrothed,' she said with a vehemence I had not expected. 'He thinks he can marry me and the Ri has given him permission to ask, but I don't want marriage and if I did I would not want him. He is a brute and not a real man either.'

'My friend Cimbrod will be pleased to hear it. He likes you,' I said. I am loyal in friendships and although this girl was beginning to work some subtle magic on me already, I knew Cimbrod would never forgive me if I were weak enough to indulge such a fancy.

'Which one is he?'

'The one just over there,' I said and pointed.

'Him? He's just a boy isn't he?'

'He is a fierce warrior and the son of a King. You could ask for no better match if you waited half a lifetime.'

'I had just thought...'

She looked at the path in front of us and then glanced at me.

'No, I am his loyal friend and we are sword-brothers. You should try to talk to him; he would be very happy. He might even persuade Drosten to give up his intentions.'

'How would he do that?'

'It is not easy to pursue romantic ideals if your head has come away from your body.'

'Oh,' she said, frowning, 'violence again. Is that all you men ever think about?'

I had no reply to that and remained silent for perhaps she was right. We had stopped outside a big hall. Constructed of timber, the building had a thatched roof. In size, it was less than half that of the hall my people built for me when we had settled in Sicambra, but it was grand by comparison to the other buildings in this place. There were large oak doors that stood open and as we approached, two guards came to Ancamma. There was some whispered conversation and she turned to translate.

'My Lord Nechtan wishes to see only your leader.'

'He won't be able to talk to him. He knows no Latin. He will need me to translate,' I said.

'I thought you were the leader.'

'No, I am only Lord Cimbrod's man. I am a warrior here and nothing more.'

'I can translate well enough,' she said in the common German tongue.

Cimbrod and I stood staring at her. She had hidden her German to hear what we said. I thought she was too clever for her own good.

'You speak German?' he said.

Ancamma smiled broadly. 'Of course I do, when I want to.'

She turned leaving us dumbstruck, and I realised I was mastering any attraction I might have had for the girl. I was unsure whether it was a touch of maturity or simple loyalty to Cimbrod. Whichever it was, I was glad of that unexpected strength. I could remember times when that had been absent and I had slept with someone who I should have known would betray me. She had plotted against me and I was the only one who could not see it. Perhaps it is often so in matters between men and women. Love blinds us to betrayal as surely as a dark night obscures what is obvious in daylight.

Cimbrod entered in front of me. It was, after all, his war band not mine. Who was I anyway but an escaped prisoner whom he had taken in?

We entered the hall. It was sparsely furnished and there

was a dais at one end where the Ri sat. He was not sitting on a throne, which surprised me. He was reclining on a sort of cushion made of straw and covered by sheepskins. Next to him was a low table on which there was a golden cup and a horn inlaid with silver. I wondered what he was drinking. I was not in the mood for ale. I hated the stuff. I would have given almost anything for a cup of wine. I missed the taste of fruit on my tongue and the smell of cherries. I could have murdered for it.

We walked to the dais and there were other such cushioned areas with skins spread out upon them. Nechtan gestured for us to sit.

I was about to negotiate for Cimbrod when I realised he was staring at Ancamma. He paid no attention to the Ri and I had to nudge him hard in the ribs to get him to concentrate.

Ancamma said, 'Lord Nechtan, this is the leader,' indicating Cimbrod. 'This man will help to translate. It might be useful if he stayed.'

'I only wanted the leader,' the Ri said, frowning.

'I cannot translate everything. It would help if he stays,' she said.

Nechtan regarded me with a look of interest but said nothing. I nodded to him and he indicated to us to sit.

It was time to talk and we sat before the Caledonian monarch and toasted his health from drinking horns servants brought to us. I noticed a number of severed heads hanging from the wooden pillars holding up the roof, and realised they had a similar culture to the Sarmatians, who took heads in battle and hung them outside their tents.

The king looked at me and began to speak. Ancamma translated, explaining again that although I was the elder,

Cimbrod was the leader. It promised to be a fruitful meeting and seemed to me to be the beginning of a useful relationship with the Caledonii.

'I may have a use for you,' Nechtan said.

'We are here to fight for the leader who is wise enough to pay us gold,' Cimbrod said through Ancamma.

'Gold is one thing; death on foreign soil is another.'

'Indeed,' I said, again translated by Ancamma, 'our comrades do not fear death for we know we will go to our ancestors as long as we have a sword in our hands.'

Nechtan looked at me as if I was talking out of turn. He turned to Cimbrod and said, 'I have a war coming, your help and that of your men may be of use. It will mean travelling north. The riches of that land are scant but I will reward loyal service.'

Cimbrod said, 'My men are at your disposal.'

'Then we go to Insi Orc, where men defy me and steal trade that rightfully belongs to my people.'

When we left the hall, Cimbrod said to me, 'Where is Insi Orc?'

'I have no idea. I thought you would have asked that.'

Ancamma said, 'It is an island in the far north, the Caledonii are at war with these people over trade. You will go with Nechtan?'

'Of course,' Cimbrod said, 'there is no greater attraction than gold unless it is a beautiful woman like you.'

She smiled at that and I realised the beginnings of a friendship was springing up before my eyes. It pleased me and it relieved me, for I had no wish for foreign entanglements for myself and least of all with this young woman. She seemed to know too well how to handle men like Cimbrod and me.

CHAPTER XV

"You have power over your mind—not outside events. Realize this, and you will find strength"
—Marcus Aurelius

Why anyone would want to live on the islands of Insi Orc defeats me. The name means 'the islands of the boar' but I never saw any wild boars when I was there, only wild men. We reached the islands by boat, which is the worst way to travel in spring as far north as we found ourselves. The islands spread out a long way across the sea, to my unbridled chagrin. I hated boats.

The ships bobbed up and down. They pitched forwards and back. They rolled sideways. After the first hour, I was vomiting over the side. The sea journey took the better part of half a day and I was glad when they deposited us on the shore. The horses had come with us and the ships returned for the other contingents. We were the advance guard and the Caledonii had probably thought we were expendable which was why we had to hold the beach while the others came.

In the event, we saw no one and when Nechtan arrived with his warriors, we had lit fires and were comforting ourselves around them. During the last few months, we had learned a good deal of the language of the Caledonii and we could communicate in a rudimentary fashion. Ancamma had taught us well but we missed her on this trip. She was regarded highly by the Caledonii as she was the best translator they had in their dealings with the Romans. They had not therefore allowed us to bring her with us.

The Caledonii camped on the beach and we set lookouts on the dunes. It was still cold and a harsh wind blew huge waves up the shore, the spray and foam almost reaching us. The rain held off I was pleased to note, and we roasted fish that the Caledonii had brought with them, but whether they had caught them on the way or bought them when we left, I did not know. I filled my empty stomach and we spent an uncomfortable night, the sounds of the rushing surf loud in our ears.

We had come to settle a score for Nechtan. The Caledonii were at war with the Orcadians; the dispute had arisen over trade. For years the main exports of the Caledonii were ironware and fine woodcarvings. Mostly it was exported through the Insi Orc islands, which were on a main sea route to countries far to the east and south-west. The Orcadian King had begun to charge high prices for the use of his domain. When Nechtan had objected, the Orcadian King refused to allow Caledonian goods to pass through his islands. It was enough to cause a war. Negotiation had failed and Nechtan had decided to attack. He was on good terms with the Lugi and Cornovii tribes who inhabited the far northern tip of Britannia so our journey north had been uneventful.

There were about five hundred Caledonii in our group and forty of us mercenaries. We were the only ones who were mounted, apart from the Ri who had a chariot and a driver. They used chariots less than the southern Britons, which was not surprising considering the terrain in which they fought.

Driving a chariot amongst rocks and hills was certain to end in a spill or a damaged wheel. They used cavalry sparingly too. Their horses were small sturdy beasts but I assumed they were no match for the Roman cavalry steeds. They seemed even less use against armoured heavy cavalry like the Sarmatians.

I looked at the Caledonii warriors. Half were almost naked. They looked similar to the Votadini who I had become accustomed to fight in the south. We mixed little with them though they were friendly enough. One of them called Taran often sat with us during the mealtimes and we became acquainted with him on the long journey north. His father had fought the Romans at the Antonine wall twenty years before and he described that war to us when we asked him. I understood only a part of the story for our language skills were limited but the overall picture was understandable. He hated the Romans almost as much as I did but he hated the Vacomagi and Votadini tribes more. It was typical of these people that they had strong dislikes of each other, indeed even the tuaths fought among themselves.

He was dark and of medium height with spiked hair. His brown eyes had a softness in them which surprised me in an experienced warrior. There were little crow's feet at the corners of his eyes for he was a man with humour and he laughed frequently.

'The only good Roman is a dead Roman,' he said, when I told him of how I had come to be in Britannia.

'I agree,' I said. 'Do all the Britons hate the Romans as you seem to?'

'Most of us in the north do. We have to tolerate their presence for they are too many to fight. They have long since subdued the southern tribes though and many have adopted

127

Roman ways. I am only relieved that they have no interest in taking our land as they have the land of the Selgovae and the rest.'

'They may move north sometime, you know.'

'Doubt it,' he said, 'they would have a bloody fight if they tried.'

'Maybe so, but they take your people for slaves don't they?'

'Yes, but we hide in the brochs and that seems to be a good way to defend ourselves.'

Cimbrod said, 'The people of these islands—how do they feel about the Romans?'

'They feel the same as we do of course. We are all the same race you know.'

'Yet you fight each other anyway?' I said.

'When we have to. Sometimes we raid each other's cattle and like now, we have trade disputes. It's all part of being a Caledonian. Much of the fighting is done to establish credentials.'

'Credentials?' Cimbrod said.

'Yes. The more heads you take and the more cattle you steal the greater your honour and respect in your own tribe.'

'There are tribes like that at home too,' Cimbrod said.

A horn sounded off to our right.

'It's time to go,' Taran said and got to his feet. We walked to the top of the dunes together and surveyed the scene in the burgeoning sunlight. The Caledonii had split into five groups of roughly a hundred men and they advanced in a most disorganised way. I was used to seeing carefully organised Cohorts with the lines of centuries precise and disciplined. It was almost a relief to see the disorganisation after the tiresome regularity of the Romans.

The cool spring morning rays of sunshine hardly warmed us and a cold sea breeze pushed us forward with gentle hands on our backs and little gestures expressed by the leaning grass. We crossed the dunes without hindrance and came to a broad flat verdant plain. In the distance, I could make out a group of houses, surrounded by a palisade.

'Cimbrod,' I said, 'shall I take some men and ride ahead?'

'No, the Ri wants us behind his men but if there is fighting he wants us to percolate through the ranks and join battle first.'

'Well, you wanted to be a mercenary. Expendability is the key to the tactics, you know.'

Cimbrod said, 'The Caledonii don't seem to go in for tactics.'

'And your people do?'

'Yes, we used short blades against the Romans and my people are fierce warriors or at least they used to be.'

'No, what I meant was that the Caledonii don't seem to have a plan of any kind. I gained the impression they want to fight anyone they come across and then go home.'

'Look! Do you see that,' Cimbrod said pointing.

'Where?'

'Over there? See it?'

I shaded my eyes in the morning sun and could make out some movement behind the huts. The huts, it turned out, were buildings sunk in the ground. They usually faced north-south with a door at either end. The movement I had seen became visible as an army. They outnumbered us by almost two to one. There were at least eight or nine hundred of them, maybe more. I estimated that half were Nudis, as the Romans called them. The expression seemed to have stuck in my mind and as they approached, I explained the term to Cimbrod.

'I suppose it is an apt name. Without armour of any kind they must be pretty vulnerable to the Romans,' he said.

'Yes, but they fight like Tiu himself. If they had someone like me to advise them I could settle the Romans for good and all.'

'How would you achieve that?'

'I don't know yet, but it will come to me.'

'Ah, like pissing in the wind?'

'Thank you for that.'

Cimbrod was smiling as we looked out upon the scene of the coming battle. I have always thought it strange, the way men talk rubbish before a battle. It is as if foolish talk distracts the mind from what is to come. Ruminating upon the violence of a coming conflict does little more than make you frightened as far as I can see.

Our men stood in a rough semblance of groups but there was even less order than among my fighting men at home.

The approaching army came closer. The naked men had spiked hair. I did not know then that they rubbed their hair with lime so it became stiff and they dried it into spikes. It looked foolish to me but I never told any of them that for fear of causing offence. Britons are tetchy when they remark upon each other and I saw more than one serious fight because one man had commented on another's appearance.

Most battles started with a chosen warrior advancing between the armies and reciting his family history and boasting about his great exploits in fights and battles. Often they had the heads of their vanquished enemies tied to their waists to show off their prowess. They seemed childish even compared to Germans for although some of our tribes take heads, they usually make them into drinking cups to insult the memory of their dead enemies.

A man pushed his way through the enemy crowd. I say crowd for they did not stand in any kind of formation. They looked to me like an armed rabble and I thought they would fall over each other in a charge.

He was not a big man. His spiked hair added to his stature but the thing that was interesting was the size of his manhood. It was erect and I wondered whether he had taken some kind of potion or become drunk before the battle. I could not imagine why he would want to expose himself in that way. In the heat of battle, I never found the ability to raise a stand, but it takes all kinds of men to make an army I suppose.

A blue dye covered him in lines from head to foot and there were dark charcoal marks around his eyes making them look sinister and sunken. He carried a round wooden shield and in his right hand, he bore a long heavy sword the likes of which I had not seen before. It was fully as tall as he was and he whirled it about his head with a practised ease that I found remarkable for a man who would only measure in stature up to my nose.

'He's mine,' said Cimbrod.

'Wait and see if the Ri wants you to fight him,' I said, but Cimbrod rode out through the Caledonii lines and raised his sword. He turned for a moment to me and said, 'If he kills me, make sure you take his head before the day is done, would you?'

I smiled and nodded. I had never seen him fight apart from the time when the brigand had felled him with his own shield, but I trusted him. His brothers rode forward and I followed. Apart from Adelmar, they were all of the same age and I could not see how they could be brothers unless their mother had septuplets. Hengeist told me later that apart from Adelmar and Cimbrod they all had different mothers and I marvelled how, in a world where monogamy was valued, a man could have six wives. I decided it was unwise to enquire too closely in case I offended them. I supposed that a king could get away with anything among the Cimbri.

The seven of us sat astride our mounts at the front of our little army. I was becoming used to the scale of things in Britannia. At home, an army of thirty thousand men is considered small. Here, a thousand men was an invasion force. No wonder the Romans found it so easy to defeat them.

Nechtan raised his arm and called in a loud voice something about killing but I did not understand what he said. Cimbrod waved at the Ri and smiled, extending an arm towards us, then signalling to the gathered warriors in front and behind. He could have been riding to a social gathering from the unperturbed expression on his face. He rode forward and dismounted. He had seen how Drosten had attacked me and he was ready. He grinned as he hefted his shield.

'Young fool,' I thought, 'watch your enemy.' I was concerned for him and I was becoming more like Cornelius all the time had I but known it.

I watched as the Nudi approached. I could feel my heart beating like a drum inside my ribcage. My mouth was arid as the plains of Parthia. I was more anxious than if I was doing the fighting myself and I realised that I cared about the outcome of the contest. I had become fond of this Cimbri Prince.

Cimbrod stepped lightly forward and said something to the advancing Orcadian warrior. The man's eyes were wide. I could see the dilated pupils even from where I sat upon my horse. I realised the Briton had taken some kind of potion, for his face was contorted into a grimace that gave him a beast-like quality. He ran forward towards my friend. The sword followed him and he swung it in a circle overhead. The reach of the weapon was tremendous. Cimbrod stepped back. He smiled again. The Orcadian brought his sword down in a diagonal slice. If it had caught Cimbrod, it would have cloven him clean to the midriff.

Cimbrod stepped back again with ease. Light on his feet, he waited until the sword was past him. He stepped forward. With a speed I had never witnessed before, even from Cornelius my mentor, he stabbed forward with the blade. Cimbrod's sword pierced the man's left cheek. Cimbrod rolled away. It was like watching a gladiator fight: multiple single blows. The victor of each, a little closer to victory.

The naked warrior, his manhood's stance now faded, let out a howl of pain and anger. He touched his cheek then lowered his hand, letting the blood run freely down his chest. His sword came up again. This time Cimbrod blocked with his shield. It was a mistake, for the striking sword was very heavy. The blow made my friend stagger back. I felt frustrated. I wished I could have told him about that. A second blow landed, then a third. Cimbrod was on his knees. His opponent dropped his shield. He raised the huge blade two-handed above his head. We could see it was over. I swallowed, my heart threatening to leap from my chest. I wanted Cimbrod to win and I knew also he was dead.

Again, with the speed of a flying Valkyr, and to my total amazement, Cimbrod rolled away and stood four or five feet away. The Orcadian, unable to control his blade as it descended found it struck the ground between the two men. I heard Cimbrod laugh. It was a quiet, confident sound and I wondered if he was simply playing with his opponent, but after his performance against the brigands, I was unsure. I had to admit, his footwork was superb.

The blue painted warrior regained his balance. He ran forward. His sword followed him. When he stopped, the blade continued to fly. He whirled it overhead, ready to rain more blows on his victim's shield. Cimbrod moved. He moved so fast I felt a surge of pride. I could not have done it better myself, even with Cornelius at my side telling me what to do.

Cimbrod stooped under the swinging blade as it reached the zenith of its traverse. He turned sideways. He used his back muscles. He turned into his man. He stabbed, hard and fast. The blade penetrated beneath the ribs. The naked blue flesh yielded as if Cimbrod was cutting fruit. The hilt remained projecting from the mad, blue, wild man. Cimbrod turned and flipped backwards. He ended standing facing the Dying nudi. I thought he was showing off now. The Orcadian dropped his blade and it fell, striking his shoulder in its descent. He did not notice. He sank to his knees. With a look of surprise on his face, he slumped forward, relaxing into the posture and shape of death, its finality overstated by the speed with which it had come to him. A pool of blood was spreading slowly around him as his life ebbed away in the lush Orcadian grass. I heard the plaintive cry of gulls overhead. I remember thinking how they would have to wait for their feast. There would be a lot more blood on the sward before the day was out.

Cimbrod reached forward, and placing his foot on his enemy's chest, tugged his blade free. He raised it over his head and screamed a war shout. The blade came down on the Orcadians' neck and completely severed it with only that blow. He grabbed the spiked hair and running, carried the head to the Ri. Nechtan smiled with pleasure. He leaned forward and said something to Cimbrod, which in a fit of jealousy I felt sure my friend could not have understood and Cimbrod rejoined us breathing hard and smiling.

'You should never have let him hit your shield,' I said.

His face fell, 'Thank you for that advice. I thought it went well.'

I looked at my friend and realised that I was jealous. I was ashamed then.

'I'm sorry. It was a wonderful and skilful fight. I admire the way you did it.'

'It was wasn't it?'

'Yes, my friend, but you may have caused a bit of resentment in the opposing army. Look.'

He glanced in the direction I was pointing and we realised that the entire Orcadian force was on the move. They yelled and shouted. It was a solid wall of screaming warriors waving battle-axes and spears with their brightly colours breeks and their red hair flying out behind them or spiked in stellate patterns on their heads. I realised at once that we were caught in the front of the battle line. We numbered only forty riders but we were all killers to the man and I felt sorry for any of the poorly armoured enemy that came near us. My horse reared as the first wave of men hit us. I found it hard to tell who was enemy and who was friend, for it was as if a sea of blue immersed us.

We rode forward. We knew that the men furthest from us were the Orcadians. It was not a formulated plan. It was instinctual. We rode hard. We rode knee to knee. All in front of us either backed away or fell to our bloodied blades. I struck with the sword to left then right. I split skulls and stabbed necks. I cared not where I hit them but wanted blood, red blood to feed my battle lust.

It had been a long time since I had felt it. I remembered old fights and battles, riding Valknir against a Roman army, against oppressors and men who would enslave me. I remembered killing on a city rampart. I saw the faces of attacking Marcomannii. I felt Cornelius at my side. I remembered the feeling of killing the man who had killed my first love. It all passed through my brain as I fought. It is the most exhilarating feeling a man can experience. My shield arm felt weightless. My right arm moved in a blur and my horse flew like Wuotan's maidens as they search the battlefields to find the ones who are ready to go with them to Valhalla.

I felt alive for the first time since I had come to Britannia. My hearing became sharp and clear. It was like some monstrous amplification in my ears. The sounds of men screaming, the noise of steel ringing against steel and the reverberating sounds of hundreds of shields, striking each other in the thunderous music of Donar's hammer.

It stopped suddenly. The smell of blood in my nostrils and the clamour of dying men and the screams of the wounded attenuated. We had ridden through the mass of enemy leaving behind a trail, a bloody path of death. Our horses were all but spent and we turned them, thirty-five of us now, but undaunted. Our brave Caledonii held out. Swamped in enemies and numbering only half of their adversaries, they fought on, individual fights bringing more death to the enemy than to our warriors. We could see it. Silent witnesses then to the bravery of our comrades, we waited for our horses to rest and calm. However much the infantry fight or die or lose, there is no point charging on an exhausted steed. It is the discipline of being cavalry. Patience despite all. I learned that from the battles against the Romans and the fighting to which my Sarmatian friends had trained me.

I had Adelmar on my left, his long arms hanging now at his sides, tired but recovering. To my right was Drogo. I almost felt he was kin, the only man who was of my tribe, a remnant of my last army. We watched as the Britons fought each other, neither side giving quarter, neither side flagging.

On our enemies' left flank I could see that our men were hardest pressed and were beginning to fall back slowly.

'Cimbrod,' I shouted above the din, 'to the left. We must go now.'

I saw that he heard me, and he nodded. We rode then. Mounted death we were. We hit the Orcadian rear hard as adamant. Our horses announced our coming and many fell beneath their sharpened hooves. We began striking and cutting with our swords, long weapons that gave us reach. The enemy flank began to crumble. They had no cavalry and although we were so few, each of us killed many. From horseback, we felt unassailable. The battle-lust gripped me again. It carried me forward; it made me fly. Strike, parry, thrust—it was all a blur; my limbs tireless, my senses sharpened. A split skull here, a severed limb there and blood that spurted, splashed and flew. I could see the enemy's blows before they even thought of them. I killed in a whirlwind of red fury, my horse bucking and kicking. We emerged again, ready to reform and rest before the next charge. I wiped blood from my bespattered face and laughed aloud for the sheer pleasure of it. I felt exhilarated for the first time since Sicambra. I wanted more—more death, more destruction.

I felt good for a change.

CHAPTER XVI

"The bravest sight in the world is to see a
great man struggling against adversity"
—Seneca

Despite their greater numbers, the Orcadians began to move
back. They did not run at first. We kept harrying their rear
and made another charge.

When it came, it happened fast. We had to rest the horses again and we stood on a small grassy knoll overlooking the
battle. Our men had moved forward to halfway across the
battlefield, killing as they came. They still whooped and
screamed their battle cries. We could see the Orcadian King,
mounted on a black pony, rallying his men. He had black
hair and a red cloak and carried a long sword.

Drosten killed him. I understood then why his fellows
respected him. The three men who stood between him and
the Orcadian King charged Nechtan's champion, but he
wielded his axe as if it were a toy. It whirled above his head.
It descended with horrible force three times as he stepped
sideways, avoiding their blows. Each axe-blow killed a man.
His assailants fell one by one. The King, astride his pony,
tried to swing his sword but Drosten hit the pony across the
neck and it fell headless and kicking on the turf, before any
blow landed. The king never got up. Drosten struck a blow
of such ferocity with his axe that in one stroke he took the
Orcadian King's head. He held the severed head high,

bloody and dripping. He screamed in his own language, his head thrown back and his legs slightly apart, like some fearsome red fury. Drying dark red blood covered his face and his rusty hair flew wild about his head. He looked ferocious and none of the enemy went near him. I did not understand what he said, but it seemed to be enough. I realised this man, whom I had defeated so easily when he wielded a sword, was all but invincible with an axe.

Two or three Orcadians saw the head of their leader held aloft and let out a cry of dismay. Others looked and they began to run. They kept their weapons, but they ran. I saw Taran, naked to the waist, his torso covered in blood chasing after them. He had a huge battleaxe in his hand and no shield. His blue-painted body was slick with red and his bearded face snarled like a wounded bear. His pupils were widely dilated as he dealt out death to the fleeing men. I was sure he must have been cold, but when I asked him later if that was so, he laughed as if I had to be mad. We watched them pass, but our mounts were too tired for more. In any case, it would have been senseless to follow. Why mete out death for no reason?

It began to rain. It was a hard and heavy shower. I did not mind, for blood and gore had bespattered me. The rainwater cleansed me and I wiped my face with my hand. I had hated the rain since I had come to Britannia, but this time it was welcome.

A quick head count showed we had lost eight men. Two of them were Chatti and one Marcomanni. The Chatti are better infantry than they are cavalry and I never rated their abilities on horseback. Cimbrod had a cut from a sword on his left arm and Hengeist had a stab wound in the thigh. Most of the men had some minor wounds but I was unscathed. I watched as the Caledonii gathered in the centre of the field, some rooting among the bodies for spoils. I could see Drosten shouting commands and ordering his men as he tied his defeated opponent's head at his waist. I thought, at least it was not my head, with blood-matted hair, tied and knotted at some man's waist. If Drosten had been able to have his way when we fought, it would have been. He had made himself scarce since the fight and I had not seen his flattened nose poking into the king's hall when I was around. I knew he bore me a grudge. Ancamma had explained a man's honour is everything to these people, but it was no different among us Germans and so I understood.

We walked our mounts down to the field. It was a field of death now, for they had killed the enemy wounded and only taken a handful of prisoners. Ancamma had told me the Caledonii did not indulge in torture but they often killed prisoners by beheading or ritual drowning. I wondered why they bothered with drowning. It would have been less trouble to kill them cleanly. Ancamma told me much later there was no way to the Otherworld—their afterlife, through running water and it was why they drowned men tied and chained to rocks in the clear white water of the Caledonian streams. It ended their life forever.

Nechtan addressed his army. My language had not reached the level where I understood everything he said but I understood enough to realise he was praising his men. When he pointed to us, the entire blood spattered gathering turned too. They raised their weapons and their voices rose in a deafening roar, making the horses rear. They waved bloodied weapons and began to sing. I looked at Cimbrod and saw him smile for he knew our battle-comrades were honouring us.

He rode forward to the Ri and Nechtan beckoned him to his side. He stood in his chariot, looking up at our leader and presented him with one of the torques from around his neck. Cimbrod bowed his head and accepted the gift. I hoped it would not be the only payment for we all needed to be paid and in gold. A loud cheer came from the assembled men and I looked around for Drosten. At first, I did not see him.

My searching gaze found him then. He had stood next to the king throughout. Nechtan presented him with another torque but I noticed it was silver not gold. There seemed to be some favouritism afoot and I did not like it. The King might just as well have made Cimbrod and Drosten fight, for the anger on the Caledonii chosen warrior's face was plain for all to see. He looked at Cimbrod and scowled. The Cimbri Prince smiled back at the red haired warrior as if he had not noticed the brooding anger. It was Nechtan's fault; he was playing the sort of games from which only kings get pleasure.

We marched on without resting. The men had stripped the bodies of anything valuable and piled up our dead ready for the return.

As we progressed up a green slope above the field where we had killed our foe, I could hear gulls screaming and calling. There was a smell of the sea, salt and fish, strong in my nostrils as we marched looking for the capital of the Orcadians. It was a small settlement of ten or so houses. They were stone-built, single storey buildings with doors at the front and the rear sunken into the ground, so when entering one had to step down. I wondered at that, for I could not understand how they kept out the damp. I did not puzzle over it for long.

I rode past a fenced area where there were sheep grazing. They acted as if nothing was wrong and they were oblivious to their impending demise for I knew these people well enough to recognise a great feast would occupy the army this night.

The Ri stopped at the largest dwelling house and sent in some men. They emerged dragging three women and two children. Nechtan said something to them I did not understand and I cursed my lack of knowledge of their language. They dragged away the children and I do not know what became of them but it is likely they were enslaved. They passed the women bodily overhead to the back of the collected Caledonii soldiers and I heard screams as they suffered. After everything I had done and seen in the last few hours, I regarded it as an anticlimax, and I scorned my fellow warriors for it. My mother was killed by Roman soldiers and although I was too young to remember it all, I do recall her screams as they stabbed her with their gladii. Is it surprising I hate the Romans and hate rape?

They used the thatch of the houses to make bonfires and herded the sheep and cattle together. A slaughter of all the livestock ensued, even though we could not eat them all. They roasted oxen whole and sheep too. It would have been a sumptuous feast had it not been for the wastefulness of it. They slaughtered fifty head of cattle and maybe as many sheep. Half the meat was wasted.

I found that as we sat around our fire that evening my nerves were on edge. I wondered if I was getting too old for this kind of life. I had seen so much fighting and killing in my time, I was becoming sick of it. Always fighting and meting out death has a way of depressing the lighter part of one's nature and I realised it was the endless killing making me serious and humourless.

It was then Chlotsuintha appeared in my mind. I say mind because no one else could see her. She stood in front of me and she pointed a knarled and crooked finger at my face.

'You must go home!' she said.

I said nothing for I knew she was in my head and not there in front of me. Visions are like that.

'You cannot tarry here. These people are not your blood-kin. Frija waits. She cannot wait forever. There is a young man who tempts her. You must go home and protect your people. Make war against the Romans; make an alliance. Keep your oaths and stop looking at women. Women are always your greatest weakness. Remember Clotildis.'

I stared at her face. There was a wart on her left cheek, high up at the front on the cheekbone. It looked so real I could have reached out and touched it. I did not however. I blinked and she was gone. I cannot explain whether it was a vision or merely a tired brain trolling through memories and wishful thinking.

The night was cold and dark and as I wrapped my damp cloak around me, Adelmar came and sat next to me.

'That was my first real battle,' he said.

'Not easy for any man is it?'

'No. I killed many men today.'

'Me too. You get used to it. The trick is not to think about them afterwards. If you think about them as people, sleeping, breathing and fucking it can make you mad in the end.'

'They haunt me. Their spirits seem to surround me and I feel bad about their deaths. Each time I close my eyes, I see the battle and the dying men.'

I felt impatient with the boy. I was not here to play

143

nursemaid to some Cimbri novice and wipe his snivelling nose. Where were his brothers? I kept quiet. I had had enough of the conversation. Afterwards, I often regretted my lack of understanding. It would have taken so little effort to talk with this young man, but we cannot any of us have back time that has gone and regrets are useless things.

We both sat looking at the flames before us and gnawed at the remnants of our feast. Cimbrod joined us then. He came out of the main hut where he had been ensconced with the Ri and no doubt eaten well.

'Galdir! It is a fine night, is it not?'

'What's so fine about it? Just another battle wasn't it?'

'Why the long face? We had a great victory. Everyone is drunk in there. Even Drosten is smiling. He keeps throwing that head up in the air and laughing.'

'I want to go home. I need to be with my people in Frankia. I think they have need of me.'

'But we need you here too.'

'No you don't. You have good fighting skills. I saw that fight you had today and couldn't have done better myself. I'm surprised you didn't pick up the head yourself and start throwing it about.'

'You know we don't do that in Cimbria,' he said. 'If I didn't know you better I would think you were jealous.'

'Of what? I said.

'Of me winning and receiving this golden torc. I only accepted it on everyone's behalf. Like a sort of communal honour.'

'Really? How will you apportion it then when we split up?' I said.

'I won't; it was the honour that was to be shared not the gold.'

'We can't all be leaders, can we?' Adelmar piped up.

'I'm sorry,' I said, 'I don't know what's got into me. Of course you deserved that honour. It was a beautiful fight and one they will make songs over when you return home. Perhaps I was a little jealous.'

I looked at the two young men and thought they understood. They both smiled and I think Cimbrod was pleased. I had no desire to start a quarrel over maudlin feelings for my own plight.

'I'm not very good company tonight,' I said.

'Cheer up,' Cimbrod said. 'Tomorrow the Ri is going to negotiate a settlement and we will go home.'

'I need to speak to him before he does that,' I said.

'Oh?'

'Yes. I'm formulating a plan that will suit us and them. If he ends this little escapade by forcing them to swear allegiance to him, then in the future if there is a need to assemble a big army, he can have their warriors too. Rome is the enemy, not other barbarian tribes. Someone ought to tell him not to be small minded.'

'I wish you luck. That Nechtan listens to no one.'

'I think Galdir is right. We could remove the Romans if we had enough men and moved south. There are really rich pickings across the wall,' Adelmar said.

Cimbrod looked at his brother, 'Little brother, you are growing up fast but I don't think you are yet ready to make policy decisions. Leave that to us grown men.'

'Since when were you a grown man?' I said.

Cimbrod scowled. 'What?'

'Pass the Nepos would you?' I said in my politest voice.

He looked at me. His face still scowled for a moment then it began to crack. It was like watching the sun come out from behind a cloud. His bright smile emerged then he laughed. He laughed and slapped me on the thigh and Adelmar joined in. Men at other campfires looked at us as we shared the mirth.

When we had stopped laughing at the silly joke, I realised my sombreness was misplaced and these young men were my friends, my brothers-in-arms.

Taran the Caledonian warrior joined us. I heard him approach and turned with my hand on the hilt of my sword, I don't know why.

'Hey, wait a moment,' said the Briton.

'Oh it's you, I said.

'A fine greeting after such a good battle. We are comrades now.'

'Yes, I'm sorry. I thought for one moment it was Drosten coming to pick a fight.'

'Drosten?' Taran said. 'He's just a bully-boy. He would no more pick a fight with a real warrior than he would part from Nechtan's side. He's quite handy with an axe, mind you.'

'I thought he was the chosen warrior in the tribe,' Cimbrod said.

'Chosen by Nechtan, but not for fighting.'

He laughed and nudged me.

'What do you mean?' Cimbrod said.

'You know, chosen.'

'No,' Cimbrod said, 'I don't understand. Speak plainly.'

Taran looked from face to face and smiled. He said, 'Well if Drosten was a woman they would be married. Now do you understand?'

'I thought that was illegal.' I said.

'Nechtan makes his own laws. It is a secret all over the

tuath. Everyone knows but no one speaks of it. Drosten has enjoyed Nechtan's protection for years. No one can argue with him or Nechtan has them banished or worse.'

'If that is true, then why is Drosten so interested in Ancamma? If he likes men, she wouldn't be much use to him. You're talking rubbish man.'

'Drosten wants status in the tuath and a family. Ancamma can provide children and he can still be about whatever business he wants.'

'No wonder Ancamma is so upset,' Cimbrod said.

'Maybe one of us should pick a fight,' Adelmar said.

'Well it won't be you, will it?' I said.

The boy looked down at the ground. I regretted my words as soon as I spoke them and said, 'Armed combat is a skill that takes a long time to learn. Experience and reading your opponent counts for much. It is not the same as a battle.'

'Cimbrod has less experience than you but he did all right today,' Adelmar said.

'Yes but he has trained in it hasn't he?'

Cimbrod said, 'I had some training at home yes, but I seem to be able to see what they are about to do before they do it and that helps me.'

'So you knew that the brigand who buried his axe in your shield was going to hit you with your own equipment,' I said, smiling for the first time.

'I... I...' Cimbrod stuttered. Taran laughed.

'Sorry, my friend, I seem to anger you even in jest tonight.'

Cimbrod smiled and said, 'No Galdir, I know you mean only a jest.'

'All the same, I would watch Drosten,' said Taran. 'He

can be sneaky and even though he isn't the best fighter we have he is a strong and powerful warrior, particularly with an axe.'

'I understand. Our problem is he thinks he owns An-camma and I think Cimbrod here will protect her from him.'

'Don't fall foul of the Ri, is all I'm saying. I must go, we can talk more on the morrow,' Taran said and walked away to his own men's camp.

The two brothers went to find their siblings, and I lay down covered by my cloak and sleep took me. My final memory of that day was of Lucia, and wondering where she might be. I could remember the feel of her soft white flesh as I made love to her under the stars. It aroused me as I slipped into a dream-laden sleep.

CHAPTER XVII

"The soul becomes dyed with the colour of its thoughts"
—Marcus Aurelius

Nechtan was a serious man. He had humour when it was appropriate but his outstanding feature as a leader was he treated his men well. I understood why they followed him with such faith. He kept little from the Orcadian raid for himself but distributed the vast majority of it among his soldiers as a reward for their valour. That ensured their loyalty and their protection. It was not surprising his men tolerated his relationship with Drosten.

One problem dogged me throughout my time with the Caledonii: it was communication. Nechtan could speak a few words of the common German tongue but only a few. I spoke a smattering of their local dialect now, so we could communicate after a fashion. Cimbrod was better at the language than I was and if Ancamma was absent, I always took him with me when I spoke to the Ri.

The sun was up and it was a fresh spring morning. Dew glittered in the sunshine and there were white billowing clouds above. We had breakfasted on cold meat and water and Hengeist had made some little cakes of wheat and barley which were a good way to start the day. For a grim warrior and a talented hunter, he could cook like a maiden.

Cimbrod and I entered the hut where the Ri slept. Drosten was at his side and there were two others but I think they were only guards. The conversation was a stuttering slow combination of German, Caledonian and sign language, but we made our thoughts clear with less difficulty than one might imagine.

Nechtan sat on a cushion covered by furs. Drosten sat beside him and glowered at Cimbrod. The Caledonii, like the Orcadians, use little furniture and a low table was the only article standing on the crude earth floor. There were often plenty of iron objects like the dog-grate iron in the hearth. Earthenware pots of various sizes lay in a haphazard clutter in one corner of the room. The only decorative item was a series of woodcarvings on the beams, depicting different animals and a hunter throwing a spear. In one of them, one hunter was busy slaying a herd of odd-looking creatures with no legs next to horizontal wavy lines I supposed the carver intended to represent the sea. These mythological carvings were common in the North Briton's homes, but as for creatures with no legs, I had to wait for the journey home before I understood.

'Great Ri,' I said, 'I come with a suggestion.'

'What suggestion?' he said. 'You are a great warrior and I will listen to you.'

'If you make peace with the Orcadians you can make them serve you in war.'

'I know this. But there is no war now. We defeated them.'

'The Romans are a cruel people. They also have a lot of gold and riches on the other side of the wall.'

'This is true,' he said nodding, 'We have long been at war with them. Now we have peace and we trade.'

'The Caledonii on their own cannot defeat the Romans.'

'No, the Roman Legions are too strong.'

'With my help, you can fight them but it will need all the tribes to fight together, like when the northern wall was taken and the Romans fell back.'

'Perhaps, but they have more men in the south and besides my people make weak alliances.'

'When the Britons in the south hear what we have done they will fight too. The Brigantes, Votadini and the Selgovae will join us. The Brigantes are a large nation.'

'It is true what you say, but why should we fight them? They trade with us and they do not seem to want our lands.'

I said, 'Because they have been sending their slavers north to take your people away for a hundred years and they will continue. It insults your nation. It is a matter of honour to fight back and drive them from your land.'

'There is much wisdom in what you say but I need to think about this. First, we will give terms to the Orcadians and then travel home. I have spoken.'

He dismissed us with the wave of a hand and I rose to leave.

'Galdir,' said the Ri, 'why do you hate the Romans so much? We hate them because they kill our people on sight. They burn our fines and tuaths and they enslave our women.'

'They are no better to us Germans. They destroyed my people and those of my friends; all my men have been sent to the East to fight for Rome.'

'Would we win, you think?'

'Yes we can win, but I will have to tell your people how the Romans fight so we can destroy them. I was a Roman slave once and they taught me much. It will be their undoing.'

Nechtan smiled at that. His white teeth shone in the

gloom of the hut. I turned and left but I heard raised voices behind as I walked up the steps. It was clear Drosten did not approve of my ideas. I was not certain it would be possible either. To draw all these warring factions together against a common enemy when they seemed to spend all their time fighting against each other and raiding each other's cattle seemed an insurmountable obstacle to me.

Cimbrod said once we were outside, 'Do you really believe this can be done—defeat the Romans, that is?'

'I am sure it can be done, but whether these people can do it or not, I cannot tell. I will need to learn more of the language if I am to succeed. Ancamma will have to teach me.'

'We could perhaps have the lessons together. That way she won't be able to get away from me so easily.'

'Get away from you?'

'I intend to bring her home to Cimbria and marry her.'

'Have you lost your senses? If you try anything with her, Drosten will want to kill us both. Even if one of us was to kill him, do you think that would bring a peaceful alliance, when we can't even be trusted with each other?'

'But killing for a woman is honourable.'

'Not if you are trying to get everyone to fight together it isn't, anyway you heard what Taran said last night. Nechtan protects him for his own reasons. You will have to control your urges my boy, until we are safely on the other side of the wall and victorious. You hear me?'

I thought I was beginning to sound like Chlotsuintha. She was always telling me to control my urges. I never listened. How could I expect Cimbrod to do what I was never able to do?

'Less of the boy, thanks. I am the leader here and I am no

longer a boy.'

'Sorry.'

'You should be.'

'Nobody heard.'

'Good,' he said.

The conversation ended in smiles but I was sure I would have to keep a close eye on my young warrior friend. The Caledonii did not seem to take monogamy very seriously, but Drosten was a brooding threat and I knew Cimbrod would be unwise to pick a fight if the Ri favoured Drosten as Taran had indicated. Although I could see that, there would be no loss of honour in Cimbrod's intentions; I also knew that Drosten's men held their warlord in high esteem and any shame attached to him would make my task impossible.

The Caledonii did not write things down. Their ancestors carved some kind of writing on stones but no one now could interpret the inscriptions. They had a strong tradition for passing stories on and they had bards as we did in Frankia. They held such people in high esteem for in the long winter nights it was the only form of entertainment around the fires. Tales of Gods and heroes told in songs and poems entertained us Germans and kept our history alive in our minds. The Caledonii were no different. They had a sect called Druids. These were wise men who knew both magic and writing but disdained putting anything down with the written word. They memorised everything and passed it on and they were keepers of wisdom and law. At home in Germania, the whole tribe shared in such wisdom to some extent but it also resides in our witches who advise on important matters through their dreams, for Wuotan visits them and imbues them with a secret knowledge, never given to men.

*

We were not present at the meeting between the Ri and the Orcadian leaders. It must have gone well for as we climbed aboard our boats to leave, three more ships arrived laden with furs and sacks of silver. Insi Orc was not a rich place I supposed, so I did not think they could have come up with much gold.

It was then I understood the carvings in the hut. I saw three creatures about a hundred yards from us. They shot out of the sea as if fired from a ballista and lay basking in the cool sun. They were the creatures in the carving. They had no legs, only fins like fish but they were fur-covered and they swam in the sea. I had never seen such creatures; they were truly remarkable. I put my hand on Taran's shoulder as he pulled at the oar beside me and pointed.

'Name ?' I said.

'Keltie,' he said.

He looked at my surprised face and began to laugh. He said something to the man next to him and they looked at me, both grinning. I think they were surprised at my ignorance and my face must have shown my amazement at the creatures. The presence of these creatures explained all the furs in the boat. The Orcadians clearly traded in these furs, which was one reason why Nechtan had taken the trouble to bring war to these otherwise quiet and beautiful islands.

We set off in the late morning and then the vomiting began, despite the flat calm of the sea. I puked for the entire journey and when we finally set foot on dry land, I felt as if the journey had torn my insides from my body. That Cimbrod found it amusing did not help. He talked incessantly the whole time and I could have killed him by the time we were halfway back if I had been capable of raising my weapon.

I set foot upon dry land feeling dizzy and faint. The nausea took most of the evening to depart. When it did, it left me feeling more tired than if I had fought a battle. I sat with Cimbrod at a fire. He had eaten some ox-meat and stared at the flames flickering in front of us, wallowing in melancholy.

'You're no seafaring man are you?' Cimbrod said.

'No I hate it.'

'No wonder you Germans never got as far as this island,' he said.

'Why would anyone want to? It's full of mists and rain. It could almost be haunted from its appearance.'

'Yes perhaps it is. I love it though,' he said, 'it has a hard feel to it. I cannot explain what I mean. Perhaps it is meeting Ancamma, I don't know.'

'There you go again,' I said. 'Leave her alone. She is not your woman. Can't you get that through your thick Cimbrian skull? She isn't really interested in you either.'

'No. She likes you. Don't think I don't notice how she looks at you. Well you can look elsewhere. She's mine.'

'Cimbrod, I have no intention of sleeping with Ancamma. She isn't my type even if I did not have good reasons for wanting to keep the peace. I have a certain woman in mind and she is far away. Now leave it there.'

Relations between Cimbrod and me were becoming strained. I could cope with his constant prattle about Ancamma, but his unfounded jealousy was beginning to rub me raw.

'Look am I your friend or not?' I said.

He looked at me with anger in his eyes and said, 'Yes you are my friend. I would trust you next to me in battle. I would trust you with my gold but with my woman? I do not know.'

'Then you are a young fool. I am a Frankish warlord. If I say something you can rely on it being the truth.'

'Yes I can but that may change, where women are concerned.'

I stood up. He was annoying me.

'I'm going to join some people who trust me,' I said and walked away before I became angry. I joined Hengeist and Adelmar at another campfire, leaving Cimbrod to simmer. Drogo was there too.

'That brother of yours is driving me to distraction. All he talks about is Ancamma. Ancamma this, Ancamma that. She isn't available to him. She belongs to Drosten and if he thinks your Cimbrod is after her he will cause serious trouble for us.'

'I know,' said Hengeist, 'I've been trying to tell him. He's my older brother and he doesn't listen to me.'

'Or me,' I said.

Drogo said, 'I think she likes you.'

'Yes, but I don't like her like that. She isn't worth half of the woman I once loved. We are here to fight, not to womanise.'

I heard my own voice but it was as if someone else had spoken. I was the one who had slept with and married my aunt. I was the one who made love to Piso's wife and here I was lecturing young men on how to control their feelings. It was absurd and I knew it. It was perhaps the one time in my life when I was sensible about women. I know Chlotsuintha would have been proud of me, she always advised me to think with my head and not any other part of my anatomy. The problem was, we are all vulnerable to the Gods. Loge,

156

God of fire is the trickiest. He plays games with us mortals in subtle ways and laughs at our predicaments. I should have known, even though I was determined that there is inside all of us a kind of weakness and the right woman can always bring that out.

CHAPTER XVIII

"There is no great genius without some touch of madness"
—Seneca

The months passed by. We learned the Caledonian language and we ate and drank. Spring wore on to summer and the valley in which the Ri had his tuath changed from a damp cold place into a lush, green valley. Despite the warm days, I had never before realised how much difference it made in temperatures to be this far north. Spring had come later than in the south and the nights were still cool. The valley was a beautiful place, sheltered from the winds and surrounded by high hills. A wooden road led away to the south. It was the main entrance to the tuath. Along the track, they herded livestock, embassies came, and warriors marched. Although the roads the Britons built were sound and useable, they constructed them of thick planks and it meant that if it rained too heavily they tended to sink and become unusable. I thought it was a pity the Caledonii did not make roads like the Romans, but everyone knows their skills are not available to us barbarians and it had always been thus with military matters too.

Ancamma and I spent many hours together. She taught me the ways of the Caledonii and the language, which was not dissimilar to ours. There were many words in common but the pronunciation was strange. Cimbrod and Adelmar often sat with us and the older brother's undeclared affections were like a garment he wore for all to see. He smiled all the time in her company. He tried hard to learn the language and although it rankles, he was much better at it than I was.

I was relieved in the end when she began to take an interest in Cimbrod and she consented to go for walks with him in the evenings. It wrought a change in my friend. He smiled more often and he laughed a lot. He brought gifts to Ancamma. Pieces of jewellery, a tunic once and often, flowers for her hair. I realised within a short time she liked him.

There were occasions when Cimbrod was not there; he had become entangled in the politics of the Tuath and often attended council meetings when the Ri wished to plan his warfare and battles. I never went with him. My only role now was to earn enough to pay Cimbrod for the life of his friend, Horsa and to wage war on the Romans.

There was one occasion when the three of us were sitting around a small fire and toasting some bread Ancamma had brought. The warm sun made it a pleasant time and we laughed and talked.

'You there, German,' a voice said behind me.

I looked over my shoulder and saw Drosten. He was scowling and he carried his axe.

'Yes, Drosten what do you want?' I said.

'I want words with you.'

'Speak away; I have no secrets from my friends.'

'Then know this, Ancamma is mine. If I catch any of you foreigners with her you can expect a lesson in steel.'

'I don't belong to you,' said Ancamma, vehemence in her voice.

'Nechtan had given me leave to wed you and you are his subject. Don't argue with me.'

'If she doesn't want you, then you should find someone else, shouldn't you?' Adelmar said.

'And who are you? You fancy yourself as her lover? If I find you with her again I'll kill you.'

I stood up. I had no qualms about teaching this man a lesson.

'Drosten, you should pick on someone who is old enough and big enough to fight back. Adelmar is only a boy. Do you wish to fight? I can oblige you. Wait here and I will get my sword.'

'I am only warning you. If I catch any of you foreigners with my woman it will be the last thing you ever do.'

He turned his back and walked away. I had no doubts he meant it, but he should have been talking to Cimbrod, not Adelmar, whose intentions had never been amorous as far as I could see. Ancamma was shaking when Drosten left and I wondered if Drosten would exact some revenge upon her.

Cimbrod trusted Adelmar. He knew his brother, who was much younger than he was, would not try to form any romantic liaisons with Ancamma since we all knew how Cimbrod felt. Some evenings Adelmar would walk out with Ancamma and they made a friendship, which no one could have expected although I could understand it. Adelmar was young, pleasant and friendly by nature. Had I not formed such a relationship with my aunt Clotildis at first, at his age?

Adelmar was young enough to be inexperienced but old enough to have desires. I knew that, but like Cimbrod, I trusted him. He often spoke of Ancamma to me but it was always as a friend and I never heard him indicate there was anything more to it than that. In the same breath, if we had a pause from sword practise or we were running across a field in training, he would liken her to the sister he had left behind. I knew there was no ulterior motive in his friendliness with the girl.

On that day, we had finished our language lesson. It was a warm evening and the sun had cast its warmth over the valley all day. The grass was long and I could hear an owl hooting far off in a copse on the hill to the south. Food was cooking and I could smell the roasting meat, its odour wafting in my direction on the gentle breeze. Adelmar and Ancamma went for a walk. I saw nothing unusual in this; it had happened many times in Cimbrod's absence. They smiled and laughed as they walked and it was a relaxing, soporific thing to see.

I lay back and rested my head in the grass. I was of course, thinking of Lucia and daydreaming what it would be like to even be close to her. I had begun to enjoy the life in the tuath. The Caledonii were a hospitable people and friendly as long as you obeyed their code of ethics. Honour was everything to them. If you insulted a man's honour, he would fight you to the death. The greatest warrior for example, helped himself to the meat first and anyone who tried to cut meat before him might have to fight him in armed combat to preserve his honour.

They were not jealous people either. They held women in high esteem, like in German tribes. The big difference was, if a Briton woman wished to, she could sleep with a man of her choice providing the husband agreed, which I found very strange. I had no interest in women apart from Lucia at that time, but a number of the mercenaries did take advantage of offers from local women.

I began to doze. The world around me was calm, idyllic and warm. It was then I heard a scream. It was a woman's scream of distress and anguish. It came from the direction in which Adelmar and Ancamma had set off walking. I had visions of her fighting the young man off and the trouble it would cause between him and Cimbrod. I sat up. I was on my feet in a second. I ran like a rat on fire.

It was dusk and I found I could not see with any clarity at first. I all but stumbled on Ancamma. She sat staring at a body. She had her clenched fist to her mouth and her eyes were wide with shock. I looked to where she was staring. It was Adelmar. I was reasonably sure it was. His head was missing. He lay with his blood still dribbling from the headless torso, pooling on the ground.

Like Ancamma, I remained still for a moment. This young man, so full of life and friendliness, had gone. I had been speaking to him only minutes before and here he lay. My feelings surprised me. I had thought I was untouched by such sights. It was common enough in battle and I had seen many. It was the setting. It was a quiet, peaceful afternoon. It was a time for youth and a time for innocence and friendship. Those things had vanished like an eagle soaring far above disappears over a dark grey horizon. Death raised its ugly hand and suddenly the idyll had gone.

My first thought was what to say to Cimbrod. My second was Ancamma. I reached for her and she stood up and ran to me, turning sideways slightly to avoid the body. She was shaking and did not speak. I said nothing either. It was obvious she had seen it and would tell me her story in her own time. Whoever had done this would pay with his life, whether it was Cimbrod who exacted revenge or it was I, made no difference. Revenge would come; I swore it by Tiu, the God of war, Wuotan's brother.

Still with my arm around her shoulders, I walked her back to the main house of the tuath. Cimbrod was chuckling to himself as he left through the doorway when I approached. He looked at me and frowned. He was about to say something when he caught sight of the blood on Ancamma's face and hands. I had not noticed it myself.

'What's happened?' he said.

'It's bad Cimbrod. Very bad. It's Adelmar.'

'What?'

'Someone has killed him,' I said, the right words evading me. I could think of no platitudes that could substitute for the truth.

'What?' he said again.

'He and Ancamma were walking over near the copse and I heard her scream. When I got there it was all over.'

'Dead?'

'Yes, my friend, dead.'

I reached out and put a hand on his shoulder. He brushed it aside. 'Where is he?'

I realised the shock of it stopped him taking it all in, so I merely repeated what I had said.

'Ancamma, did you see who did it?' he said.

She said, 'Yes.'

Her voice was all but inaudible and she stared at the gound.

'Who was it?'

She began to cry. I could not make out the words, some were Germanic and some were Latin.

'Ancamma, who did this thing?' I said, taking her by both arms, her face close to mine. There was a long pause and she spoke his name quietly.

'Who?' said Cimbrod, raising his voice.

'Drosten, it was Drosten,' she said again. She looked up at Cimbrod and said, 'He came from behind. He did it with an axe. Adelmar had no chance. He said to me if I ever told anyone he would kill me too.'

'Drosten... I'll kill him. Where is he?'

'I don't know. He went towards the Ri's house.'

'We should see to Adelmar's body first. Revenge can wait.' I said. I had no desire to start a full-scale war against the tuath. I knew they would protect Drosten.

'His body. Yes.'

Cimbrod seemed confused for a moment. I could see his eyes moisten. He was only a young man and it was beginning to show. I put a hand on his shoulder again and squeezed it.

I said, 'We need to do this right or we will end up fighting everyone. No sense in dying for a death, my friend. We have all the time in the world to exact revenge.'

'I want to kill this man. My brother was only a boy. The absurdity of what he said never occurred to him. There were only a few years between them and I had always considered Cimbrod a boy too.

'Let us burn his body and then ask the Ri for justice. He admires us. He knows we can kill Drosten and he won't want to fight us,' I said.

Cimbrod looked at me. The anger seemed to be fading and I thought he took in what I said. We walked the half-mile or so to where the body lay. Ancamma went to her sleeping place and tried to calm herself. The body lay as we had left it.

'But...But where's his head?' Cimbrod asked.

'His body is as it was when I found it. Drosten has it. You know he belongs to that cult.'

'My brother's head, for Donar's sake! I'm going to get it back. We can't burn his body without his fucking head.'

'Cimbrod, slow down. We will retrieve his head and add the head of Drosten to that pyre but now we burn your brother. Let's carry him back to our camp.'

He regarded me again for long moments. His eyes were wild. I could not predict what he would do. He was young and I knew how at that age, I too, had been unpredictable. My temper had always let me down. I had never had anyone to advise me apart from my friend Duras and he was much lighter in manner than I had become. Besides, I had never listened to him.

'Cimbrod,' I said, 'we will get revenge slowly. First, let us honour the dead. Worry about the living in good time. I know about these things. Listen to me or we will all be undone.'

He looked at me. I could see the agony of mixed emotion written on his face and I could have shed tears had it not been for the harshness inside me my own position had instilled. I functioned now as the pragmatic warrior I had become. It was my nature and that nature and inherent steel in my soul was what had kept me from descending into a pit of despair in my own past. I was alone except for these Cimbri men whom I respected. I knew what it was to feel loss but I was still here, functioning and lucid. I had survived and had to ensure my friend Cimbrod did too. I wondered if the Gods had planned it all. They had taken away Livia my greatest love when I was even younger than Cimbrod. They had removed Cornelius, and Duras who, although still living as far as I knew, was a world away in Dacia. I had to help my friend to be like me or at least persuade him not to yield to the basic passions I could see evolving in him.

'Cimbrod, let me be your Nepos.'

'What?'

'I will be your Nepos as Cornelius was to me.'

He looked at me again. Had he not been so grief-struck I think he would have smiled. As it was, I think he understood.

'You're a strange man,' he said his face showing a precarious calm about which I was unsure. It was a relaxation I did not trust. I did not want it to fly away as soon as he saw Drosten. I approached the boy's body and began to lift it onto my shoulder.

'No, Galdir, it is for me to do this thing,' he said.

I let him take over. He hefted Adelmar's corpse onto his shoulder and we carried it between us. I remember thinking how light a body becomes when all its blood has poured away.

We struggled with his remains even so. The body was slick with blood and I recall noticing it was still warm. In the camp, Hengeist and the others flew into the anticipated rage and it took all my powers of persuasion to stop them from exacting a justified revenge immediately.

We burned Adelmar's body on a pyre of oak and beech. By the time the body had arched its back and its limbs contracted, my friends had calmed enough to see the sense of what I had said. We drank beer that night and none of us slept. The brothers shed tears and took oaths of revenge. We would approach Nechtan in the morning and ask for justice.

I thought about that boy often after that. I had liked him and I knew he looked up to me. The injustice of the killing made me as angry as my friends were, but I still had to persuade the Caledonii to war and I could not do it if we were the cause of bloodshed and dissent. I had to play it carefully. My future hinged on driving the Romans from the wall and accessing the south without anyone discovering I had broken my oath, but Adelmar's death, unpredictable as it was, could only interfere. I began to realise that if I lost control of the mercenaries my influence here might also be lost and with it my chance of fermenting war.

CHAPTER XIX

"Time discovers truth"

—Seneca

'Yes, I was expecting you,' Nechtan said, 'Drosten has told me all about it.'

'He told you?' I said.

Cimbrod, Hengeist and I stood facing the Ri. Drosten sat next to him. He was stony faced and stared back at us defiantly. The hall was gloomy and dark. There were no windows but the fire in the dog-grate burned brightly and flickering torches stood in brackets along the walls. There was a smell of freshly baked bread in the air and despite myself, I realised I was hungry.

'Yes, they fought over a woman,' Nechtan said, and shrugged his shoulders.

'That is not the way it happened,' I said. 'He attacked the boy from behind with an axe. It was murder.'

'Drosten said it was a fair fight.'

'The only wound on the body was his missing head. He had not even drawn his sword. He was also only a boy, the youngest of the mercenaries,' I said.

'And where is the body?' the Ri said.

'We burned the body before dawn.'

'So you can't prove there were no other wounds can you?'

'No. Do you doubt my word? You can ask Ancamma yourself.'

'The word of a woman is not acceptable by our law. A man is always right.'

'What?'

'Our laws do not allow a woman to speak against a man,' Nechtan said.

Cimbrod stood next to me and his eyes narrowed as he regarded Drosten. He raised his hand and pointed with a steady index towards the killer.

He said, 'That man killed my brother by sneaking up behind him and cutting off his head with an axe. I demand justice. Even by Caledonii custom the least you can do is sanction a fight between us and the Gods will decide the truth of it.'

'No, there will be no fight for revenge. I do not want to lose the services of either of you. Drosten does not deny killing your brother over the woman and he came to me willingly with regret he slew Adelmar. In the absence of a Druid, I mete out justice here and my decision will be obeyed. Drosten will pay weregild for your brother, the sum to be agreed between you and there will be no fighting.'

'They did not fight. Adelmar was murdered,' I said.

Nechtan stood up. I had overstepped the mark. He pointed at me.

'You are not blood kin to anyone here. You may not speak further on this matter. Cimbrod leads and it was his brother. Weregild will be paid and there is an end.'

His eyes flashed and he drew his flat hand, palm down from right to left. There was no point arguing, I knew that. The audience was at an end and we left the hall seething but silent.

When we reached our camp, Hengeist said, 'It does not matter to me what that little chief says. I will kill Drosten one way or another.'

'It might be unwise to do that before he pays us the weregild, brother,' Cimbrod said.

'Wise? What had wisdom to do with it? He killed our brother. We have sworn to kill him. It is a matter of honour.'

'Hengeist,' I said, 'there is plenty of time. I liked Adelmar and I considered him a friend. I too want revenge, but I know it has to wait. Drosten is going nowhere. Let him pay the gold and when the time is right, one of us will kill him.'

'He wasn't your kin. This does not concern you.'

'Perhaps, but I am one of you am I not? If I am not, there is no need for me to stay.'

'Stop this quarrelling,' Cimbrod said, 'Galdir is right. He is one of us and I will heed his advice. We wait, and however long it takes, we will exact our revenge when we are not so hot with anger.'

Hengeist realised it was no use arguing. He looked from one to the other then shrugged in resignation.

Cimbrod and I went to find Ancamma. Her bower was behind the Ri's hall. I had always found it amusing to think of this hall as a kingly dwelling because of its small size. My own hall in Sicambra was huge by comparison though I wondered whether my people had managed to mend the roof.

We knocked on the wooden door. Her bower was a small hut to one side of the Ri's dwelling and was made like all the other houses out of wicker covered in mud which was smoothed inside and out. The roof was thatched.

She stood at the door but would not let us in.

'You must go,' she said. She had a strained look on her face and I could see she was still shocked. Cimbrod stepped forward and gently pushed the door open. She did not resist.

He stepped towards her and took her in his arms. Tears came. She sobbed into his shoulder and I realised I was out of place. I had no need or right to be there.

'He said he would kill any man who came near me and that I am his property,' she said.

Cimbrod smoothed her hair and said, 'If you do not want to be with him, I will protect you. I will kill him for what he has done. The Ri might afterwards exact a huge weregild but I don't care. You will be safe with me.'

They stood like that and I had nothing to offer so I left. I walked away and thought about these events.

Drosten was a dead man he just did not know it. He had made so many enemies now any of the mercenaries might kill him in revenge at any time. His jealousy had so devoured him I could not see the Ri's protection being strong enough to delay his death. It pleased me. It was an unjust and unnecessary killing, and Adelmar was only a boy to my mind.

I thought about how this might affect my plans. I wanted a war with the Romans, and the northern Britons were without doubt willing to fight. They would be attracted by the obvious wealth in the south. I needed to persuade the Ri to send out emissaries and arrange a council. He respected my fighting abilities, but had never considered me worth including in his councils. I would have to use Cimbrod, who seemed to have Nechtan's ear. In the end, it was easier than I had thought. Perhaps Wuotan took a hand or Loge playing his tricks amused himself with me.

*

My opportunity came sooner than I had expected. A week after the killing Nechtan summoned Cimbrod, Hengeist and

I. He sat as ever on his cushions and furs and was drinking ale from a horn he put down on the low table as we entered. He looked up and smiled.

'Cimbrod, good of you to come,' he said.

'You summoned us,' said Cimbrod, his tone of voice flat and unyielding.

'Tomorrow we have visitors. An embassy from the Vacomagi tribe who live to the east, is coming to discuss some matters in which they want our help. It may involve you and your men. I wish you both to be there. There will be a feast at midday. That is all.'

We said nothing more, knowing he had dismissed us. We walked out into the sunlight and Cimbrod said, 'What was that all about?'

'I suppose he wants to help the Vacomagi in some war.'

'Suits me. I'm sick of hanging around doing nothing but thinking of my slain brother.'

'An alliance with them would be useful if we are to persuade the Caledonii to start a war.'

'I don't understand why you want to fight the Romans so much.'

'No, but you will.'

'What do you mean?'

'It will become plain enough in time,' I said.

We walked in silence to our camp. Taran was there. He was in the habit of eating meals with us for he was curious about our homelands and interested in our customs.

'I am often surprised by what you tell me,' he said squatting next to the fire outside Cimbrod's tent. 'To think your people have such different attitudes to us.'

'We aren't that different,' Cimbrod said.

'Well the role of women for example.'

172

'What do you mean?' I said.

Taran said, 'Here women are allowed freedom. They speak their minds and are much honoured. Some even train as warriors.'

'We have warrior women too,' Cimbrod said.

'Is that because they fight better than you Cimbrod?' I said.

'What?'

'A joke. Sorry,' I said.

'Our warrior women really can fight. Often they ride in chariots and they get out, kill a few men and then the chariot picks them up again,' Taran said.

'Do they fight nude then?' Cimbrod said.

'No such luck my friend. Our people are modest. Only the male warriors fight naked.'

'I don't understand,' I said, 'how you tolerate the cold the way you do.'

'It's Druidic mushroom magic, Galdir.'

'Magic?'

'Yes, the Druids make a potion from mushrooms. It is wonderful stuff but you have to get the right dose or it can drive you mad.'

'What does it do?' I asked.

'Well, it is strange. In small doses, it makes colours seem brighter than normal and straight lines bend before your eyes. Sounds bend too and seem louder and clearer. You still have control, and before battle it whips you into a fury.'

'If you have too much?' Cimbrod said.

'Well imagine if you sit by the fire and stare into the red glowing heart of it. The shapes change don't they? Well imagine all around you looking like that. Nothing is real and you see things not only altered, but things which are not there.'

'Not much use in battle if you can't see the enemy,' Cimbrod said.

'In small doses, you don't feel the cold and you feel the enemy as much as see him. I have taken it many times before a fight and it is exciting. Do you want to try some?'

'No thanks,' I said, 'I have enough problems with wine and beer thank you. Cimbrod? Do you want to try?'

'No, it sounds too tricky for me. I like to keep control of myself even when I don't fight.'

'Go on, my friends I have some here,' Taran said and he stood and proffered a tiny earthenware bottle. He smiled as if he had bested us in some test of courage but I knew Cimbrod, like me, did not trust the potions of these wild people any more than we trusted their leader.

'Well, maybe I could try a little,' I said not wishing this Briton warrior to outdo me.

'Have a care Galdir, a little is good but too much and the world will desert you!' Taran said. He was laughing as if this was all some great Caledonian jest. I frowned but drew the courage from somewhere.

I took the bottle; it was made of wood and felt comfortable in my hand. It had a small stopper of elm-wood and I removed it, suspicious its contents might poison me or do me some kind of ill-defined damage. I pressed it to my lips and looked around me.

'Go on, go on,' Taran said, 'just don't take too much, it's very strong.'

I sipped a little from the bottle. It was a dark, bitter liquid but after a moment, I detected a strange musty taste on my tongue. It was not as disgusting as it sounds but had a flavour of just mushrooms and herbs. Nothing happened so

I sat down next to Cimbrod. I waited.

I am certain I heard him say, 'You're mad. Crazy. Briton rubbish. How do you feel?'

'I feel...nothing,' I said.

'You have to wait a bit,' Taran said.

I waited and thought perhaps Briton potions had no effect on Germans. I looked at my companions and everything felt the same as before. I was wrong of course. The first thing happening was subtle. I looked at Cimbrod and his face became distorted in a strange way. If I had been asked to describe it then, I would have said he had become wolf-like; his nose was long and his teeth fierce. I heard the sounds of the men around me but they were not human voices; they had somehow bent, twisted; they sounded as if I heard them through water or some such thing.

I looked around me. The trees were on fire, the grass was bright red and then I looked up at the sky. It had changed colour too but if you ask me to describe what colour it was I could not. There were purples, reds, and greens all swirling in patterned shapes and then I saw them. The Valkyries had come. One swooped down towards me and I covered my head, throwing myself to the ground to avoid her. She was terrible to see; her face was a mask of grim and bony death and in her hand was a blood-dipped spear. On her head, she bore the winged helm of Wuotan and her flying steed breathed fire as it swooped down at me. Cimbrod told me later I screamed and I cowered, curled up on the ground.

I had to escape them; my time was not now. I could not go to Wuotan yet. I ran. The ground beneath my feet was a mire of blood and skulls. I crunched on men's long-dead faces as I ran and reached the river. It was a deep green in colour and I stood rooted to the spot staring down at it. I looked and its surface changed into a strange pattern, squares and circles seemed to intermingle but all still a deep emerald green. I felt as if I was looking down into a vast well of verdant colours and patterns. Deep, deep down there was a face. Indistinct at first but shimmering, it became larger and larger until I could make out the features. It was a woman. She was beautiful with blonde hair and it hung loose about her shoulders as she laughed and regarded me. I looked into her grey eyes and I felt comfort as if I had been alone but now was not. In her hand, she had a sword and clear as day, I saw her replace it into a leather scabbard at her waist. She looked up at me and pressed her index finger to her lips then turned away. When she faced me again, she was holding an infant in her arms and the child cried a strange mewling sound, seeking some maternal comfort perhaps, but all the same crying aloud, almost as if it was in my ear. She looked down at the babe in her arms and then looked up again. She said something to me then she waved and began to recede into the deep green water whence she came. I know I stood still then and a sudden a feeling of well-being filled me and I felt as if I was floating. I turned and walked towards where I thought the others waited. I felt worn to a ravelling. I sank to my knees through fatigue and I remembered no more until dawn. The last thing I recall was Taran's laughter.

Cimbrod told me next day my friends had carried me back and laid me in my tent. I still have flashes of those visions and I know who the woman was, though I had yet to meet her. I never took any foreign potions again. It may have been the loss of control but I knew I had experienced real fear as well as strange scenes. It was not a trip I would recommend to anyone.

CHAPTER XX

"In a crowd, on a journey, at a banquet even, a line of thought can itself provide its own seclusion"
—Quintilianus

In front of the Ri's hut was a flat clear space. I had imagined it was an assembly point. It was here the Caledonii entertained in the summer and I assumed large tribal gatherings did not happen in the winter for there was nowhere else for a large group to gather. The Ri had sent for us. Cimbrod, Hengeist and I walked slowly towards the Ri's compound wondering what would unfold.

It was late afternoon and the sun still held enough warmth to make it comfortable for us to wear tunics although we all carried our cloaks, for at night it became cold. Our feet kicked up dust from the dry cracked earth as we walked along the path and I could hear a corncrake screech its ear-tingling cry as we rounded the corner of the nearest hut. The smell of the roasting meat made my mouth water. We had not eaten at midday, knowing what the feast would be like if it was anything like the ones we had in German lands.

'I must say I'm not very impressed with these Caledonii,' Hengeist said.

'Why?' I said.

'Because they don't even seem as civilised as we are at

home. Our father has a great hall where we feast and entertain guests. We don't just leave them to camp where they want and have feasts in the open air.'

'It's not so bad,' Cimbrod said, 'halls become smoky and crowded; at least outside we can breathe.'

'Perhaps,' Hengeist said. 'Is Ancamma going?'

'Yes, she's translating for us. There isn't anyone else who speaks her quality of the common German tongue.'

'You really like her don't you?' I said.

'I already told you that,' Cimbrod said.

'No, I mean you really do want to take her home with you.'

'Yes. I said so didn't I? I will have to get some gold first to show my father I haven't wasted my time and I want to kill that bastard Drosten, then I'll return home.'

'I am hoping I can make my way to the southern ports and take ship across to Gaul. After that, I can go home. Even then there is a risk to my people if I openly lead them while Marcus Aurelius lives, so maybe I will be unable to declare myself for a long time.'

'Perhaps it's better if you don't go home. You said the Romans would slaughter your people if they knew you were free and openly trying to start a war.'

'Maybe. If we raise a rebellion here then I may at least get as far as Gaul in the confusion. You could come with me if you want,' I said, glancing sideways.

'No; I want my woman and I want revenge, then nothing will stop me going home.'

'Looks like the guests have arrived,' said Hengeist as we turned the corner.

The square in front of the Ri's hall was milling with warriors and their women. Half of them had red hair and their body-smells mixed with the smells of roasting meat and occasional wafts of spices. It was like being in a big city but focussed on a little square in Caledonia. They all looked the same to me and I found it difficult to tell who was a Vacomagi and who was Caledonian. They were waiting for the Ri.

One of the Vacomagi drew my eyes. She was half a head taller than most of the men and had long, dark, shiny deep-red hair the colour of autumn beech leaves. It sparkled when she moved her head and I noticed around her neck was a golden torc of intricate design. Her pale skin was freckled like mine and I thought she was a beauty. She moved with grace and her smile was like a rising sun; it lit up her whole face and her grey eyes shone. Her face looked like the one I had seen in my drug-induced vision by the river and it accentuated the thrill of looking at her. Until I saw her, I would have told anyone I was not interested in women but I confess my heart leapt and I felt stirrings in my groin.

She wore a patterned tunic, not a robe, tied at the waist with a gold belt, and she wore a sword, which surprised me. I had not seen any warrior women among the Caledonii, although we had such at home. She was bold enough to walk straight up to the apex of the half circle in which the cushions were distributed and sat on the one to the right of the Ri's. I was about to approach her and warn her, when Nechtan appeared in his most resplendent tunic of red and green squares. Around his neck he wore his four golden torques and considering he had given one to Cimbrod at the Orcadian battle, I supposed he must have many.

The warrior maiden stood up when he arrived and I smiled for I thought she had clearly realised her mistake and was about to apologise to her host. Nechtan greeted her. He bowed. He smiled, showing his pearly teeth, and he gestured her to his own seat. I realised I was looking not at a warrior maiden, but at a Vacomagi noble, or even a Queen.

We all sat in a broad semicircle and they served the food. They gave the Vacomagi woman the first of the meat, which in Caledonii feasts meant either she was the strongest warrior or she was a very honoured guest. I noticed also that Drosten was the next in line after Nechtan. I understood then why the Ri would not tolerate revenge for the death of Adelmar. He clearly thought Drosten was his greatest warrior or else Taran had spoken the truth. I was impatient to prove Nechtan wrong about Drosten's warrior skills but I knew politics reigned here and not brawn.

I ate the roast ox and tried to talk to Cimbrod. He was taciturn, and answered in monosyllables at first until he had imbibed enough beer to start ranting how it was a shame murderers were allowed to dine at a king's feast. Happily, no one heard him apart from me, so no one took offence.

'Keep your voice down, by Donar,' I said.

'Why? Why should I? I am a prince in my own country and I do not expect to be silenced.'

'Cimbrod, you are my friend. I would do anything not to offend you, but if you cause trouble here at this feast, I will stop you myself. Hear me now,' I spoke in a low voice, 'Drosten will wait. We will avenge Adelmar. Patience is necessary to achieve what is needed here.'

Although I spoke to my friend, I was looking at the beautiful Vacomagi woman. I could not take my eyes from her. She rewarded me as I spoke, with a brief glance. Our eyes met and we both held it that little bit longer than might be considered polite. I became hopeful. I made plans. I wanted her. I needed to be close to her and noticed by her, but above all I wanted her.

I smiled. She continued to look impassive. I could discern no hint of a smile but I reckoned sitting next to Nechtan would draw the smile off anyone's lips. Cimbrod had now drunk enough to feel belligerent. He stood up suddenly and put his hand to the hilt of his sword. I stood up too. I put my hard and calloused hand over his. I squeezed. I am a strong man and it must have hurt but still he tried to draw his weapon. I put an arm around his shoulders and dragged him away. The feast had hardly started, yet I had to leave. I wondered if I would ever see the beautiful woman again.

Cimbrod became angry.

'What are you doing?' he said, once we were out of earshot of the feasting Britons and staggering towards our camp.

'I'm saving your life. I know you can take Drosten when you are sober; but drunk? I am your friend. Be patient! I keep telling you and you just don't listen do you?'

'All right, all right,' he said, waving his hand in my face, his speech slurred, 'you win. I'll forget the killing of my youngest brother. I'll pretend it never happened, should I? I can pretend he rides next to me when we fight. I can pretend I will hear his laughter and see his smile, but I won't. You know it Galdir. Don't you understand?'

I had never embraced a man as closely as I did Cimbrod. I felt his pain. I understood what he was feeling and perhaps it was his youth but I put my arms around him and clutched him to me. He fought me off at first then calmed and I could hear and feel him weeping onto my shoulder.

After a few minutes, we walked together to the mercenary camp and I left him in his leather tent to sleep off the beer. I had drunk little and decided to make my way back to the feast. I walked towards the music and the firelight and approached the outer huts. A figure appeared.

'I saw you helping your friend away.'

It was the Vacomagi woman.

'Yes, a little too much beer.'

'Too much to drink is a contradiction in terms,' she said in clear and cultured Latin. 'One cannot have too much, by definition.'

I noticed how beautiful her face became when transformed by her smile. I realised I was smitten.

'My name is Galdir.'

'I know. You speak Latin. Ancamma was telling me.'

'You know her?'

'Of course. Everyone knows her. She does most of the translating with the traders for her tribe but she works for me too now and again, when they come from far-off places. Not everyone speaks Latin you know.'

'You speak Latin well enough. You could do your own bargaining.'

'I do not bargain with traders, it is beneath me, I am a Warrior Princess. Besides, it is better if I know what they are saying without them knowing. It is politically shrewd. I thought you might understand. They tell me you are a king.'

'No; I was the Warlord of the Franks until Rome defeated us in battle and annexed my lands. Tell me, how is it you speak Latin?'

'I was enslaved for a time. When I was a child, Roman slavers captured me, north of where Dalriada has been built. They took me to Lemonum and sold me. My owners had an estate in northern Gaul. The family were kind to me, although I was of course expected to work. The master died and they freed me when the family returned to Rome. I made it home, but few others did.'

'We have much in common, you and I,' I said, scratching my stubbly chin.

Our eyes met and I could see behind the grey cold of their colour there lurked a flaming fire. It was with some satisfaction I realised it was directed at me. I could hardly disappoint a Princess. I stepped closer to her and she leaned towards me smiling. I inclined my head, closed my eyes and kissed—thin air. She had dodged my kiss and stepped back. She was still smiling but I felt foolish. It irritated me.

'I don't go around kissing complete strangers you know, I am after all a Princess.' She turned and walked back to the feast. I wasn't sure, but I thought she wiggled her hips a little more on the way back than when she had approached me.

'Does the Princess have a name?' I called after her.

She half turned, barely pausing in her long stride, and said, 'The Romans called me Flaminia but here my name is Oenna.'

I stood for a moment looking at her back, before she disappeared around the corner and I lost sight of her. I was sweating and there was a faint tumescence beneath my tunic.

'Oenna... Oenna,' I murmured to myself and smiled. To me it was a beautiful name. My failure to embrace her did not discourage me. The hunt was on and I wondered if that was what she had intended. Wittingly or otherwise, she had aroused my interest in the chase and I was never a man to refuse such a challenge.

I had become a patient man. I did not lose my temper unless provoked but in matters of the heart, many including Chlotsuintha, recognised I could be weak and hasty and in that respect, I remained Galdir.

CHAPTER XXI

"What a woman says to her avid lover should be written in wind and running water"
—Catullus

The feast was progressing well by the time I returned. There was music and some people were dancing in a manner I found strange and risible. I have learned since in my travels there are many forms of dance and perhaps all of them are pleasing to the Gods, but the way they danced that night made me smile. They danced in pairs, men and women, and they hopped from one foot to the other and turned circles to the sound of a drum and a flute. They waved their arms about their heads and held each other's hands. The amusing spectacle continued at intervals throughout the night and I was surprised they did not become tired. If they were that nimble in battle, then fighting would be no obstacle to these crude people.

I drank more beer, wishing all the time it was wine, and my head began to spin a little from watching the dancing. I ate some more of the roast ox and a mashed yellow vegetable whose name I do not recall. I looked frequently at Oenna. She seemed to be deep in conversation with the Ri, but every now and again she raised her head and laughed. Occasionally I noticed her looking at me but as soon as I returned her gaze, she looked away again. I wanted to get up and interrupt her conversation but I was still sober enough to know it would not have been wise. They are tetchy these Britons and they fight with anyone who they perceive might be besmirching their honour.

Oenna stood and came towards me, as I was about to leave. She stopped in front of me, looking down and smiling.

'We can dance if you like,' she said.

'What?' I said looking up.

'Dance.'

'I don't think...'

'Of course you can, I'll teach you.'

'Is it not unseemly for a warrior to jig about in this way?' I asked. 'I don't want to make a laughing stock of myself.'

'You won't. Besides, everyone is so drunk it would be surprising if they remembered.'

She offered me her hand and I took it as I stood up. She was almost as tall as I am and our eyes were on a level. How could I resist her invitation?

'I don't know the steps,' I said.

'I will show you, it's easy.'

She took me to where they were dancing. She showed me where to put my feet and hands. As I turned, I saw Ancamma grinning at me and I knew I must have looked stupid. I wondered why I was doing it. Oenna had made me feel foolish when I tried to kiss her and now she was turning me into some kind of clown.

I persevered. I began to get the rhythm of the music and after a while it became pleasurable. I still resented it but seemed, with the help of Oenna's patient tutoring, to be learning the steps. Looking at others around me, I realised I was not as foolish as I felt. There was no one staring at me. I could have been invisible to all of them.

185

'Why are you frowning?' she said.

'What?'

She cupped her hands over her mouth so I could hear and she asked me again.

'I'm not frowning, I'm concentrating,' I said.

She thought this was funny and laughed at my reply.

'Come' she said.

She took me by the hand and led me away towards the mercenary camp. We rounded the corner of the first row of huts and I stumbled. She grabbed my arm. She at least, was sober. I turned and reached for her. This time she did not avoid my lips and we kissed long and passionately. A first kiss is always memorable and I can almost feel it on my lips as the memory stirs.

We walked hand in hand towards the little stream outside the tuath, talking of our respective pasts. It was a warm night and I saw a bat dart from a tree then flit across the stream. There was an owl hooting in the wood as we sat by the stream in the long grass, with the moon looking down upon us and the sound of the water tinkling in our ears.

We made love. The first time it happened too fast and I found myself apologising. I had not lain with a woman for a year or more. She laughed a little; she showed understanding and tolerance of my haste. The second time was perfection. She was patient and gentler in her touch than I could have imagined in anyone who wore a sword and described herself as a warrior. Flesh touching, fingers exploring, caressing. I felt timid at first, unused to the intimacy, but I overcame it and realised as we touched each other with more confidence how well suited we were. When we had finished, we lay naked, entwined in each other's long limbs, caressing and talking in the cool night air as lovers do. I could hear the faint sounds of music still from over the hillcrest; the feast would go on all night but I had no wish to return to it. I drew my cloak around us both.

'So you were enslaved too?' she said.

'Yes, did Ancamma tell you?'

'She told me enough.'

'She knows all about me so maybe she did tell you enough.'

'I keep no slaves myself. After what happened to me, I find it abhorrent.'

'I agree,' I said. 'When I was Warlord, I never had slaves. Servants, yes, but no slaves.'

'It is strange we should meet, you and I,' she said. 'We are as you said, much alike.'

'Happily not physically,' I said, smiling.

'No, not that.' She was smiling too.

'Why did you pick me out? There were many men there tonight.'

'I noticed you the moment you walked into the feast. Do you believe a man and a woman can be created for each other? That the Gods intend them to be together? It felt like that.'

'Yes, it was instant.'

'A destiny perhaps'

'Inevitable,' I said running my fingers down her back. 'You said you are a Princess. Does that mean your father is the king of the Vacomagi?'

'No, he's my brother. He wants me to marry, but he can't force me to do that. I told him I would choose in good time. I think he feels intimidated by me for he has never raised the subject since.'

'I can understand how he feels. You have a power in you.'

'Yes. I've heard that before. Even old Nechtan drools over me. He will do anything I ask him.'

'He wants you?'

'Yes, but he can't have me.' She was smiling again.

'And I can?'

'You can.'

She stroked my cheek with a gentle open hand.

'So what do you want from Nechtan?'

'My brother wants help to fight the Venicones who live south of us. They have been encroaching our borders and they send raiding parties to attack tuaths and fines in our land. They steal our cattle.'

'What did he say?'

'Nothing yet. He won't talk until tomorrow when the Druid comes.'

'Druid?

'Our wise men. They have all the knowledge and learning of the tribes in their heads. It is too big a decision for Nechtan to make alone.'

'We don't have such people. We allow the local kings to decide legal things and the warlord makes decisions about war.'

'You make other decisions too?'

'I decide who I make love with.'

'I'm glad you do.'

We kissed and then we both seemed to sleep for a while. I awoke with a headache, it was still dark and in the moonlight, I looked at her sleeping face. It was a beautiful face, with high cheekbones and full lips. She lay close up to me, her breast moving against my chest as she breathed. Her soft, warm white skin was almost luminescent in the moonlight, like milk or alabaster. I closed my eyes again. This was the first real happiness I had felt for a long time. I dreamed of Livia, my first love. She was smiling and she offered me her hand. I reached towards her and then she was gone.

I was alone when I awoke. I wondered at first in my sleepy confusion if it had been a dream, but I knew such vivid pleasure could never be the stuff of dreams. I washed standing naked in the stream, thinking of Oenna, and dressed to the sound of the water rushing by and the cry of a sawbill calling its mate in the woods across the stream. I splashed more water on my face and walked in a daze to the mercenary camp to look for Cimbrod. I could still taste her and smell her on me and kept thinking how lucky I had been, wondering when I could be with her again.

'What's so funny?' he said when I found him.

'How do you mean?'

'That smile on your face. You keep smirking.'

'That my boy, is not a smirk, it is a reminiscence. I had a very good night thank you. Hey, Drogo!' he called over his shoulder smiling, 'Galdir's found a woman.'

Drogo emerged from his tent. He smiled too but said nothing at first. Then he looked at my face and still smiling, said, 'I hope it was someone more worthy than your Queen Clotildis.'

I looked at him and my puzzled expression made him say, 'I meant no disrespect, Galdir.'

'I did not think you did. Clotildis was wicked. She tried to kill me. This was an entirely different kind of woman, just as beautiful but sent by the Gods.'

Cimbrod said, 'If she was sent by the Gods, you had better pray it was Frija or Idun and not Loge.'

We all laughed at that.

'We have a council meeting to attend. I have permission

to bring you and Hengeist,' Cimbrod said.

'Yes. Do you think they will let me speak?'

'Why?'

'They may need to see the bigger picture, that's all,' I said.

'And they'll get it from you?'

'Yes.'

'Perhaps you could let me into your secret before you open your mouth and drag us all into some Frankish scheme. Don't forget I lead these men.'

'Well, it's like this,' I explained. 'I am going to persuade Nechtan to send out envoys to all the surrounding tribes. I mean all of them. They could raise an army big enough to take back all of Britannia and free the southern tribes from Roman domination forever.'

'You're mad. One night of love has gone to your head. These people are more barbaric even than our own people. They cannot maintain a siege, nor can they stop themselves from fighting and quarrelling with each other long enough to take on the Romans. They have no discipline like the Romans have.'

'Nor do the Germans.'

'We Cimbri are known for our discipline in battle. That was how we managed to take on Roman legions in Raetia and northern Italia two hundred years ago. The Caledonii do not have that ability.'

'You seem to know a lot about them.'

'Ancamma has taught me much,' Cimbrod said.

'Then our job will be to unite them. It could become a common cause. The Romans have been coming here and taking them away for slaves for hundreds of years. If that were your people would you not want to free yourself of them?'

'That is what the brochs represent. It is their way of defying Rome. As soon as the slavers are sighted, they hide in the brochs and escape them. You will never get them to fight openly.'

'We will see. I can be persuasive. Ask Drosten.'

Cimbrod smiled, but said nothing more and we walked together in silence towards the Ri's hut, but Hengeist stopped. He said, 'I won't go with you,' and turned to go back to the camp. 'Why?' said Cimbrod.

'Because I don't think I can control myself in the same hut as the man who killed our brother and frankly I cannot understand how you can.'

'Hengeist, we've been through all this already. It is best to wait.'

I said, 'Cimbrod is right, we kill him when the time is right. Temper has no place in politics. I can tell you a story of my own about how I lost my temper at a council meeting and almost paid with my life. We all want the man dead.'

'You are a friend but not a brother. I can understand your reluctance, you want something from these people, but I want revenge, only revenge. I wish we had never come here. Cimbrod and his half-baked ideas.'

He walked away; his firm tread raised dust behind him that hung in the air for a moment before a breeze dissolved it in the warm morning sun. I realised his lust for Drosten's blood would not dissolve in a similar fashion and I wondered whether there was some way to end this, for it risked turning Nechtan against all of us. As long as Drosten had Nechtan's protection, he was inviolate. It would not last forever and when it ended, I would be there sword in hand, for Adelmar had been a friend.

CHAPTER 1

"It is much easier to try one's hand at many things than to concentrate one's powers on one thing"
—Quintilianus

Many things in life go according to plan; many do not. The quality of a man, however, shows itself when he rises above his adversities. The council meeting did not go according to any plan I had in my head at that time. We entered the smoky dark room together and a servant or slave showed us to a cushion to the far right of the Ri. Drosten sat at Nechtan's immediate left and Oenna on his right. The room soon filled with silent men and women waiting for the meeting to start.

I began looking around at the faces but when my gaze rested on Oenna, I found we could just as easily have been alone. I had eyes for no one else and felt mesmerised. Presently Cimbrod nudged me hard. He whispered in my ear.

'Stop staring at that woman. Do you know her?'

'Yes, I know her.'

Vexed by my vague reply Cimbrod persisted until he noticed the object of my attention seemed as inclined to stare at me as I was at her. He desisted then, murmuring, 'So it was her was it?'

I said nothing, but he had ripped me from my reverie and I began to look at the others in the room. They were all dressed in tunics although the women wore gowns of wool, coloured in different shades of red, green and brown. It was like peering through a fog and it reminded me of the halls of my own people. They had no more idea of a chimney than they had of building with stone.

The guests passed horns of beer between them but I declined. I felt nauseated just by the smell of it and I could think of nothing I wanted less than the bitter brew they served here.

Nechtan stood and said, 'We are here to cement an alliance, but first Oenna, Princess of the Vacomagi, will state her brother's case so all will understand their need.'

'I am here,' she said as she rose to her feet, 'to enlist the help of our friends the Caledonii. The Venicones have raised an army and they march towards my brother's land bearing arms. Our men are strong fighters but the Venicones are numerous and have almost twice as many as we have. I come here to ask Nechtan to bring his brave men to help us. There will be rich rewards for those who fight with us.'

A number of the chieftains present stood and spoke. They were all in favour of crushing the Venicones whom they too regarded as enemies. A figure dressed in a long white robe stood behind Nechtan. I had not noticed him before, but he might have come through the doorway at the back of the hall while the chiefs made their speeches.

He was fully as tall as I am, with long silver hair and a beard of equal length. The hair and beard mingled as they hung from his thin and wiry frame. He stooped as he stood, leaning on a staff. On the end of the staff was a silver emblem of a half moon or perhaps a rising sun, I did not know.

His face was wrinkled; long years were portrayed in furrows on brow and cheek. The striking feature of the man was the dark eyes peering from his long face like living black coals. They darted back and forth from face to face around the semicircle of warriors while others were speaking. They were intelligent eyes and their look was one of deep sagacity. They reminded me of Chlotsuintha my old witch. Her eyes were like that even to the end before she died or maybe chose to leave—I was never sure which. Only a witch can one minute announce to you she is going to die and next minute do it.

I held up my hand. Nechtan ignored me at first but in the end acknowledged me and I stood to speak.

'Great leaders of the noble Caledonii and Vacomagi,' I said looking at Oenna, 'I was once a slave among the Romans and they taught me much. I became a Warlord of my nation, the Franks. I have fought the Romans and won many times in an alliance with Germanic people like the Marcomanni and the Chatti and even with the Sarmatians. When Marcus Aurelius came, he defeated us because we did not stand together. If you unite and stop fighting each other, if you rise up like one Britannic Nation, you will throw off the oppression of these Romans, fight their slavers who steal your people away, and take back what is yours.'

I looked around at the faces, all of them turned towards me, flame-light flickering in reflection from sweating foreheads. They were stony faces, none of them nodding in agreement. I went on.

'I will help you to unite the tribes. I will show you how to fight the Romans and how to win. I know these things because I have fought against them many times and we won battle after battle until the alliance broke up in northern Italia. It broke up because my people fought among themselves like children. Do not go the way of the German nations; learn from our mistakes. It can be done.'

There was silence. I sat down. No one seemed to want to speak for or against my words. but after a few minutes, I saw Nechtan whisper in Drosten's ear. Drosten stood and pointed at me.

'This man is a Roman traitor. He could even be a spy. He comes here with his German friends and thinks he can lead us. I do not trust him; even if I did, I would not follow a foreign traitor. Do we not all know mercenaries betray anyone for the slightest reward?'

He sat down again, a smile flickering on his red-bearded lips. There was murmured agreement with Drosten's notion that I was a traitor. Nechtan patted him on the shoulder and I wondered, angry, what kind of relationship they had. I stood up again to reply when the tall white-clad man pushed past Drosten and entered the semicircle. He spoke slowly. His voice was deep and booming, belying his frail appearance. He pointed his staff directly at me. I noticed the end did not waver or shake. He must have been much stronger than he appeared.

'I know you,' he said slowly.

There was a quiet, a silence so profound, one could almost reach out and touch it.

'I know you. You are the one. It was foretold and expected.'

'Me?' I said, wondering what he meant.

He sniffed the air in my direction.

'Goibhnui the God of this tuath speaks to me.' He drew his opened palm from left to right between our faces. 'He tells me you have always been here with us. Your spirit has always been the leader,' the Druid said. 'There is another voice in my head too. It is a woman's voice. She is small and bent, but she knows things; she points at you and her wrinkled face is cracked in a smile. She knows you and she loves you, though she says you can be foolish. She tells me you are a filid, a man who sees the future and I can see it in your eyes and smell it on your breath.'

He was talking rubbish of course. I had no more prescience than the next man. It was true I had a few dreams now and again. Livia appeared to me sometimes and gave me hints of what was to come but I am not like our witches at home, who knew Wuotan sent dreams and messages to them. I stood in silence. There was no response required.

'It has long been foretold a leader would come,' he said, turning to the seated warriors, glancing from face to face as he spoke. His words seemed to hang in the air.

'My brothers and I have always known it; it has been passed down among us for generations since Maelgwn the Great dreamed it many long years before.'

He rested the point of his staff on the ground and raised his other hand. No one spoke. It must have been a trick of the light but his whole figure seemed to shimmer and flicker as he stood before the assembled chiefs, his face reflecting the torchlight.

'This man is like the iron hoop holding the spars of a barrel together. He will bind us and take us in war against the Romans for it is thus prophesied. It is known that a man, a king, will come from a far off land. He will defeat our best warriors with only his hands. He will bring the people together and defeat a great monster. That monster is Rome. You would do well to listen to him.'

He turned and looked at Nechtan, 'You think you are a great King. No one will remember you for even ten seasons after you go to the Otherworld, unless you take heed of the plans this man offers. I have spoken. By Brighid and by Oghma I swear this is true. By the holy tree and stream I swear it.'

There was silence for a few moments as the Druid pushed past Drosten again and stood behind him. Suddenly everyone spoke at once and there was a hubbub of confused argument. I sat down again. They would not be able to hear me even if I shouted. I looked at Cimbrod. He was smiling, though why he thought it so amusing was beyond me.

Drosten stood to speak. The Druid struck him such a blow on the head with his staff that it drove the helmet down over the man's eyes. Drosten sat down again and struggled to lift off his helmet. I heard Oenna laugh. Drosten's face turned purple with rage but he remained sitting and did not get up again.

Oenna stood. Her tall frame, regal in bearing, made me realise again, the depth of her beauty. I could hardly understand what she had seen in me. All thoughts of Lucia had vanished. It was a relief. Unrequited love is such that unfulfilled as it is, another can take its place if the new feelings are potent enough.

'Caledonii. You have heard what our Druid has to say. This man,' she said, pointing to me, 'can help us draw the nation together. He can help us with our struggle and lead us in battle. We must listen to him.'

Nechtan was sneering in my direction and I realised he had no regard for me, although he had little choice but to capitulate. The entire council was behind Oenna and therefore backing me too. When the meeting broke up it was early afternoon, and outside in the bright sunshine, another feast had begun. These barbarians seemed to feast often and I for one did not mind, for it gave me an opportunity to speak to Oenna. She stood outside the Ri's hall holding a horn of beer. A servant brought one and shoved it into my hand. I was reluctant to drink after the night before, but drink I did.

'I wonder why the Druid supported me. Do you think he believes in his prophesy?' I said.

'His name is Lutrin. He travels far and wide like the other Druids. I've known him for years. He told me he wanted this to happen months ago.'

'You mean he planned it?'

'Well you didn't believe all that nonsense about a foretelling, did you?'

'Well, yes.'

She laughed then. A soft little laugh it was, like the sound of birdsong to my ears. I shook my head. I had believed. He had described Chlotsuintha when he referred to a small old woman who had loved me despite all my foolish weakness.

'There truly are people who can see into the future. I know it,' I said.

'Perhaps, but Lutrin is no filid. He is a knowledgeable lawyer and wise man but he is not prescient. He wants a united Britannia that will throw off the Roman domination, but he knows that as long as our people fight each other all the time, the Romans will rule supreme. He has a score to settle with the Romans because they've killed every Druid south of the wall in the last hundred years. The southern tribes have not had druidic guidance within living memory. He hates the Romans for that.'

'All I want is to go home. I want to rule my people. If there is war and confusion here there is a good chance I can slip across the sea and escape to Gaul.'

'I thought you said as long as Marcus Aurelius was alive

you could not rule openly in your homeland? Are you not endangering the Franks by returning home?'

'No...Yes... I don't know. All I know is I don't belong here.'

'Will you come with me to my homeland? If you can convince my brother to make peace with the Venicones, then perhaps even the Damnonii and Votadini may join us. It could be the biggest army our land has ever seen.'

'I will see if Cimbrod will release me. I swore to him I would pay him for a man I killed when we first met. An oath is an oath.'

'No, I want all of you to come with me.'

'They won't go unless there is gold and fighting. It is all the Cimbri want at the moment. They aren't interested in anything else.'

'That's not what Ancamma tells me,' she said smiling.

'Really?'

'I am sure she can persuade Cimbrod. He is smitten with her.' She smiled as she spoke.

'As I am with you,' I said, looking into those grey eyes.

'I know. It has been a useful... council meeting,' she said.

'Exhilarating.'

'The best for a very long time. You are a persua-sive...speaker.'

'It depends on the reception one gets.'

'Such a reception might come again.'

'The sooner the better,' I said.

'Tonight I may be busy.'

'Too busy?'

'No.'

'Until then?'

She said, 'Council meetings have never held such excitement for me.'

Cimbrod interrupted us by slapping me on the back, spilling my beer.

'Hey! Better spill blood!' I said.

'Sorry,' he said, 'you did well there my friend. How you got that Druid to support you I still wonder.'

'I think perhaps Oenna may have had a hand in it,'

She smiled sweetly.

'So what have you got planned now? Will you go and negotiate in your usual fashion?'

'No, it might not be politic; brute force doesn't always work. Oenna wants all of us to go with her to her home. We have to persuade her brother to make peace and create the beginnings of an alliance.'

'I don't want to leave.'

'Don't worry my friend, Ancamma will go too. She is the translator.'

'That isn't what I meant.'

'What then?'

'I have burned my brother's body here and the one who did it has not paid the weregild and he still breathes the same air as I do. You expect me to turn my back on that?'

'Cimbrod, you are a Prince at home. You are a leader of men. You cannot simply drive everything ahead of you because of a personal battle. Drosten will die. I have sworn it and so have your brothers. Time is not important, only honour.'

'You speak of honour. The only honourable thing to do is to kill him.'

'You know, Cimbrod, we have now talked about this so much I despair of you ever understanding. You are worse than Hengeist who is also unreasonable in his own way.

Wait, be patient and let us create a war. We will have revenge. We will retrieve our honour.'

He looked at the ground and I could see, through his pain, he understood. Dwelling on revenge for the loss of his brother risked becoming an obsession, and who could blame him? Adelmar had come with him from far across the sea, trusting his brother and relying on his protection, only for a crude and barbaric man to kill him in a cowardly attack. I understood all this, but I was unrelenting in my own plans.

'When do we leave?' I said turning to Oenna.

'Tomorrow,' she said. 'Cimbrod, I would be honoured to ride with you and your brave warriors. Come with me and I will ensure one day, whatever happens to any of us I will see justice done. I swear it upon Epona the Mother God of my tribe.'

Cimbrod looked her in the eyes and smiled a wistful smile. 'For your sake I will go. I will gather the men at first light and we will ride with you.'

He turned and walked away, leaving Oenna and me to talk about plans for a future of war and an alliance of north Britons to dwarf all others.

It had been a good day.

CHAPTER II

"The only problem with seeing too much is that
it makes you insane"
—Phaedrus

I awoke with Oenna in my arms. Our night of passion had not spent itself until first light. Tired, happy and content I could have stayed in her bower for days but as she stirred I realised there was much to do. I had forgotten my fantasies of Lucia and it was no doubt a good thing, for she was another man's wife and my thoughts about her had always been dishonourable. I had now beside me, a beautiful woman who was free to be with me and it elevated my spirits as nothing else could have done at the time. We packed our gear.

Cimbrod came to the door and banged on it with his fist.

'Are you two coming or are we going to have to wait all day? There won't be any point in going at all if you don't hurry.'

We emerged, all smiles. He looked up at the sky in a good-humoured way and we mounted our horses.

I had no one to say farewell to. Nechtan did not even bother to come out of the hut, and as we rode away I wondered when I would see Drosten again. I had much to say to him as yet unsaid.

Lutrin the Druid rode with us. He had business at a stone circle on the same route as we were taking. He had no need of protection however, for no one attacked Druids. They were holy men and could put a curse on you if you crossed them. He spoke little but I knew he listened well.

'Cimbrod,' I said, 'did Drosten pay you the weregild?'

'No,' he replied, 'I don't think he ever will.'

'Pity,' I said, 'it means you have no way to pay the men.'

'I know that and so do they. They're grumbling.'

'You could divide that torc you got from Nechtan and give them each a piece.'

'I don't think a torc would go very far among thirty five men. Do you?'

'It was just a thought.'

'My brother will pay you if you secure a treaty with the Venicones. They will have to pay compensation. A treaty is much cheaper than a war. Even our loyal people don't fight unless they are paid,' Oenna said.

'They won't pay any compensation unless your brother marches with his army to request his dues from them. It is perhaps better to negotiate through strength than weakness.'

'You will need to explain that to Drest yourself. He doesn't listen to me.'

'Drest? Is that his name?' I said. I frowned at Cimbrod. It was an odd sounding name and I was half expecting him to make some joke or start laughing as he did over Cornelius' name.

Lutrin said, 'If you can tarry a while and wait for me one day and night, I will finish my business here and come with you. Drest will listen to me.'

'We would be honoured, Lutrin,' Oenna said.

We rode on in silence. The hills were beautiful. The verdant rise and fall of the country contrasted with the deep blue of the summer sky. It was a warm and pleasant journey and the comparison with my arrival on Britannic soil was not wasted on me.

We came to two hills. They were grass covered and separated by a broad, wooded valley through which a stream flowed fast and merry. Boulders interrupted it here and there, making deep clear pools where the water seemed almost still.

We rode into the valley to the sound of birdsong and camped close to the stream. Lutrin walked to the clear waters and lying on his stomach, he reached beneath the surface close to some tree roots spreading into where the stream undercut the bank. With a suddenness surprising us all, he flicked his arm and a fish appeared. It struggled and fought as it writhed on the grass, its jaws and gills opening and closing as it searched the air for its native water. Presently, he produced another and then another. They were silver sided fish, with dark blue backs and they were each the length of a tall man's arm.

'I wish I had time to tell you all how to tickle the fish in this way but it is something learned gradually. One has to mimic the water and its flow by fluttering the fingers along their scaly sides and then take them by the tail. If they do not wish to come, they fight. Some can drag you into the water behind them if the Gods favour them, for they contain much secret knowledge of the Otherworld and this world too,' he said as he stood up 'Perhaps you all should try, while you wait for my return. Look to the dawn of the second day and I will come back to you. This is a holy stream and one which has much mystery to it. Treat it with reverence and do not upset it with cruel words or evil thoughts.'

Lutrin mounted his horse again and rode to the top of the hill. It was a distance of perhaps a mile but his horse seemed not to falter for even a second as it took him up the slope. The whiteness of his hair and robe made a clear contrast with the green of the sward as he departed. I watched him go with wistful thoughts. He reminded me of Chlotsuintha. He talked in the same cryptic way and he led his life intertwined with his Gods and the spirit world, just as she had done. It seemed an age since she departed to the Allfather's side, although in reality it was less than a year, but I recalled all of her prophecies. I also recalled how Lutrin had said he could hear an old woman with a wrinkled face telling him who I was and I wondered if it was she, reaching out for me when I needed her.

'Where's he going?' said Cimbrod to Ancamma.

'He goes to worship. It is nearing the time of Lugnasa and he needs to pray to the Gods of river and stream for a plentiful harvest. He is a great man with much knowledge.'

'Likes fish then?' said Cimbrod and he laughed for a moment but stopped when he saw Ancamma's frown. I wondered if perhaps she had worked a charm on him for his sense of humour seemed under control.

'Perhaps so, but he goes to the stone circle on the hill above us where the Gods can see him when he prays to the sun,' she said.

'I thought you were from Gaul. You seem pretty convinced of the Caledonian Gods and their presence,' I said.

'I have been here long enough to realise the power of the Britannic Gods. They can work wonders. They can protect us with a mist, they can make streams swell to repel invaders, and they can produce lightning, striking down the unbelieving Romans when they wish. I have seen it.'

'I saw no evidence of lightning when I fought at the wall,' I said.

Oenna said, 'When you have been with us a while Galdir, you will understand. The Gods in this land are our Gods, they are strongest in this land and they protect us. They always have. Have you any other explanation for the Roman's lack of success in invading our lands?'

'Well, yes I have.'

'What then?'

'It's economics. There is little to interest them. It would be a costly war if they waged it against the northern tribes. Rome is very cost-conscious. If the newly subjugated land does not turn a profit, they have no interest. I realise you think it is the valour of your people or your Gods, but I'm afraid it only comes down to money in the end.'

'My dear Galdir,' she said, 'you have much to learn about this country. It has beauty and mystery, but it has strength. The land is the people and the people are the land. They are inseparable. Their power is mutual. These northern lands will never be truly defeated by any invader. We are strong.'

I looked at her and realised she might have been right, particularly in her case. She had an air about her of strength and forthright determination I had never seen before and I admired it.

Drogo, still on his horse looked down at me with a frown.

'This seems to be a good place to camp.'

'Yes,' I said.

'We are not easily overlooked from the hills above.'

'You seem nervous Drogo,' I said.

'No, not at all. Should I be?'

'Of course not,' Oenna said. 'There is no one around here to attack us. Brigands don't move about in large enough numbers to do that. Besides, Lutrin picked this place.'

We made camp and although the men tried to emulate the Druid's fishing skills they were all unsuccessful. Most ate food we had brought with us, but Oenna roasted the fish on spits and we all tried some. I am not fond of fish but these had a deep red flesh and few bones so I had to acknowledge they were a beautiful feast in the end.

The night passed uneventfully. Oenna and I longed to lie with each other but it was obvious there was no possibility of that, surrounded as we were by the men. In the morning, even when I suggested we ride to the top of the hill Cimbrod insisted Ancamma and he should come with us. It irritated me, but I knew Oenna and I would be able to be together when we reached our destination.

We rode through a pine forest and emerged on the slopes of the hill. It was a grassy slope and the horses seemed to enjoy the ride. The dew had made the turf soft underfoot, but the going was firm enough. It took twenty minutes before we reached the top and looked out upon a lush green land of pine forest and grassy slopes. In the far distance, looking north, I could see mountains but unlike Frankia, there was snow on their peaks. We sat astride our mounts enjoying the view.

Then I looked back and caught my breath. At the entrance to the valley below, I could see Roman equites. There must have been fully two hundred of them, their red-plumed helmets reflecting the early morning sunshine. They were riding at a fast gallop down towards our camp.

'They're attacking us,' I said.

The others followed my line of sight.

I called out as loud as I could to warn our men. I waved my arms above my head in desperation. They could not see the Romans from the gully where we had camped and I had no way to reach them in time. I began to ride down the slope. Oenna called to me.

'There's nothing you can do.'

Cimbrod followed, his face gaunt, unsmiling.

'Wait there,' I shouted to Oenna and Ancamma.

'No we're coming too,' Ancamma yelled.

There was no time to argue. We rode. We were half a mile away when we heard the sounds of battle. We were on a small, forested track which emerged near the grassy bank of the stream where we had made camp. I heard riders coming towards us. I drew my sword, ready to fight but I realised almost immediately they were our own men. We stopped short. They were armed, bloodied swords drawn and riding as fast as they could towards us pursued by a large number of the Roman cavalry. We waited.

It was a narrow path, with dense pine forest either side. It was only wide enough for three or four horses abreast. As soon our men were close, we turned and rode before them. The equites were close behind. We rode hard. It reminded me of a race I had ridden in when I was in Dacia. It seemed an age since then.

Emerging from the tree line, we galloped hard up the hill. We had covered perhaps half a mile and ridden almost to the summit before I was able to glance over my shoulder. I could see the survivors numbered only ten, Hengeist and Drogo among them. Four of Cimbrod's brothers were not there. The following equites were now slowing. I thought it was because their horses were blown. They had ridden hard into our camp and fought already, so our horses were the fresher.

We stopped and looked back when we reached the summit of the hill. Still they came on, a slow procession of cavalry, whose intentions were clear. Once their horses could move on, they would follow us. There was at least one turma of about thirty and I could see an officer with them. They had two scouts who rode in front. We had to move on.

'We will have to split up,' I said to Cimbrod.

'Yes, we can divide into two groups. We are outnumbered two to one. Hengeist, Ancamma—with me. We will meet here in three days if they don't catch us,' he said. I looked at his face and our eyes met. I had never seen his gaze so hard, so angry. He had lost much because his brothers were with him as his followers and it must have hurt him doubly that any of them may have died. They were his responsibility and I knew he would have imagined he had let them down.

We split into two groups as he had suggested. Oenna and Drogo were in my group and there were seven of us. One of the two remaining Marcomanni was with us, his name was Marcomir. Cimbrod rode due south, Ancamma with him; we rode south and then east towards the Vacomagi lands. We knew the Romans would not follow to the coast. We had three days in which to return.

'How far to your people's lands?' I asked Oenna.

'A day's hard ride. We can get there and summon help.'

'Would your brother risk a war with the Romans?'

'He would not allow them to kill me if that is what you mean,'

'What?' I said. It was hard to converse riding at a canter.

'He would not let them harm us.'

I looked at her face. 'No, I would die before I would let that happen.'

She smiled.

We stopped at midday on another high ridge and looked back, screened from view by a copse of aspen trees. My horse was breathing hard and sweating. The Romans had dwindled into tiny dots riding slowly down a slope but still on our trail. There must have been fifteen or sixteen of them. I could see the scout get off his horse and examine the ground. He was dressed like a Gaul in bright, striped leggings and a tunic. It was too far away for me to make out his face. He pointed in our direction and they rode on towards us.

'I don't understand why they are still following us.'

'They must want us very badly, I suppose,' Drogo said.

'But why? It is almost as if they knew who it was camped by that stream.'

'Yes, they came from two directions as if they had planned it. If Hengeist had not been awake, they would have slaughtered us before we could arm ourselves. He heard them before any of us saw them.'

'What happened to Cimbrod's brothers?' I said.

'Hengeist fought his way out like the rest of us. As for the other brothers, all dead I think. I saw Lugius cut down with a spear, it went right through him as he hacked at the rider's horse with his axe. Boior killed two with a sword but his weapon stuck in a horse's chest and unarmed as he was, three of the Romans stuck him with spears. I had my hands full and saw little else. We lost all our gear too.'

'You were lucky to come out of it without a scratch. I'm proud of you Drogo, your fighting skills are coming on well.'

Oenna said, 'If the Romans knew about the meeting in Nechtan's hut they might have sent men to stop us.'

'You think there's a spy? Surely no one could be spying for the Romans in that gathering?' Drogo said.

'How else would they know we were there?' I said, 'Maybe it's Lutrin?'

'Don't be silly. He's the one who convinced the council to

create an alliance and to believe in you,' Oenna said.

'But he was conveniently absent,' I said.

'I have known him for many years. It is inconceivable a Druid would do such a thing,' she said, gripping her reins with pallid knuckles.

'Well who then?'

'There were many chiefs present at the meeting. It could be almost any of them. We had better move on. They're getting close. How do we lose them?'

'I don't know, but they seem pretty determined.'

'Their officer is with them, look you can see his plumed helmet,' Drogo said pointing, 'there's only half a turma. Perhaps if we ambushed them, we could win.'

'There are only seven of us; they outnumber us by two to one. I don't like the odds. Anyway Oenna is a woman,' I said.

'Don't let that worry you, it wouldn't be the first fight I've been in,' Oenna said. I looked at her and smiled. I knew she had spirit and I admired her more with each passing moment. She smiled back and the look in her eyes was one of understanding.

I looked down at the Romans. They looked like hard veterans from their appearance. I said, 'These men are professionals, you can see from the way they carry themselves. We ride.'

We headed for a forest about a mile away; I decided it was safer to hide than to fight. The persistence of the followers was disturbing for there seemed to be more afoot than a simple attack. They could have been after me or Oenna but their dogged pursuit showed us they were not only dangerous but tenacious.

I began to wonder if they knew I was the same man who

had been lost in the fight at the wall. If they did, it could cause problems at home. The Romans would kill my entire tribe if they established I had betrayed them and was leading a rebellion. These were dangerous times. I said a short prayer to Idun of the golden apples and bade her keep the Gods contented so they would help me. I should have prayed to Loge the trickster, he would have helped me find a spy if there was one, that was his sort of game after all.

CHAPTER III

"The mind ought sometimes to be diverted that it may return to better thinking"
—*Phaedrus*

The forest was a deep, dense barrier of pine. There was only one opening; a small deer-path winding like a snake between the furrowed boles of the looming conifers. Mossy tree roots seemed ready and waiting to trip the horses and dense thicket grew beneath the woven canopy of branches, hiding the slippery rocks. There was a stillness inside. A dark, sombre, brooding place it was; a perfect place to hide.

I followed up the rear and Oenna led. We dismounted as soon as we entered the tree line and led our mounts. It was hard going at first but we found it easier after a few hundred yards. There was a stream trickling across the path and Drogo suggested we use it to throw off the pursuit. I thought it was a foolish suggestion because the path was too narrow and the hoof-prints would be easy to track in the green moss-covered mud. We continued along the winding track for almost an hour and found a grassy clearing where we stopped. The sky above us was overcast and the light was fading a little as dusk descended.

'If we leave the path we may get lost. These forests are vast,' Oenna said.

'We have little choice. The Romans may well be right be-hind us and they are too many to fight. I had hoped the path

215

might branch and we could lose them.'

Drogo said, 'There is an equal chance they would follow the correct fork and we would be no better off.'

'No, I think they would split up. We would have some chance of taking them then.'

Marcomir said, 'There is a way. It is an old Marcomanni trick.'

'Yes?' I said.

'If we double up on the horses, I can take three of them on some firmer ground and they will think we have split up. I can come round and meet you, or follow your tracks if you double back. We can meet here. If I avoid the mud they won't see the hoof-prints are less deep.'

'It won't work; all of them might follow us instead, surely we need to stick together?' Drogo said.

'We have little choice. We have to count on them splitting up. You might find they all follow you and leave us alone though,' I said.

'I will take my chance. It would be an honourable death.'

'Indeed,' I said, 'we go with your plan.'

'May I say something?' Oenna said, irritated.

'Of course,' I said.

'If they have an experienced tracker he will know exactly what we are doing. Drogo could be right. You are assuming they are stupid. They may follow either track and come back, then follow the other.'

'I think they are fighting men. They would still feel they have a good chance even if our numbers equal theirs. If they are not that confident, we have a problem.'

Oenna frowned but agreed with obvious reluctance. We split, as Marcomir had suggested. He rode one horse and led three. The rest of us doubled up two to a horse and picked the stoniest ground on which to force a way through the undergrowth. It was hard going, but we had to keep to a straight line heading north so Marcomir could find us again. He was a good woodsman and he moved faster than we did.

After an hour we stopped. I could hear the sound of pursuit. They made no secret of their coming. I hoped they had divided forces and our six would equal their seven or eight. There was a small clearing, where three could stand abreast and we stopped there. Drogo and Oenna and a doughty Cimbrian hid at the neck of the entrance. I stood with the others at the far end of the dark space. We expected to face mounted soldiers and I confess the prospect did not bring any confidence. If they had already caught Marcomir, they might be in full strength. We did not know.

They came at speed. There were only seven or eight of them. They were Tungrians such as I had fought alongside at the wall. Each man carried an oval shield. They had spears in their hands. Fighting a man with spear when you have a sword and no shield may sound daunting but despite their reach, once you get close enough they have no chance.

I moved forward fast. The first spear thrust came. I turned to my left and parried the horizontal spear. I riposted to my right and with luck caught the man across the face. The blood ran down and it blinded him. The man behind him was stabbing at my head and I ducked. I stabbed at his legs, but he was fast and stepped back into the shield of the man behind.

The Cimbrian on my left was down, a spear transfixing him. He writhed and groaned on the forest floor. I knew he was dying. His assailant drew his sword and stabbed at me. I had to give ground. I had a spearman in front and the swordsman to my left. The Cimbrian to my right fared better; he had despatched one man with his short sword, pushing up close. He too stepped back. Then it began in earnest.

I swung my blade to my left, fast. I contacted some part of my opponent. The spearman stabbed again. I grabbed the shaft and pulled him near. I could smell him he was so close. The look in his eyes was one of hate, his face contorted. I reached over his shield in a second and my blade penetrated his neck and on into his chest as it descended. He screamed and fell at my feet.

The fight became a blur. Cut, thrust, parry. Step back, keep turning, moving. Kick. A blow landed. Pain in my side. Legs wobbling. Force a step backwards. A tree against my back. Cut, thrust parry. A man down. Strength returning. A sudden shout. Oenna and Drogo coming from behind. A shout from the Tungrians. Blood everywhere.

Death and then calm. I stood breathless, leaning against the tree. The Cimbrian with Drogo and Oenna had fought well and despatched two and Oenna had wetted her blade too. Drogo had been a hero. He had killed two, one from behind and one as the man turned with his spear. We had lost only one man. The five of us surveyed the scene.

Our Cimbrian comrade had ceased his death struggles and now lay twisted and still in a pool of blood soaking into the grass beneath him. The spear had passed through his chest. It was a mortal wound as soon as the spear had hit him. I wondered then whether I could have done more to prevent his death but I knew I had been fighting for my life too.

'I have never done that before,' Drogo said, a smile on his lips even though he was out of breath.

I looked him in the face. His apparent smile annoyed me.

'You think the death of these men is enjoyable? You think it is a thing to smile at? To take the Gods' greatest gift from a man for no good reason we know of and then to smile, is that a good thing?'

'I... I only meant...' His voice trailed away and young as he was, he seemed hurt by my seriousness.

'I'm sorry. It's just that it could be any of us lying there now, bleeding and dying. And for what? We are not fighting to defend our homes. We are not fighting for our women or families. They attacked us, but we should honour our opponents for their strength and courage. If they had none, then we have gained nothing ourselves by their deaths. It has always been so. The mightier the opponent the more honour you achieve. If they were nothing then we are nothing too.'

'You are too hard on Drogo,' Oenna said. 'He is young.'

'Yes,' I said, 'I suppose you're right. It's just I can't understand these men. They are Germans like me and they fight on the wrong side, far from home. It is a waste of good men who should be fighting against these Roman bastards, not helping them.'

She said, 'That is as may be, but they attacked us not the other way round and besides, they killed those Cimbri boys, Cimbrod's brothers.'

I nodded and walked to the bodies lying in their varying postures of death. I had never before worried about the death inflicted upon an attacker. I had always seen it as honourable to defend myself and to obtain blood-revenge when needed. This day, I felt only sorrow at the irony of killing my own kind, far from their homes, because of orders from some stuck-up Roman commander who used us all in his scheming. It underscored my feelings about them. Rome with all its machinations and cruelty stood for everything I believed was unjust and unfair.

I staggered, and putting my hand to my side recalled the pain which had made me step back. My hand came up covered in blood.

'Are you hurt, Galdir?' Oenna said.

'A scratch I think, here in my side.'

'Let me look,' she said.

'It will keep,' I said.

'No, let me look.'

I pulled up my chain mail and realised it was more than a scratch. There was hole in my mail and the spear point must have penetrated, for there was a small cut on my left flank. It had pierced through the mail vest and through my abdominal muscles, but it was superficial enough to miss any vital organs. I remembered I had twisted sideways when the blow struck home. I hoped the Tungrian had cleaned his blade regularly and it had not been dirty. It was painful now the fight had ceased, but I thought it should not be too serious. Oenna wanted to rub it with moss which I disdained and so she bandaged it instead with a strip of cloth from a Tungrian's tunic.

'And now?' said Drogo.

'Now we push on to the north. If we move slowly, we should come across Marcomir. We need to go in a straight line. Then we will have to fight the remaining men. It only shows, you should never split your forces in battle,' I said.

'Let's move,' said Oenna as if she was in charge. I smiled at her. She looked beautiful as she cleaned her bloodied blade on a slain man's tunic. Every inch a warrior. I had never seen her like. She was a sword-maiden and beautiful at the same time; her red hair draped over the mail coat she wore, her face grim and her eyes glinting in the faint remainder of the daylight penetrating from above, subdued by the tall filtering pine trees.

I had at first thought she would be only a passing fancy but seeing her like that, brave and beautiful, made me realise my feelings for her were deeper than such a short acquaintance should have created. I knew we were kindred spirits and suited to each other like sun and sky. I did not want to part from her, but the need to go home troubled me. I had promised Frija I would return to lead my people and she had said it was my destiny. I knew I had to try to control my feelings for Oenna but the weakness which has always been my downfall made me think of her every moment of every day. It was like being young; nothing mattered, as long as we were together.

We pushed on in the darkening forest. The dry pine branches, grey and brown, reaching from the boles of the tees grabbed at us as we made our way through their dark and narrow corridor. None of us spoke. There was nothing to say. We all knew what lay ahead if we were to survive: another fight and more death. That prospect had a sobering effect on us all and my mood was sombre, not least because of the pain in my side. Would we be as lucky in the battle next time?

CHAPTER IV

"The bow kept taut will quickly break, kept loosely strung, it will serve you when you need it"

—Phaedrus

It was dark by the time we made the clearing where we had separated. There was no sound and the forest seemed silent as a dead man. We halted close to the trees at the south end, and ate some of the bread and salted pork we had with us, though none of us dared light a fire. We posted two guards and tried to sleep, for we could not tell how long it would be before Marcomir returned, if indeed he was alive.

It was damp and cold in the forest. An owl occasionally called its ghost-like melody and the smell of the pines would have been pleasant had it not been for the circumstances. We expected the Romans to follow closely on the trail of the Marcomanni warrior, if they had not already caught him. We could not leave and double back for none of us wanted to desert our comrade.

The wound in my side prevented me finding a comfortable position and I could not sleep. I rose and went to where Drogo sat guarding our sleeping comrades.

'Drogo, I can take this watch. I cannot sleep,' I said.

'No, Galdir. I will do my duty. To be truthful, I doubt if I can sleep either. I keep thinking about the fight and what you said in the forest.'

'Mmm'

'Yes,' he said, rubbing the back of his neck as if he was uncomfortable with his thoughts.

'What troubles you then?' I said.

'It's just I have only ever killed in that battle against the Orcadians and this was different somehow. I could see their faces clearly and I was close enough to smell the men I killed.'

'That is quite normal. Fighting in small numbers is not like in battle. You even see their pupils wizen as they die. It is something you get used to.'

'It's not that, it is just I killed them unfairly. The first one did not even know I was there and the second had no time to defend himself. Is it not dishonourable?'

'Drogo, my friend, you fought them honourably enough. They would have killed you without even thinking about it. It is the way of things. If you live through battles, it is always because someone else has died. You cannot spare them or they would have your blood on their swords instead. That is the nature of the times in which we live; it is buried deep inside our very being. Kill or be killed is basic and it forms the cornerstone of our nature. We cannot escape or run from it. It is a different matter to wonder why we do this. Some might ask, why kill others at all? Why cannot men live side by side in peace? I almost achieved that in Frankia you know but the Romans came and they are not a peaceful people. They want the world to be theirs and if they cannot make the world Rome, they destroy it. They are like some great machine plodding on, inexorable and solid, crushing every-thing before them and caring not one bit. We have to fight them, if not for revenge, then for freedom. To die as a free man is a hundred times better than to live to old age as a slave. Believe me I know.'

'And when we have fought them, and when we have killed them all, will we have peace, Warlord?'

'It will be as the Allfather wishes. I suspect peace is only a temporary respite and even if it were not the Romans, we would fight each other as the Britons do. It is these people's greatest weakness. They fight continually among themselves and never seem to have strong enough alliances to join and defeat the Romans. But hear me. We Germans have shown repeatedly our alliances are weak too. There was a time when Marcomanni, Chatti, Cherusci, Franks and even Sarmatians had coalesced. We fought the Romans all the way to their very own country before the alliance broke up because of petty squabbling and nothing else. No, the Romans will falter in the end and their downfall will come, if not by external might, then by divisions in their own ranks. I intend for our nation to be there when it happens and our people will rise eventually ruling all of Gaul. It has been foretold.'

'Foretold?'

'Have you not heard of a witch called Chlotsuintha?'

'Er...Yes. I grew up hearing stories of her. She remained in Sicambra did she not?'

'No, she died before the end of the siege. I thought everyone knew and grieved for her.'

'I had not heard. I'm sorry.'

'Then know this now my friend, she saw the coming future of our nation. Not only the close future but also in a historical sense. Wuotan gave her a vision of a wide and beautiful country, green and pleasant, ruled by Frankish people who will take their place among nations and became whole and great. I like that thought, that future. I want to be part of the foundation of that nation and such is my goal.'

'You can't do that from here. Is that why you want the Caledonii to fight the Romans?'

'Yes, of course it is. I hate the Romans but I know that unless we drive them from here I cannot return home. It is impossible to travel through Britannia let alone Gaul, without a pass and credentials. Do you think they would give them to me for the asking? If there is a war, I don't care if it is successful or not, it will provide sufficient distraction for me to return home.'

'I will go with you; I am your man and no other's. I never swore an oath, but you are my Warlord and I owe you my trust and respect. Will you let me come with you?'

'Drogo, I would be honoured to have you by my side.'

He stood then. I thought I could see the emotions expressed in his eyes, for the eyes tell you everything about a man. He made to embrace me but I resisted. It was not his masculinity putting me off, it was because I was his Warlord and although I had told him to put away formality, I did not want his emotions to cloud the hierarchical nature of our relationsiip. It was a weakness in me, perhaps borne of the loss of my own self-esteem, but I pushed him away all the same. I should have been more attuned to the emotions of others, and more astute, but at that time, self-pity and gloomy ruminations of my own failures consumed me.

'I apologise, Warlord,' he said, 'I did not mean to overstep the line. I am after all only one of your soldiers.'

'Drogo, I am privileged to have you with me but I am your leader, not your mother.'

There was only Drogo and I who were Franks in this little group of warriors and I should have made it matter. There was something about the lad holding him away from me. I could never put my finger on it however. He seemed distant at times and sad too. I always assumed it was the grief we shared over the fall of our nation, it had stolen much from me and I guessed it was so for him too.

We heard Marcomir before we saw him, and Drogo and I roused our comrades, expecting to fight. He entered the clearing, with rents in his clothes and a broad smile breeching his face.

'Marcomir! Well met indeed,' I said in low tones. 'How long before we have company?'

'I'm afraid I can't tell. I think they made camp, at least I could see a fire lit behind me. Maybe I lost them after that,' he said.

'Unlikely,' I said, 'we must go.'

We roused the others and saddled our mounts. The forest was black as cinnabar as we made our way out, leading our horses into the narrow path we had followed that afternoon. We were all in good spirits, for we now thought we could avoid another fight and make our way back to meet Cimbrod and the others. It occurred to me however that perhaps they had not been as lucky as we had been. The pursuing Romans could have killed them, for all we knew.

It was still dark when we emerged from the tree line and struck out south, needing to distance ourselves from our pursuers. We had another day of this chase before we could cut back to meet Cimbrod, if indeed he was there at the meeting point.

Dawn found us looking down upon a wide vale of oak forest. I had never seen such a large group of oaks. In Germany, they grew in copses often mixed with other trees but not in this fashion. Each tree stood more than ten yards from the other and between them was a flat, grassy sward. Small bushes of hazelnut and juniper crawled beneath in places but it was as if these kings among trees drove off all other competition to spread their hundred-year boughs towards their kin all around.

My people at home believe oak trees are holy and the priests often use them for displaying sacrifices and offerings to the Gods. The Marcomanni nail the bodies of their torture victims to the trunks, but such things we Franks always regarded as barbaric. The sunrise cast straight beams of light into the trees and there was a strange feel to the place as we entered. It was still and quiet, almost sinister. We knew it would be a poor place to hide for the trees did not grow close enough together to create a screen.

'Oenna, do you know this place?' I asked.

She rode beside me and I realised we had conversed little until then.

'Yes, it is a holy place for the Druids. They come here almost as regularly as they visit the stone circles. Lutrin says this forest is particularly blessed by Cernunnos, the God of woodworking. Only those blessed by him may cut trees here and only the best craftsmen may be so honoured.'

'We have similar beliefs at home'

'Tomorrow we meet Cimbrod. I think if we stay here we will be safe.'

'But we can be seen from the hills above can't we?'

'Perhaps, but it is said a mist surrounds this forest and enemies cannot see through it.'

'You don't really believe that do you?' I said.

'Yes, I do. I have a very good feeling about this place. My people have an affinity for these trees. They have always been here and they will always remain. Lutrin said so.'

'Will we have a chance to be alone here?'

'I don't think so, not until we reach my home.'

'No, you are right. I need you though.'

She smiled, 'You won't be much use for it with that hole in your side.'

'It is often surprising what a man can do when need drives him.'

Laughing she rode ahead and shook her head. As she looked back at me I could see she was laughing still. I looked around and there was a faint mist beneath the trees. I found myself staring into the clearing haze and a feeling beyond my control descended upon me somehow. It was as if there were faces staring back at me. They were fierce warrior faces. I could make out their indistinct forms, mail clad and carrying axes and spears, their blades dark stained as if from blood long dried and clotted. I shook my head and the vision dissipated.

I found I was trailing behind the others and could not catch up; the pain from my wound was increasing all the time and after a further hour, I had to stop to rest. We halted in a clearing. In the centre of it was a tree stump, cut about two feet from the ground, its surface smooth and flat and six or so feet in width. There were stains of a reddish brown hue on its surface and someone had inserted small metal stanchions at the corners. The purpose of the tree stump seemed clear to me and I had a feeling of foreboding as I dismounted.

Another strange waking dream came to me. I looked all around beneath the trees and I could see again crowds of misty and wraith-like figures. Their faces were indistinct but they all looked at me with an incandescent glare from eyes as red as burning coals. A voice in my head called my name and I began to feel faint. I leaned forwards and reached out to the tree stump for support. It felt as if a lightning bolt jumped from it into my arm, spreading pain rapidly upwards. A bright light flashed before my eyes and I was aware of falling forward onto my knees. I heard my companions calling my name with echoing tones. My eyes closed and all went quiet and black.

I opened my eyes and stood up. I looked down and could see my five companions, some kneeling and the others standing around a big fair-haired man. Their bodies had a strange translucency, a radiance too. It was a kind of all-pervading brightness and the entire world seemed lit by a hundred suns. I realised it was my body lying there. Blood flowed from my side onto the green turf, but I found I could walk and see.

'Oenna, what is happening?'

She ignored me. No one turned or even acknowledged me. An eerie silence pervaded the scene. I reached forward and touched her on the shoulder. My hand seemed not to contact her and I shouted.

'Can't you hear me?'

A voice to my right said, 'Galdir, you are in the world of spirits you silly boy. No one can hear you. Be at peace.'

I turned and saw Chlotsuintha. I knew this was another vision but wondered if I was dead.

'Am I...Am I...?'

'No my silly boy, you are just close to the spirit world in which I often walked in life. It is the place between the Gods in Asgard and Midgaard, the world of men, made from the body of Ymir, where you foolish mortals play out your little games. You are here because you are ill and the place you find yourself in is holy even to our Gods.'

'What will happen?'

'I've told you many times what will happen. Did I not

explain you would lose the battle against the Romans?' Did I not tell you, how you would return home? You know these things. Be at peace.'

'Will I succeed?'

'Success can be measured in many ways, my foolish, impatient boy. Perhaps following the path the Allfather has prescribed for you would be success. You always struggled with it. The fire burning in those loins of yours scalds you still. It is not until you have control over your passions that you will be able to fulfil your destiny. Be at peace I say again. It is time for me to go. When your first love returns to you heed her words and all will be well.'

The little wizened figure held up her hand. She reached forward and touched me on the chest, over my heart. Everything faded away again as if I was falling backwards into some dark cloud or pool. I awoke with a start, fighting for breath and gasping.

'Galdir, are you all right?' It was Oenna.

'Yes my love,' I murmured; I was feeling emotional. 'There are spirits here. I saw them.'

'We saw nothing. You fainted. Looking at the blood you have lost it is not surprising. I have bound your wound again but I don't think we can move from this place today,' she said.

'Give me some water, I'll be all right.'

'Drogo,' she said, 'make camp here and we had better not light a fire. It would be visible from the hilltops. I am sure those Romans will still be following.

Drogo for his part did as Oenna told him. It was as if he acquiesced because he recognised the bond between the Vacomagi Princess and his Warlord. I was indisposed so Oenna became the next in line.

Marcomir sat down next to me.

'You know Galdir; there was something strange about the Romans following us.'

'What?' I said.

'I can't put my finger on it. It was just they seemed to know too much about us and where we were going. Their persistence was unusual. I left no trail in the woods, at least none a normal man could follow, yet they followed with an accuracy that was uncanny. I can't explain it.'

'You're imagining things. They just have a good tracker. Tomorrow we meet up with Cimbrod and continue our journey. All will be well.'

'If they were out on a punitive raid or a patrol, how could they plan to attack the camp in the way they did? Even if it was so and they simply scouted ahead, why bring a Gallic tracker? It makes no sense.'

'You think they knew we were there?'

'For a start they covered all the avenues of escape from the camp and they had enough time to divide up to attack from three directions at once. They knew where we were all right.'

'Perhaps there is treachery afoot. I can't think who would do that though. I trust Oenna and Drogo implicitly. I wondered about the Druid though.'

'Me too. He disappeared at just the right time. It was all too convenient.'

'He was the one who wanted to support a war with the Romans. It doesn't make sense either—if he is a traitor that is,' I said.

'All will be revealed in time I suppose,' said the Marcomanni.

'Yes, in time' I found myself drifting off into a deep sleep despite the early hour. My limbs felt heavy and the pain in my side had reduced to a mild burning sensation, now that I was still. As I closed my eyes, I pondered the Marcomanni warrior's words. A Roman spy in the wrong place could thwart all my plans.

CHAPTER V

"The intelligence of few perceives what has been carefully hidden in the recesses of the mind"
—*Phaedrus*

'Galdir.'

I heard the echoing voice as if it was far away. I thought it was my mother at first. Perhaps I had been dreaming of my early childhood before the Romans killed her. Sleep fled from my eyes and I was aware again. I must have been in a deep sleep for I had difficulty orienting myself and I had dribbled onto my cheek as I slept.

'What? Where?' I said, wiping my cheek with my hand and propping myself onto one elbow on the damp grass. The pain in my side stabbed as I moved.

'They are coming.' It was Oenna.

'Who's coming?' I said, not fully awake.

'Riders, they can only be the Romans. They must have followed us.'

I stood with difficulty and tried to follow what was happening but my mind seemed clouded. The wound in my side gave me pain but it was tolerable. I walked to my horse with a stooping gait, holding my side and mounting with difficulty.

We began to ride. I had trouble following where we were going but Oenna reined in her mount and drew level to me.

'Make haste, my love,' she said. 'We have no time.'

'How could they find us?' I said

'I don't know, but we could hear them approaching while you slept. If we go to the spirit world, I want you to know I...'

Before she could say it I had spurred my horse on, but the pain in my side slowed me down. We had ridden only half a mile and the others must have realised I could not ride at full tilt behind them for they stopped, turned and faced the track behind us, weapons drawn.

'Ride on, ride on!' I said.

They remained formed up in a line so I joined them and drew my sword. They had decided their plan and they would not heed me. Better to die in a fight, I supposed, than from some carelessly acquired wound like mine. The truth was none of them would leave me behind. Oenna loved me and the others were my sword-brothers, my battle-kin.

We stood our ground as the riders approached. We were ready and expectant. I knew I had to take the first few and I edged my horse forward, talking in soft tones to him all the time. It is the best way to calm a horse especially before a battle. I had learned that long ago.

In the burgeoning dawn light, we saw the dim shapes of riders appear beneath the oak trees and I could feel my heart racing. Their hooves thundered on the turf and I guessed they must have had reinforcements for there were certainly not seven or eight of them, the transmitted vibrations told me that.

I realised then there were at least a hundred men facing us and it was hopeless. I was prepared to die. I hoped Oenna would flee if she saw my death, and in that hope I faced my end with pleasure. Had I not been in a similar state of mind at Sicambra? I rode forward and raised my blade above my head, my horse cantering.

A voice among them said in the Caledonian tongue, 'Galdir! Hold! We are not Romans.'

I halted. I lowered my weapon as I realised these riders were barbarian horsemen. It was Lutrin who spoke.

He rode out in front of the riders and raised his hand. His white robe flared out behind him and he raised his staff in greeting. He smiled as he approached, his furrowed features smoothed by the half-light. I felt more reserved than perhaps was wise. Had he not disappeared when the Romans attacked the camp?

'Would you fight your friends?' he said.

'No,' I said, 'we thought you were the men pursuing us. I'm sorry.'

'They were not far ahead of us when we came here and they could not put up much of a fight. They scattered and escaped. It is good to see you alive. Drest had feared the worst and sent as many men as he could quickly muster.'

'You have driven them away?' I asked.

'Yes,' said Lutrin, 'we are here to help.'

I dismounted. The feeling of firm ground beneath my feet was a relief.

'We thought...'

'I understand,' Lutrin said. 'When I saw what happened at your camp I rode to Bannatia, the Vacomagi town and explained. Drest cares for his sister as you can see.'

Oenna said, 'Lutrin, we are pleased to see you. I knew you would come. I came here for I thought it was the safest place.'

'Yes, the Gods of river and stream, tree and branch live here. They spun a mist to hide you from the enemy. Where are the others?'

'We are only six. They killed one of us in the forest and now we are six. Cimbrod and six others escaped too. We meet them tomorrow near the first camp.'

'Then we camp here and find your friends tomorrow. My heart is relieved to find you.'

'Galdir has done much to protect me.'

'This even your brother knows now.'

They set up a wide camp and bivouacked for the night. They had no worries it seemed in making fires and they set up pickets to ensure no repetition of the attack on our camp by the Romans. My nerves had been on edge for days and I was glad to relax in the company of these Vacomagi. They differed from the Caledonii in that they were both good horsemen and sea-going fishermen for they lived on the east coast.

For once, Oenna and I slept next to each other. It was almost as if she wished to demonstrate to her tribesmen that a bond existed between us. Of course, even in the depths of the night, there was no more than a reassuring physical closeness but we both seemed to derive comfort from the other's proximity.

I had more strange dreams that night but I put it down to the wound. It had ceased bleeding when Oenna inspected it next morning and I felt stronger in any case. We rode to meet Cimbrod after a small meal of oat-porridge made on fires of dead oak. The smell of the fires was not as I had anticipated. Burning oak has a peculiar odour all of its own, it pervades everything but is not unpleasant. Lutrin said that was because the oak has strong inherent spirits but I did not understand what he meant. These northern Britons were a strange people and their beliefs were stranger still.

I recalled how many Romans there had been and was

not optimistic the Vacomagi could challenge so many mounted equites but I thought it unlikely they would have tarried after laying waste to our camp. We did not know if there had been survivors who fled in a different direction, but it seemed unlikely. We mounted the ridge above the destroyed camp expectantly. There was no one there and we set lookouts and rode on to where we had camped three days before, next to the salmon-stream.

The wreckage remained strewn across the site of our now abandoned resting place. The green sward had brown stains where men had bled and the bodies had begun to deteriorate already. We dismounted and began what we knew we had to do to honour our dead. I set Drogo and Marcomir to building a pyre and the others dragged the rotting flesh that had once been our comrades onto it. We stood in silence as the bodies twisted and charred in the heat of the flames, the smoke rising in a black spiral on its journey to the Gods. I gripped Oenna's hand tight in mine as we watched.

Oenna said, 'Do you need to rest Galdir?'

'Rest?' I said, 'No, I am fine. It's stopped bleeding anyway. We will have to wait at least one day for Cimbrod and Hengeist, it will be long enough for the wound to start healing. I feel better than when we entered that oak forest. It was a strange place.'

'My people revere it. It has powerful spirits living within.'

'Do you believe in such things?'

'Of course, don't you?'

'I believe there are many Gods and I believe they influence our lives in subtle ways. I think they communicate with us in dreams and portents but I give little credence to the idea spirits wander the earth. I have never seen one except when I have been ill or close to death and I suspect most such things are part of our imagination.'

'You should not ignore the spirit world.'

'I don't, but I have yet to see a spirit wield a sword or spear and until I do I will not fear such things.'

I said nothing of the visions of Chlotsuintha. I thought they were all in my head in any case; either that, or the stuff of dreams where my imagination took charge of my thoughts. I wondered if perhaps they were some form of wishful thinking spawned by the fact that Chlotsuintha always cared about me and our nation. Her death had been a grave blow to my people's morale.

I did find it hard to cast aside a vision I had in Rome before I ever knew who I was. I had looked in a barber's mirror and seen mounted Frankish warriors fighting Romans. I could still picture it with ease and I had never known if it was my father or me, but they pulled the warrior down and he disappeared in a sea of red tunics.

It was midday before we saw Cimbrod and his companions. They were all there and they paused before they approached. Oenna and I rode down to meet them and when they saw us, they advanced up the hill.

'Cimbrod!' I said.

'Galdir, Oenna. Well met indeed. I see we have company.'

'Yes,' Oenna said, 'my brother sent us an escort.'

'Did the Romans chase you?' I asked.

'Yes,' he said. 'We managed to lose them but it was close. We had to journey for almost a day in a deep stream.'

'It opens into the Tama River,' said Ancamma.

'You fared better than we did,' I said and explained what had happened.

'Hurt bad?' said Cimbrod.

238

'Mainly my pride,' I said, smiling. 'We have dealt with the bodies. We lit a pyre and committed them to the smoke and flames. We did not know when you would come.'

'Where to now?' asked Cimbrod. He gave no indication he had even heard me.

'We ride for Bannatia. It is where my brother has built a very large tuath. The halls are much bigger than those of the Caledonii,' Oenna said.

'Stone?' I asked, recalling the only stone structure I had seen so far was the broch near the coast.

'No they build in wood,' said Ancamma, 'like the Germans and Gauls. You will be surprised by the accommodation after Nechtan's hall.'

'If the entertainment is as good as the hall, ride on,' Cimbrod said spurring his mount down the hill. Hengeist paused and looked at me.

'Cimbrod hides his feelings, Galdir. We lost four brothers in that fight you know.'

'I know.'

'If there is any way to get even with the Romans I will take it.'

'Then stay your hand against Drosten. We all want him dead but a war will brew if we keep all the Britons together.'

He said, 'Whoever betrayed us will bleed at my hands too. Before you contradict me, there was no way the Romans could have known where we were and how many men they needed to take us.'

'I have the same thought in mind. We need to discuss this when we arrive at Bannatia. It is always easy to suspect, but proof is hard.'

'I do not need proof. Suspicion is enough. I think it was Drosten. I saw him sneaking away from the Caledonian tuath on the night of the feast. He did not return until the next day.'

'He could have had a tryst Nechtan would have disapproved of. It means nothing.'

'No. But it raises my suspicions and that, after Adelmar's death, is enough.'

'Remember our agreement Hengeist. War first, revenge later.'

'I hear you.'

He rode ahead and I wondered how to contain his bitterness and anger. I understood how he felt. The Romans were a far off vague and unknown threat. Drosten was real enough. If I had been Hengeist I think I would have killed Drosten long before, but my temper has always robbed me of wisdom and perhaps Hengeist had better control of his.

I had no idea what Bannatia would be like. I had now seen so many different places and people nothing could surprise me. I had lived in Rome, Lovosice, east and west of the Rhenus and now here in Britannia I was still learning how different people can be and how customs and lives may vary.

CHAPTER VI

"A bad beginning makes a bad ending"
—Euripides

The east coast of northern Britannia is different from the west. In the west, there are wide green hills and mountains with pine forest and rain-soaked fields. The rocky inlets and the lakes provide places of shelter and security but this is not the case on the east coast. There, the land is flatter and less densely wooded. There are long yellow beaches and sandy hills where sea-birds call and the cold grey seas ebb and flow. The eerie sound of the waves was like a dull drumming in my ears as we rode along the beach in the mist that Oenna told me was always there. The beach was wide and flat reaching out to our right as we rode, like a shallow sea-filled plain even at high tide. On my left, I could see grass-bedecked dunes twenty feet high, fluttering a verdant greeting in the breeze.

I was still in pain from the wound in my side and Oenna who rode beside me, frequently asked if we should stop for she could see the strained look on my face. I wondered if she was reluctant for our journey to end.

'I've had worse,' I said.

'Really?'

'Yes, my own cousin Guntramm stabbed me with a spear on the other side. It became infected though and I was in a lot of pain for a while. This wound is nothing by comparison.'

We rode on in silence and I saw she was biting her lip, then, 'My brother's town is only a mile or so along this coast. His hall is big, not like Roman buildings, but like the halls the Gauls build in their country.'

'Of course,' I said, 'I was forgetting you were in Gaul for a while. You must hate the Romans as much as I do.'

'No, I don't hate them. Life is not all black or white; there are grey areas too. I hate the slavers who captured me but not all Romans are cruel. The family who bought me were kind people. They were farmers and treated me well. They had a daughter the same age as me and she was always kind.'

'I hate them all. If I had my way, I would destroy every last one of them for what they did to my people and the Sarmatians. Their war upon us was unjust.'

'You cannot destroy Rome. Their Empire is vast and besides they always return in greater numbers. My time in Gaul taught me that. You should have learned what their 'Divine Julius' as they call him, did to the Nervii.'

'I remember saying much the same thing to my uncle once. He thought he could fight them too.'

'And was he successful?'

'Only as long as the German alliance continued. Once it broke up the Emperor took on all the tribes singly and wiped them out.'

'Won't the same happen here? Perhaps you are leading us all to destruction? They will just bring more legions here.'

'No, it is too costly for them. Britannia is an island and the cost of importing troops is very high. That's why they use auxiliaries.'

'You are hiding something. I can see it in your eyes.'

'Me?'

'Yes.'

'I need to return to my people; that's all. I cannot stay here. When the war is fought, and the Romans are thrown out of Britannia, I will return home.'

'And me?'

'I... I don't know. Would you come with me?'

'No, I cannot. If we are to be together you must stay here with me.'

'Then we are both stubborn and stupid and have no future.'

'Why is your future more important than mine?' she said, frowning.

'I am a man.'

'So? I am a woman.'

'You don't understand.'

'Perhaps it is you who lacks understanding. Marriage for me is a political thing anyway. My brother wants me to wed a man who will be politically advantageous. I have a younger sister and she too must forge a wedding alliance for the benefit of our people.'

'Being with me has no political advantage to your brother. He will hardly allow me to marry you.'

'He might if you are the leader of the armies of an all-Briton alliance. Are you asking?'

I looked at her. Her eyes were laughing at me. I do not know why, but the conversation had fostered anger in me and I spurred my horse on. Oenna rode behind me for the remaining journey. If any of my companions had asked me, I could not have said why I was irritated. I was still in love with her but there were too many things coming between us. She seemed to be giving me a choice but it was one which could cost me my honour. I could not stay in Britannia for love or anything else. I had sworn to lead my people and that was my destined path. I wanted to be with Oenna despite. These opposing desires created such conflict in me that it translated itself into anger, I know not why. If anyone should have understood political expediency, I should have.

I found the Briton's women irritating in any case. In Rome, men and women who were married did sleep with others but it was always secretive. It was Germanic to take only one wife. Here, if a woman wanted a man she would have him openly and no one objected. Oenna told me that the secrecy and dishonesty of the Roman way was dishonourable and that truth and honesty were greater virtues than any Roman deceit. She was teaching me something I knew already, but I had slept with Piso's wife and even my married aunt and the dishonour of those relationships had not stopped me from forging ahead with them. I had always had a weakness for women. She made me feel guilty I suppose, for the very strength of her views and the ingrained morality that was so strong in her was something I had never been able to achieve myself. It accentuated my own weakness.

Bannatia appeared almost before I was ready for it, for my ruminations had taken me far away. What I found as we rode towards the gates, pleasantly surprised me. There was a proper wall ten feet high and gates manned by proper warriors. We had to wait for admittance as is correct in a real town. I was astonished, for it was the first evidence of sensible civilisation I had seen since the Roman's towns in the south. I began to realise why Oenna was so different from the rustic Caledonii with whom I had been living for such a long time.

My beautiful Oenna called up to the guards and they

opened the gates for us. As she rode through, they bowed in respect; she was after all, a Princess. I had expected Bannatia to be another tuath with small buildings of mud and lathe but what I found was a large town like Dalriada in the west. There were winding streets and shops with a blacksmith near the gates. Children played in the dusty streets and ran with balls, chasing each other and laughing. The sound of their pure childish glee was music to my ears and I revelled in it.

It seemed as if I had heard no such unbridled and innocent laughter for many months. Even Cimbrod had ceased to laugh since his brothers had died. I realised he carried an intolerable burden now but I saw few signs the feelings had erupted. It is often so; events lead to emotions expressed much later or even not at all. Anger and hatred can fester and change a man. I hoped this would not be so for my friend, but equally I knew there was nothing I could do to reach out to him, any more than I could change the past. Besides, I had my own problems at that time and my sensitivity to other's problems was never great in those days. I was always better with horses.

The main street of Bannatia was a long winding lane with low, thatched, wooden houses lining its meandering progress as it scaled a small hill where a second walled compound stood. The back of the compound was set close in to a rocky cliff rising high above. A small spring trickled clear, cold water down the edge of the cliff forming a little waterfall here and there in its descent as it ran down to a pool behind the King's hall. Beyond the stockade, I could see the hall—a large building made of rough-hewn wood with iron-studded oak doors and pillars of wood flanking the entrance. Outside stood two spear-carrying guards who acknowledged our approach by crossing their weapons over the doorway and barring our entrance.

'Uid,' said Oenna, 'You know me well enough not to obstruct my entrance. I live here!'

The guard looked at Oenna and smiled. He had long grey hair, once blonde, and he stood erect, as a soldier should.

'My lady, you know well what the king would say if anyone came past me unannounced. He would take away my weapons and say I was an unreliable old dotard. Surely, you would not wish that upon an old man? I cannot admit armed men to his presence.'

'I am as ever, comforted by your diligence. That is why my brother put you here. I have with me a Frankish Warlord and a Cimbri Prince, not to mention the Druid, Lutrin.'

'I would be honoured to announce you, but I wonder if your noble friends would kindly stay here until I do. My lord has had worrying news from the south and he has given strict instructions which I dare not disobey.'

'These are strange times Uid, are they not? A Princess of the house of Talorc left standing on her own steps?'

'It is only the presence of the strangers that concerns me. They look...Err...Warlike.'

'Uid,' said Lutrin, 'have you become foolish since I left only three days ago? Do you bar my way? I will go and tell Drest I am here with friends and I vouch for them, if you don't. Hurry. I do not like to be kept waiting; we Druids are an impatient folk!'

Uid scurried away to do the Druid's bidding.

'So Oenna,' I said, 'Are you always greeted in this way when you return?'

'Galdir,if you looked a bit less like a killer and a bit more like a prince this would never have happened.'

I was about to reply when the guard returned and bade us relinquish our weapons. That done, we followed him into the Vacomagi King's hall. She was right of course, I wore a chain mail tunic with a sword and dagger at my waist and my helmet was dented and tarnished. I must have looked dangerous to anyone.

'Oenna! I am so glad you are safe.'

The voice came from a carved wooden chair, elevated about a foot from the ground by a small dais. Benches stood before it. The speaker was a tall man whose height was recognisable even though he remained seated. He was thin and angular, his long arms like sticks.

We crossed the floor space and as we approached, he stood up and embraced his sister. It was a warm greeting; I could see they were close and I could sense their affection for each other. I studied Drest. I realised as soon as he stood up he was taller even than I had thought. He was half a head taller than I and his limbs seemed to move in a jerky and rapid way reminding me of an insect. His clean-shaven face was long and narrow and his russet eyebrows were bushy, meeting in the middle above his freckled nose—like a bush on a cliff-top. He was balding at the front but his red hair lay in a long tangle on his green patterned tunic which narrowed at the waist, embraced by a silver decorated sword-belt. His grey eyes were knowing and sharp, darting from one to the other of us, weighing us up even when he embraced his sister. I wondered if he was nervous.

We walked forward and I recognised the hall was very similar to one I had lived in many years before in Dacia. I looked up. There, among the rafters was a chimney of intelligent design. We had one such in my own hall in Frankia. It took the smoke from the central hearth right out through the roof and was not a common feature in any barbarian hall. I wondered where the idea had originated from for its presence seemed incongruous among a people whom I had thought were less advanced than even the Germans.

'What has happened Drest, that you should bar your doors to strangers and post guards at your hall's entrance?'

'I'm sorry my sister. The guards were only doing their duty. The Romans have sent assassins to remove me from power. Forcus killed one of them yesterday, so I have been cautious since. They seem intent to back our enemies the Venicones, who have made a peace treaty with the Romans and even have trade rights with them. But sit please, my sister and tell me who your friends are.'

He smiled broadly at Lutrin, who grinned in return.

'Lord Drest,' Lutrin said, 'We have travelled far and...'

'Lutrin, my dear friend,' the King said, 'refreshment is on its way. I know your appetite for wine.'

Lutrin sat and smiled as he looked up at us. Oenna introduced each of her companions. Drest sat on the benches with us as if to induce an air of informality and I realised he was honouring us by doing so. A servant brought wine and water in the Roman style, which surprised me again. I realised the Vacomagi were a very different people from the Caledonii and seemed to have taken on some semblance of civilisation when compared to the other northern tribes.

'So you came to help me fight the enemies of my people did you?' Drest said to Cimbrod.

'We came with that intention but our numbers are reduced to a third after the Romans attacked us in force.'

'How many?' the King said.

'Only fourteen now. There were forty of us to start with but we fought a battle in Insi Orc and now the Romans have reduced our numbers further.'

Drest considered this and said, 'I cannot use fourteen men as a fighting force. You are too few. Perhaps I can use you as a bodyguard. I certainly have need of one; that is, if Oenna will vouch for you.'

'Lord Drest,' I said, 'I have a slightly different intention.'

'Oh?'

'Yes, I am here to enlist your help in drawing together all the northern tribes and throwing the Romans out of Britannia forever.'

'You are?'

'It will take a lot to do this but Lutrin is as convinced as I am.'

'Don't you understand. We are at war with the Venicones. They will side with the Romans in any case.'

Lutrin said, 'If you call a meeting of all the kings they would attend with the others. This is the time foretold. It is the time of our people, Drest. We shall throw off the yoke of Roman rule and live the free life our Gods want for us. One kingdom, one people, one land.'

Drest looked from Lutrin to me and back again. He said, 'This man isn't one of us. He is a Frank. Our people will never listen to him.'

'No,' Lutrin said, 'but they will listen to me and my brothers. It is the prophecy. There have been great stirrings in the spirit world. Our High Council has debated this for some years now and we know the time has come. Do you doubt me?'

'Lutrin, I trust you as a law-giver, as a religious leader and as a friend. You are, however, naive in your belief that all men trust Druids. Politics, trade and hatred may be stronger than respect for our religion.'

I said, 'Will you not even consider what Lutrin asks?'

'I will consider it, yes. I need time to do so but there is little time. The Venicones are on the march even now. They have raised an army and the Votadini have aligned themselves with them. Both tribes are in the purses of the Romans with their trade deals and exchanges of hostages. If I sent an envoy, they would burn him. They don't want to listen to talks of peace and harmony.'

'Lord Drest, we are not preaching peace here but war. All I want to do is reflect that back at the Romans. I will go with Oenna and Lutrin to talk to these people. You do not know it, but you can trust me.'

'German, I do not trust you but I have trust in my sister and in the Druid. I will consider what you have asked and will talk further with you in the morning. My steward will show you and your friends to where you may rest. Later we will eat together.'

He turned to Oenna. He placed a hand on her knee, 'I am so glad you are safe. I worried for you.'

'Then listen to my friends. You will not need to worry if you do.'

Drest smiled at his sister. I could see his love for her reflected in his eyes. He clapped his hands and a small elderly man appeared dressed in a green tunic and with a huge helmet upon his head. It kept slipping down over his forehead and he had to push it up to see where he was going. I wondered if the helmet was part of Drest's new precautions but said nothing. He escorted us to rooms opening off the main hall, noisy rooms, but comfortable. To my irritation, I shared with Cimbrod and Hengeist. I wanted to be with Oenna but she had her own bower at the rear of the hall and I did not know whether I would see her again that day. I lay on the cot without speaking, staring up at the wooden rafters of the ceiling. Presently, a man came with fresh clean bandages and a paste he smeared on the wound in my side.

The door closed noisily behind him and I began to speculate on where all this was leading. I was now in another king's hall. I loved his sister and hoped to forge alliances between peoples about whom I knew nothing, in the expectation I could ferment a rebellion against the most powerful nation in the known world. My hopes began to wane. Who was I anyway but a jumped up ex-slave with a few fighting skills and nothing else to recommend me?

It was then a picture came into my head. A memory of how I had killed Piso's father. The anger, the frustration of that moment began to insufflate my mind. I had let my rage drive me. My master had been a dishonourable man who thought he could take advantage of a young girl in my presence as if I had been nothing – furniture, to stand and witness what he, in his abject corruption was about to perpetrate. I had snapped and the adventure my life had become began there. I had no regrets. I was glad of it all. It gave me strength and hope for I had come so far and I would finish what I had begun. I would triumph over these Roman conquerors and drive them from this island. I had to. It was for honour as well as revenge and I knew then I would not cease from mental strife, nor let my sword sleep in my hand until I had achieved what I had set out to do, in this green and pleasant land. I began to relax and felt sleepy.

'Galdir? Going to sleep?' Cimbrod said from his cot.

'What?'

'Are you dozing?'

'Not now. How can I doze if some Cimbri keeps shouting at me?'

'I lost many whom I loved in this last week. The Romans killed four of my brothers. Do you have any idea what that has meant to me?'

'Get used to it my friend. It doesn't stop here.'

'What do you mean?'

'Since I escaped from Rome and travelled north, everyone I have become attached to has died. The only survivors are Duras the displaced King of Dacia and Lazygis, my Sarmatian friend.'

'You think your bad luck will extend to me too?'

'No, only those whom the Gods love, die young. Your ugly face is unlovable.'

Cimbrod laughed, despite himself and sat up, 'But I'm beautiful,' he said, swinging his legs over the edge of the cot. 'Anyway, I want this war too you know.'

I noticed Hengeist was snoring, exhausted from the journey of the last few days.

'I know.'

'You do?'

'If you didn't want revenge on the Romans, you would not be the man I took you for. It is now a matter of honour for us both.'

He said, 'No, not that.'

'What then?' I said.

'My brothers came with me out of loyalty. I loved them and they have died. They feast now at Wuotan's side and they fight and revel. That is not a bad thing, although their love and their company are denied me. If I return home empty handed, my people will despise me for losing my brothers. It is a defeat and it means they died for nothing. If I return with a wife and gold in my hands, they will see my brothers' death as honourable and victorious. I will follow you in this business for these reasons.'

I sat up then and looked my friend in the eyes.

'Imagine if your victorious return would spell the death of all your people—every man, woman and child who depend upon you. If you could see that future you would understand why I cannot return home as a triumphant warlord. I will have to hide and rule secretly where the Romans cannot find me and when Marcus Aurelius is dead there may be a chance, a slim one, but a chance all the same.'

'I am not of a defeated tribe. Whatever happens, my people are safe. I do understand you though. What about Oenna? Is she just a diversion?'

I looked at him again; my head pounded. My face must have changed then for he said, 'Galdir, it was only a casual question. No need for anger.'

I realised I had reached for my sword and I dropped my hand to my side as my sudden fit of anger subsided.

'Cimbrod, I'm sorry. I really cannot speak about it. I want to stay with her but my duty demands I leave. What would you do in my stead?'

'Me? I would worry about that when the time comes. The Gods often play us false when we make too many plans.'

'Perhaps you are right. Cimbrod?'

'What?'

'I am glad we are friends. Meeting you in those woods near the wall was a fortunate meeting.'

'Who knows where it will lead? We work well together though,' he said.

'Yes, I think our destinies are intertwined.'

There was a long silence and I was again aware there was much between us. I also understood it had often been so in my life; there were strong bonds between us warriors—often stronger than blood. It was a fellowship and one few things, apart from greed and lust, could sunder. None of us can know what the Norns spin. If I had known their plans then, I suspect it would not have altered anything I did later. We have all after all, to be the person we are for good or ill.

CHAPTER VII

"The mind ought sometimes to be diverted that it
may return the better to thinking"
—Phaedrus

'Oenna,' I said, 'does your brother hate you?'

'What?'

'Does he not value your life more than this?'

We rode up a grassy slope southwards in the early dawn
in good spirits and glad of each other's company. The sun
rising beyond the cold, grey sea cast purple and golden light
across the sandy shore to our left and I could hear gulls
crying to the sunrise as we rode. A gentle breeze wafted
odours of salt and fishy smells to my nostrils as my horse
stumbled, struggling to find a grip in the loose earth. The
dunes to our left were topped by dark, damp sand, but it
would dry and lie as a golden crest on each yellow and green
mound by mid-morning, for it was a mild autumn.

'You ask such foolish questions at this hour of the day.
He values me above all others.'

Lutrin smiled beside me and spurred his horse on, tired
of our bickering. He knew perhaps that the words we spoke
were not the ones in our minds.

'Why, if he loves you, would he send you with no escort
apart from an old Druid and one warrior to meet an army?'

'He told you last night.'

'He said he did not want to send his army with us lest it

255

started a full scale war. I thought he would have sent Cimbrod and his men with us at least. The Romans could still be after us.'

'Are you scared?' she said.

'No. I am concerned for your safety.' I said. 'I value your well-being, you know that.'

'Perhaps, but not enough to stay with me after all this is over.'

'I have my honour and a debt to pay to my people.'

'Have you no debt to pay to me? Last night when we made love you seemed happy enough to honour me with your body.'

'Oenna, why do you do this to me? I cannot stay and you would not want a man who has no honour.'

'There is more to life than honour. Can you not feel it too?'

I reined in my mount.

'Oenna, we cannot do this. Fighting over what might or might not be in the future is senseless. We need to wait and see what happens, then we shall make a decision together. We do not know what the future holds.'

She glanced at me over her shoulder and frowned. We did not speak again until we stopped half an hour later.

'Where is this army then?' I asked Lutrin.

'They are marching north and we are riding south. We will meet them as certain as the breaking wave will meet the shore, Galdir.'

'Why can't you just say yes or no, or answer a simple question in a simple way?'

'A simple word may say much more than it is intended to say. A long one can equally say nothing at all. Do you think the length of a speech is the important thing or is it perhaps what it tells you about the speaker?'

'There you go again. Talking in riddles, like Chlot-suintha, my witch at home.'

'If you remember my words carefully, you may find they aid you when we meet the Venicones. It may not be what they say that is of interest, but how they say it, that is all.'

Oenna laughed. I scowled at her but she laughed even more, raising her hand to her mouth. The simple femininity of that gesture made her seem even more beautiful to my eyes and my irritability softened.

'What?' I said, almost able to smile.

'Galdir, you cannot get sense from a Druid, they all speak like that. Don't you my dear, dear Lutrin?'

'The manner of speech is not...'

The first arrow missed him by the narrowest margin and I leaned forward and pulled both Lutrin and Oenna to the ground as a second passed above us. The hollow in the dunes in which we now lay made us invisible to an approaching enemy but it was equally impossible for us to see where our assailant might be. We crawled to the edge of the dune and peered out through the long verdant grass. We could see nothing. The dunes stretched out before us and there was no one visible. I signalled to Oenna I would circle round. She nodded and I crawled to my right. I dragged myself to the edge barely raising any part of me from the sand. I could feel it cold against my stomach as I used my arms to pull myself along. In the next hollow, I rolled down the slope and knew no one could see me from the shore where the arrows had come from. I continued in a semicircle until I reached the flat, wet beach and began to climb back up to where my companions lay hidden from view. The wind was getting up and blew sand down towards me as I climbed, sword in hand.

I reached the edge of the hollow and was surprised at what I saw. There were four horsemen seated on their mounts and Lutrin was looking up at them. I could not hear what he said but his voice was curt and angry. Presently, one of the men dismounted and stood before the Druid.

I climbed the slope and joined Oenna and the riders eyed me with suspicion, scowling in my direction. I smiled at them in return.

'What's happening?' I said.

'They are Venicones. Advance guard. Lutrin is explaining to them what happens in the Otherworld to people who threaten or kill a Druid.'

I looked at the three mounted men. They appeared, as far as I could see, identical in every respect to the mounted soldiers of the Caledonii. I wondered how one could tell them apart from any other of the north Britons. They all looked the same to me, but I did not voice my thoughts. One of them pointed in our direction.

'If you harm those under my protection your spirits will be pursued by Otherworld wolves until the end of time. You know this to be true.' He waved an open palm across the man's face. 'We need to speak to your king and you will lead us to him in peace. Although you have come with an army, Lord Drest does not wish to fight and so he has sent us as envoys.'

'Who is the woman?'

'I will tell that to your King and not to his servants.'

The old man glared at the dismounted soldier. His pallid cloak flew out behind him and his long, white, wispy beard trembled and fluttered in the breeze as he spoke. He looked like some gigantic seagull, all white against the golden sand.

The soldier looked at Oenna and me and scowled.

'My lord Morleo may not wish to speak to you. We have been sent to scout ahead; we do not arrange the King's appointments. He has secretaries for that. We are warriors.'

Lutrin raised his staff. The wicked silver half moon at its tip flashed in the burgeoning sunlight and ended almost touching the man's throat.

'You will honour my staff and honour my wishes. There is no law that punishes a Druid for taking a man's life if he insults what we all believe in. I represent the Gods of hill and stream, wood and sky and will not be obstructed by mortal man. I may help you to become a frog or a mouse perhaps, if you keep me from the Gods' work. Would you like that? Do you hear me?'

A look of abject terror overcame the soldier's face and he knelt before Lutrin.

'I meant no disrespect. Please do not curse me. I am only a warrior.'

'Then let us ride. I wish to speak to your lord and speak I will.'

*

The day was waning by the time we saw the Venicones' army. We climbed a rocky, turf-covered hill and as we gained the summit I could see a wide plain below. To our left was a cliff-face plummeting to the rocks below and the angry surf beat audibly at the foundations of our viewpoint. The great army of the enemy was only a war-band by my standards and I realised why I scorned the north-Britons. There were perhaps two thousand warriors, half of them with braccae and cloaks, their bodies painted like Taran's. The ebbing

259

sunlight reflected from the spear-tips, and they raised a little dust in their wake as the sea-breeze took it, wafting it away into the hills on the army's left. They walked and rode in a mob. A Roman quotation came to mind, though it might have been Greek, which said that to send an untrained man to war was no better than to throw him away. These men would have been thrown away if they fought Romans or even a German war band.

I knew these people could fight like furies, but they had as much discipline as a flock of starlings. Could they really throw off the Roman grip? I began to have doubts again. It was not that I doubted myself now; I began to have misgivings about the whole idea of uniting a rabble like this. They clustered in groups as they walked, grim-faced and serious, looking around at the land passing either side. Tousle-haired and wiry, they moved their limbs like strong fit men but I still had my doubts. Fierceness is good in a fighting man, but discipline is better.

To this point they had followed a Roman road, flat, straight and smooth, but it had stopped a few miles south and it must have slowed them down. I could see carts in the vanguard and horses drawing empty chariots, the terrain too rocky for drivers to remain stable inside them. Their cavalry rode behind in the van and I was surprised they had no mounted warriors riding the left flank but they probably felt secure in their numbers and did not expect to an ambush.

'So this is an advance guard is it?' I said.

'Don't mock Galdir. You know it isn't,' Oenna replied.

'My point is they number only two thousand.'

'True, they are only a small army by Roman standards but they are a big one by ours. Each of them is a staunch warrior and they fight like cornered bears when they need to.'

'They fight like barbarians. The Romans have silence and discipline. To them it is just a job of work. They also have stout leather armour and cutting and slicing at them does little. Men like these with no armour and long swords die easily fighting Romans. Against heavy Sarmatian cavalry it would be like watching a farmer reap his corn.'

'There are many more warriors in my land than there are Romans. Every one of them sees death for their land as an honour,' she said.

'How many tribes are there in your country?' I asked.

Lutrin said, 'Eighteen. Four are too small to help. Each of the others could produce around two thousand men if they have time to gather. The Caledonii can muster almost five thousand according to Nechtan. The order to muster has to go by word of mouth for my people have no written language by which to communicate. Only we Druids can write.'

'The Romans say the pen is mightier than the sword you know.

'Where did you hear that?' Oenna said.

'Don't know exactly, but I think it means that commanding an army gives greater power than fighting in one.'

My companions looked at me as if I was mad but I was sure I had heard the expression somewhere. We rode down slowly towards the leading men, flanked by the Venicones' scouts. I could see a big man riding a white horse. He had bright red hair and a hairy, blue, bare chest. I thought he seemed familiar, but could not place his bearded features.

I asked Oenna who it was, but she did not know him. He held himself proudly on his steed and I guessed he was a Venicones lord for he looked haughty.

The Venicones' scouts rode past us and sent one of the

front marchers back to announce us. A horn sounded and the entire moving mass of men came to a halt. Lutrin shifted uncomfortably in his saddle and I was about to dismount until Oenna placed her long, cool fingers on my hand.

'Wait,' she said.

I looked at her and could see a warning in her glance but could not understand why.

A short stocky man dressed in a blue tunic under heavy chain mail walked towards us. Tall dark warriors similarly dressed, flanked him and carried huge spears such as the Romans use for boar hunting. At their waists, they had long swords and each had a shield.

The short man raised dark eyes and looked straight at Oenna. He frowned and said, 'So Drest sends a woman to beg for his life does he?'

'Morleo, you were ever unwise, but to insult the bearers of glad tidings of peace brings you close to stupidity,' Lutrin said from behind me.

Morleo, the King of the Venicones looked at Lutrin. He sneered and I could understand why Lutrin was scornful of him. He had nothing kingly about him. His hair was un-kempt and around his neck was a cheap silver torque such as Nechtan had given to Drosten after the battle in Insi Orc. He had a mean, furrowed face and he was bow-legged, giving him a strange waddling gait which seemed as regal as a duck on a beach.

'I have no quarrel with you Druid. I know well what plans and schemes you spin in the cold, dark halls of the northern kings. I care nothing for you or anything you may say. I have never killed a Druid but there can always be a first time, so have a care.'

Lutrin sat silent but I could see him turning pale with

anger. Expressed on his white-skinned face the added pallor gave his face the hue of a dead man. He spurred his horse on suddenly, pushing between Oenna and me, but I reached forward and grabbed the bridle, bringing him to a standstill. There was murder in his eyes.

'We come in peace Lutrin, do we not?' I said.

The Druid cleared his throat but said nothing; he had not mastered his voice and I realised whatever the danger to his life he would have attacked the King.

I dismounted. I stood opposite the King and looked down at his sweating face. I could smell him.

'Lord King. I am a leader of men from a far off land. I was Warlord of the Franks and came here because the Romans forced me. I have fought with the Romans and against them. I have fought beside Nechtan of the Caledonii in the islands far to the north. Oenna, sister to King Drest, and I have fought Romans together on our road to the Vacomagi town of Bannatia. I come with a message of peace and a hope for future freedom. Will you hear me?'

'I march to war and brook no mealy-mouthed speeches that try to delay me while my enemy gathers his weakling forces. Whoever you are, you have nothing to say to me. Stand aside.'

Morleo made to push me out of his path but I stood steady as a rock and his hand stopped on my arm as if fixed there. I was close to drawing my sword but I knew it would be suicide.

Morleo turned his head and said over his shoulder, 'Take them. They will burn in our fires this night.'

Men all around us began to close in and this time I did draw my sword. The nearest man was Morleo, and my blade could easily have taken his head, but something stayed my hand. As it happened, it was wisdom. The two warriors either side of the king had raised their shields and thrust their spears at me, protecting their lord. It seemed the embassy was doomed to failure and death, when with a suddenness that surprised, there was a flash of white and I was knocked to the ground by a white horse. I must have struck my head for there is a moment or two missing in my recollection. Next, I caught a blurred glimpse of a blue stained body standing over me.

The rider had dismounted; he towered above me and roared. It was hard to understand what he said, but it seemed to be enough to bring the melee to a standstill. I was aware of a curly red head leaning down towards me, and a huge strong hand grabbing my arm, pulling me to my feet. I realised where I had seen his face before. It was the Votadini warrior from the clearing, that day when I had killed the Tungrians. The clear blue eyes had steel in them and he said in accented German, 'You know me?'

I smiled but had nothing to say as I gained my feet. I looked over my shoulder and saw Oenna still mounted and with sword drawn, holding a crowd of men at bay. Lutrin sat on his horse next to her, his face impassive now, as he swung his staff at any who came close.

The Votadini roared an order, and quick as a wink mounted blue Votadini warriors surrounded us. With no apparent difficulty they had pushed their way forward and formed a cordon holding back Morleo's men. I mounted my horse and looked down at the Venicones' king. His face was a deep shade of puce and he was speaking fast and loud at the newcomer. I could not understand him, but I learned later his expletives were not ones to which I had yet been introduced.

Our Votadini escort rode with us, surrounding us closely until we had reached a clear space on the army's left flank. I could see scowling faces directed at us and I was now certain my aims had been thwarted. How could such a rabble of malcontents ever become a fighting force capable of destroying the iron discipline of Rome?

'Oengus, my lad,' Lutrin said, 'I am glad you were there to save Morleo.'

Oengus smiled broadly. He looked at Lutrin and said in the Briton tongue, 'Yes, I am pleased I could intervene. He doesn't seem to care what killing a Druid can do for his future.'

Oenna said, 'You are Oengus the Mad?'

'Few people dare call me that to my face, Hen.'

She dismounted and looked him in the eye. 'I am Oenna of the house of Talorc, sister to Drest, Lord of the Vacomagi. I say what pleases me and I can fight for that right if you wish.'

Her gaze was unwavering and I could not help the feeling of pride arising in me as I looked at this maiden of adamant. She stood straight and tall; her pride and beauty shone like a beacon in the night. The thought that she loved me warmed my very soul and I realised all those months when I was in Gaul, moping for Lucia, the unattainable and unreachable, had been a waste of time. Oenna was truly a Princess among her people and among all people as far as I could see. I felt honoured to be with her.

Oengus smiled broadly and I realised I liked this man. Something about his demeanour reminded me of my Dacian friend Duras. Big, laughing and yet still powerful. He reached forward and with a gentleness unexpected from so large a man, patted her on the arm.

'Be that as it may Hen, you were unwise to come here. Morleo is not a man of compromise.'

Oenna smiled and was about to say something.

'And you are?' I said.

'You have learned our language?' he looked at me with surprise. 'I march with Morleo because I am forced to. The Romans are much closer to my lands than they are to the Vacomagi. They have taken hostages and demand unfair trading terms. My people cannot do other than what the Romans demand.'

'Do you not wish to fight them?' I said.

'They hold half of my nobles and kin as hostages. I dare not move against them. I can only raise three thousand warriors in any case and they have more. They have heavy cavalry too, who ride among my warriors and kill them as if they were mowing barley. We cannot stand against such men.'

'The heavy cavalry were disbanded.'

'They are back together now. They rode fully five hundred strong against us in the spring and we sued for peace in the end. My people say they take heads like we do.'

'And if they did not fight? What then?'

'It would still take ten Votadini tribes to remove the Romans from the wall. It cannot be done.'

'If I can talk to you and Morleo, I think there is a way to defeat the Romans which I can explain to you.'

'Morleo does not talk. He only wants to fight. He is...well, limited,' Oengus said and smiled that broad beaming smile of his.

Lutrin joined in, 'There is much we have to talk about. Great things are happening in our lands and Morleo is but a little man who can be removed from the world if need be.'

266

'He has a thousand men here and it would be foolish to try.'

'You know I am the Magus of the Druids. All men of the true faith will hear me,' said Lutrin.

'Then we will talk. I will speak to Morleo first. He does not listen readily but he needs me. My army is equal in strength to his and without my men, he has no hope of defeating Drest. We will talk tonight. Camp here and I will leave some of my bodyguard to protect you. I will come to you. I would fear for your safety if you come into our camp.'

He mounted his white stallion and rode away towards the army, which had stopped its march and was setting up tents on the plain. I saw him lean forwards and murmur something in a low voice in his horse's ear. The steed shook its head and blew audibly, digging its rear hooves into the turf as it cantered away. I heard him laugh aloud for sheer pleasure as he rode off. I liked him more for that. To be one with a horse, a man has to communicate with it and it is a trait I have seen only in certain men, men who are part of their natural world—men with feelings. Even we killers have those emotions; expressed at the right time, they add to our power.

I looked at Oenna now with an even greater feeling of admiration. I had seen her strength and realised she was different from any woman I had ever met. Proud and strong, she had much more to her and she was mine for the taking. But at what price? To forsake my own people who needed me? Could I pay that price? Could I really stay here in this green and pleasant land and would my world really be built here, amidst these dark and war-like brochs?

I led the horses away, fed them and tethered them to a bush and when I returned, Lutrin and Oenna were deep in conversation. They looked up as I approached and fell silent.

'What?' I said.

'Lutrin thinks we may be in danger tonight. Morleo is not a man who gives up easily,' Oenna said.

I pointed to the ten warriors who had camped twenty yards away. 'I think they will keep us safe tonight. Besides I will persuade Morleo that the Romans can be defeated and if he refuses, I will kill him.'

'Don't be a fool Galdir,' Oenna said 'If you did that we would have a thousand warriors after us in a second.'

'It might be the only way to adduce a settlement here.'

Lutrin said, 'We need willing help not war. Between us we will be persuasive, short of violence, my boy. I am not a man who favours violence in any case.'

'It was not immediately apparent this afternoon,' I said.

'I am human. I can be moved to anger like any other. Let us eat and perhaps the Gods of this place will show us the way.'

As the sun sank, we ate our meagre rations of corn and vegetables, and waited for Oengus to return. Ill at ease, my mind was in turmoil.

CHAPTER VIII

I disliked Morleo as soon as we began talking. He was a king and the Romans had never defeated him, but he had none of the regal qualities I associate with kingship. He was unkempt and emanated a reek like his horse. He was quarrelsome and bad tempered and I never saw him rise above any occasion that allowed him to conceal his bad temper. Despite all that, he led his men well. They gave him their trust and he repaid them by rewarding bravery and stamping out dissent. When he came to us with Oengus he came fully armed and prepared for a fight, which seemed inappropriate considering his alliance with his companion.

'I am here because Oengus wishes it. Keep it short; it has been a long day.'

'May I introduce myself?' I enquired.

'You've done that already. You're some defeated German aren't you?'

Oengus said, 'He has qualities you do not display yourself Morleo. He saved my daughter from the Romans a year ago, risking his own life in doing so. I owe him much. I want you to listen to him.'

The Venicones king scowled at the Votadini and I wondered what hold Oengus had on him.

Oenna remained silent; I think it was because she won-

269

dered what I was going to say. Lutrin sat expressionless by my side. We sat around the fire and its flames cast a flickering yellow light illuminating our faces in a ghastly parody of reality, ghostly and vague.

'My people were once part of an alliance of tribes in Germania; Chatti, Marcomanni, Batti, Quadi, and Teutones all combined in one army. We numbered a hundred thousand men at one time. We stood against Rome, and Sarmatians and Scythians joined us too. We fought Roman armies, one after another, and knew no defeat.'

I paused for breath but could see the look of boredom on the face of the Venicones' leader.

'We took our forces all the way to northern Italia and could have sacked Rome herself. It was because we were united in one goal—the defeat of Rome and throwing off the Roman yoke of slavery.'

I was impressed with my oratory but I could still see Morleo had no understanding of the size of the forces I was describing.

'Morleo, you have a thousand men here. You think you are strong. Imagine how strong you would be with ten times that number. Then multiply it by ten again and that will tell you what kind of army I was part of in those days.'

'Yet the Romans defeated you! Your nation was weak. The Romans are strong. I do not wish to be defeated and displaced like you. You are a weak man from a weak nation and I cannot see why I should sit here listening to the talk of such a cowardly weakling.'

He was challenging me. If he had spoken in that way to any proud Briton warrior it would have resulted in a fight, and he knew it. It would have taken little effort on my part to kill him. I only had to draw my sword and bring it across his throat in one movement and it would all be over, the talking, the irritation. I thought he was an obnoxious little man, but still I stayed my hand. I was learning to be patient.

'It was not weakness,' I said. 'The alliance fell apart because all my people quarrelled. When it broke up, many went home. The Romans then marched north, took each nation separately, and Marcus Aurelius crushed us one at a time. Does that not teach you anything?'

'It teaches me to stay away from Germans who cannot win wars,' he chuckled.

'It is vital to unite the north Briton tribes. They can defeat the Romans with numbers and tactics. It can be done. Is there nothing you would accept as proof?'

'I would accept as proof an example of a new way of fighting, some new way of convincing even the Damnonii to fight alongside me and my men. Twenty years ago, we had an alliance. We threw the Romans all the way across the northern wall! We realised then we hated each other too much to stay as one nation for there is no man of sufficient worth to command us all. You come here with your plans but you have no men yourself. Is it your life you offer? No. You offer to lead us in a way that served your own people badly. I will never permit you to bring down my people as yours were brought down by the Romans.'

The verbal conflict between Morleo and me was senseless and I was becoming tired of it. There seemed no possibility of compromise as we stared at each other across the flames. We were both scowling at each other and I knew, deepest in, I was achieving nothing. I had almost decided to kill him and have done with it. It was then Lutrin spoke.

'Almost two hundred years ago the Romans entered this island. They came and they conquered the southern tribes. It caused ripples in the Otherworld for they have no respect for our Gods and none for our people. They killed and persecuted all the Druids in the south and what is a tuath without access to druidic wisdom? Just as Galdir has told you, they took on each tribe in turn. The Catuvellauni, the Brigantes, the Iceni, the Selgovae, have they not all capitulated? Our people failed to unite and many were driven north. Have you not seen how many have settled in your own land? They are the defeated people. They are the ones who have allowed this Roman disease to spread, like a plague, a pestilence among us; eating our land. Can you not see it in their eyes? Their people's defeat is clearly painted there. It was foretold long ago that there will come among us a man from far away, he will bring us all together, and we will defeat the Romans. Listen to him, or is there only air between your ears?'

Morleo stood and was ready to draw his sword, had not Oengus restrained him.

'Peace, my brother,' he said. 'Lutrin speaks from the heart about a prophecy of which even you have heard. Why do you struggle with it so?'

'I struggle with this German who thinks his coming here will change things.'

Oenna said, 'His coming here has already changed things. He is a peace-maker who will draw all the tribes together and help to lead them against Rome.'

'Bah! Peace? You speak of peace, but where is your brother? He raises forces even as we speak. His people have encroached upon my land; killed and raped in my tuaths. Does he think I will stand for that?'

I said, 'And if each of you makes restitution to the other is there then a reason to fight, when the real enemy lives well and fattens himself in your land?'

'It is true what he says, Morleo,' Oengus said. 'The Romans are more our enemy than other tribes who belong here. Can you not see that? If they did not have heavy cavalry we would have driven them back across the southern wall in the last war. My hands have been fettered by the hostages they have taken, yet I think now I will still fight. Losing some kinfolk but regaining my honour must be my destiny.'

'Oengus,' I said, 'even the hostage problem can be overcome. I have plans.'

'What would you have us do?'

'Return with your men and Drest will call a meeting of Kings. Plans must be made and favours brought to bear. If you ride with us to Bannatia it will be a start.'

'I don't trust you German,' Morleo said.

'I trust him,' said Oengus. 'I will go. Would you leave me to deal with this without you? You might never then know if the German speaks truly.'

Morleo scowled at that and muttered under his breath. Oengus and the Venicones' King stood and walked to their horses.

Lutrin called after them, 'We will wait for you in the hall of King Drest. There are many plans to make and many destinies to fulfil.'

When they had gone, the night was still and quiet. We said little for we were all aware we stood on the brink of a precipice that would change our lives in some way.

CHAPTER IX

"Let each man pass his days in that wherein his skill is greatest"
—Propertius Sextus

Drest paced the dais in his hall. He showed his perturbation by waving his hands in the torchlight. He looked like a petulant, scalded insect with his long thin limbs expressing his emotions. His fists clenched and unclenched and there was fire in his blue eyes.

'How could you do such a thing?' he said. 'That dirty little man has demanded I pay two barrels of silver in compensation for a raid my men carried out in retaliation. What possessed you?'

Oenna said in calm tones, 'My dear brother, you have to make compromises sometimes in matters of state. It is the spirit of compromise that neither party is truly happy, is it not? The benefit is we avoided a full-scale war with the Venicones and the Votadini and we are all allies now against the Romans. Was it not worth a few silver ingots?'

'This is all your fault, Galdir. I should never have listened to you. And you,' he said pointing a long stick-like finger at Lutrin, 'you have caused nothing but trouble since you arrived. You never appear unless there is trouble in store and that is usually of your making.'

Lutrin stood up. We had been sitting on the benches before the dais and a fire blazed behind us on the large square hearth, keeping the cooling autumn weather at bay. It had rained for days and we were all glad of the warmth. He drew his open palm across his face in his now familiar gesture.

'Drest, my boy, listen to me. Have I not known you since you were a child, suckling at your mother's breast? Know now that what you have agreed to will bring peace among the tribes and with that peace will come a mighty alliance. When all the fourteen kings meet here in only ten days, you will see how we will drive the Romans away from their wall and the riches of Britannia will be yours. Admittedly, you will have to share with the other kings, but it will be a considerable amount of plunder. Even you can see that.'

I had remained silent throughout the discussion. It was not my place to interject in matters of state.

'How many men can these kings raise?' I said.

'Each kingdom should be good for two thousand men. Some will bring more, others less, but there should be about thirty thousand warriors. About two thousand will be mounted or in chariots and the rest will be on foot,' Oenna said.

'It may be enough' I said.

Cimbrod, sitting next to me shuffled uncomfortably. 'Lord Drest, your people still fight with long weapons. They think rushing at the Romans will be enough but one cannot rely on numbers alone in a war.'

'You have fought in many wars have you?' Drest said.

'No, but I have had good teachers and history speaks for itself. Your people have never won a war against Rome. A few battles here and there—like on the northern wall, but never a war. My people have. The Romans settled many of them in northern Italia because they had to make peace.'

'Don't tell me,' said Drest. 'They had tactics we crude

275

Britons do not understand.'

'I can train them to fight the Romans if you will give me a chance,' I said. 'I have fought many battles against the Romans and I know how they think. We have a real chance of success but I must have control of all the forces or nothing will come of the muster but a rabble who will die before the Roman wall, achieving nothing.'

Drest bit his lip as he looked at me in silence.

'Well?' I said.

'If you can convince the kings of this plan then I will back you. Oenna assures me you can do all you claim but let me warn you, my people do not tolerate failure from their leaders. It is your life you gamble with. Make no mistake, it will be forfeit if you fail. I have spoken. Now go, all of you, I have much to do to prepare for this council. The tribes have never all been represented in one place before, and it will take careful planning. Some of them would kill each other on sight.'

We stood to leave. Oenna caught my eye and she smiled. I knew what she meant, for although I was sharing accommodation with Cimbrod and his brother, I spent my nights in her bower. It was a secret all over the court, and in true north Briton fashion everyone tolerated our liaison without comment or condemnation.

When the meeting broke up, I went to the room where Cimbrod and I quartered. Hengeist was not there and we sat on our cots talking.

'Are you sure about all this?' Cimbrod said.

'What?'

'This war. It could cost you your life.'

'Better that than simply sit here and never return home. Just think. We may drive the Romans out of Britannia forever. It would be a great achievement.'

'I have no interest in it. All I want is to return home rich and with Ancamma at my side.'

'Where is she anyway?'

'Drest has sent her to the Venicones to arrange the handing over of a fortune in silver. Not surprising Drest is unhappy.'

'Well, I could do with a walk,' I said, stretching and stifling a yawn.

'I could go with you.'

'No. Really. I will be better on my own.'

Cimbrod smiled and said, 'Why do you persist in trying to hide your relationship with Oenna. It's tiresome.'

'Not my idea. She has difficulties with the whole tribe knowing about it unless I marry her; she thinks Drest would forbid it.'

'Why?'

'Because he knows I have nothing to offer him politically.'

'He'll change his mind if you defeat the Romans for him.'

'Yes, but I would want to return home then. I can't win.'

'You have to.'

'I know; I heard what Drest said. I'm going.'

I had allowed Oenna sufficient time to reach her bower, which was in an adjoining compound only a short distance from the King's hall. I crossed the hall to the doorway and the guard there smiled his usual knowing smile as I stepped out into the rain. He shut the oak door and it saved my life. Some large drops of rain fell as the vibration from the closing door dislodged them and they struck the back of my neck. Cursing I pulled my head back and in that instant the arrow flew past. It hit my left ear lobe and caused a painful cut but had I not reacted to the rainwater I would have been skewered, transfixed through the eye.

The arrow embedded itself in the door behind me with a twang and remained there, buzzing with a soft, audible vibration as if to remind me of its presence. The guard, thinking I had knocked, opened the door. I pushed past him and he saw the arrow projecting from the door.

'We are under attack?' he said.

'I don't know,' I said, 'it was only one arrow.'

'You are hurt?'

'No, it just scratched my ear. I was lucky. Did you see anyone?'

'No, I will call the others and we will search. As you say, one arrow means one man.'

I sat down and waited, dabbing at the cut on my ear. Presently, he returned wet and irritated, with two others.

'No one there. We saw footprints but they led away across the town and petered out. I will report this to my captain. You had better stay here.'

'No,' I said. 'If he's gone then I doubt if he'll come back. It was a clumsy attempt anyway. Now that I'm on my guard he won't be so lucky next time.'

'As you wish. Would you like one of us to come with you to the Princess's bower?'

'How did you know where I was going?'

'The whole court knows where you go at night. It is impossible to keep secrets around here.'

'Whatever happened to discretion?' I said. 'No, I am quite safe now I know to be on the lookout.'

I took my leave and walked looking around me with more than usual caution. I knocked on Oenna's door. When

I told her of the attack, she said, 'Who would do that Galdir?'

'I don't know. I think it may be something to do with the Romans. They were very persistent when they chased us and they seemed to know who they were pursuing. It is not impossible someone has told them of our plans and they want to remove me. It would be a typical Roman scheme.'

'Who would do that?—Betray us I mean. Until we came here, no one knew how successful we have been. They did not try to kill me and I am as responsible as you are for the forthcoming alliance. It doesn't make sense.'

'It must be someone from the Caledonian tuath. Whoever it was, must have set the Romans on us before we left. I have a strong suspicion it was Drosten. He spoke against me in the council until Lutrin rapped him on the head.'

'Yes, he killed Cimbrod's brother too.'

'I think he hates me for breaking his nose. Besides, he was seen leaving after the meeting in which Lutrin persuaded Nechtan to his plans. He could easily have been passing on information.'

'It makes sense, but I just think he would have been at greater lengths to appear above suspicion. Surely Nechtan would suspect him too, if he is always disappearing before some tragic event? Do you really think it's him?'

'Maybe. Cimbrod and I have both sworn vengeance but the man is favoured by Nechtan. We will bide our time. We need Nechtan on board for his people are the most numerous. I don't trust him entirely either.'

'We must be careful, but as for who is responsible for all this remains uncertain. I wondered at one time if Drogo could be the one. I don't like him,' she said.

'Drogo? He's a Frank and he looks up to me. I think he is

above suspicion for I know my people and they would never capitulate. Why him?'

'I don't know. It's something about the way he looks at you when you aren't looking at him. Hostile somehow.'

'I have not been very supportive with him that's all. He needed more from me than I was prepared to give in the forest when we fled the Romans. Anyway, he killed two of our pursuers. That proves he is one of us.'

'He had no option. If he had stayed his hand it would have been obvious.'

'I don't agree,' I said, getting irritated, 'now leave it alone.'

'If you like. There were many Caledonian chieftains at that council meeting. Any of them might want to remove you from the scene if they don't want the prophecy to be fulfilled. Is it painful?'

'Terrible pain. Now that I'm wounded you'll have to be very gentle with me,' I said with a smile.

'I'm always gentle,' she said.

'I hadn't noticed that.'

She reached for me and we came together. Our lovemaking was pure and passionate throughout the night and we slept little. It was as if the act of love itself released us both from the responsibilities we had assumed together. It was often so for us. Our shared life was an escape and a refuge from the world outside. When I reflect upon it, it was one of my happiest times.

We none of us know how the Gods will interfere in our existence. That is one reason to mistrust happiness and until I fell for Oenna, I had always felt ill at ease when life was good. It never works out the way I plan—after all, different Gods rule different aspects of our existence. Although at times I have prayed to Wuotan, it is still often Loge the trickster who interferes. He is ephemeral and unpredictable, like a fiery flame that flickers and changes, so we cannot see how he will change our lives. I missed Chlotsuintha in those days with her prescient guidance, but even she used to speak in riddles. I have never been good at riddles, any more than I have been able to see my future clearly, but that might be a good thing for if we all knew what is in store for us we might never embark upon the greatest adventures of our lives.

CHAPTER X

*"I hate and I love. Perhaps you ask why I do so.
I do not know, but I feel it, and am in agony"*
—Catullus

When the kings began to arrive, the weather changed. The rain became torrential and Drest had to order his men to dig deep trenches around his compound lest a stream form and threaten the foundations of his hall. No one in Bannatia had experienced such rain before: it poured down for the entire week before the council, and the accommodation plans for the meeting had to be constantly changed. The water ran in torrents down the rocky hillside above the town and I think the only creatures who did not mind were the geese that swam on the new pond which had formed in the field below the King's compound.

The visitors came gradually, some delayed by the weather, others because travelling long distance is always unpredictable, particularly in north Britannia where there are few roads apart from the ones built by the Roman invaders. I often wondered if the difficulties with the terrain were part of the reason the Romans had never made headway here, but I supposed it was more likely they had no real financial interest in the place.

On the appointed day, the kings of the fourteen tribes or their representatives gathered in the King's hall at Bannatia. There was a damp smell in the room from the wet travellers who stood nearest the hearth. Steam issued from the cloaks of those nearest the hearth and visibility was not good despite the torches standing in brackets, lining the walls.

There was no raucous conversation, no backslapping, and most of those present were silent, regarding each other with a degree of mistrust that seemed stamped on their faces as their eyes moved from enemy to friend. There were over forty men and women, seated and standing, around the hearth. Each king had a bodyguard and an advisor. I noted Nechtan had not come personally but instead had sent Drosten and Taran. I had greeted them at the door. Taran embraced me as an old friend and slapped my back.

'Still in one piece?' he asked. He was soaking wet like all the other new arrivals.

'It would seem so, Nudi.'

He smiled at the term and said, 'It rained so much on the way here I was glad I had not used body paint.'

'Yes, bad weather for travelling. There again, you aren't made of salt so you won't dissolve.'

'For an ignorant German, you seem full of wit today.'

'I am surprised a dull Briton could understand my wit.'

'Like a drink of my potion?' he said with a wide grin.

'Just go and sit down. You're a wicked poisoner,' I said, smiling back.

Taran laughed and I did too. I was glad to see him for we had shared much when I had stayed with the Caledonii.

Drosten remained silent and pushed past me. I was unbalanced slightly and stepped back. There a look of scorn on his face. I was tempted to say something but decided that however much I hated the man, this was not the time. I wondered if he was trying to start a fight. Taran shrugged and followed Drosten.

'We can't all choose the company we are in,' he said over his shoulder.

I was distracted by Drest who began by asking for silence in a voice so loud I would never have thought his narrow chest could produce it. I thought his was an odd beginning for almost everyone was quiet in any case. Lutrin then stood and gave a similar speech to that which he had given in Nechtan's hall. He introduced me to the assembly.

I began much as I had done when I spoke to Oengus and Morleo, supported by the Druid. When I had finished, there was silence again. It was as if I had never spoken. I looked around the hall. The firelight gave the assembled leaders the appearance of ethereal beings, the red light reflecting from their shiny foreheads, yellow from their eyes.

Drosten stood then. He said, 'Lord Drest. I have travelled far, not as far as many here but a long way all the same. My lord Nechtan has sent me and I need to present his words to his brother Kings. The Caledonii have fought many of you in the past. We have always had peace after our wars, forging alliances from the dust of our strife. It is the way we have lived all our lives since the time of our ancestors. There is no need to migrate to the south. We are happy here. There is nothing across the wall but trouble and armies we cannot defeat.'

I was about to respond when Morleo jumped to his feet. He looked no more regal on this occasion than he had when I had met him with his army. He wore a small bearskin cloak and his silver torque glinted in the firelight.

'Nechtan is an old woman. He skulks in his hall and dares not even meet with us. He sends some fat, so called friend, to do his talking for him and his words are those of a coward. We all know the Romans have huge wealth stacked up behind that wall of theirs. They are weak now and they are confused since a pestilence has spread across their armies in the east, and Commodus, the new Emperor, has had to pay for peace with the German tribes across the Rhenus and Danubus. I hear he prefers a negotiated peace with the Germans, unlike his father who fought and never negotiated. He cannot send more troops and the local troops are few in number. Nothing will stop us if we fight now and fight together.'

Oengus stood to support him and slapped him on the back, saying, 'The Votadini will fight, so will the Venicones and the Vacomagi. Anyone else with balls here?'

I was nonplussed. I wondered where Morleo had heard there was a new Emperor. I guessed he might have changed his views because of that. It could only mean Marcus Aurelius was dead. Dead at last. My chance of returning was real, not imagined. If I could return home and negotiate with Commodus then perhaps I could rule my people again. The thought flitted through my mind in a second.

'Are you saying Marcus Aurelius is dead?' I said.

'Yes,' said Oengus, 'Have you not heard?'

Drest said, 'We have had no news of that. Morleo, when did you hear it?'

'We heard it from some Roman traders two days ago. It can only mean our chance of overrunning the wall is even better than before. The enemy is headless as a chicken with a wrung neck!'

Lutrin stood then and held his staff up for silence.

'It is indeed a good omen if the Romans have lost their leader. Does anyone here know anything about the new one?'

Galam, the new king of the Orcadians stood. 'I have

heard of this Commodus. We have learned about him from the many trading ships that come to our islands for the fur trade. He is a son of Marcus Aurelius and he is young and inexperienced. Although I can only give five hundred warriors, my men will fight, for I think the Romans have no great leader. Who leads them here in Britannia?'

'Marcus Licinius Piso is the General on the wall,' I said. 'He was sent here because my people defeated him after a long siege. Marcus Aurelius then came with five more Legions, which was the only reason we were, in our turn, defeated. Piso is here in disgrace. He is not a popular or clever man. If you let me advise you on how to fight the Romans, we have a very good chance of driving them away forever. It depends on the strength of the alliance.'

The discussion waged back and forth for several hours and each king had his say. Oenna remained silent throughout and I wondered at that. She seemed pre-occupied. She glanced once in my direction and smiled a soft almost disconsolate smile. I could not understand what it meant. Was she encouraging me? Had something else happened? I could not work out why she seemed so distant; the matters under discussion were the most momentous decisions ever made here in living memory, yet she seemed to be day-dreaming and locked in her own thoughts. I concluded women were enigmatic and for a man to understand them requires him to think like them. It is a trick I have never managed to acquire.

'Galdir,' said Oengus. 'You said there was some hope for the hostages.'

'I have a friend among the Romans and it may be possible to ensure their safety but it is not something I can discuss openly lest it be relayed back to the Romans.'

'Surely you can trust the company you find yourself in here?

'Of course. I give trust as well as expect it from you. All the same, it affects only you and Morleo and I will tell only you and nearer the time. The plan must remain secret until then. Meanwhile I will discuss with you how to train the troops and how to deploy them against the Romans.'

Morleo said, 'You know already how to fight them?'

'Yes. There was a great Carthaginian leader once, called Hannibal Barca. With a small army, he marched all the way from Hispania into Italia itself. He defeated huge Roman armies repeatedly, usually drawing his troops up in a certain way. I have used the same technique against them successfully too.'

'But you lost the war,' Morleo said.

'We were successful against Piso, but they had fresh armies. It was, in the end, a disaster because they outnumbered us and came when we had just defeated Piso. They will have no fresh legions this time. They can be defeated.'

After more discussion, we decided I would visit each of the tribes in turn and discuss tactics and weapons preparatory to beginning our campaign in the spring. It gave us five months. It was a short time but it had to be enough. They were warriors not farmers so the degree to which they required training was mainly in tactics. We needed, in any case, to take advantage of the confusion a new Emperor would create.

The debate lasted until the afternoon. Afterwards some of the guests remained, some left. Those staying for the feast that night, included Oengus and Morleo, who had been instrumental in changing minds over the likely success of the forthcoming war. Curious, I approached him.

'Lord Morleo, we meet under different circumstances this time.'

'Yes, German we do.'

'You seem to feel differently about the prospect of war with the Romans.'

'Yes.'

'Because?'

'Although I am not in the habit of explaining myself to anyone, I will tell you. Oengus and I are kin on my mother's side. We have always fought beside each other and our tribes are almost like one, we trade and we share women. He is so convinced of the prospect of success that my reticence threatened a very fruitful and long-standing closeness. He also told me about what you did for his daughter, Nerys. She said you killed four Romans to protect her. Anyone who could do that is worthy of trust. There was no reward for you but death if the Romans had found you out. Oengus and I know this.'

'I lost my temper. Anyway, even we Germans have some honour.'

'So it seems.'

'Would you really have burned us that day when we met?'

'No, we don't burn people but we do drown them sometimes. It was a figure of speech.'

I looked at him with doubt in my eyes.

He said, 'No, really.'

We both smiled and I realised I had misjudged the man. He had backed me fully against Drosten in the council meeting and I could not help myself but to be grateful, although I wished he would bathe. It might have made him seem more palatable.

As Oenna and Oengus approached us she was smiling and laughing. There was a radiance in her eyes I had not seen before and I wondered whether Oengus had some special charm which I did not. I hardly believed he was pursuing a sexual encounter but I felt irritated by it.

'So, my friend. We are allies and will fight together next spring,' Oengus said.

'But we need the Caledonii,' I replied. 'If Nechtan refuses to fight it will make a big difference to our numbers. Lutrin thinks there could be as many as five thousand Caledonii warriors.'

'I have no doubt it is so,' Oenna agreed. 'Drosten said when he left he would tell Nechtan of the council's decisions but did not promise anything else. Nechtan may need to be persuaded.'

'Or killed?'

'No, that is not our way. I am sure he will listen to reason. Even the Damnonii from the west want this alliance. If the Caledonii do not comply they will be left behind and lose out with the plunder,' Oengus said.

'It will be a final chance for our nation to expel the Romans from our soil. I will ride to his tuath and I am sure I can persuade him,' Oenna said.

'I hope so. When I return home, I will begin the business of ordering my troops, ready for the spring. Where will we muster?' Oengus said.

'That is yet to be decided. Do your men favour swords or spears?'

'Both. They will fight with any weapon they can get.'

'They need to have shields and additional short swords or they have little chance against Roman legionaries.'

'So you say, endlessly.'

'Can that be achieved in five months?'

'We will see. I must go in the morning. Perhaps we will meet tonight,' Oengus said.

Oenna and I took our leave. We walked through the rain to her bower. I had been tense in the meeting and the relief expressed itself in desire. I reached for her and as our lips met she hesitated.

'Oenna?'

'It's all right, I just don't feel well.'

'What's wrong? A fever?' I said, fearing the worst.

'No' she said, 'I just feel sick.'

'As soon as I kiss you?'

'No, silly. I felt sick before that. I've felt nauseated all day since I awoke, to be truthful.'

'Should I ask Lutrin to have a look at you?'

'Lutrin is a man. He is very wise but he is a man all the same.'

'What difference does that make? If you are ill you need someone with wisdom.'

'You really don't know what I'm talking about do you?'

'What?'

'Oh never mind, just go will you?'

'But Oenna my love, have I said something wrong?'

'Men! Just go. I will be fine. I know a wise woman who can help. Go, can't you?'

She pushed me bodily through the door and for a moment, I stood puzzling over her behaviour and feeling hurt. I shrugged and I walked back towards the king's hall nonplussed. I have never been good at understanding women. Even Clotildis, my first wife had known that. It was how she managed to persuade me to kill my uncle Odomir. Oenna was unlike any other woman I had met before, and I knew it. The fact I did not understand her was not germane to the issue. I had thought at first our relationship was superficial, but I knew I loved her more deeply with every passing day, and the rejection clawed at my soul.

CHAPTER XI

"The best way to keep good acts in memory is to refresh them with new"
—Marcus Portius Cato

Oenna waited a full two weeks before she told me. She said she had wanted to be certain. I rode to Damnonia with a permanent smile on my face. Would it be a son? Perhaps it would be a beautiful, tall, fair daughter to make me proud. Finally, there was something to be happy about in this wet, Gods forsaken little country.

It seemed odd to me I had been to so much trouble to construct a war here and I now did not care whether it took place or not. Now I was to become a father. Priorities. That is what drives us all in the end. It is seeing one's priorities with clarity that creates motives, and I had strong incentives now to stay and forget all about returning home to Frankia. Oenna was adamant she would bring up her child as a Briton and I had no intention of leaving her behind. It was as if this new and wonderful event was the one stimulus I needed to stay. I wondered if this was what the Gods had intended for me all along, but like a fool I had been blind to it.

None of us, who are not witches, can see into the future with any accuracy after all. If you pray to the wrong God, the answers never come. The reason Chlotsuintha and Frija had such accurate dreams was because they prayed to the right Gods at the right times. It is no use praying to Idun for the outcome of a war, or Loge for a harvest to be successful.

The miles flew by as we rode. We travelled from the land of the Vacomagi through that of the Caledonii towards the west coast, where the Damnonii dwelt. My purpose was to assess what kind of fighters they had and ensure they would be able to follow my battle plans. They were a large nation but somewhat insular in their politics and their leaders seemed to scorn their neighbours. They treated the Caledonii with little respect because Nechtan's people lived such separated lives and only came together in large numbers at fairs and markets or feast days.

There was a light, glistening frost whitening the grass as we rode and to our right the hills rose high above us, snow-capped, bleak and forbidding. The smell of the mud and crushed heather beneath our horses' hooves was fresh in my nostrils and a lone crow or raven circled high above as if it had business with us but dared not impart it. Wuotan uses ravens. They sit either side of him and whisper in his ear. They tell of what goes on in the world of men and he sends them with messages for those who can hear them.

We followed a faint track skirting a hill adorned by a copse of birch and ancient beech trees, their leaves red-brown and gold in the faint morning sun.

I was so deep in thought about Oenna and her pregnancy I failed to notice the sound of following horses. Cimbrod noticed. He at least did not have his head in the clouds. He was less of a dreamer and more serious than I had yet seen him since the death of his brothers. He reached over and tapped me on the shoulder, a frown on his face.

'Following horsemen.'

'What?'

'There are horsemen behind us. I can hear them.'

We stopped and I could indeed hear the far-off thrumming of hooves behind us but I could have sworn there were similar sounds in front too.

'More of them ahead,' I said.

'Yes.'

'If they are hostile we could have a problem.'

'Indeed,' Cimbrod said.

'Follow me.'

I spurred my mount to the copse on the hilltop above us, startling a pair of pheasants who called out with indignation their wings making that familiar whirring noise as they flew away. We entered and turned, hidden by the trees and watched the track below. Even from our vantage point, I could see a clear trail where our horses had trampled the heather. It lay there like a black and purple spear pointing us out to whoever was following.

Then I saw them. There were four men on horseback. They were not local tribesmen and I noticed they wore leggings like those worn by warriors in Gaul. Their breeks were white, green and red striped and they all had spears and shields. The riders wore cloaks of blue wool over their bare chests and their helmeted heads looked down at the heather to discover where we had gone. In a moment, they would see our tracks.

'They look like that tracker from Gaul who followed Oenna and me on the way to Bannatia. They must be Roman auxiliaries,' I said.

'Let's kill them then. They don't look too tough. If we surprise them they won't stand a chance.'

'Cimbrod, I want at least one of them alive. I need to know what they know. The Romans must have been aware we were coming. I want to find out who told them. If we don't find out, planning our campaign will be useless. I need surprise on our side.'

'What do you suggest?' he said.

'String them out and kill the first three, then hope we can take the last one alive.'

'Suppose they wait for the others who were coming from in front of us?'

'They won't. They are four and we are two. They don't know you are a brave and fearsome Cimbri Prince.'

'Don't mock me, Galdir.'

'All right, just a joke. Let's go.'

We turned our horses and rode through the beech trees. There was one large dead tree standing alone in a clearing. The trees around the glade grew dense and dark and I indicated for Cimbrod to hide on one side. Working with him was always a pleasure; there was never a necessity to explain, he knew what to do. Despite that, I insisted on instructing him so he looked at me with irritation as I spoke.

'Take the third rider, I'll take the first two and we can capture the fourth,' I suggested quietly. He stared at me as if I was teaching him to pass urine.

He hid himself behind two tall beech trees. I slowed my pace for I did not want the trackers to lose me. I turned at the far side of the grassy slope and waited. A wintery sun tried to pierce the dark grove, and the clearing shimmered in its light, for the ground was frosty. I could hear the boughs above me sighing and groaning in the wind and wondered if these would be the last sounds I would hear before I saw the halls of the Allfather. I grasped the hilt of my sword tighter to ensure I would not be lost on the way to Valhalla but these anxious thoughts dissolved almost as soon as they appeared, for when the pursuers came, they came fast.

They were riding two abreast, which must have made them cramped as they approached. I had not expected that and had to rely on surprise to give us an edge. They saw me. The front two screamed a war-shout and charged.

They levelled their spears. They sped towards me, shields vertical. Both looked up from beneath the helmets protecting their heads. It was a look of triumph. I realised my mistake. These were no ordinary soldiers. I had no shield and they were both approaching together. Fending off one spear meant the other would strike home.

I slipped from my horse. The two riders had my horse in the way. They had to ride round him. Even with my long sword, it would be hard for me to reach. Their horses hit my mount and the collision unhorsed one of them. I forgot about him. It is a long way to fall from a horse and he was moving fast. The second reined in and turned his steed. I was there already. I struck the horse full in the face with my weapon. He reared and bucked as I stepped back. The rider dismounted. His horse could not see, nor could he command it. The blinded beast ran. It left me facing the spearman. He had a sword but no time to draw it. I lunged at him. He stepped back. I noticed the first man was sitting behind his comrade shaking his head as if to clear it.

Despite my opponent's longer reach, I stepped forward with small, fast steps. He backed away as his colleague stood up. The fallen rider must have been disorientated, for he did not even see my blow as it struck him. I missed his neck. I cut his right arm above the elbow, almost severing it. I felt the blade crunch through bone. I stepped back and had to parry the spear thrust from the second man.

He was good with a spear. I wondered where his comrades were. He whirled his weapon above his head. He swung it in a wide arc at my head. I ducked and he stepped forward. He gathered his spear and had it in both hands above his head. It was as neat a move as I have seen. Neither of us had a shield. I was sure the first to land a good blow would kill the other. He stabbed forward, the spear level with my face. I parried. He advanced. I feinted low: a stab to the midriff. He pulled in his stomach and the spear descended. He aimed it at my throat. I brought my sword up. I parried again. I knew how to take him then.

Cornelius, my mentor had trained as a gladiator in Rome. He had fought the finest swordsmen and the greatest spearmen who ever graced the sands of the Colosseum. I could almost hear him say it.

'Get close but keep your blade back, like this.'

The phrase kept repeating itself in my head as I backed away. The spear spun in a circle again. The spearman reached forward with it as it moved in its graceful arc. It missed my face by a hair's breadth but as it passed I stepped into it. I held my sword back as I put my left foot forward. He stepped back and tried to reverse his spear-stroke. It was too late. My sword was long enough. I rotated onto my right foot as I stabbed. Being a tall man, it doubled my reach. It was a satisfying feeling as my blade entered his midriff. It was not finished yet though, for the spear was descending and I knew it. I rolled away to my right as my opponent tried to sink his weapon into me. There was a gush of bright red blood as my blade came away. That stab was the last thing he ever did. I could see him grimace with pain as he sank to his knees and I knew he was gone. He knelt for a moment then slumped forward. He was still kneeling, his blood soaking the golden brown leaves carpeting the glade all around. I pushed him with my foot. He crumpled and lay on his side. He had been a good fighter. I knew he was no ordinary tracker; he was an assassin.

I heard a twig break, off to my right, and raised my sword, but soon smiled. It was Cimbrod. He was limping but at least he lived.

'Sorry Galdir. I killed them both. I saw you dismount and did the same. They were hard men.'

'I know. I think one of mine is still alive. The others may be here any second. Are you ready for more?'

He smiled and stumbled forward, his leg collapsing beneath him. There was a deep cut in his calf. Clearly he had his own story to tell, but I lost no time in asking, and bound the wound for it bled heavily. I approached my first adversary, struggling to get to his feet. The blood he had lost had weakened him and his right arm hung from his side partially detached, suspended by a strip of skin. I pushed my sword-tip indenting the skin on his throat and he lay still. I cut the useless limb from his stump. He grunted but that was all. I bound his arm with a tourniquet made from the hem of his comrade's cloak and the blood loss slowed. He grunted again, but said nothing.

'Who sent you?' I said in Latin then in German. Still he said nothing. I smiled. 'When we get you to the Damnonii I think they will persuade you to talk.'

He looked at me but still said nothing. Cimbrod had remounted and I did the same. It took precious moments to find one of the assailants' horses and when we had, we tied the assassin to it and set off. There was still no sign of pursuit and it puzzled me. Perhaps the riders on the road ahead had not been from the same group or perhaps they could have been friends. Either way I had no inclination to wait there in the wood and find out. I had no desire for another fight with professional spearmen, for I thought we had been lucky and I felt no desire to tempt the Gods twice in one day.

We rode down the other side of the hill and circled to resume our journey. We had no sooner set out again, leading the now pale and faint Gaul than we heard riders behind us.

'They're coming,' Cimbrod said.

'Hide.'

We rode as fast as we could for a gully off to our left and there we dismounted, pulling our prisoner down with us. He groaned as he hit the ground but neither of us felt much sympathy.

I peered around a gorse bush, waiting to see if the approaching men had spotted us, and was surprised when the riders came into view. I recognised one of them. They were blue-painted men on the usual north Briton ponies. One was Taran. I stood up and waved my arms, calling his name. They almost rode past us but the rearmost rider turned in time and called his fellows. They picked their way carefully among the rocks and rode down to us.

'Galdir. We heard you were crossing our lands and Nechtan sent me to escort you. He thought you might get lost.'

'In this little country it would be hard to get lost. We are relieved to see you though. Four Roman assassins were after us. Cimbrod killed two and I killed one. This one is for questioning. I'm sure the Damnonii will be able to extract information from him.'

Taran frowned. 'Are you both all right?'

'Yes, Cimbrod has a spear-cut in his calf but otherwise we are fine. It is a bit of luck you found us.'

'The Gods have smiled upon you. We will ride with you to the west. There may be others.'

We mounted up and I found it hard not to express my pleasure at meeting Taran again. We reminisced over the battle against the Orcadians and talked about the forthcoming war.

'So how will you defeat the Romans? My people have been trying to do that for a long time,' Taran said.

'Be patient my friend. You will see soon enough,' I replied.

'They have such discipline that my people have died in huge numbers every time we fight them. Is there some secret I do not know of?'

'Like I said, be patient.'

'Answer me one thing, I'm curious. You said you had a friend in the Roman legion. Can he be relied on? Who is it?'

'I can't tell you, my friend. His very existence would be threatened if anyone knew. Surely you can understand that?'

'I do. I was only curious. I hope you don't mind me asking?'

'No, of course not. This Gaul here will be useful to us. I think the Romans have a spy and he may know who it is,' I said.

'No doubt. We will question him when we arrive.'

'How are things in the tuath?'

'Much the same as before. Nechtan is angry with Drosten though.'

'Really?'

'Yes. It seems Nechtan gave him strict instructions not to comply with the plans to fight the Romans and Drosten gave way. They have quarrelled and Drosten keeps leaving for days at a time. No one knows where he goes.'

'You think he is our traitor?' I said.

'Drosten? No; I'm sure he would never betray his people. He is one of our great warriors. He was shamed by your defeat of him, but among us he remains the man with the greatest war-record and the most heads, so he has the most honour. He knows it too.'

'It doesn't matter. We will question this Gaul and I am sure he will talk in the end. I don't like torture but sometimes it is necessary, according to Cimbrod anyway.'

'You always say that Galdir. I don't understand you at times. You have strange customs in your land,' Cimbrod said.

'Well we aren't Marcomannii you know. They torture for the pleasure of it and they think they gain power from another man's pain. It is not the way our Gods have taught us to behave.'

'Maybe so,' Cimbrod said shaking his head.

Riding in silence we made good time, and camped by a small stream where both Cimbrod and I bathed. After the fight we stank of sweat and thought it was not a good way to introduce ourselves to the Damnonii who were expecting us in two days. I dressed Cimbrod's wound which although deep showed no signs of turning septic. The Gauls, I thought, must have looked after their spears and kept them clean. We set one of the Caledonii to watch and managed to sleep by our fire.

I slept deeply that night, dreaming of Oenna and her forthcoming baby. I was excited at the prospect of becoming a father for the first time. It seemed to me my luck was at last turning.

CHAPTER XII

"No man is happy; he is at best fortunate"
—Solon

The next morning we found the Gaul was dead. We assumed he had lost too much blood and it was a bitter event for us. He had the key to the traitor's identity and I wanted to avoid any further attacks. I also knew it meant I could speak to no-one without some chance of my plans reaching the enemy. We struck camp and I mulled over the death of the assassin. It was strange, for he had been weak but not dangerously so. Besides, when I found his body his face was a strange shade of blue and his tongue protruded from his mouth as if he had choked. It made no sense. He must have lost consciousness and swallowed his tongue in the night.

We rode at a leisurely pace for we could not arrive before nightfall and we had not far to travel on the last day according to Taran. He knew the layout of the land and we were both relieved to have a guide. The added numbers were also reassuring, for our blue-painted companions looked doughty and strong. None of them wore cloaks although the weather was frosty and cold. I marvelled at their capacity to put up with the freezing wind but supposed they were used to it.

The country around us changed from green rolling hills to rocky slopes with dense pine forest all around us. The pines emanated a deep gloom, reminding me of home, and it thrust a melancholy feeling into my thoughts. I tried to think of my future with Oenna but the same picture kept coming into my head: Frija, as she stood there on that last day after the defeat. She was so certain I would return to rule. That she could be wrong had always seemed obvious to me, and I had been desperate to go. Now I wanted to stay. Who could blame me for staying anyway? It would keep my nation alive. There would be no threat to the Franks as long as I did not return. My mind still could not rest. I had an uncomfortable feeling I was playing out some divine game, the rules of which I remained naively oblivious.

At midday, Taran elected to ride ahead and ensure there were no enemy riders in front of us, and we thanked him for taking such a risk.

'Don't worry, I know the land. I can be silent and invisible when I need. We Nudis are like that.'

He smiled and rode away.

'I'm glad we found Taran,' I said.

'Really?' Cimbrod said.

'What?'

'I just don't entirely trust him. He seemed to appear too conveniently.'

'You heard what he said. Nechtan sent him.'

'How would he know where to look? I mean we could have been anywhere.'

'There can't be that many roads to the Damnonii lands. He must have known where we would be. You should learn to trust. He is a good warrior and he fought well in Insi Orc.'

'Maybe you're right. I don't know. If we have any more bad luck today I shall be seriously suspicious.'

'You worry too much.'

Cimbrod looked me in the eye and I could read his concern but I felt no disquiet.

I said, 'I suspect Drosten is the Roman spy. He keeps disappearing from his tuath. He knows all about the plans and could easily have passed them on to the Romans. Anyway, he hates us. If he told the Romans who and where we are, they would send assassins.'

'Too obvious. He makes it plain what he thinks. He's not the type to betray us.

It has to be someone who knows what is happening. Someone who was at both the council meeting of the Caledonii and the meeting of kings in Drest's hall.'

'Not necessarily. Our departure might have been talked about. It's over a week since we planned it.'

'Perhaps. I'm no good at this sort of thing.'

'No nor am I,' I said. 'Maybe Lutrin will solve the problem. He has wisdom few others display. I had thought he might have set the Romans on us at the camp where your brothers died. He brought Drest's men though and if he wanted us dead, it would have been foolish. It could be anyone I suppose.'

'Well it isn't me and it isn't you; after that it could be anyone.'

When we had eaten a meal of mainly sausage with bread, we set off. The Caledonii warriors seemed reluctant to talk, but one of them rode with me and he at least made a little conversation. His name was Deort and he was older than his comrades.

'It was a good thing you came along when you did. Taran seemed to know where we were.'

'Yes.'

'How could you tell?'

He smiled and looked at me as we rode over a hilltop. He

had greying hair tied loosely on the nape of his neck and he had a silver torc around his neck. He never released his spear nor did he put it in its leather loop on his saddle. I could tell he was an experienced warrior.

'There is only one easy way to ride across to the Damnonii. We knew you had to be near there. Taran seemed to be certain anyway. He wanted to find you alone so he rode ahead and when he didn't find you we had to look for tracks.'

'He rode ahead did he? Like now?'

'Yes he is full of the idea that he tracks better alone than we do together, but he is too young to understand the subtleties.'

'Subtleties?'

'Yes, I have been tracking and hunting in these lands for thirty years, since I was a youth. I know every hiding place, every little crevice around here.'

'Odd you didn't see the tracks of our attackers.'

'It was because Taran took us ahead of where you would be and we were riding east towards you when you were attacked.'

I said, 'He has an ability to read the future perhaps?'

'Don't think so, but he has good hunches.'

'Have you been to the land of the Damnonii before?'

'You talk a lot for a warrior, don't you?'

'Yes,' I said and we both smiled. I realised too much talk is a sign of a fool and I had no wish to appear foolish to this man.

We rode in silence after that. It was an easy journey, for we had ascended during the last three days and now we were riding downhill most of the time towards the coast. Taran reappeared when we made camp but he had nothing to report. He had seen no one and picked up no tracks.

We sat around the fire as night came and talked about the forthcoming war. None of us expected the Romans to be prepared and it was with some satisfaction that I said, 'We will drive them away from Britannia. They will have to make peace and learn respect for the so-called Brittunculi.'

Cimbrod laughed. 'You talk as if it was easy. There are many tough battles ahead.'

Taran said, 'Where do you intend to attack the wall?'

'Why?' I said.

'I just wondered. There has to be a point where they are especially weak. That must be the point to launch the attack.'

'Drest and I favour Camboglanna in the west, south of Dalriada. It is more difficult for the Romans to move their troops from Vindolanda and it will take them so much time we may be across in full strength by the time the Second Legion arrives. The terrain is hilly around there and we can attack them as they march.'

'It sounds good to me. So it is an all out attack in force?'

'Of course.'

'I just thought there would be several points of attack. They can't defend the whole wall at once.'

'No, we will pick a single point of crossing and march south from there.'

He was silent and Cimbrod looked at me with a meaningful glance, for he knew the plans as well as I did.

I covered myself in my blanket and none of us spoke again as we settled down for the night. The next day was an easy one with only two or three hours ride, and after the rigours of the journey so far, Cimbrod and I were relieved to rest. I slept lightly and awoke often as if I needed to be cautious but I was unaware of any immediate threat.

As I closed my eyes, I thought of Oenna and the events of the last few months. I had started life in Britannia with the Romans, Lucia embedded in my thoughts. I was here now, thinking of Oenna and the prospect of staying with her and a child. I had known her such a short time but felt as if I had known her forever. We seemed to be a perfect match; we even had similar events in our past. I felt luck had finally come my way and I had at last found a partner who loved me for who I was, with no other motives than to make me happy, just as I wanted her happiness.

Becoming a father meant much to me too. If I had stayed in Rome all those years before and not reacted to my master's dishonourable behaviour, no doubt I would have married and perhaps had children. They would have been children thrust into slavery by an accident of birth. They would have learned to be obedient and without souls; condemned to move only at the will of another, subject to cruelty and oppression for their entire lives. My children would never have been able to experience the kind of life I had lived since I had left Rome. They would have had no choices and no freedom. Their will to fight and to rebel would not have existed; subservience and obedience would have been in-grained in their personalities, even their souls. My escape had guaranteed their lives in freedom and an ability to fight. It gave me satisfaction as sleep took me, to realise how one initial act of murder had preserved the future of my offspring as well as my own.

*

The Damnonii were separatists. They had no truck with

their neighbours. They traded, it is true, but in culture they were singular. They lived a more civilised life, by which I mean they lived in larger conurbations and although they did not build in stone, they lived in houses grouped together in towns. The agricultural life of Britannia was still very evident but they had industries of iron working, wood carving and building, and they created artistic jewellery that was sold and traded all over the north of Britannia. In short, they had characteristics making them like the Romans, but their development had not advanced enough to truly emulate them.

It is unusual for Britons in the far north to live in conurbations and to think about nationhood. This one thing separated the Damnonii from the other tribes. They were haughty and aloof in their dealings, and this arrogance gave them a reputation of being proud. Not that the Damnonii minded, they did not care what their neighbours thought.

A guard ushered us into the King's hall and the similarity in construction to the dwelling-place of the Vacomagi's leader was obvious. There was the same feel of size and the same square hearth in the centre of the hall. Benches were laid out around the hall and Cimiod, their king, sat on a low couch made from wicker covered by furs and skins. He welcomed us and a servant brought us horns of ale and snacks of skewered meat. He was a tall man for a Briton and had brown hair tied into braids at the side of his head. He, in contrast to Morleo, had all the bearing and appearance of a kingly personage. He spoke slowly with a deep baritone, and he smiled often. I gained the impression he was a happy man and I liked him as soon as we began to converse. We made some polite and appropriate conversation at first.

'You have come to share secrets with us I understand?' he

said.

'Secrets?' Cimbrod said.

'Yes about training armies to fight the Romans, have you not?'

'In a way,' I interjected, 'it is not so secret that the Romans do not know. Their histories abound with ways to defeat them.'

'And you know these histories?'

'I was taught such as a slave in Rome when I was only a boy.'

'And what do you intend to teach us about fighting? We have been a warrior nation ever since my long ancestors and we defend ourselves with great success. Do you really think, in your arrogance, you have something to teach us? We know valour and we know death. Is that not enough?'

'Valour has its place in an army but it is meaningless when it is applied by individuals against the Roman war-machine.'

'What would you have us do?'

'I need to know about your people's way of fighting, so I can advise on the best way to employ your men. The Damnonii have promised three thousand men. Are they all swordsmen or spearmen?'

'And do they use armour and shields?' said Cimbrod.

'Armour? Shields? Those are for old women. Men do not hide behind shields. My men are true warriors.'

'Then you must change. The Romans use both armour and shields. Their heavy cavalry can ride among you and kill at will for even their horses have mail kirtles.'

'We cannot change our style of fighting. My men would feel it was dishonourable.'

'Then I cannot use them. We will fight, plunder and ravage without your men who in their pride and arrogance wish to stay at home.'

Cimbrod said, 'Lord Cimiod, Galdir means no offence. He knows the Roman tactics from long experience of fighting them and he can defeat them if all the north Britons fight together as one man.'

Cimiod was silent, thinking about Cimbrod's words.

I said, 'The Romans use a tactic in which they attack with their infantry and engage the men in front of them. They then attack both flanks simultaneously with their cavalry. If they have heavy Sarmatian cavalry they will be successful, for none can withstand a charge of heavy horse, even the Romans. They can even use them in the centre of the front lines to punch a hole in infantry. That is why Marcus Aurelius wanted the Sarmatians to fight for him.'

'How do you suggest we fight them then?' said Cimiod.

'There was a general from Carthage called Hannibal. Have you heard of him?'

'Hani... what? Is he the one you spoke of at the meeting of kings?'

'Yes. It is ancient history. He defeated the Romans time and again and employed tactics allowing his smaller army to defeat huge Roman armies with ease and he always won.'

'It sounds interesting,' Cimiod said, 'tell me how this miracle can be achieved.'

We then discussed tactics, and after some hours Cimbrod and I left. The servants showed us to accommodation which was palatial. It was a large hut outside the King's compound but inside the town's palisade. There were two wide cots and the maidservants who showed us to our sleeping place asked with ardent gestures what else they could do for us. Embarrassed, we both declined the offers of any other favours and I think our resilience comforted us both.

It had begun to snow heavily as we crossed a muddy street to another hut to meet the leaders of the Damnonii warriors. They were not an organised army to my mind, but I was able to instruct them in how best to use spearmen against Roman cavalry. I explained how to use infantry to stand against the Legionary shield wall. I made much of the use of shields, which they scorned at first as unmanly. When I told them of the type of opposition they were facing, and what my own experience had been in Germania, they began to understand what was required. It began to dawn on them that defeating a Roman army was more than attacking in huge numbers; they needed tactics and new weapons.

Cimbrod and I had many such visits to make and the aim was to construct a new army, one which could communicate across a battlefield and which, with little training, would threaten Roman rule for good.

The next day when we left, I knew Cimiod had understood both the plan and the strategy. He agreed to have his commanders train their men in a way that would allow the forthcoming battles to follow the pattern I had laid down. For once, I had no doubts. Cimiod was a reliable leader and his men, I had surmised, were obedient and serious.

CHAPTER XIII

"Discipline is an index to doctrine"
—Tertullian

Spring came and winter's snows receded even from the peaks of the tall hills all around us. We had delays in assembling the army because the different tribes all wanted to wait until their festival called Beltane. In that festival Druids came into the tuaths and the people lit huge fires. They drove their cattle between the fires so the smoke could purify the beasts ready for the long summer. I found it hard to control my impatience with the tribes for they were argumentative and they allowed their religious and ritualistic behaviour to interfere with everything I planned.

Oenna was happy. Her pregnancy was progressing but had only just begun to become obvious in the late spring for she was tall and thin and her build and fitness had hidden the wonderful promise of what was to come.

We walked hand in hand upon the long beach where we had ridden to Drest's hall in the previous autumn. The wet, ridged dark yellow sand displayed our footprints behind us as we walked. Seagulls flitted across the shoreline and there was a sea mist on the far horizon obscuring the sunlight. There is no sensation comparable to holding the hand of one whom you love and I felt happy and at ease. Oenna too had relaxed into the idea of becoming a mother and when we were alone we made plans. The thought of me leaving to go home had receded and neither of us saw it as a possibility any longer. I knew my place was here with her in her land.

'The army will assemble in a week,' I said.

'Yes, you have brought together tribes who have been at each other's throats continually for years.'

'It seems to me the timing was the important factor. The men are restless and now have this war to look forward to.'

'I think stopping them from raiding each other's cattle was the best idea. They have little excuse for fighting without that.'

I said, 'Now they have trading agreements most of the fighting will stop. It is the one thing that will cause their downfall, fighting among themselves.'

'Which of the three attacks will you lead?'

'I have to attack Verovicium. It's the closest to Vindolanda where Lazygis will be posted with his men.'

'I would prefer,' Oenna said, 'to fight from a chariot, it is what I am used to. The driver will drop us at the flanks.'

'You? You're not fighting.'

'Yes I am.'

'You're pregnant. You will have to stay at home here in Bannatia.'

'I don't think so. I can wield a sword and that hasn't changed. I'm a little slower on my feet but not much.'

'I absolutely forbid it. You can't take risks with our unborn child.'

'You said yourself there was little risk involved when you told me the plans.'

'I didn't want you to worry that's all. If you are there, you will distract me from my purpose. You can't go.'

'You are not my husband yet and even if you were, you would not have the right to order me to do anything. Women have fought in our wars for centuries. Remember Boudicca?'

'She wasn't pregnant. Have some sense now. You are not going and that is that.'

'You can't prevent me, I told you.'

She was frowning now. 'I might go to one of the other two attack points if you won't have me in your army. Cimbrod will let me. I will get Ancamma to influence him.'

'Why do you have to be so difficult? Why can't you be like other women?'

'If I was like other women maybe you wouldn't like me,' she said and smiled. It was a disarming expression and I was almost inclined to give in. I took her in my arms and our lips met.

'Darling Oenna. It is only out of concern for you and our unborn son I have to have you safe. I can do anything in this war, whether it is easy or hard, but only if I know you are safe. Please be reasonable.'

'It's you who is unreasonable. Can't you see that? I am a Briton. I have fought before and I have been through hardships of which you can only guess. Do you think I travelled alone all the way from Gaul and sailed home in luxury? I had to protect myself then and I have learned sword skills since. I can look after myself.'

'I won't allow it. Even if I have to lock you up.'

'I'm going.'

'No.'

'Yes, and you can't stop me, so accept it.'

'Compromise?' I said.

'What?'

'You can come and observe. No hand to hand fighting and you stand with me. I will be directing operations and will only enter the fight if things are going badly in any particular place. I'm not just a soldier after all.'

'Agreed. I will come as your aide.'

'No, you will come as my wife.'

'As you wish. There, that wasn't so hard to give in was it?'

'Women!' I muttered.

'Without women there would be no men, so don't underestimate us.'

We walked on in silence. Oenna smiled as if she had achieved a victory and I recall feeling as if new problems had arisen to trip me up on the path to victory.

*

The muster was a gradual thing. Thousands travelled from the farthest reaches of the north of Britannia. Each travelling war band brought food and fodder for their horses, in huge quantities. None of us knew how long we would campaign and none of us knew with precision how far south we would be able to penetrate before we found new supplies. It was not a migration and so the men in our armies had left loved ones and families behind. No one was staying in the south. The aim of our campaign was to free the island from Roman rule and return home.

Caledonii made up the backbone of our infantry and they numbered almost five thousand. Nechtan came with Drosten at his side and Taran commanded two hundred of the cavalry who followed in the van. There were a thousand chariots. They were shock troops useful on the flanks or the centre.

Squads of Votadini spearmen, infantry from Insi Orc, swordsmen from Damnonia, Vacomagi infantry all rubbed

315

shoulders as if there had never been wars between them. They camped next to each other, fraternised, gambled, bartered and drank ale. To me it was a beautiful sight, a massive field filled with blue bodies and black and white ponies. Many of the mounted soldiers slept with their steeds, which was common in Dacia, and frowned upon in my home. None of these minor differences mattered in this army which, when the other tribes arrived, numbered over thirty thousand men.

One week after Beltane, all the armies assembled on a plain south of the Caledonii borders, north of the huge lake where I had met Cimbrod's men months before. I held a council of war. I had decided to fully reveal my plans and set the boulder that was our army rolling down the hill to smash the Roman wall. We met in the open for there were almost thirty men, all of them warriors and kings. We had no tent large enough for such a gathering and I hoped it would not rain. Britannia is a wet country and I should have known better than to trust to the weather, for rain it did. The assembly became a damp and bedraggled collection of seated warriors holding cloaks over their heads to keep the rain out.

After an hour, we erected awnings around the periphery of the council and that seemed to help keep out the weather enough for us to speak.

'Brave Britons,' I said, 'we have gathered our forces, and exactly as we planned together, they are divided up into infantry, spearmen and mounted warriors. I am here to tell you how best we can deploy them. It will mean co-operation and you will have Votadini spearmen on the flanks of Damnonii infantry to protect them from the Roman cavalry. There will be Caledonian chariots attacking the flanks while Venicones attack the legionaries head on in loose order in the way we have trained them. We can make all this work as long as we recognise that we fight a common enemy, an enemy who has enslaved all your peoples for hundreds of years and threatens to take your land from you.'

I waited for a response and Drest stood next to speak. He wore a round helmet, with a beaten insignia of a boat with sails on its front.

'My friends,' he said, 'we are here to do battle and all that remains for us now is to hear the details. Each of us has a role, and like all armies we must all obey one man. This man is Galdir who has done more to unite us than any other in our history. I beg you to listen. I urge you to adhere to the plan.'

I went on to explain what was required. I had decided to split the army into three smaller armies each of ten thousand arranged with the infantry in the middle, spearmen at the flanks. The mounted troops were to hang back and attack the equites when they tried to outflank. I set out each army so the thinnest lines were in the centre and the strongest troops were on the flanks. The chariots, hanging back to prevent the Romans from out-flanking us, would then stop any Romans getting through the line in the centre. The seasoned, hardest troops on the flanks could then envelope the Romans and crush them. Hannibal had done that and the Romans had taught me how he had been successful to the point of invincibility. The one spike in the sand was the Sarmatian heavy cavalry and I realised we had to do something to prevent their attack.

The gathered leaders seemed to understand and when we had decided where we would mount our attacks, there was silence as if all those warring factions were weighing up whether they could stomach fighting alongside their old

enemies. I had set Cimbrod to command one army at Bro-
colitia, a mile castle northeast of Vindolanda.

Drest commanded the second army and they were attacking between Aesica and Magna, two other mile castles to the
west. I was to lead the central forces at Verovicium north of
Vindolanda where Lazygis and his men would be if he still
lived. I was sure he did, for his death wish always seemed to
keep him safe. The plan was to attack between the mile
castles where the troops had to be summoned from either
side and once our men were over, to regroup and reunite.

I had defeated Licinius Piso before at the siege of Sicambra so I knew it could be done. His hatred for all Germans
would be visited upon him I was sure. If I had a chance, I
would humiliate him for the way he had treated my friend
Lazygis and his Sarmatians.

Revenge however, is a poor excuse for barbarity, and I
knew this inside if not consciously. I am not a vengeful man
by nature because when it comes to it, I know honour
counts for much more in a man's life than vengeance.

Oenna walked to our tent and we talked in an animated
and excited way for we had much to look forward to and we
both felt an inexplicable optimism. The thought that we had
the rest of our lives together filled us both with a joy it is
hard to describe.

CHAPTER XIV

"Men naturally despise those who court them, but respect those who do not give way to them"
—Thucydides

There was a faint cold moon above as I splashed through the water and mud. Long shadows pitched and rippled across the pool in the ditch below the Roman wall and stabbed at the darkness beneath. I carried a ladder and knew I was invisible from above. I had watched the sentry as he walked up and down the wall-walk and had counted how many paces it took him to walk his beat. I could hear him, still marching away from the centre of the walkway as I raised my ladder. I climbed. One, two, three, I counted paces as I slipped onto the wall. He did not look round. Ten, eleven twelve. Lower the ladder on the far side. Ten more and he would turn and see me. Ladder up, place it on the other side and climb down, flatten myself against the wall in the shadows and wait for his next return.

All was still and black around me, the only audible sound the slapping footsteps of the Roman guard in his nail-studded sandals, if indeed he was Roman. It was a quarter of a mile across the military road and the vallum beyond where our spy had tethered a horse for me. I hoped with desperation it was there. We had paid him well and he knew what would happen to his family if he failed. I knew too Oenna would never permit anyone to harm the woman and child but I had to give the fellow some incentive.

I ran crouching for the road. It was ten feet across and there was a ditch either side. I could see the brickwork, as I lay flat against it. The Romans build their roads as if they are sunken walls, six feet below ground level. It is not surprising they last so well and seldom need repairs. It is strange the things passing through a man's mind when he is in danger. I remembered Cimbrod, helpless with laughter just because of a name, and I smiled to myself, for it was infectious still and always brought that laughter from deep within me.

The sentry was walking away again after exchanging a few words with his companion in the middle of their section. I waited until they were almost at the end of their steps and then ran across the road, a moonlit mile smelling of horse-dung and danger. On the other side of the road, I squatted. I was sure they would not see me and if they did, would not challenge me. They were after all, there to keep people out—not to check on those within.

Walking due south, I knew there was a farm and the horse should have been tethered to a post on the path meandering uphill towards the little farmhouse. An owl startled me as it screeched overhead. Looking up I could see the soft white down of its underside as it descended, claws first, to take some small and hapless creature in the grass. I felt like the owl's prey waiting for some shout exposing me to a massive Roman eagle.

I found the steed without difficulty and eased myself into the saddle. I knew where to go, had I not been an auxiliary here? It seemed like years since Lazygis and I had returned from Cataractonium to find his men dispersed along the wall. I knew their separation was too much to hope for. I wondered if it was my own Greek letter to the Governor working against me. It seemed ironic.

I rode trying to look unconcerned, almost casual to any observers on the military road. I knew well there would be checkpoints along the way and since I spoke Latin and knew how to act as an auxiliary commander I felt sure I could get through to Vindolanda.

It took only a half-hour before I had passed a checkpoint and ridden south to the Sarmatian camp. They were in the same field they had always occupied and I knew where to find my friend. He was a creature of habit and I had no difficulty locating his tent, for he always decorated it with a red insignia his wife Ayma had made for him, long ago. The fire arrows had clearly not consumed it on the day I had been captured. Ayma had been a hard, serious woman who tolerated no insults and could fight like a man, shoot a bow and use a light war axe without any difficulty. Despite that, she had a keen sense of humour and a soft streak for her son Panogaris. They were both gone now to the home of their Gods, Pan and Ma. I knew how Lazygis carried their memory in his heart and he prayed to his Gods daily to be reunited with Ayma and his only son.

'Lazygis,' I shook the tent-pole, 'Lazygis are you awake?'

'In the name of Ma, who is that?'

'Me,' I whispered as loud as I could.

'Who in Britannia is me?' came the muffled voice. 'I'm coming out.'

He looked sleepy, his slanting eyes more slit-like than normal and I could see bags under his eyes. Inactivity is never good for a fighting man.

'Galdir?'

'Yes my friend, I've come to visit.'

'Galdir,' he said repeatedly as he stood in front of me. He

reached forward and hugged me, which was a strange thing to do, as it is not part of the usual Sarmatian repertoire of gestures.

'We can sit in your tent, I have much to tell you,' I said, lifting the leather flap.

'No,' he said.

'Yes. I can't afford to be seen.'

'Well we can go over to the horse field, it's always quiet there.'

A woman's sleepy voice interrupted us.

'Who is it?' the voice said, in the common Britannic tongue.

'Never mind my darling, an old friend,' Lazygis said.

I looked at my friend with my head cocked to one side. This was not what I had expected. Lazygis had shown no interest in women since he became a widower and I had assumed there would be no change in that.

We walked in silence now to the where the horses were tethered, picking our way between the sleeping men and their tents. It was a large flat field with posts sunk into the ground and row upon row of ropes strung between, to which they tethered the Sarmatian mounts overnight. The only sound audible was the occasional whinnying of the horses and we crouched down among them out of sight. He looked at me and his eyes gleamed in the moonlight in a way I had never seen before. Could he have found what I had, here in this wet, unforgiving country with its painted warriors and constant rain?

I smiled. 'You have a woman?'

'Yes.'

'Yes – is that all you can say?'

'She is a Briton of the Selgovae tribe. I helped her when

322

the Romans killed her husband. She loves me.'

'And you?'

'It isn't a betrayal Galdir. Ayma would understand. She always was practical you know.'

'I know. I have a woman too.'

'You understand then?'

'Lazygis, I am a Warlord again. I have raised an army of Britons and we will drive the Romans away from Britannia forever.'

'Army? What army? Slow down will you? Minutes ago, you were dead and now you come back with a woman and an army? What is going on?'

'Sorry. Time is short, but if this works out for me then we will have plenty of time to catch up. For now I need to know what your status is.'

'My status Galdir is that moments ago I was asleep with a beautiful young girl and now I am squatting in the moon-light among the horses with a dead man.'

'No, I mean military status. Are you and the others stay-ing here in Vindolanda? You must have heard there is a war coming?'

'Yes but Piso's intelligence is that there will be a full-scale attack at Camboglanna. He said when he briefed us how he had an inside man who had found out the Brit... your plans.'

I thought for a moment. That was what I had told Taran to shut him up and stop his incessant questioning when we rode to the Damnonii. I knew now who the traitor was. I knew what to do to him too.

'That is good news.'

'I don't think so. He is moving all of my troops and most of the Legionary Cohorts to Camboglanna and hopes to launch a surprise attack on the invader's flanks. It sounds a good plan. It's your army is it?'

'In a way. It is a confederation of Britannic tribes. They seem to have been able to put away their differences for the moment. I only hope it will last long enough. Our German alliance didn't.'

'I can't fight for you.'

'What?'

'I can't break my oath to Aurelius. My men have sworn on all we hold sacred and there is no way we can change sides like mercenaries. We have been defeated by the Romans but we still have our honour.'

'I don't want you to fight anyone.'

'How do you mean?'

'I want you to go to Camboglanna. We aren't attacking there. I knew there was a spy and I spread a false plan to fool the Romans.'

'I still can't turn on the Romans. My men would never be oath breakers. That was why we have put up with the treatment we have had from the Romans all this time.'

'All I want from you is a slow response. I want you to be very slow in coming when they summon you. By the time you arrive, there will be upwards of thirty thousand men on this side of the wall and Camboglanna is far enough away to make it difficult to get here before we are across. No one would expect five hundred Sarmatians to attack a whole army would they?'

'It might work. Won't the Romans see where you are marching to?'

'No, we are breaking up into scattered war bands and some will be seen heading for Camboglanna. They will only be old men and women but from a distance they will look blue and half naked.'

'It may work. They won't expect us to go south to join the Second if there is a huge army between us and them. We could perhaps stay around here.'

'You could consider settling here. I am.'

'You won't go home? What about your people?'

My face must have changed then. He reached out a hand and placed it on my shoulder. 'Galdir, you have changed since we last spoke. What about the Franks?'

'I know. I have a choice between living here with Oenna who is expecting a child and leaving her here. I'm staying.'

'I think I understand. It's just that last time we spoke…'

'I met up with a band of Germanic mercenaries and found I owed them more than I owed the Romans. I guessed they would think I was dead anyway.'

'Yes, Cerialis told me that himself. For once, he wasn't frowning. I wish we could join you but I cannot betray my oath. I am surprised you can. Love and women my friend, they can change many things.'

'When do you go to Camboglanna?' I said.

'In two days. It will take most of a day to get there.'

'We are attacking at…'

'Don't tell me, old friend,' he said, putting his hand up.

'But I would trust you with my life at any time.'

He said, 'If I don't know, then no one can accuse me of lying or treachery. It can't even be tortured out of me if I remain in ignorance.'

'I must go, but there is one more thing I need.'

'What?'

There are some Votadini hostages. I need them freed.'

'I will see what I can do.'

'I really must go now,' I said.

'Not so fast my friend there is one more thing to do.'

'What?'

'How did that whistle go you always called your horse with?'

'Like this.'

I whistled. Then I understood. I heard a whinnying and a stamping of feet off to my right. Valknir. I called his name and he must have tried to come for I could see the horses, restless and moving, off to my right.

'You found him?'

'Yes. That was why we thought you were dead. There was blood on the saddle and a Batavian found him roaming the battlefield. He won't let anyone ride him, so we used him as a pack-horse. He is a troublesome beast that one. Does things if he wants to, but if he doesn't, nothing will persuade him. Even Panador can't influence that horse.'

'No, we have a bond,' I said as I unhitched him.

'We have a saying in Sarmatia, "a horse without his owner is like a man with no legs—just moving meat". It doesn't translate well.'

'I can't take him. He can't jump the wall.'

'No, but I can take you both to the gate. I am friendly with the gate-guards. I spend a lot of time gazing north these days. I was always looking for you perhaps.'

'I know, Lazygis. You have always been a true friend from the first time we met. You saved my life then. Do you remember?'

'I remember an incompetent boy who almost got himself killed.'

He smiled.

Lazygis gave me a saddle. The stirrups were a little short but I could easily have them lengthened. We rode to the gate and he told the guards I was on a secret mission for the Legate and they were not to divulge they had seen me to anyone. They believed us I think because these were dangerous times and such things were quite likely.

I rode Valknir away from the fort and I shook my head. My horse. It felt good. I leaned forward and spoke to him as I always had done. He shook his head and blew in response. Reunited at last like old friends we took up where we had left off without any difficulty. He raised his front legs, dug his rear hooves into the soft grass and cantered happily beneath me. I felt complete at last.

Meeting Lazygis again had lifted my spirits even further. I realised what a close friend he had become. I did trust him completely and knew that not only would we not have to kill my friends, but our chance of success was higher than ever before. I rode with my head held high, onward to a grim beginning and a successful war. If only the Gods would this once, not play me false, I would have a future. I had become a Warlord again and had begun to believe I was indeed one of these doughty Britons. Despite my feelings of expectant elation, there was something nagging at the back of my mind. I wondered as I rode in the moonlight whether somehow I had made a wrong decision on the road to this future. I think now it was a prickle of conscience. Could I really disengage from the destiny Chlotsuintha had predicted? She had always said it was a prophesy coming from Wuotan himself.

Who am I to try to change such things?

CHAPTER XV

"Without a sign, his sword the brave man draws,
and asks no omen but his country's cause"
—Homer

It was a bright spring night. I could see the bright far off stars and the moon cast a baleful light behind us, as we gathered in the vallum beneath the wall. We had crawled in the damp grass and mud and the five thousand men with me were begrimed and wet.

The ladder carriers were ready, and on my command they ran forward, as silent as shadows, to the Roman wall. A guard shouted from the wall only once. An arrow found him in the dark, silencing him forever. There were more shouts. I could see my men silhouetted on the skyline as I looked up at the wall. The secret was the number of ladders. So many men had ascended at once that opposition from the troops on that section of wall was impossible. There could only have been about twenty Romans and they died fast. The first men up the ladders were our toughest warriors and they had practised this manoeuvre repeatedly for weeks. The guards managed to light the beacon after which we abandoned all efforts at secrecy.

Five thousand men is a large number when it comes to transferring them over a twelve-foot wall on ladders, and my concern for Oenna who had insisted she come with us, hampered me. I hung back to ensure she was safe. We climbed the wall together and watched as the last of our men assembled below. The procedure took precious time. Once they had formed up, a full cohort of Tungrians approached marching towards us from the east. I knew Cimbrod and his men would be behind them. He had instructions to get across and march west, to join up with us. I still had five thousand men waiting on the opposite side of the wall at the gate where the intervening mile castle raised its ugly bastions.

The enemy formed up in their regular centuries as if they were on parade and the moonlight cast their shadows long and eerie on the dark wet ground.

I called down to them.

'Who commands you?'

A stocky figure emerged, and recognising him, I climbed down and approached, careful to remain out of range of the legionaries' pilae.

'Flavius Cerialis,' I said. 'We meet again.'

'Sarmatian traitor.'

'I was always on the other side, you should have known that.'

'I knew there was something about you I couldn't trust.'

'Look, if you and your men lay down your arms and step back fifty paces, we will spare your lives. There is no need for you all to die. We outnumber you by ten to one and we have more troops crossing the wall behind you.'

'You think I would betray my oath to the Emperor like you did? Never.'

'Your men are Germans. They aren't Roman. Why throw their lives away?'

'You know nothing of honour do you?'

'Yes, I know about honour and I know that to live is all

we have in this strange existence. We will give you safe passage from the north Briton territory if you lay down your arms, or you will all die. We cannot take prisoners; we march on when we have finished here. Listen to reason.'

He glared at me, then turned around and marched back to his men. I felt that at least I had tried.

'What was that all about?' asked Oenna when I joined her.

'Nothing, I offered them their lives. They wouldn't take the offer.'

It was a short fight. I realised early on the Britons had learned their lessons well. The central warriors carried shields and their swords were new and shorter than any they had used before. They still screamed war shouts and snarled as they fought but it was unlike any similar skirmish I had seen before in this place. Shield to shield, the fierceness of the Britons counted for much. The Tungrians knew how out-numbered they were and within half an hour some threw down their shields and begged for mercy. It shamed me. They were Germans and should have accepted it was their time for the Valkyries to take them to Wuotan. Instead, those who threw down their weapons died without their swords in their hands. It was pitiful to see.

I saw Drogo push a Tungrian over by tripping him and he stood, sword poised above him. Then the boy turned as if to give quarter. A Briton pushed past him and hewed the Roman with his sword. It was over in a moment, but I wondered if my fellow Frank needed to learn how in battle, death is the rule not the exception. I watched as he stood looking down at the dead legionary, pensive despite the din of the battle raging all around. I tried to imagine what was going on in his head.

The spearmen on the flanks, eager to be in the melee, became restless. I had kept them on the flanks in case the Tungrians had cavalry, but they did not. Our line overlapped the Romans, and I sent the flanks round on either side. Our spearmen enveloped the Romans and in the end attacked both their flanks and rear. It was over very quickly. None of the Romans survived. We regrouped quickly, for this was to be a fast efficient victory and we had to march to the next mile castle to open the gates. We achieved this with all speed and by the time Cimbrod arrived, my army was complete.

We sent out mounted scouts to locate any enemy for we knew the bulk of the Romans were far away to the west where I had misdirected them through Taran. I felt sorry for Taran, then, for I recalled the scene when they executed him. The Britons do not torture or burn people but in exceptional cases they do drown them. They took Taran the traitor to the river and weighed him down with rocks chained to his head and feet. He begged for his life, he clutched at the men around him, he cried. It was of course to no avail. They fed him to the icy water slowly. Lutrin had told me what it meant. I could see the look of terror in Taran's eyes as the freezing river took him. Like his executioners, he knew there was no way to the Otherworld through running water and no way back to this one. All I could see then was the red hair like a dark stain as the freezing water swept him away. I had no regrets, for his friendship had been false, his humour and his potions a veil to his treachery. I was angry with myself for being duped, but also questioned how a man like him could have been a traitor. I remembered the look in his eyes when first we had met and the time when Cimbrod and I had found him on the road to Damnonii. I thought it was the first time in my experience a man's eyes could look true, yet be so false. I recall hoping I was right about him. I knew that had I been wrong, the Romans would have manned the wall in strength. Our success was the measure of his guilt.

An hour later Drest and his army joined us and we were at full strength. All we had to do now was to wait. Licinius Piso would come. There were too few men to the east to launch even a skirmish for our numbers were so great. I wondered if they would come in the night by forced march, or whether they would set off at first light. I did not intend to give them time to rest when they arrived. I remembered how Hannibal had attacked one Roman army before they were fully awake and how the fall in morale with fighting on empty stomachs had helped the Carthaginian General.

'We hardly had a fight at all,' Cimbrod said.

'No nor did we,' Drest said, looking down at us both from his horse. 'How many Tungrians did you kill Galdir?'

'About five hundred. Our men fought well. Piso will come from the west and he will have about five thousand men.'

'It will be like swatting a fly,' Drest said.

'No it won't. The Sarmatians could alter things so much the balance would be equal, believe me,' I said.

'But you said…'

'Yes. The only problem is if they can't avoid coming. There is only so much Lazygis can do to disobey orders. If Piso keeps them close they may have to fight.'

'What now? We have taken the wall.'

'We wait. When we have fought Piso there is another army at Cataractonium and then there are no others until we are in the deep south.'

'I am proud to be a Briton tonight,' Oenna said.

'Save you pride my love, wait until Piso lies dead and we have taken the wall.'

'You hate him don't you?'

'No, but he has been part of what happened to my people, and he deserves both defeat and death.'

'The men won't find it easy to wait,' Drest said.

'Always impatient aren't they?' Oenna said.

'I wish you had stayed with the baggage,' I said, looking at her.

'I'm not baggage and this is where I belong, at your side.'

Drest looked at her and shook his head. I think he must have wondered why I had so little control over his sister, but he should have understood for he knew her better even than I did.

We posted lookouts and waited for the scouts. My men knew what I required of them and even Nechtan cooperated. His men were the toughest infantry with a combination of swordsmen and spearmen. The night passed slowly and I stood on a grassy knoll and looked at the sunrise. The slats of cloud were long and grey, stretched in a horizontal line below which the dawn showed red and mauve. The sun's rays reached out towards us but there was no warmth there.

By the time our scouts returned, the sun had risen high in the spring sky. They said there was no large approaching force in the west heading our way. They had not seen any troops, not even the gate guards. Had Piso outwitted me? Had he kept all his troops near Vindolanda?

We had to wait for our eastern riders to come in before we would know what was happening.

'If the Romans are off to the east, they may try to delay us until the Second Legion arrives,' I said to Drest as we stood looking east on the little hill. The ground was verdant and grassy and I saw no movement on the Roman military road to indicate the return of our scouts.

'But our men reported them heading west. It was why Taran paid with his life. We weren't wrong, I'm sure of it.' Oenna said.

'No, I think he was there, otherwise the Tungrians would not have attacked in such small numbers. There were only five hundred of them. They would have waited for reinforcements from the east if they had known Piso and his army were marching this way. They had no idea of our numbers I think.'

Cimbrod called from below us, 'Maybe they won't be back. Should we send more riders?'

'No,' I called down the slope. 'We have to be patient. They will come. I know it.'

Drest looked at me; I could see beads of perspiration on his forehead. I wondered whether he had the temperament for war; there was nothing to be worried about here.

'We could send men north,' he said. 'They may have crossed the wall and are making their way east out of our sight.'

'Why would he do that? He must know by now we hold the wall. He would have to assault his own defences to attack us.'

'Not necessarily. The furthest eastern extreme of the wall at Hexacoria is still in Roman hands until we march there and take it from them. It will take us time.'

'He would have to march very fast to get there before we do,' I said.

'Yes, but he may know we are waiting here. We have to locate the Romans. They can't just have disappeared from the face of the earth.'

'We'll send riders north.'

'We then have to wait here for them to return, or split the army. He's cleverer than I thought,' I said, shifting in my saddle. Even with the longer stirrups, fashioned by a Caledonian saddler, it was not as comfortable as my own. With years of riding in the same saddle, the leather becomes used to your shape and eventually fits you like a glove. I wondered whether perhaps the previous owner of this saddle had been a strange shape for it nipped and rubbed in several places.

'We send the riders, Galdir,' he said.

'Yes,' I said, 'and I was telling Cimbrod to be patient!'

'There is one thing bothering me. If they head east from the north side, they may come across our camp. Most of our supplies are there.'

I sat still, dumbfounded by my stupidity. The Romans could take or destroy all our supplies. I had left only a small defence force at the camp for we were expecting to send for the supplies once the wall was secure. Worse still, Ancamma was there.

'Drest, I said, 'Ancamma is still at the camp.'

'We had better send our fastest men to ride to warn them they may have Roman company.'

'I don't want to lose our supplies either. In all probability, the Romans won't find the camp. There is no reason for them to go so far north in any case. Relax Galdir. She will be fine.'

I rode down the slope.

'Cimbrod,' I said, 'Ancamma is still at the camp and the Romans may be north of the wall. I presume you will want to go with the scouts. I cannot leave here; there are many things depending on me, otherwise I would be tempted to come with you. You could take Drogo and Hengeist.'

Cimbrod frowned, 'I should have thought about that before. It was stupid. Of course I'm going. If anything has happened to Ancamma I will stay to kill every Roman in Britannia.'

'Go with the speed of Sleipnir,' I said.

'I'll outride the Valkyrs if I have to.'

'Bring her back safe,' Oenna said.

He turned his horse and left, shouting commands to right and left as he rode through the ranks of our army. I could see Drogo mounting his steed and Hengeist joined them as they rode. I hoped I was wrong but realised there was a real danger Ancamma might be a prisoner and used as a bargaining chip by the Romans.

'I hope she is safe,' Oenna said.

'Yes. I don't know what Cimbrod would do, if anything happens to her. Well, we can't change the past or the future so we just have to wait and see. I'm glad now I didn't leave you back in the camp.'

'Leave me in the camp? You really do think you control me don't you?'

'That's not what I meant.'

'Just concentrate on the war Galdir, I'll look after myself.'

'Sorry, I'm just a bit tense about Piso. We can't fight an invisible army and the scouts should have located them by now.'

'Yes, it's a waiting game.'

'When the battle does start, you will stick with me won't you?'

'Oh for the love of the Gods! Stop whining. It isn't like you. Keep your concern for the war; I can take care of myself.'

I wished I had Lazygis by my side. He always had a level

head and a cool mind. I could not focus on the matters at hand; all I could think about was where Piso could be. I knew I had to make some decision but determined to wait for the eastern scouts to return. I decided I would give them an hour.

They returned in less time than that. They looked tired and we gave them a few moments to catch their breath before they were able to tell us what was happening. They had ridden clean to Vindolanda and seen no one. The eastern part of the wall had been abandoned that far and it seemed to me Piso would have taken his men to Onnum, north of Hexacoria, the first military town east of Vindolanda. If he had withdrawn all his wall cohorts to there, he would have almost ten thousand men, many of them Roman legionaries but a sizeable proportion would be auxiliaries raised locally. I knew the dangerous part of his army were the Tungrians and Batavians who made up most of the regular troops.

I wished I had paid more attention to the numbers on the wall during all those months I had been an auxiliary. It seemed to me I had spent too much time grieving over my own plight and mooning over Lucia. Had I used my time better in those days, it would have helped me make up my mind.

Despite my doubts and fears, I had to decide the next move. I resolved in the end to march the army east and hoped Piso would give battle there, even if it were on ground of his own choosing. We had thirty thousand men and I knew we could defeat the Romans, but I was well aware those odds were ones many successful Roman armies had faced in Germania, Gaul and in lower Britannia. Those barbarians had not had me there to guide them and organise them though. I felt sure we could defeat the Romans if my men stayed together. I held a council meeting with the leaders of every tribe first.

It might seem this wasted time, but there is nothing wasteful in such councils of war, for it was the surest way to gain the cooperation of the mixed tribes and their leaders.

We sat in a circle on the little hill. There were thirteen of us including Cimiod, Nechtan, Drest and to my annoyance, Drosten. Oengus and Morleo were there too and I was glad of it. Oengus had been my solid support throughout the muster and I owed him much for that. Nechtan sat with his hand on Drosten's shoulder and smiled, revealing his perfect dentition. Oenna sat next to me—her support and encouragement for me, was like gold.

Drosten stood first, to my intense irritation. He said, 'So far this uprising had achieved nothing. We have killed a few hundred Romans and gained neither plunder nor slaves. There is a huge Roman army loose somewhere and we can't even find them. Nechtan, for whom I speak, does not feel we have achieved anything. We want a change of leadership. We risk everything yet what does the German risk? Nothing.'

He sat down and whispered into Nechtan's ear and I noticed Cimiod nodding silently. For a few moments no one spoke. Oengus stood next. He was scowling at Nechtan and I could see the anger in his eyes.

'This campaign has lasted half a day and the Caledonii are bleating on about having no plunder. Friends, we have to fight and defeat the Romans before we get their gold. Our plans have been solid and worked out well in advance. The Romans are clever though. We think they have crossed the wall and even now are heading east to join up with the remains of the wall cohorts. We don't need a change of leader; we need better intelligence. As for Galdir, he has been right about everything so far and I see no reason to trust him less because Nechtan bears him some grudge.'

Nechtan, still sitting, looked up at Oengus. He frowned at first and then began to smile. The quality of his teeth began to irritate me; I felt they were wasted on him.

'I have no grudge against the German,' he said, looking from face to face, 'but I have no faith in his decisions, for as Drosten says, he has little to lose. For the time being the Caledonii will follow his command but if his decisions are found to be lacking we will withdraw or continue on our own and there is nothing any other faction can do to persuade us, for we are the largest contingent.'

Drest said, 'This alliance is the thing that matters most. If you listen to the lessons of history, you will know our people have never worked together like now. Lutrin has already told us we are embarking upon a future long foretold. We must follow the destiny our Gods have set in place for us. That destiny is to follow Galdir to victory. I, for one, will follow him and take my men east and rub out the Romans. If any of you have doubts, then consider this. Our strength depends upon the methods of battle the German has taught us. Our power depends upon us staying together as one army. If our tribal differences make us separate we will all fall separately to the Romans. We must stay together as one army. Let us stay united and fight for our homeland. We are brothers in this at least.'

Lutrin who had been silent until then stood up. The assembled leaders regarded him in silence for he had a forceful presence and commanded respect as if it were his natural right.

He said, 'At last the time approaches. I hear the sounds of

a great battle to come. It is a time of unity. We are gathered and ready. Know this: you all carry the hopes of your country within you. You will not fail—it has been foretold. But remember, when you stand victorious over the skulls by your feet, it is only because you fight side by side and together that victory is achieved. Know also, the Gods are watching. Hill, stream, and rock observe us and smile upon our endeavours. To win favour from the Gods keep your blades in reserve for the enemy's soldiers and not for each other.'

Further discussions took place but the result was the army would move eastwards and expect to fight Piso's legion and its auxiliaries. I knew they would follow me now but I had no doubts about the precariousness of my position. As long as we were successful, they would support me. As soon as we failed, I would be ignored or lose my life. I also knew Drosten would be delighted if that were to occur and would no doubt be the first to acclaim a new leader. I wanted to kill him.

Oenna whispered in my ear, 'Our son will lead these fools one day, I can feel it.'

I smiled back at her for I think I could see the same future. I was confident I could achieve what we had set out to do as long as I had her by my side and the Britons worked together. When we had taken Britannia back for the Britons I had no strong ambitions to lead them but if that was what the Gods decided, who was I to argue?

Of all the assembled leaders, I was most glad of Lutrin for he forced respect from these barbaric and uncivilised men. They believed in everything he said and I did not care whether he made it all up for political advantage, or whether he was a true seer. As long as the alliance held together the means cementing it was of no concern to me.

CHAPTER XVI

"*As to gods, I have no way of knowing either that they exist or do not exist, or what they are like*"
—*Protagoras*

My main worry as we marched was for Oenna. She was the single most important reason for me to consider a future here in Britannia. I felt that without her by my side, this island meant nothing to me. I had given up everything that mattered to be with her and I would have sacrificed anything for her safety, if it came to it. It was an exchange of one responsibility for another and I still had strong doubts whether I had made the right choice. It nagged me. It ate away at my thoughts and I had trouble concentrating on the army in which I rode. I scanned the horizon continually for Cimbrod, for I was concerned for Ancamma too. I had become fond of her and her friendship meant much.

We marched in columns. I realised with irritation these were not the military columns of a Roman army, neat and straight. They were untidy groups of barbarian soldiers carrying their weapons and shields, and jostling each other as they meandered along on the Roman road. I had never been confident I could organise them into a disciplined fighting force capable of annihilating the Romans. Something in them however had made me trust them. I knew they all wanted this war. They wanted to be free of Roman rule and the constant threat of the Roman slavers who cruised the north Briton shores, endlessly seeking profit from the misery they created. Had I not been a slave myself? Did I not recognise the evil such slavers could do?

By midday, we had reached Vercovicium, north of Vindolanda. The flat, green landscape was quiet, and as far as the eye could see, the Romans had withdrawn. As we headed south towards Vindolanda, a cool, spring sun shone down upon us and I would have found it cheering had I not had the odd feeling that we were ignorant of much that was happening around us. We did not know enough about what the Romans were planning. Still I looked north from time to time, searching the horizon for Cimbrod. Where was he? I could see the distant rolling hills, green and pleasant, but no sign of my friend. I wondered if he had come across the Romans and had to wait until they had passed. I hoped they had not captured him, and the absence of news became more disconcerting with each passing moment.

Drest, who rode with me showed equal concern.

'Galdir, Cimbrod should have returned by now. I worry for the baggage camp. If the Romans get all our supplies we will be in grave difficulties feeding the army. Foraging is a slow process. Ancamma, if she is still there, will have to flee north if the Romans come, it could make Cimbrod unreliable. I suppose their scouts would have got there first, but I don't think Piso would re-route his entire force just to take our carts and supplies.'

'I hope she has fled north. If she had warning of the Romans coming then she will be safe, but the Romans may use her as a hostage if they find her. Like you, I feel uncomfortable about this. I wouldn't worry about Cimbrod. If he knows his woman is safe he will be strong.'

'Look, I'm also concerned for my sister. You can't take a pregnant lover with you to a battle. Anything could happen.'

'I know. She even wanted to fight.'

'She told me. She has too much spirit that one.'

'I want her for my wife, Drest. It would be my one reason for staying in Britannia forever.'

Drest looked at me. He was frowning and I could read in his eyes there was a faint look of disapproval.

'Galdir, if she marries you I have to consider the political consequences. You bring with you no alliance. You have no troops on whom we can depend in a war; you don't even have land. Anyway, if you can't control her as a lover how do you expect to when she is your wife?'

'If we win this war I will have plenty.'

'Let us cross that bridge when we come to it. If we lose this battle against Piso there will be no way back for any of us.'

'I know,' I said.

He turned in his saddle scanning the horizon as I had done so many times. I was about to speak when he pointed. 'I can see a rider.'

There was one lone rider approaching as if every Roman in the world were chasing him.

'It's Drogo,' I said.

Drest and I turned our horses and rode towards my countryman as he approached. I looked at his face as he drew near and my disquiet increased for he looked distressed. He pulled up in front of us, breathless and strained.

'Lord,' he said, 'the Romans.'

'Drogo, take a few breaths and tell us what has happened,' Drest said.

Drogo breathed deeply for a few moments and although

impatient for the news, we waited, looking at him. His breathing began to settle enough for him to speak and I was unsure whether he was breathless from exertion or distress.

'They're all dead,' he said and looked down at the ground.

'Who is dead?' I said.

'Everyone at the camp,' he said.

'Everyone?'

'Yes. I found Ancamma's body among them.'

'Ancamma dead,' I said, my heart sinking. 'Drogo. Are you sure? What did Cimbrod do?'

'I... I... saw her.'

'Drogo! Tell me.'

'She's dead.'

'Pull yourself together man! Where is Cimbrod now?'

Drest said, 'What happened Drogo? Where are Cimbrod and his brother?'

'Cimbrod and Hengeist sent me back to tell you. They rode on after the Romans but their anger has made them foolish. They are pursuing a huge army. We estimated from the tracks there must be ten thousand of them, and they will reinforce from the troops at the east end of the wall. What can two men do?'

'Nothing,' I said under my breath. 'There is nothing to do. What about the body? Did you just leave it there?'

'Lord, we made a pyre from what was left of the wagons and we burned her and then they sent me back.'

'The supplies?' Drest said.

'All gone or burnt by the Romans.

I wondered now if Cimbrod would be lost to me. If the Romans caught him, I would never see him again. It was another blow to my heart. I had come to love him as a close friend, for we were sword-brothers and besides, he looked up to me. It was a grudging respect but one I valued; truth to be told I admired him too. He was one of the fastest and most skilful swordsmen I had ever seen. My heart was sore for Ancamma. The last time I had seen her was when we left her behind and I remember Cimbrod kissing her in front of the whole army. It was a sign of commitment from them both and everyone knew what it meant. I could imagine what was going on in his mind. Had I not lost in my life too? The feelings this evoked in me brought sorrow and relief at the same time. I was glad I had Oenna with me and relieved I had not left her with the baggage like Ancamma. It was a pointless way to die in many respects. She would have been better staying with us after all but she was not a fighter and Cimbrod had left her where he thought she would be safe. We had, after all, no way to predict that our plans would change so dramatically, nor that Piso was such a tricky opponent.

The smoke from Vindolanda was apparent before any structure declared itself. A huge column of black became visible ascending the horizon and darkening the sky ahead as we approached. The Romans had burned everything in the place. The main street, dark and ash-strewn ran straight as a spear through the remnants of the desolate little town. Piles of blackened, smoking, timber and smouldering thatch, the remnants of the shops and taverns, homes and cattle stalls, now rose on either side of the street where the thatched buildings had once stood. If our men had come with hopes of plunder then they would be disappointed, for there was nothing left to steal. All was as black as I imagined Cimbrod's thoughts would be as I rode through the remains of the town. I thought constantly about him and the pain he must be suffering.

I had memories of the bathhouse, now sagging, roofless and sad, with one wall missing and the roof caved in. I had hated my time as a soldier here, yet there was something deeply melancholy about the silent smoke and ruins, where people had lived and laughed, gambled and drunk. Mixed in with my almost nostalgic reminiscence was a deep, intense sense of loneliness and frustration which even Oenna riding beside me could not assuage. I looked at her and saw tears in her eyes and running down her cheeks. I knew what she was thinking, for Ancamma had been her friend too.

The Romans had left nothing they thought we could use. They already had our supplies and now they intended for us to be very hungry before we fought them. I had however, anticipated the possibility of running short of food, for I could not foresee how soon the wagons north of the wall would be able to join us. Against all advice, I had insisted every man had with him four day's supply of rations. It was fortuitous in the end.

We had to bring Piso to battle and soon. Our supplies would run out, and with empty stomachs, the men would not fight well—if at all. As the news spread that we had lost the supplies, men grumbled and I saw frowns and scowling faces everywhere. That they blamed me was clear, but it puzzled me why it should be so. Such events as losing supplies are common in war—one cannot account for the unpredictable.

We made camp as the sunlight began to fade, picking a spot north of the Vindolanda conflagration. The troops had no trouble lighting fires for they transported glowing embers from the ruined town and kept warm making fires from the death of the place, for it had no meaning to them. I sat at the entrance to my tent, which was a short stone's throw from where Drogo kept a lonely vigil, staring at the ground by his feet. What he had seen in the camp had depressed him I thought, but I felt very little for anyone but Cimbrod and I doubt now whether I even spared Drogo a meagre thought. I should have had concerns for him as my compatriot. I knew he had gotten to know Ancamma well and I should have seen how upset he was by her death.

Oengus came over while I was deep in thought, mulling over the loss of a close friend, poking disconsolately at the fire, and Oenna was inside our tent, tearful and emotional. She had said little since I broke the news to her. She and Ancamma had been close.

'I am sorry to hear of the loss of your friend Ancamma. I knew her too. She often traded on behalf of Drest among our people.'

'She did?'

'Yes, she was a fearsome trader. If you consider yourself an accomplished warrior, she was the same with the use of speech. Some of my people referred to her as "Thief, the Gaul". I remember once she bought a herd of cattle for Drest, and when she paid it cost her half of the worth of the herd because she had so charmed the owner he said "yes" when he meant "no".'

I said, 'I am sad losing her but I think I am more worried by her death than grieving. The fates can bring an end to any man at any time and everyone here in this army knows it. Ancamma was realistic and she was nobody's fool—she knew the risks as well as any of us. I am more concerned because of Cimbrod. His behaviour might become erratic. He is young and headstrong. You know Drosten killed his brother in cold blood.'

'No, I didn't'

'Well Cimbrod and I both want the man dead but he is protected by Nechtan. I have had an almost impossible task keeping my Cimbri friends from killing Drosten. It would make the alliance fall apart if it happened.'

'That is obvious. You think he will do something stupid?'

'I don't know. Much depends upon what we are doing. We have to find the Roman army and give battle. Once that is achieved Cimbrod will be engaged in the fighting and it is a good way to forget oneself, I have found,' I said.

'Yes, battle lust does that but we have to find our adversaries first.'

'I think Cimbrod will return with news of them.'

'Good intelligence is worth ten thousand men, Galdir. As you said, we need to locate the enemy soon and give battle before starvation defeats us. We have to find them.'

'We will have to give Cimbrod and Hengeist time. They will find the Romans, if they still live that is. With Ancamma dead Cimbrod may be crazed enough to attack the Romans with only the two of them.'

'We need Cimbrod. He is a great warrior.'

'Yes,' I said. 'We have to give him until tomorrow evening. Piso will choose his ground carefully. If I were him, I would pick some high ground from which to fight. He is not a very imaginative man you know, but he is no fool. I think his battle plans will be predictable.'

'I leave the battle plans to you. I came to express my unhappiness at your loss and to assure you I will support you when the council meets in the morning.'

'Oengus, I never doubted your support. I am glad to have you behind me.'

'You saved my daughter from those beasts. I owe you her

life.'

'I did it for honour's sake. I lost my temper too. There is no debt to repay.'

'My friend, that is not the Votadini way.'

He squatted beside me and reaching forward, touched my shoulder and I understood. He was a kinder man than I had realised. He had been trying to distract me from the disaster of losing the supplies and focus my thoughts for a few moments on the matter at hand. I knew deep inside he was right. When I went into my tent I embraced Oenna, and she for her part reached for me in a sleepy state and murmured with a soft voice something about our future son. I slept only in fits for there was much on my mind.

Soon before morning, the scream of some poor creature caught by a bestial prowler, startled me. I thought it might have been the death-scream of a hare, loud and surreal. I wondered if in some vague way it was symbolic. Perhaps it represented the shade of someone who had loved me, passing in the dim pre-dawn light and stopping to communicate pain or distress. I thought about Ancamma. She had been a good friend to us all with her constant teaching and guiding. She had been our link with the Caledonii and I felt weaker for the loss. I pictured her happy smiling face whenever she was with Cimbrod. It made me shudder for I wondered how I would react if the same fate came to Oenna.

I began to see things in a different way and wondered if my whole life was unlucky. Was it my nature or the Norns leading everyone around me to some grim and unpleasant fate? Then a thought came to me: how lucky I was in this strange misty country. I had found Oenna and she bore my child, my future. I had lost a friend but I had the one thing giving meaning to the whole strange vista before which I found myself.

Interspersed among those thoughts, my mind conjured up the last moments of my mentor's life. Cornelius had taught me much; he had loved me in his fashion, if indeed he was capable of loving anyone other than Livia, his niece and only surviving blood kin. His death had been miserable. He had an infection from a splinter in his foot and it was a strange, unjust way for such a man to die. The tiny wound festered and poisoned his whole leg, and a stupid farmer smothered him to speed his end and get us out of his farm. Cornelius had fought and killed men in fair fights for many years and he had taught me his gladiatorial skills. For such a man to die of a splinter in his foot seemed ironic and cruel. It only confirmed to me that the Gods are tricky, playing pranks on us for their twisted pleasure. Chlotsuintha had of course never seen it that way. She had served Wuotan since childhood and would have told me it was the God's intervention in our lives setting hurdles and pits to make us strong and give us incentive. That night was the first time I felt she was wrong.

Perhaps I had dozed off again after all, or perhaps it was another waking dream, but I saw in the roof of the tent, a tiny picture moving and then fading. It was a scene in a large hall. There was a King or Warlord seated on a golden-painted throne. He had a long grey beard and he sat straight with a look of anger on his face. On his head was a wide brimmed hat and he had only one eye and his left hand was missing. He pointed towards a tall blonde man with braided locks and a mail vest, who stood in front of him. I could only see the man from behind and could not identify him at first. The Warlord's lips curled in contempt. He held a huge spear in his right hand and his gown shimmered in the firelight. Either side of the chair, perched upon its back, were two ravens moving their heads from side to side as if curious to see the man who stood there before their Lord. At his feet were two wolves who sat, each with its head cocked to one side, also regarding the mortal who stood there.

I could hear the words 'Go home my son. Your people, my chosen ones, need you. Go home.' I noticed then that the one-eyed king ceased frowning, his face cracked into a smile like the rising sun, and he laughed aloud.

Then I heard him say, 'Complete the tasks I have set for you. Then we will feast and fight forever.'

I got up deciding sleep was impossible, with my mind racing as it was. I sat down outside, staring into the embers of the fire and pondered what I had seen. Was it my father communicating with me from Valhalla? Was it Wuotan himself, commanding me to return to Frankia?

I began to think that perhaps Oenna was deflecting me from my true path. If Chlotsuintha had always spoken truly then I was not supposed to be here at all. My tired mind seemed to deny the validity of what I was embarking upon. I had to have this war and I knew deep inside it was no longer for any of the reasons I had persuaded myself before. It had started as revenge on the Romans for all they had destroyed in my life but had become more than that. Oenna and the child she bore had changed my motivation, changed my plans. I now wanted my child to grow up in a free land, far from Roman meddling with those elusive things that had always before escaped me in life—happiness and freedom.

CHAPTER XVII

Cimbrod was the key. He and Hengeist led us to the Romans. He came the next morning; he held his head up, his eyes shiny with moisture, close to exhaustion. The dark shadows beneath his eyes were a testament of his feelings. There was no trace of a smile on his face and I realised he was older now, not in years but in his mind. So much loss in his short life had changed him. When he had embarked from his homeland he had been young, carefree and laughing. It had all been a game to him. This was not the same man who rode into the camp that day. The boy had died with his woman. The man had appeared and I alone, of all the assembled men who watched, understood. I had also lost in my life, and our losses formed a bond between us. It was friendship and grief bringing him to a halt at my tent.

We said nothing. There was nothing to say; we both knew that. Ancamma had been everything to him, as Oenna was to me, despite the short time Oenna and I had been together. He dismounted and looked into my eyes. Silence hovered between us like a morning mist.

'Ridden all night?' I said, breaking the silence in the end. I heard Drogo approach from my right. I had no need to look for only he would be foolish enough to interrupt.

Cimbrod said nothing. I could see the strain written on his face as obvious as if some tattooist had anointed him with an indelible dye. There was anger, hate and grief in his questioning eyes and still he stood looking at me in silence.

Drogo said, 'Cimbrod, I bore the tidings like you told me.'

Cimbrod, torn away from his thoughts, said, 'You did well Drogo. Leave us.'

'I am sorry for your loss Cimbrod.'

Cimbrod looked at him and Drogo stepped back as if Cimbrod had struck him. It was not that there was enmity there in that look, but there was danger all the same. The boy realised it and he knew no words were welcome here in this sad meeting of comrades. He turned and walked away leaving us staring at each other, knowing there was nothing worthwhile to say. I gestured the ground by the dying fire. We sat and eventually Cimbrod broke the silence, his voice flat.

'We followed the Romans after we burned Ancamma. They made an easy trail for there were many of them. I left Hengeist there and he will return if they move on.'

'They will pay.'

'Yes.'

'You have lost much my friend. We will kill Romans to-morrow. We will kill all of them and then find more. I swear it on Donar's hammer.'

'And Drosten, when we have finished.'

'Yes and then Drosten, for Adelmar.'

'Galdir...'

'What?'

'Nothing,' he said and put his head in his hands. I was

not the only one who had passed a sleepless night.

'You have no time now to think of what might have been, and grieve as a man should. We have work to do. We have vengeance to seek. I shall not rest until every Roman in these parts is dead.'

'Galdir, I wanted to take her home with me—to be my Queen. She... she...'

It may have been that I realised I was the older and I knew he respected me. I was the one with more life experience and he was looking to me for comfort and support. I understood too, it was one of the responsibilities of age at times when others need you. I had been Warlord of the Franks, should I not be able to counsel a friend in grief?

'Cimbrod,' I said, reaching across the grey and dying embers to touch his shoulder, 'whatever you have lost, you have more to do before the end. You recall my friend Lazygis, the Sarmatian?'

'Yes,' he said, weariness such as I had never heard before, apparent in his voice.

'He is a great warrior,' I went on. 'Marcus Aurelius killed his wife and son so he has a death wish. He rides and fights like some Fury from the underworld. He is always unscathed in battle as if the Gods refuse to let him die. He fights on and hopes for death, but they deny him. You can become like him or not, but you must not give up. There is nothing in this cold wet place left to live for, so should you not fight and die and join your loved one again all the sooner?'

He looked at me. He understood. He was young and should have had a long and prosperous life ahead, but he accepted what I had said and nodded with a fire of determination in his eyes. I realised almost as soon as I spoke I had kept back that Lazygis had mellowed and had a woman to care for now. I was telling Cimbrod what he needed to hear and I had not lied to him, I knew that.

After he left, Oenna joined me.

'Funny, I didn't dare come out.'

'What?'

'I don't know, he frightens me somehow.'

'Cimbrod? He's my friend.'

'I know that, but I sense there is something about him that is changing. I wish Ancamma was still alive. I valued her so much as a friend.'

'Me too. I find it hard she had gone.'

'No it's not that. I think she was the voice of reason and she kept him from his true nature.'

'Nonsense. He is just a young man. He is full of spirit and it has to come out somewhere or it will fester within him.'

'Perhaps,' she said.

'I still don't trust Drogo.'

'What?'

'Drogo. There's something about him I can't place but it's as if his eyes say something his tongue doesn't express.'

'What are you? A witch?' I said and smiled.

'We women have instincts you men could never fathom.'

'I don't doubt it but I know my countrymen, none of them would deceive their Warlord. They are brought up to believe him to be sacred and chosen by Wuotan.'

'You and your Gods. In this place our Gods are stronger.'

'Perhaps all Gods are the same, but they just take different forms.'

'Even Roman Gods?'

'Even Jupiter Optimus Maximus, yes.'

'You might be right, but our child? He will believe in the

Gods of his land.'

'You always seem so certain it is a boy.'

She said, 'You don't understand women. I can feel it. He moves inside me. Little quickenings I thought were just wind at first. He communicates with me.'

'I wish you had stayed in Bannatia.'

'No, my place is at your side.'

'Then that is good too. At least I can keep you safe,' I said.

She smiled and her eyes showed some deep thought, but I could not fathom it then. She had her own plans and hopes and who was I to stop her doing anything she wished? I was not yet her husband and if the Romans were not defeated, I never would be.

We ate a little bread and drank some of the vicious Britannic beer, and I went in search of the leaders of our army. I wanted to run over the points I had so often made to them. but in the end there was little to discuss. We had all come to fight, and now we had located the enemy there was no need for further delay. I thought the Britannic tribal leaders greeted the news with enthusiasm, even Nechtan seemed in good spirits as we broke up to organise our forces for the march.

We marched east. I was glad to see our men in better alignment and order than on the previous day and hoped it indicated a modicum of discipline, but I was always sceptical about that; I had fought with barbarian hordes many times in Germany and Gaul and knew how loose was their orderliness. Despite that, I thought that with thirty thousand men I could defeat any Roman Legion.

We came to a point where the military road ceased. I had no explanation for that. I assumed it was because we were nearing Hexacoria where the Romans would have headed. We were all relieved when Hengeist rode into our midst with the news the Romans had re-crossed the wall and were camped only a few miles east of our position.

The weather had brightened into a warm spring day and I knew if it held, my army would have good enough morale to do what I required of them. We laid plans that night and elected to move east again at first light. I cautioned the leaders that our men would fight best if they rested for an hour or so and ate before we attacked our enemies, recalling only too well how Hannibal had won the battle of Trebia by not allowing the Romans to eat beforehand, and I wondered if we could do the same. In the event, it proved impossible to engage them in time, or maybe the Romans had learned their lesson all those years ago.

When we arrived it was two hours past dawn. We ascended a rise ahead of us and saw them drawn up on a hill opposite, across a wide plain. Thin, wispy clouds passed overhead and the morning sun stood well above us as we obtained our first glimpse of the Roman army. It was a fearsome sight for many of the Britons. They had no doubt counted on their numerical superiority but I think they realised quickly this was a professional force of Roman soldiers ready and waiting for our advance across the field. Their silent ranks lined the hill like a palisade.

We sat on our mounts on the hilltop; Oenna, Cimbrod, Lutrin, Drogo and I, surveyed the scene. Say what you like about the Romans, they know how to organise an army. The regularity of the troops and the tidiness of their formations rankled as much now as it had done on the raid I had been on north of the wall. It must be understood I had never been used to fighting among men whose main aim in life was to fight in a tidy way. "Tidy" was the word that came to mind as I looked across that verdant Britannic vale at the assembled Romans. Tidy is all you can say. In Frankia, my men had been impossible to keep in any kind of disciplined order but they fought their hearts out anyway. They shouted my name as they died in droves, battling against overwhelming odds, for they loved me. I never understood how the Romans still fought with such passion despite the dreary discipline with which they did everything.

I stared across the valley and Oenna commented, 'Orderly fellows those.'

Lutrin laughed, 'It won't save them. Galdir, how does it feel to be the instrument of the Gods?'

'I don't think that is what I am. I am just a leader and nothing more. Only time will tell whether I am worthy of that role or not.'

'Galdir,' Oenna said, 'you are worthy of it. Have faith. Don't lose your nerve now you are so close to achieving our aims.'

'No, precisely what I was going to say,' Lutrin piped up.

I frowned as I looked at my woman. 'I'm not losing my nerve and I won't do either, as long as you stay here on this hill whatever happens. Do you hear?'

'I will do what is required of a sword maiden of the Briton army. If you want anything else from me you will have to find another woman on which to sire your pups.'

I flushed but said nothing. There was no controlling this woman and deepest in I knew it. I looked across the valley. I examined my troops and my eyes wandered to the Roman army again.

I could see him then. Marcus Licinius Piso. He was riding his white stallion behind the ballistae at the top of the hill. His shiny helm, which had a purple horsehair plume, hid his fair hair. His armour was black. It was a habit in the Roman army not to burnish armour if you were a general for it made you an instant target for archers. I could not make out his face with any clarity, but I had seen him often enough in Vindolanda to know how he would look. His face had acquired lines and wrinkles from the stress of being in command here in the far north of the Empire. It always amused me. Had I not been indirectly instrumental in his posting?

I had only ever spoken to him three times. Once was when I had returned his wife to him in exchange for Frija and he had tried to trap me with an ambush of equites. The second was when he explained my position in the Roman army.

He had said, 'You are nothing now. I will reduce you further. You are my dog, my slave, to run errands, to fight whomsoever I tell you to and never to question. If there is dissent, your precious Franks will suffer. Oh and Galdir? Just remember I forget nothing. I recall how arrogant you were on that hilltop in Frankia. I am in command now and you will remember it.'

I had no regard for the man anyway because he was a political animal and little else, but it was as if he and I were linked somehow in our hatred for each other. My destiny had damaged his and at times, I felt the converse was also true. I suppose one cannot blame him for being bitter; like me, he was an unwilling guest in this bleak country and like me, he was fighting for his life.

I stared across the verdant plain straight at him. I saw him pause then, as if some ghostly hand held him in its clutches and although neither of us could see the other with clarity, it seemed he noticed me. Perhaps at that distance he recognised Valknir or perhaps he really did know who confronted him. I remember thinking there were many things he did not know. He did not know I had been a slave in his home and I escaped by killing his father. He had even less inkling I had slept with his willing wife when she had been my prisoner. I despised him for his ignorance. It was akin to what I had felt looking at him in his Praetorium on the wall, standing next to Lazygis while he ranted and raved at us. It seemed an eternity away yet fresh in my mind.

I smiled to myself. It was as if I had taken everything that mattered from this man right in front of his nose and it had prepared him for this day, when he would die. That knowledge made me feel powerful. It was like plucking a chicken ready for the pot. It would be a red day on which one of us would spend our venom on the other and mete out the death and destruction that only Tiu the War-God takes such pleasure in promulgating. I could almost hear the Gods laughing at the irony of this struggle between us, for the Roman knew nothing and his ignorance made him foolish and weak in my eyes. I am ashamed of those thoughts now. Despite his words when he ordered Lazygis and me to Cataractonium, all I had done to him in the past was dishonourable. I regretted none of it but should have seen that honour should be everything to a man and I had betrayed mine. Sleeping with another man's wife behind his back was like a Roman; killing a man by bludgeoning him with an oil lamp too, was not the act of an honourable man. It had brought me to this day; I was here not for honour but revenge, and vengeance is a poor motivation for anything in life. Bitterness after all, breeds nothing but bitterness.

Our men drew up along the brow of the hill opposite the

Romans. We were out of range of their ballistae, the bolts from which could skewer two or three men at once and had an enormous range. I looked at the opposition. They must have numbered about ten thousand as Cimbrod had rightly judged. Only seven thousand of them were regulars and the rest were auxiliaries. I was pleased to see there were no Sarmatians. They had their cavalry drawn up at either side no doubt to out-flank us as we ran up the hill towards them. I had thought that was what they would do so I had the majority of our spearmen at the flanks. Horses do not like spears. I remembered Hannibal, but to my knowledge he had always picked his own ground and had not fought uphill in any of his battles. Weighed against that was the fact we outnumbered them by almost three to one, disadvantaged as we were by our lack of good armour.

I could see the ranks of the legionaries neatly formed up, still and silent in their staggered centuries. I was uncertain whether they would open out their ranks when we attacked, but more likely they would stand together and use their shields side by side hoping my men would crowd and push each other onto the Roman short swords. I had thought of that too. My infantry in the centre were mainly half-naked warriors and they had long swords and axes. They were careless of their own lives, but we had instructed them to open out and surge forward in waves so the men at the back could replace those who had tired in front of them. If they did not pack too tight they could use their weapons without closing on the Roman's front ranks, but if they did, they had shields of a sort and short blades at their waists.

Our cavalry and chariots remained on the hill. If the Romans broke through the Nudis in the centre, then our mounted forces would assail them, protected by our spearmen, while the second layer of our infantry turned inwards to attack the flanks. It was a good plan but nothing happens the way you plan it in a battle. There are too many unpredictable factors, many of which require changes of direction at a moment's notice.

I knew Piso would stay where he was. He would have been stupid to advance upon us. We too were on a hill and if he attacked us, our numbers would tell very quickly.

The Romans are sticklers for routine. I knew precisely when they would have their next meal and I instructed my men to eat heartily in advance. I wanted to attack before the Romans could eat. They would be the ones to run out of stamina before us. It was a minor element of strategy, but after a few hours of fighting men get very hungry and soldiers know to eat well before battle. The only missing piece of the puzzle was the Sarmatians. I hoped Lazygis had managed to avoid being here. If they arrived, they might have to fight.

CHAPTER XVIII

"The wise learn many things from their foes"
—Aristophanes

An hour after we spread our forces out upon the hill, we advanced. My mouth was parched and my heart beat like a drum. I sat upon Valknir and watched as my men moved fast across the grassy plain below in the warm spring sunshine. It reflected off their weapons and helmets and they looked a vast and fearsome horde. I hoped they would keep their heads like the Romans on the hillside above them, but it was all so uncertain. Cimbrod sat on his steed next to me, quiet and thinking deeply. His face showed none of the anxiety I felt. Oenna's horse seemed restless and kept moving around for it was a feisty stallion, a gift from her brother before we set out.

'Look,' I said, pointing to two neat rows of wooden machines at the summit of the Roman hill, 'ballistae.'

'I see them,' Cimbrod said.

'Nechtan had better get his men spread out. Concentrated as they are, they'll take huge casualties.'

'Don't worry Galdir, they know what to do. I can see Drosten there just reaching the lower slopes.'

'I hope a ballista bolt doesn't get him. I want him alive for later.'

'Yes.'

'Drest has the right flank, I trust him you know.'

'Yes, me too, but I have worries the mixture of tribes he's commanding might not obey him. If they don't, we could have a very bad day.'

Cimbrod shifted in his saddle. He seemed ill at ease and I knew what was perturbing him.

'You want to be down there don't you?'

'Of course.' he said.

'Why don't you go down to the left flank with Oengus? He and Morleo would make good sword-brothers.'

'Perhaps I'll take your advice. I'm better fighting than watching.'

He turned then and cast me a glance of expressionless calm. Oenna smiled at him and he replied with a wan betrayal of a smile, for it meant nothing. I could still feel his pain, but like him I recognised a battlefield is no place for sentiment.

Valknir was restless too beneath me. He was battle trained and had fought with me many times. I think he was eager to join the progressing battle and I had to keep tight rein on him and talk often in his ear to stop him moving forward. I cast my mind back to another battle when I had ridden with my uncle's forces against a similar force. In that fight we had encircled the Romans, and the Sarmatians, a thousand of them, had decimated the Roman legionaries. Lazygis seemed conspicuous by his absence and I wondered what had happened to him. If Piso failed to use the Sarmatians, he was an even bigger fool than I had thought.

I had six messengers with me and it was their job to ride with any new instructions if a change was required. Drogo was one. I explained to him what I thought would happen.

'One of two things is likely,' I said.

'Yes Galdir,' he said.

'If my plan works, then the centre will give ground and our flanks will turn in to take the Romans as they advance. Our cavalry should hold them. If the Roman centre gives way then the more distant men of the flanks will fold around like we did with the cohort we fought back there on the wall.'

'I have never seen so many men together since Sicambra. I was only fighting those last few days for I joined our army from the south after the siege had begun. My mother said I was too young to fight.'

'From the south?'

'Yes, I ran away from home in the end. I stole my father's sword and shield.'

'How did you get into the town? Two days before the final battle we had everything locked up tight.'

'The gate guards knew me for a Frank. They let me in.'

'Where did you say you were brought up?'

'In a small town south of Sicambra, Eudes was our King.'

I looked at him with a frown. There was something wrong about what he had said but I had no time to think further on it.

'Drogo, ride over to Drest and tell him to keep his spearmen back. His flank is wide open to the equites on the hill. Why don't people listen?'

Drogo rode away and I could see him heading towards Drest with arrows flying around him. He rode with his head down and his shield up which seemed sensible to me.

Alone now, apart from Lutrin and Oenna, I surveyed the scene. Our front ranks had spread out and the Roman missiles had begun to take their toll of the bare-chested blue-dyed Britons. Men lay in the sward, bleeding and writhing. I could see one bolt that had penetrated two men and one of them was still moving, trying to free himself from his bloody twin. Blood was visible layered on the once verdant ground even from where I sat, and all the time I could hear the battle cries of my men and almost hear the silence in the Roman ranks. Our left flank had moved forward a little slower than the right and it gave the swarm of native warriors an unbalanced appearance from where I was watching. We overlapped them and had twice the depth of warriors. The barrage of ballista bolts continued until our front ranks were twenty yards from the Romans and then the Pilae came flying overhead. The Roman javelins transfixed men and shields and many of the Britons had to abandon their shields for they could not extract the javelins whose tips had bent on contact with the hard wood.

Lutrin said, 'it is a great moment and one I have worked for all my life.'

'You have?'

'Since I became a novice at the age of ten. I learned what the Romans did to the Druids in the south. I swore by Cerrunos we would be avenged upon the Romans and we would take back that which is ours. Now is the hour and this battle is only a beginning.'

'Well if Drest doesn't pull back his spearmen it will be a very short beginning. Look.'

'That's not what you told him to do,' Oenna said.

'No. Maybe poor Drogo didn't get through.'

'I saw him get there. Look that's him,' she said, pointing, 'you can see his horse.'

'Drest must be ignoring Drogo's message. It's not like him.'

I looked to the left flank. I could see our men pushing forward steadily and pushing back the Tungrians, not by numbers, but by the ferocity of the open-order attack of Oengus' men. They had spread out and were using their long weapons to tease the Tungrians out of line. As each man fought, once he stepped forward, my men would use the advantage of their longer weapons and the Romans would die. The Votadini had not pressed forward but were fighting hard. I could see Oengus with Cimbrod beside him and they stood forward leading their men in the melee. I think my men's unwillingness to crowd forward must have surprised the Romans. Our battle lines surged forwards almost rhythmically. It is often so in battle for at the front line there is no constant pressure; for five minutes or so there is fierce fighting then one or other side drops back and there is a pause before another wave of slaughter begins. It is like watching waves striking the shore.

The left flank was tidy and as the Tungrians began to drop back, bands of the heavy infantry began to curl around to attack their right flank, exactly as I had planned. The spearmen held off the cavalry who were powerless, despite launching several charges. They could not outflank us because of the length of our lines.

My heart leapt. We were winning and the Britons were displaying a tight discipline I had never imagined they possessed. The right caused me some concern for the spearmen had still moved forward and the Roman cavalry had moved around successfully. In a few minutes, they would be behind Drest's men and charge home. They would beset Drest on two sides and I felt uneasy because I knew the immediate response would be for the Britons to bunch up, which was exactly what the Romans would want with their short weapons. The centre was holding as well, which came as a surprise to me as I had expected them to back away to lead the middle of the Roman army onto the plain where we could assail them on three sides.

I had a thousand men on horseback lining the crest of the hill from which I watched. Oenna, Lutrin and I were alone apart from my messengers. I saw no sign of Drogo. I had to make a decision. It was too late to send another rider to Drest. There was no time. When needs must a man has to act, as they say, and I knew we had to attack the Romans cavalry before they had a chance to charge. I summoned the commander of the mounted Britons, a small, broad, black-bearded man called Odgar. He had a talent for riding and his people, the Venicones, favoured him because of his skilful horsemanship. Although he wore a leather breastplate his arms were bare and blue-painted, and he smiled as he approached.

'Quite a fight,' he said.

'Odgar, we have to attack the Roman cavalry now. There is little time. You see them riding around the right flank?'

'Yes, but there are two thousand of them at least. We have only half their number. Their horses are much bigger than ours too.'

'Since when does that make a difference? We are warriors. When Drest sees us ride down, he will send his spearmen. I have sent a rider to him. Blow your horn man.'

Valknir reared and I knew he could sense what was to come and was excited at the prospect of some action. I had no illusions we could defeat twice our number but we had to punch through them or the whole of the right flank would fold as the Romans advanced.

I quieted Valknir for a moment, and turning to Oenna told her firmly, 'You stay here. I have to move on and lead the cavalry.'

'Of course.'

I glanced back at her over my shoulder. Doubt came for an instant for her reply was so uncharacteristic of the stubborn girl I knew her to be. She was smiling too. My attention flew away however, for Odgar blew his horn.

The entire mounted force formed up, at least as much as any barbarian cavalry ever did. By that I mean they conglomerated, but they did so with admirable speed and I walked Valknir to their head with Odgar beside me. He looked up at me and smiled, 'I thought I would never get into the fight, no warrior wants to watch from a hill.'

'My friend, you echo my thoughts with an accuracy of a mirror.'

Beaming, I was riding to battle; it felt good. Until then the fighting had been a vague far-off thing, something to take seriously, but not a matter that drew the vigour coursing through my veins as I experienced now. I could feel my pulse rising and a heady feeling began to take me as always happens when my blood is up. I heard Lutrin begin one of his damned chants. It did nothing for me, but it may have encouraged the Britons, so I felt no real irritation over it. As we rode forward his voice disappeared into the clamour and the sound of hoof beats beneath us.

I was beginning to realise that like Cimbrod, I wanted with mounting desperation to be in the thick of it and in the front line. Perhaps it was immature of me to want to fight, but although I was the over-all commander I was becoming more and more restless, seated on a fine warhorse doing nothing but move the pieces on the board in front of me and break wind. If that was what being a general was all about, then I preferred not to be one. We rode.

It was then things began to go wrong. How badly wrong

became obvious as the day wore on. My purpose was to engage the Roman cavalry, not to drive them off, for we were outnumbered. I had hoped Drest would see what was happening and obey the orders I had entrusted to Drogo. I was riding at a gentle trot at the head of my men, when it occurred to me perhaps Drogo had been killed by some stray arrow or javelin, but even so I trusted Drest and knew he would observe what was transpiring so close to his flank.

We cantered to within a hundred yards of the Romans, then slowed a little for the horses to gain their breath, and as soon as Valknir's breathing had settled we started our approach. The Romans had seen us of course and they had detached half their number to swat us away. They expected us to be easy prey to their bigger horses and their long spears. Although a few of my men, mainly wild northerners, did charge straight into the Romans, almost all of us stayed tightly formed up together. We were in a rough wedge—when I say rough, I mean a very rough wedge formation, for these were wild men, not Romans.

Our pace picked up slowly at first. With fifty yards to go, the Romans came on too. They were in a square formation, ready to wrap around us when the apex of our men had penetrated them. We rode down a slight slope towards them. Our pace increased to a canter at thirty yards. We accelerated. I could feel Valknir beneath me, his withers rising and falling. My horizon bobbed as I put my weight into my stirrups. My hand held a spear not unlike those we kill boars with in the woods. The tip was of heavy iron and I could swing it as well as use it to stab. On my left arm, I carried a shield. I remembered how Oenna had given it to me. It had a bronze boss shaped like an eagle and she had laughed when she presented it. She said it would be eagle against eagle. I could ill afford the sentiment beginning to arise in me so I put away all feelings apart from rage and it gripped me like an adamantine fist.

I am not a man given to war-shouts like most German warriors, but the battle rage had me in its folds and my blood was up. I screamed, 'Wuotan!'

That scream echoed from my throat over and over again. I realised then why men do that. It released me from the pent up fury devouring us in a charge. In silence, I think I would have burst. I vented all my anger in those first few moments. We hit their front row of horsemen, with a sound rising in the air like some massive cataclysm. Valknir reared. He was excited too and even with stirrups I had a hard time to remain in the saddle.

His hooves were flailing; he whinnied and blew. The horse in front collapsed with its head crushed. He began biting anything in sight. It was as well we were in front or he would have chewed the rump of one of the little Votadini ponies. The trick is never to be still for a moment. If you stop, you are dead; dragged to the ground or stabbed with a spear. My momentum took me well into the Roman ala. Had I tried to continue they would have attacked me from behind. I wheeled my beautiful, wonderful steed and he responded as I had trained him, bucking and biting. The noise of horses whinnying, men screaming and the cries of wounded men trampled underfoot filled my ears and my spirit. It must have echoed all the way to Asgard for the Gods to hear. I think looking at the outcome they must have been well pleased by our efforts.

I buried my spear in the throat of a Roman as he tried to strike at one of my men. I wrenched it free. I continued to wheel, striking blows with the spear. Man after man fell before me. Blood flew in a spray all around. My spear wedged in a shield but I tugged on it and it came away. A spear struck my shield hard. It almost unhorsed me. Another struck my helmet. I was wild and angry; hot, red rage consumed me and I felt invulnerable. I battered all around me.

Considering I was the leader of every man on the field that day, I should have had more sense than to be there, right in the middle of an ala of Roman cavalry, battling and raging, but it felt more exhilarating than anything else could in the world.

The little ponies were not in the least dismayed at their opponents and they did exactly as I did, their riders wheeled and struck with their spears and shields. It is an odd thing but the difference in height between our opponents and us did not seem to give the Romans much advantage at all. Our ponies were fast moving and sturdy, whereas the Roman horses seemed clumsy by comparison when we were all pressed together.

I came up against a big man with a sideways mounted plume. He was an officer. He came at me with a snarl. He thrust his spear at my face. I turned my head just in time. The tip scraped my cheek-guard. I fended off his weapon with my shield. I replied with my spear. It entered his chest with an audible thud, even in that noisy fracas. For a split second, I could see the look of surprise in his eyes as he slumped sideways and his blood ran down the shaft of my lance. It stuck fast of course and although I had another, I had no time to unfasten it. I held up my shield as I drew my long sword. It was a heavy German weapon and although it had not the reach of a spear, it was well suited to its use. I had often practised riding fast, leaning forward and skewering an apple on the sward. I remembered Cimbrod then for he had teased me telling me I would make a good cook but he could do better.

Valknir began to tire; he was big a horse and must have burned up much energy. I could feel him breathing hard and knew it was time either to emerge on the opposite side or to turn back and wait to mount another charge. I realised then the main reason why my men, fierce as they were and strong as they seemed, were able to continue. Many had fallen but the little ponies were very hardy and strong. They seemed as fresh as if they had just trotted a hundred yards in the spring sunshine on a day out in the hills. They continued to run rings around our Roman foes. The Romans could not fell our mounts because they were low on the ground but that was not true for my men. The Britons had a way of stabbing the Roman horses in the belly, which brought many of them down. I think this was one reason why we were so successful against our big Roman adversaries. They did not stop and the Romans began to fall back. I could see the dismay on their faces for they had thought they would be fighting children, perhaps because the Briton's mounts looked like children's horses next to the big roan and chestnut Roman horses. Bigger is not always better I realised with a grin.

I fought my way back in the throng. I hacked one man's head so hard, my blow split both leather helm and skull. I swung the sword around me in circles. I emerged beyond my men and turned. Blood and gore covered me but I felt good whatever the outcome was going to be. If the Valkyrs came for me it would have been a good day to go to the long feasting with the Allfather, but it was not to be; I had much more to do in this life and I knew it. All around me and in front there were little fights. The main body of Romans was drawing away gradually. They found it hard to withdraw too for my men came after. I could see Odgar swinging his spear and wailing like a tornado. No wonder the Romans were loath to engage him: he rode striking at anything coming near, blood covering his shield and arms. I pursued him and gave my orders. He blew his horn and we withdrew to within fifty yards. We had not routed the Romans but they needed to rest their horses. Ours seemed as fresh as when we had started, so this time I took Odgar's advice and we charged them again. Valknir was very tired but not blown. All the same, I rode slower this time and it gave me time to think.

It was then my heart sank. It was Oenna. I saw her at the back of our formation out of the corner of my eye. It made me furious. It was an anger borne of concern. She had followed despite what I had said to her. I saw her horse rear as she disentangled herself from the Roman equites. She waved her bloodstained sword in the air. A Roman approached and she grounded her steed and rode straight at him. She was on a bigger horse than the other Britons and she charged like a professional, her arm outstretched before her and a cry on her lips like a Valkyr. My jaw dropped as I saw her fight. The mounted soldier facing her was a big man. He carried his spear steady and firm. He aimed straight at her chest. His longer reach made my heart leap for it gave him such an advantage. I knew he must kill her. I rode towards her. To my amazement she continued, unabashed and still whooping. The spear-point reached forward. It had almost reached her. She swivelled in her saddle and struck the shaft. It deflected and she regained her upright position. As the rider passed her on the right she struck, backhand and fast. It hit the Roman on the neck and he flew from his steed. It was a quick, fast blow and worthy of the best of mounted swordsmen.

My mind was in turmoil. I had thoughts of anger at her disobedience. I had feelings of envy for it was a fabulous stroke. I felt concern for her and our child; unborn, yet part of a great and cataclysmic battle. Over-riding it all however, I felt pride. This was my woman and she was a Valkyr. She was a true warrior and a kind of woman I had never seen before. Beautiful, gentle and emotional but built of the fires of Jotunheim, a giant among women and my true sword-sister.

She smiled when I approached.

'I told you I could fight,' she said grinning.

I frowned and said, 'I see now I was wrong, but please go back to the hill, I have to have someone to watch the battle. Please.'

She looked at me with a strange sadness in her eyes.

She mouthed the words across the din of the battle, 'I love you.'

Then she rode away to do my bidding and it released me in a strange way, for I had not now to worry over her and I could concentrate better upon the matter at hand.

Where was Drest? He must have seen us drive into the Roman cavalry. He knew as I did; the spearmen were our best defence against the cavalry, yet no one seemed to pay any attention to the heroics engaging my mounted men. Where were his spearmen? I slowed to rest Valknir and grabbed a man at random by the arm.

'I need you to ride to Drest over there,' I said pointing.

He almost took me with him as he turned his horse around and the stupid man seemed not to understand I wanted him to deliver a message.

'Wait,' I shouted.

He paused then and I told him what to say. I was brief and began with an even briefer assessment of his intellect. He rode away shaking his head and I followed behind my men towards the now tiring Roman cavalry who turned and faced us. I could see their mounts were close to exhaustion, sweating and blowing. It turned out they had run short of fodder days before, as we discovered later, which explained their poor showing that day. Onward rode my intrepid Brittunculi, the Nudis and whatever else the Romans called us. On we came and we had blood on our minds and anger in our hearts, none more so than I.

Hate is a poor emotional basis for anything in life and it clouds your judgement. It is possible to achieve the greatest things in life in the name of love, but what is there in history that is worthwhile, that was ever achieved by hatred? I focussed on my enemy and my detestation was getting the better of me. Perhaps the death wish Lazygis had carried for the time I had known him had infected me, I cannot say. My place was not there in the midst of a group of fighting horsemen; it was on the hilltop with Oenna overlooking the scene as a whole for I was leader and not a fighting man. It is often a hard lesson to learn.

CHAPTER XIX

"Force has no place where there is need of skill"
—Herodotus

On the left flank, things had gone well. Oengus, Morleo, Cimiod and Cimbrod executed the plan with a precision that, knowing barbarian warfare, would have made a Roman martinet proud. On their right flank, the Romans had kept their two thousand Gallic cavalrymen well back at first and predictably, used them to threaten our left flank. They rode around us, as one might expect, to charge into the rear of our men's lines. They had to ride a long way, for our lines were longer than the Roman infantry ranks ranged above us on the slopes of the hill.

The Damnonii were fanatical swordsmen. They had groups of axe-men too, but the novel alterations I had brought about were the formation of squads of spearmen with both the usual spears but also long wooden poles which could be employed against cavalry by bracing one end in the ground and angling the sharpened, fire-hardened ends up to make an almost impenetrable wall. If they got the timing right it would skewer the front rank of charging enemy horses and deter further cavalry activity. There was no way the infantry could rout the cavalry of course, because I had taken all the mounted men we had to our right flank in my attack on the Roman cavalry there, and spearmen cannot run like a horse can.

The Votadini, Damnonii and Venicones had engaged the Tungrians and kept to open order as I had trained them to do and this was successful for our men did not squash up behind. The Romans changed tactics and opened their lines but it was a disaster for them with their short weapons against the longer weapons of the Briton's warriors. Our casualties were much lighter than is usual in these battles, and after the first hour we pushed the Romans back. Our line began to overlap and assailed the Romans on their flank and their front. The spearmen kept the cavalry away and the Roman right flank began to fold. They routed, chased by Oengus and Cimbrod.

In the centre, things did not go well and I do not know whether it was Nechtan who decided he knew better than I did or not, but he bunched his men and the result was the predictable slaughter the Romans so enjoy. The Batavian cohorts pressed forward into the Britons and that forward pressure pushed the Caledonii even more densely together. Their long weapons were of little use and it decimated them with each surge of front-line activity. They gave ground and it drew the Romans forward. When the Roman right flank gave way, half of them turned to face Oengus' men.

I of course, was oblivious to all this. Our second charge had driven off the Roman cavalry and my men had given chase. They whooped and screamed as they tried to chase the bigger Roman steeds. They did catch a number, because the Roman horses were blown, but most of them escaped back to where their fresh one thousand cavalrymen waited. Odgar tried to sound the retreat but no one heeded him and the battle fury drew us inexorably towards the fresh Roman cavalry.

378

I stood out in the mass of men, for Valknir was a tall horse and I was at the same level as the Romans. There must have been some archers nearby although I had not seen them, for a sudden hail or arrows came and they had aimed most of them at me. I protected myself with my shield as well as I could, but as the man to my left fell, gurgling blood, skewered in the throat by a missile, I felt a searing pain in my thigh and Valknir reared. The arrow had pierced the outer side of my thigh and passed through the saddle beneath, pricking his chest. Another arrow hit my right shoulder but bounced off the mail I wore, leaving only a bruise. I could neither ride straight nor could I dismount. I was pinioned to my horse whose behaviour became more and more erratic with the constant pricking from the arrow tip.

I gained enough control over Valknir to turn him, and cantered back a hundred yards. I stood alone. I was breathing hard as I broke the arrow and with both hands lifted my leg off the shaft. There was pain, but I think my battle-fervour was still filling my veins for it was bearable. Blood ran down my leg over my greave but I was able to move now. I lifted the saddle flap and removed the arrow, tugging it free from the thick leather with difficulty. It was then I gleaned some knowledge of what was transpiring. To my left I could see the Caledonii line moving back and at last, in front of me, I saw Drest's Vacomagi spearmen pressing forward into the Roman cavalry who were busy slaughtering Odgar's mounted warriors. The fresh thousand Roman cavalry had charged and our men were fighting like Furies just to stay alive.

The overall plan was still intact. I needed to prevent the centre of the Roman army from turning and attacking

Drest's men. We still had a thousand chariots up on the slopes of the hill and I rode in that direction ready to lead them down. I could see Oenna, astride her horse talking to Lutrin and pointing at something to her left. The reassurance that she was safe gave me strength.

I had never liked chariots in a battle and regarded them as unreliable. A driver and a light infantryman occupied each one. The design of them was to be fast. They dropped off their man and then returned when he had done the intended damage. The problem that had made me reluctant to use them here was the terrain. The grassy plain was full of hummocks and mounds and I anticipated a good many of the chariots falling to pieces even if the occupants could stay inside.

I arrived on the hill and shouted to the chariot commander, a sturdy Caledonian called Uvan, to attack the Roman centre and reinforce Nechtan's men who were on the point of routing. The Roman centre had driven them towards the now empty left side of the plain. Uvan smiled as if I had gifted him my horse. He turned, still grinning, and signalled his men. They charged full pelt down the hill as if they had been waiting all day for the command, which I suppose they had.

I rode with them and to my surprise the chariot riders must have been used to driving in those conditions for spills were infrequent despite the helter-skelter pace. In spite of the pain from my leg, I rode at their head and as Nechtan's forces parted to let us through, we struck the Romans hard on their left flank. The first charge carried us through the lines of legionaries and I found myself once more gripped by a rising rage. Chariots around me mowed down the unhappy Tungrians and I heard them die screaming. I struck with my

five men with drawn swords and a lone rider, weapon in hand, approaching them at a gallop, oblivious of their numbers. It took my breath away as I rode Valknir down the slope to try to help. I was reminded of Lazygis attacking Romans at the siege of Sicambra—hopeless odds, but staunch and rampant courage sweeping all away before it.

Cimbrod, for it was he, swung his sword to left and then right in almost one movement. It happened so fast the blade became a swirling, flying blur of light, caught in the rays of dying daylight. Both men fell from their horses and he was on to the remainder who had scattered. He had no chance and I knew it. If only I could spur Valknir to one, last spurt of speed. It was hopeless, I had seventy yards to clear, but there was no way I could get there in time to save my friend. Fool! How could he give his life away like this? It was suicide. There was still an element of jealousy dominating my thoughts like every other time I had seen him fight. He was fantastic, a natural, and perhaps I had most difficulty with the fact he had no need of me. I came to terms with it in the end for I admired him, but the thing that rankled was I realised he was better than I was and it always sat ill with me.

Cimbrod turned his mount neatly and moved him sideways. He slammed into one of the bodyguards. The man fell from his horse, the stupid Roman saddle giving him little support. There were two men left protecting the General. Piso was trying to regain control of his mount for it had panicked when the Cimbrian had entered the fray. It was a beautiful horse that, but not one I would ever have wanted in a real fight. I saw Cimbrod turn again. Never still, he swung his sword at the remaining two mounted bodyguards. He slashed one across the face. With a speed I had never thought possible he turned to his left and parried a blow from the other. He spurred his horse past his opponent and struck him backhand as neatly as Oenna had done. There was only one man left. It was Licinius Piso.

I could see the look of terror on my enemy's face and he began riding away, Cimbrod following. I had to slow Valknir then for I realised he was blown at last, and no matter how much I dug in my heels, he could not canter any longer. A wise cavalryman never over-rides his horse. A good horse will ride until it dies for a master it loves and one has to be very careful and observant for the signs of exhaustion in a mount like my Valknir. What a horse, what a companion!

I could see Cimbrod in the distance following the Roman General, gaining on him inch by inch as the Legate tried to get away from this horrific blood-drenched monster who followed with such clear intentions. They rounded a copse of oak and aspen trees and I lost them for a moment. When I could see them again, I saw Piso's white stallion first. He stood disconsolate and quiet with his head down, trailing his halter.

As I approached, the steed did not move; he shook his head but remained where he was. I looked down at the bloodied ground and saw, to my irritation, Piso lying there, with an ugly rent in his throat and a grimace on his face, his mouth a crimson mockery of his delicate Patrician lips. There was no escaping the truth that Cimbrod had beaten me to it. Killing a Roman General was a major event in the battle, and I felt satisfied, even though I was disappointed I had not done it myself.

'Quite a battle that,' a voice behind me said.

I turned and greeted Cimbrod who rode his horse towards me. Weariness consumed me. It had not been like any battle I had been in before. I had always ended laughing and joyful to be alive. This time I was just tired.

'Yes,' I said, 'how did you fare?'

'As well as I wanted.'

I gestured towards the fallen bodyguard on the hill. 'You killed them all.'

'Like you said, even when you try to die the Gods don't let you.'

'No. I suppose not. That reminds me. I won't have prisoners taken, you had better tell the men.'

'My men are already making sure of that. Oengus knows what to do.'

'I have never seen a warrior with the skill you show on horseback. I am honoured to call you my sword-brother,' I said.

'I told you I could fight.'

'Yes my friend,' I said with a half-smile, 'but when you insist on head-butting your opponents shield's one moment, you can expect to surprise your comrades when you outshine the best in another.'

'It seems like an age ago now, Galdir.'

'I think we have both changed since then.'

'I can't stop thinking about her. All through the battle during the killing and even when I cut the bastard's throat, I had her face in my mind. It hurts so much. The pain is almost more than I can bear.'

'Time will pass and it will help. It won't heal but in years to come the pain will come less often; all we can hope for is the Gods give us other things to distract us, or else we die in battle. Before I met Oenna I no longer cared which to be honest, for I had lost many who were dear to me too.'

I reached forward and squeezed his arm.

'At least we won the battle,' he said.

'Cimbrod, there was an odd thing that happened and it nearly cost us the victory,' I said as we rode.

'Oh?'

'Yes, I sent Drogo to tell Drest to keep his spearmen on the flank. He put them in the middle instead. You don't know whether or not Drogo was killed do you? Maybe he never delivered the message.'

'He was alive an hour ago. I saw him. He was riding as if the Valkyrs were after him towards the retreating Gallic cavalry. I suppose in a way a Valkyr was after him, I saw Oenna riding after him, to get him back. She called to him to stop. I hope she caught him because the Romans might have killed him, but I suppose his battle-lust had swallowed him whole.'

'That's twice she's disobeyed me. I told her to stay up on the hill with Lutrin.

'You expect a woman like that to obey you? You're mad.'

'Perhaps,' I said, seeds of doubt growing in my mind. 'We need to call a council and decide where we go next. There must be three thousand Romans left who made it to Hexacoria. We have to choose between following and besieging the place or sweeping south towards Cataractonium and Eburacum where the plunder is to be found.'

'Not just plunder. The Second Legion is at Eburacum.'

'We will swat them away. We still outnumber them almost three to one. The Britons have learned how to defeat the Romans and I know they can do it again. Don't you realise what we have achieved for these people, you and I?'

'Galdir, it all has no meaning for me now without Ancamma. Do you understand?'

'I understand, my brother.'

We rode together back up the hill, two tired men, warriors both, with an historic victory to tell our children about. Riding back to the army we stopped on the brow of the now empty hill and looked down into the valley of destruction we had created. All across the slope occupied by the Romans such a short time before, lay the carnage of their destruction. Roman bodies and dead Britons lay in their twisted, mangled death postures. Blood stained the sward and there were the sounds, so familiar to my ears, of the end of a fight. Men calling, some screaming, and then the silence in between as if the very earth was swallowing it all up.

It was then I saw Oenna's horse. It stood off to the right in the floor of the blood scored vale. Blackbirds circled overhead and the mount had its head lowered in a grazing posture but there was little grass there. My heart skipped and I scoured the plain with my eyes to see some sign of her red hair but could not locate her. Full of dread, I rode Valknir down the slope, he was tired but he always obeyed me.

'Hey where you going?' Cimbrod called after me.

I did not reply and I think he must have ridden off to where the commanders were assembling on the opposite hill. I looked from side to side on the ground as I rode. Surely, she could not have fallen from her horse? A bad fall can be fatal. I shivered as a chilly sensation gripped my neck and my heart began to beat faster as I neared Oenna's horse.

I drew closer and the scene I beheld took on a surreal quality. I felt numb. I heard nothing. Time seemed to pass me by and I seemed to function automatically. I had no feelings then, for what I saw took my mind away. I observed as if I was outside myself, for the shock of that moment was more than my mind wanted or was capable of taking in.

Oenna lay on her front and her horse nuzzled her head, the red hair splayed around her shoulders like some deep wine-coloured storm. She moved a little and I saw her fingers flex in a tiny but clear signal she was not dead. Hoping against all hope, I dismounted and came to her side. I felt a tear run down my cheek and realised I was weeping. With a gentleness borne of love, I turned her and looked at her face, searching for some sign of life and consciousness, some clue to what had befallen her.

Her eyes opened but she said nothing. I looked down at my hand supporting her under her shoulders and realised blood ran down it dripping onto the ground. She saw me and her face became animated, frowning. Her lips moved but no sound came, only blood trickled down her chin. I had nothing to say. I knew there would be no future now but I still could not master my emotions enough to do anything but look.

Presently, she coughed and whispered. I had to lean forward with my ear close to her mouth but I heard her.

'Drogo,' the whisper said.

'Drogo did this?' I said.

She looked into my eyes and I knew the truth.

'Drogo did this?' I said again for my mind had no other words. I did not know what to do. I looked around and there was no one near. I could not carry her for fear of making the injury worse and I would not leave her.

'Yes,' she whispered, 'it was Drogo, he betrayed us.' She smiled then and said, 'I told you so.'

Her whisper trailed away and I saw her eyes staring, fixed and unseeing. Her pupils dilated and filled them. I knew with certainty she had gone. I could do nothing; feeling totally numb, I sat there immobile, the dreadful knowledge of what had happened seeping into my mind. Tears ran down my cheeks dripping onto her hair. I stroked her face with my left hand and whispered to her. I cannot recall what I said but I know it was about our lost future—mine, hers and our unborn child's.

I cannot tell how long I knelt there, holding Oenna in my arms, rocking to and fro but I noticed it was dark when the pain in my legs brought me back to reality and what a reality that was. I felt the world had ended. I could see no point in doing anything. I argued with myself. I blamed my own negligence and weakness that I had not prevented her from coming to this place to die. I asked myself over and over again why this had happened but came up with no answers.

It began to rain and I still could not muster the energy or the will to move until I heard a rider approach. I did not even look up. A hand appeared on my shoulder. The gentle grip made me aware of his presence. It was Drest.

'I have been looking for you both since the end of the battle. Cimbrod said you had gone to look for Oenna and I realised something must be wrong.'

There were tears in his eyes too and his voice was thick and choked.

I had nothing to say, and perhaps the stark reality of what had happened was so obvious words were unnecessary.

'I warned her. I warned you both it was foolish for a woman to be here.'

'She accepted no warnings from either of us,' I said.

'She was ever headstrong but brave also.'

'She was murdered.'

'How do you mean?'

'Drogo did this. He must have been the traitor all along.'

'But he was a Frank, one of your own.'

'There were signs. Oenna warned me. I didn't listen and

now she lies here blood-soaked, and her spirit seeking vengeance.'

I could feel anger arising within me. It was cold anger and it fed my resolve that I had one more thing to do if it took all the rest of my life. I would kill Drogo. I would find him and put an end to his miserable life if it was the last thing I ever did. Slowly and with care I put down my beloved's body. I had difficulty standing for my legs felt numb. I could not feel even the arrow wound on my thigh, all I felt was anger.

'We must burn her body as she deserves,' I said.

'Yes,' said Drest.

We carried her between us and let the horses follow behind. Valknir would not run away and the other two followed him.

A constant thought kept running through my mind. Revenge, blood and death. It was all I could think now and I wanted to exact it somehow, even if the whole war collapsed around me and the Britons were defeated, I would avenge her death.

I knew though, Oenna had wanted her people's freedom. Deepest inside we had known that unless we had both been free of the Roman yoke, there would have been no life for either of us in Britannia. The Romans would have ruined it for us with their order and their laws. They were Roman laws not the Briton's or the German's laws. Laws making the foreign rulers superior to their conquered Brittunculi and Nudis. They had no respect for foreign cultures, and their arrogance, I was sure, would be their downfall in the end. Today they had learned that the Nudis and the Brittunculi were capable of thrashing them and I was glad of it, but I thirsted for revenge not just for the slavery I had endured from childhood to my teens, not just for Sicambra, or even the death of my mother, but now for the death of the woman I had loved.

A picture came into my mind as we carried her and it is strange the way one's mind works, for it was an image of a Roman, who had treated a slave well in my presence. It was the night when I had bragged to Lazygis about my skills at tasting wine. I could see the face of Clodius Super as he indicated how, if you treat a man as a fool, then all one accomplished was to create foolish behaviour, and I knew he was right. Had I not been a slave myself once? Treated like a fool, I had never realised rebellion was an option. Would I kill such a man too? It dawned upon me it was not every Roman I hated but perhaps certain of them. I was glad Piso was dead that was certain. I also wanted Drogo to die a slow, painful death for what he had done to Oenna and for the treachery and the way he had deceived me. I was a fool; I had accepted him because I wanted to have a fellow countryman to ride with and teach. He had pulled a curtain across my eyes and I had ignored even Oenna's warnings because of that. Even if I found him and killed him, it would not bring Oenna back to me but it would make me a man again instead of the fool I had become.

A nagging doubt tugged with incessant urgency at my sleeve though: what man was I now without Oenna?

CHAPTER XX

*"The worst pain a man can suffer: to have
insight into much and power over nothing"*
—Herodotus

Drest, Cimbrod and I burned her body when we returned to camp. Lutrin stood with us and performed some Britannic rites too tedious to mention in detail. In my country, we do not do valedictory speeches like the Romans. We fire our dead and have done with it. The finality of death is a falsehood for we believe our spirits continue in some form or another. I was sure I would see her again, and although it helped me, my bitter grief sat upon my shoulders like some brooding black crow, as I watched the flames take her.

Her body arched in the flames and her long arms flexed as the charred remains began to crumble into the dust of her pyre. I still had not understood that I had lost her. For days, I seemed to expect her to lift the flap of our tent and laugh the way she had always done, for the sheer pleasure of living.

Despite the turmoil in my mind, I managed to continue. I was able to see to the things a Warlord needs to in his army. I even attended the meeting of kings after the battle.

There is no necessity to dwell upon the council meeting. It was a long evening of drunken, heroic self-extolment as barbarian meetings always become. I recall Eddarronn, the King of the Lugi, a tribe in the far north, explaining in extended detail how he had slain a Roman Tribune and

391

devoured his cohort. It sounded as if he had done it single-handed, but I am sure others were involved too. There was then a debate on what the army should do next. The arguments went back and forth but no one supported Nechtan's suggestion that we should move south to plunder. I was certain it was unwise to leave three or four thousand Roman soldiers behind in Hexacoria, ready to attack our rear when we fought the Second Legion at Eburacum. They decided to march to Hexacoria and attack the fort there and then they would have taken the entire wall. The north was wide open as far as Eburacum and they could almost taste their spoils.

I found it hard to concentrate on what the Britons said. It had only distracted me from thoughts of my woman for a short time for guilt and remorse tortured me. I began to resolve it however, because I knew what Oenna would have wanted. I knew she was as much a part of this war as anyone there and I would continue in her name, and continue I must. I also recognised the only relief of pain for me was to try to focus on the matters at hand and I tried my best to hide my grief from these savage men with whom I had sworn to fight. I still puzzled over Drogo. I had been sure he was one of my people and I had trusted him. I thought he looked up to me and the thought he might have been a traitor all along began to nag at me like a thorn stuck in my very soul. My mind was still far away and turning over the terrible events of the day, when the chieftains began to leave. In a strange way, I regretted the end of the meeting for it would leave me alone with my thoughts. I needed company so I tried to unravel the guilt or otherwise of Drogo my fellow Frank.

'Drest,' I said, when the council meeting broke up. 'Why did you keep your spearmen away from the Roman cavalry for so long? We almost lost all our mounted warriors and the Roman cavalry would have attacked your flank.'

'You told me to.'

'Me?'

'Yes, Drogo came and told me you had changed your plan and you wanted all the spearmen in the front line. I had no idea he was a traitor then. I kept some back despite, because I could see the cavalry moving up on our flank. He said you wanted to rout them yourself and I was not to attack the cavalry'

'I told him to make certain you had them on the flank. I could see the Roman cavalry moving forward. That was why I made Odgar attack. Drogo's treachery could have cost us the battle.'

'It is all one can expect from such a man. Do you think he was always working for the Romans?'

'There was something he said before I sent him to you. I had no time to question him over it. He said Eudes was a king from south of my capital. He was in the north. If Drogo had really lived in Frankia he would never have got that wrong. It would be like forgetting your way home in daylight.'

'What about Taran?'

'Perhaps he was a spy too?' I said. I closed my eyes and could see his tearstained face as they dragged him to the water's edge.

'Two spies?' said Drest.

'No, maybe not. Perhaps Taran was only guilty of having a loose tongue. He may have told Drogo and that was how the Romans learned where we were supposed to attack.'

'But Drogo was with you all the time, even when you escaped the Roman pursuers in the forest.'

'I have often wondered about that. He was very upset at having killed two Tungrians. I assumed it was only because he was a novice. Perhaps he had sworn an oath and thought he had violated it. He may have had others to pass his information to.'

'Poor Taran. We killed the wrong man,' Drest said.

'Yes, it has an ill feel to it, does it not?'

'You know, Oenna told me she disliked Drogo. I didn't pay much attention to it at the time. When I asked her why, she could not give any good reason. It was instinctual.'

'I... I can't talk about Oenna yet, Drest.'

'I'm sorry. One day we shall. Her absence is a vast emptiness in me too.'

I could not reply. My emotions threatened to get the better of me and so I took my leave and went to find Cimbrod who was possibly the only person in the massive feast who felt as I did.

He was sitting at his tent. He had a leg of roasted mutton in his hands but he was not eating.

'Here,' he said, thrusting the meat at me.

'You should eat, my friend. There are more battles ahead and we both have to keep our strength up.'

'You eat it then. I can't. All I think about is my woman and her absence from my life. I don't want to live without her.'

'Have you talked to Hengeist?'

'Hengeist?'

'Yes, he is your blood kin. He loves you and would not see you like this any more than I want to.'

'He isn't speaking to me,' he said.

'What?'

'He is angry because we have let Drosten live and feels I

have dishonoured our family's name.'

'Perhaps now it is time to settle the score?'

'I don't feel like doing anything just now. Don't you see?'

'Cimbrod, when someone you love passes to the place where our spirits go you don't lose them entirely. I know Oenna waits for me. I am in pain just like you and I ache for her constantly, but we have to continue. We have to live the life Wuotan in his wisdom has shown us.'

'He hasn't bloody shown me anything.'

'Your eyes have been closed to it. What do you think brought you to this land? Adventure? No, it was because it is part of your destiny. It is the path the Norns have spun; the one Wuotan wants us to follow. He punishes us for diverting from that path by inflicting grief. I think that is why Oenna and my unborn son were taken away, but I feel deep inside I have much to do before the end.

'The Gods have given me strength and skill; should I abandon their chosen path because I miss my woman? She was strong and she knew life has risks. We took those risks together and it has come out against us. Should we complain about how the Gods have treated us or accept what fate brings and fight to be the men we are destined to be? Hear me my friend; moping won't bring back Oenna or An-camma. Let us share our memories and grief but let it not deter us from the true path chosen by Wuotan.'

'You're a madman,' he said and shifted uncomfortably. He was becoming more agitated as we spoke.

'No, I am right.'

'Shut up and eat the bloody mutton. I've had enough of all of you.'

'When did you first come across Drogo?'

'What?' he said.

'Drogo, when did you first meet him?'

'Why?'

'I'll tell you in a moment.'

'Well he came to me with the Tuetoni and the Marcomannii who you know.'

'And he told you what?'

'He said he had fled from Frankia and he wanted to go with us to Britannia to fight and to adventure. He seemed a nice lad even though he was a little unskilled in fighting but Hengeist liked him, so we took him along.'

'I think he could have been a Roman spy all along.'

'Why?'

'He knew a lot about my homeland but something did not ring true. I hope I find him. I owe him a long and painful death.'

'That he killed Oenna is enough to make him pay but how did he betray us?'

'He took a message to Drest which could have caused the collapse of the right flank and he said it was from me. He ran to the Romans afterwards. Oenna must have seen him try to leave with the equites. I think he heard from Taran we were attacking in the west and passed that message to his masters. I also think he is in Hexacoria right now.'

'What did the council decide?'

'They're all for attacking the remaining Romans and then moving south towards Cataractonium. I hope we find Drogo alive. I have questions.'

'Yes,' he said.

'Is he really a Frank?' I said more to myself than to Cimbrod.

'I don't know. Surely you have a better knowledge of that than I do?'

I scratched at a louse in my armpit; it had been annoying me all day. I realised I had not washed for some days. Oenna would have been disgusted with me.

'Look, I thought he was my sworn man. I didn't question him closely. I trusted the lad. When we attack Hexacoria we need to find him, he must not escape. He killed Oenna like Piso killed Ancamma and I had Taran killed because of him. Taran's death still haunts me. He was killed in a way that meant he could not reach his Otherworld. I wish I could have all that time back and make the right decisions.'

'Like you said, there is no going back Galdir,' he said.

'No, no going back.'

I proffered the mutton leg. 'Eat my friend. We need strength to fight tomorrow. By the way, you fought like a God today.'

'Like a God?'

'Truly.'

'You exaggerate. My blood was up that's all. I'm glad I killed their General though. Ancamma's death as you say was because of him. I have a bitter anger now against the Romans. I will never forget what they have done to my life.'

'Then let us fight them together. Put grief away for the time being. You have all your life to grieve, as have I.'

He said, 'I need vengeance.'

'Maybe so, but not all the Romans are responsible and maybe not all of them are bad. Vengeance gives no lasting satisfaction you know.'

'I intend to find out.'

I took my leave of him and found my own tent. I lit my fire with difficulty since it had begun to drizzle slightly and I looked up at the dark grey sky wondering if perhaps my woman looked down on me. The clouds put paid to that idea and in the end, I went to bed early with thoughts of Oenna nagging and prodding me. I slept that night but was tormented by dreams of Frankia and my home. It was as if Wuotan denied me dreams of Oenna so as to keep me focussed on my goals.

*

We took Hexacoria in three days. For an army of barbarians fighting Romans who hid behind their fortifications it was a great achievement. They fired their ballistae at us but we used screens of thick wood, and from behind those we filled in their trenches which were full of evil little wooden spikes; then we pulled down or burned through their walls. Outnumbered ten to one they had tried to parley and make peace but we had none of it. We killed every man in the place. The women and children were enslaved and sent north.

I found Drogo. I noted he was dressed as a Roman officer. He was dying from a wound in his gut and I realised with satisfaction it would be a slow and agonising death. It was not like me but I had pictures of Oenna's face in my head and it made it easy to want the worst for Drogo, if indeed that was his name. His young face grimaced as I spoke to him, for he was suffering. I was glad it would become more painful before he died and made sure no one despatched him to make his passing easier. I think I had guilt over Taran's death too and Drogo's pain assuaged it, which is a sad reflexion of the twisted emotions that vengeance fosters in a man.

He begged me for water.

'You are a traitor and you die as you deserve,' I said. I

stood between two burning houses in a wide street and the smoke wafted down towards me. He spoke, but I could not hear him so I knelt closer to him.

He grimaced through his pain and said, 'I am no traitor.'

'No? You spied for the Romans and caused the death of many of your companions. You killed Oenna. How could you?'

'I betrayed no one. I was true to my oaths. I have been working for my Emperor since before I even laid eyes on you and your barbarian scum.'

I looked at him, puzzled. I said, 'You were a Frank long before you were ever a Roman.'

'I was no Frank.'

'Who are you?'

'I grew up in Rome and my father took me along when he traded in Germany where I learned the language from the Chatti. Marcus Aurelius himself sent me to gather intelligence. My Emperor knew my name and that in itself is a greater honour than any you uncivilised people could understand. I travelled around and they ordered me to go to Britannia. Our Emperor knew Britannia was on the verge of war and he needed intelligence.'

'Pity he's dead then isn't it?'

'Commodus needed my information too. He will come and destroy you all,' he said, coughing a little blood onto his chin. I reflected the wound must have been worse than I had realised at first. I felt nothing at that. He had betrayed me. He had killed Oenna.

'How did you know all that about Chlotsuintha and Clotildis?'

'It is common enough knowledge for anyone who keeps their eyes and ears open.'

'I thought we were comrades and friends.'

He sneered through his pain and said, 'I am a loyal servant of the Emperor and have never been anything else. You barbarians are all the same. You try to raise armies and destroy the Roman way of life that has so much to offer. You can never achieve peace and order yourselves; it requires Roman law, forced upon you, to achieve either of those things. Commodus will come. He will devour you. I am only sorry I will not be there to see it. Now finish me.'

'No. You will die slowly. You killed Oenna.'

'I had no choice.'

'No? You took away all that mattered to me, including my unborn child.'

'What makes you think it was yours? These barbarians sleep with anyone they fancy.'

I knew what he was doing. He wanted to goad me enough to make me kill him.

'You killed my woman and I will not release you from this world. I want you to suffer for what you did.'

'Give me water. For the sake of humanity,' he said.

'No. Did you think about Oenna when you killed her?'

'I had no choice. She followed me away from the battle. She wouldn't go. I tried to run but she came after.'

'And so you killed her so you could escape to these Romans?'

'I had no choice. She was trying to kill me with her sword. All I did was defend myself. If you must know, I was fond of her. I never wanted to kill her.'

'Not fond enough.'

He looked up at me. He was sweating and I thought perhaps his spilled bowel was infecting him.

'No one here will end this suffering for you and no one

will give you water. Taran cannot reach the Otherworld because of you. Think on these thing as you die. I hope you have plenty of time to do so.'

I moved my head from side to side. I began to realise I was not angry with Drogo the man; he had only served his Emperor. I did not feel sorry for him though and I knew he was wrong. The Romans would not have any spare legions ready to come to this far-flung colony. They had their hands full on the Rhine and in the East. They could ill afford another front. I wondered why Drogo did not know what I did, or was he putting a brave face on his inevitable demise?

'I won't kill you nor will any man here;' I said in a loud voice so my men could hear, 'you will die slowly in pain as you deserve. You have shown you are the worst kind of man. You let Taran suffer for the crimes you committed. He died because of his careless talk but you used that to further your own spying activities. I had thought of you as a friend but you fooled me. You killed my woman. May your Gods look after you for there is no one here who will help you.'

I turned from him, and he said as I did, 'Oenna died because of your carelessness. If you hadn't brought her with you into this battle she would still be alive. It wasn't Piso's fault she died. He was just doing what any commander would have done in his place.'

I walked away. I could see no sense in killing him, although it might have given me some slight satisfaction. I felt stupid. I had trusted him and had I not taken him at face value or questioned him with greater care I would have realised he was not one of my Franks. As things stood he had duped me and I had been so ready to have one of my own near me I had swallowed the bait. He was right though. Oenna had died because of my ineptitude, even though his

401

taunting about it had been only a little spite he threw my way at his end. It hurt no less for that but I had already reasoned it all out myself, and when a man blames himself as much as I did, there is little room left for condemnation from others.

We left Hexacoria behind us burned to the ground. The men had found a quantity of silver coin and some other valuables and it seemed a satisfactory start to them. The important thing was that we had found enough supplies to carry us through the rest of the campaigning season. We marched south toward Cataractonium and the Second Legion and I looked forward to the conflict.

CHAPTER XXI

"It is not right to glory in the slain"
—Homer

I sat astride Valknir on a small hillock, pensive and watching the setting sun, thinking of Oenna. The sky was all reds and pinks, streaked with grey horizontal clouds the tops of which looked like distant mountains. I knew my grief was a form of selfishness. The dead do not experience the loss. They are gone. Grief twists us and forces emotions of guilt and blame, yet in truth it is a selfish emotion and I was aware of it. I felt sorry for myself, for my loss and the state in which I found myself. Self, self, self; that was what entered my mind and I resolved to shed my grief—at least for the time being and get on with the business of life and war. There was more in life than wallowing in self-pity. I think I grew up at that moment.

I recalled how Cornelius had always said a red sunset heralded a clear day on the morrow. I smiled a wan smile as I recalled how once he had berated me for my poor performance when we had been training. I pictured how he had laughed at me when he had tripped me flat on my face as I overbalanced thrusting a Roman short sword at him. My smile faded as soon as it had come for I pictured him lying on that straw palette when he died, his face blue and his tongue hanging out of the side of his mouth. I shuddered. I was not able to keep the bad thoughts away and however

403

hard I tried such things kept pursuing me.

Dismounting I walked Valknir down the hill, talking gently to him. He followed with a meek tread as if it had been an uneventful day and he had been on a stroll in the countryside; he seemed unperturbed by the battle we had just fought. I picked my way among the fallen, and reflected upon how these bodies lay. It is a strange thing when men die in battle, their bodies do not find a natural posture. Some lay with their limbs twisted at strange angles while others lay with their heads turned that bit too much to one side for life still to be lingering. I stopped at one Roman corpse. The face was familiar.

Clodius Super had fallen beneath his horse as it had died, a spear embedded in its chest. I could see how the cold and lifeless body of the horse still trapped his leg beneath it. He must have tried to continue fighting for a Votadini warrior lay close to his head with the Roman's gladius projecting from his rib cage. Someone else must have finished off the Tribune with an axe. He had a wound almost splitting his chest in two, but his face looked calm, which I thought was odd at first. I remembered him as a decent fellow—for a Roman— and such was a rarity in my estimation.

While I stared at him, it occurred to me my hatred for these people was not a simple all-encompassing abhorrence. There were still some Romans I did not hate and I supposed it meant it was their actions and policies I found so distasteful. True, I grieved with constant bitterness for Oenna and blamed the Romans for that pain, but I blamed myself too and the more I did, the less hard I was on Drogo the Roman spy who killed her.

I knelt for a moment at the body and reached out for an object glinting in the fading sunlight, almost obscured by

Super's lifeless form. It was a dagger, its silver scabbard encrusted with rhinestones and the hilt bound with copper wire. It was no fabulous weapon, but when I drew it from the sheath there was a cold blue reflection of the dying embers of the day as if the sun still peeped at me from the horizon. The blade was an unusual shape. It began parallel-sided then tapered in a gentle curve for ten inches towards a viciously pointed tip on one side. On the pommel was a Roman God's head. I don't know which deity it was, but it was made of gold, hammered into the copper. It was a well-balanced weapon and I put it in my belt. It would serve to remind me of one of the few Romans I had respected. I saw no others I recognised.

There was something sad about the battlefield, not because of the dead, but because of the finality of that moment. All around me lay the rack and ruin of the slaughter. So many dead, and for what? Greed? Vengeance? This field so recently occupied by the Second Legion, now littered with dead, was all that remained of a once proud and arrogant army. It seemed to me then to be all foolishness.

I had fought all my adult life in battles. Hand-to-hand combat had been the mainstay of my daily existence for over ten years. It was as if I had sprinted through all that time, never stopping to reflect upon the nature of what I had become. I was a killer and the violence of my life was visited upon me and my own throughout. I wished I could have been a more peaceful man; one who raised cattle perhaps, or a trader, or almost anything where I did not have all those I loved taken from me in violence. I was not becoming used to the brutality; that was the trouble. I was becoming more sensitised to it instead, and every death I caused and every loved one I lost made the futility of my violent life starker and more palpable.

With my head down, I began to make my way towards the Briton camp. Cimbrod was waiting for me. He needed my support and I thought he and I were the only ones suffering in this massive army of celebrating barbarians.

I heard an approaching horse to my left and turned my head.

'Lazygis?' I said.

'Galdir. Well met.'

'Where have you been? I lost sight of you after I left you with the Romans that night.'

'Yes, Piso sent us south and we had instructions to skirt your forces and to join him at Hexacoria.'

'But you didn't.'

'No, my brother, I didn't.'

'Piso was destroyed with all his men.'

'I know. It was a great battle. Like the one you fought here.'

'We outnumbered them two to one you know.'

'For a barbarian army, that is still a great achievement. I wish I could have raised our Sarmatian banner in your ranks but I think you understand why we did not. We saw it all from the hill over there,' he said pointing to the west.

'How did you find me?'

He laughed, but his voice was more serious, 'I simply looked for a battlefield filled with dead Romans and I knew where you would be. It is as if war follows you wherever you go my friend.'

'What will you do now?'

'My men are tired of being lackeys to the Romans. They would never break their oaths but they do not have to go south to join the remaining Romans now. Piso has gone and no one knows about us.'

'So?'

'We will move west. There is a place near the wall where Panador and I have a mind to settle. There are wide green places where we can raise horses and you know I have a woman. She has friends there and if we do not cause trouble to the Scotti I think we can live in peace.'

'Can you live in a farmhouse?'

'All things are possible. You may recall how when we first met it was Ayma who baulked at sleeping in a tent; it was not me. I can sleep almost anywhere these days.'

'But there are no Sarmatians who can live in houses. You told me that yourself. You said you could only be yourself in a wagon or under an awning.'

'Galdir, people change. When will you learn that? You have changed too. You have a woman now and you thirst no longer for the fires of your fine hall and the Franks whom you found after your sojourn in Rome.'

'It has all changed for me. Oenna is dead; killed by the Romans along with my unborn child. There is nothing left for me now in this damp, cold place. I may return home after all.'

'Home? You don't have a home. If you return as the War-lord, the Romans will carry out their threat or at the very least, you will have a war on your hands. What kind of war that would be when you have no warriors I cannot guess. The Romans do not forget. They write things down and pass it on to generations beneath them. You surely realise you cannot go home. It would make a mockery of our oaths and the reason why we are here in Britannia.'

'Lazygis I...' I said.

There were deep emotions stirring in me and I had no

words left. He dismounted and embraced me. I had a vivid picture in my head of Cimbrod after Adelmar's death when I had supported him in a similar way. I did not blubber. I did not weep, as I wanted to except deep inside. I preserved the illusion that is manliness although I think Lazygis would have understood if I had betrayed that pride. All the same, I chose not to give vent to my feelings.

The embrace was brief.

I said, 'I wish you luck and happiness. I hope your new woman is fertile and kind and that your first child is a masculine one, my brother.'

He drew back from me and looked into my eyes.

'Galdir, we cannot replace those people we have lost in our past. We owe them a duty however. We owe it to them to carry on and to make the most of every moment that Pan and Ma have given us. There is no more precious gift from the Gods than life and we owe it to ourselves too, to be true to that. I will make a life here because there is no other option for me and I will love it. I will love my new wife as I loved Ayma and I think it will make her spirit glad to see it. Your grief is mine and I will always feel what you do, as a friend, but I must change. A wise man said to me once that it is better to bend in the wind of change than to fracture like some old broken tree. We none of us has the privilege of being able to change those things that have happened. Accept what has gone before and learn from it my friend. You have become a great leader among these people and I am sure they know it. Continue to lead them. Make them strong as we Sarmatians were never able to become. Unite them and defy those Roman bastards. Move on. It is all we have in life and by Ma I will do so for the sake of my dead family. I will make a life I am proud of when I do join Ayma and Panogaris.'

We stood then in silence. I had nothing to say to my friend. I knew he was right but it was too soon for me to take in what he was telling me. I still had a flame of vengeance burning within me and I wanted the Romans gone. I wanted them to be out of Britannia and knew there was also much left to do to cement the Britons into one nation. There was however a kernel of thought that my friend had sewn in me. I could do this and I wanted to do it too for Oenna. I could bring them all together for I had learned in Germany how the Romans divide and conquer and our childish fighting with each other had been their best means of defeating us. I missed Oenna, but I owed it to her memory to stay and do what I could to build alliances here, at least for a time.

'I must go,' Lazygis said.

'Will you not come with me and drink a last horn of beer or wine if we can find some?'

'Panador is waiting just over that rise.'

'Bring him too. If you are with me, then no one will challenge you.'

So it was the three of us rode through the Briton camp as if we were victorious leaders, and the men greeted us with loud acclaim. We rode past them and men stood, cheered, and waved their battle-spoils and booty. Apart from the dagger taken from Super, I had nothing. True, I would get my share of the silver taken from the Legion's pay chest but I had not stopped to loot other bodies. I was the Warlord after all.

We entered Cataractonium as the light faded. There were fires burning here and there and a massive blaze lit in the town square. Cimbrod was easy to find for he and Hengeist had buried their differences, and although they kept themselves to themselves, they were still with the leaders. I found the Briton Kings in the General's villa. Their men had ransacked the place but they had lit a fire in the hearth and food had been prepared, laid out on the General's table in the peristylium. I saw Marcomir on the other side of the garden. He and the other mercenaries were gorging themselves and staggering. I knew I did not need to disturb them. They would soon be incapable of social behaviour in any case. They were Germans after all.

Cimbrod approached when he saw me.

'Who's this?' he said.

'This is Lazygis, my Sarmatian friend. I told you about him.'

'Yes, of course. Welcome. If you are a friend of Galdir's then I am your friend too. Hengeist,' he called over his shoulder and we made our introductions. We ate and drank together and talked about the battle. Lazygis was able to give us information about the remaining Roman forces and it seemed the only remaining legion in Britannia was in the far south near Londinium. I thought it unlikely they would march north after what we had done here so we had the whole of the north in our grasp. Our victory had been complete. My job now was to keep the army together if indeed we were to march south and finish the task we had begun.

When we had eaten and drunk our fill from the Legate's stores Lazygis made to leave and it was with deep sorrow I realised I might not see him again.

I walked with the Sarmatians towards where they had tethered their horses and Cimbrod and Hengeist came too. As we crossed the square, I noticed a crowd of men and heard a familiar voice. It was like a prick from a thorn, a sudden reminder of unfinished business. It was Drosten.

We crossed to see what was causing such a stir amidst the revelling warriors. My jaw dropped when I saw what was unfolding. There were thirty or so drunken warriors standing to one side of a huge fire. The yellow light reflected from their eyes, their faces contorted in a bestial fashion. They were calling out and holding up arm rings and jewellery.

The object of their attention was a woman. They had stripped her naked and her hands were tied behind her. Drosten stood before the crowd holding a halter fastened about her neck. Caked, dry blood obscured one side of her face and her cheeks were streaked by tears running down towards her chin. Her black hair hung in straggles, matted with dried blood on her forehead. The beautiful face looked swollen and bruised. A fresh cut on her lower lip stood out in glaring testimony to the abuse she had suffered, but there was no mistaking those bewitching green eyes for they had fire in them still. It was Lucia. My heart leapt.

'Not enough' he said, 'this is a high-born Roman filly. You can't mount her for less than a sword's weight in gold.'

A man came forward; he was a tall heavily built dark man in braccae with blue painted skin and a huge barrel chest. In one hand he held his battle axe and in the other a leather bag. He put the bag down in front of Drosten.

'Mine,' he said in a deep baritone.

'Still not enough,' laughed Drosten. 'Who has more? Just look at these titties.'

He reached behind and pulled Lucia to him, fondling her breasts. She spat a mouthful of blood and spittle in his face and he struck her open-handed across the face. She fell to the ground and remained on all fours whimpering, exposed, violated and beaten before this audience of leering warriors.

I could stand it no more and pushed through the crowd. The time had come. It was not love or a wish for revenge pushing me; it was the same anger I felt when I killed Piso's father all those years before in Rome. I would not allow this to continue and unreasoning and illogical as it seemed, I was determined to act.

I stood in front of Drosten trembling with rage and he scowled at me.

'You want a piece of this? You can go to the back of the queue.' He looked up at his audience sneering, 'Germans come last.'

It raised a laugh from one or two of the watching men, but I knew what I was about, temper or no temper.

'Drosten, I will take the woman. I defeated you once with no weapons. Think what I can do to you with a sword in my hands. Now give her to me.'

Lucia looked up in my direction. Her eyes opened wide for she recognised me. A look of relief came over her face and I knew she trusted me to protect her.

The big man with the axe was standing next to me on my left. He half turned and with his left fist struck me a blow in the face. It caught me by complete surprise and caused a shower of sparks to appear in my brain. The punch almost took me off my feet despite my size. He raised his axe above his head and amidst the swirling colours filling my vision, I was dimly aware of the snarl on his face. Had I been fully aware, I would have feared for my life but the blow he had struck me left me dazed. I closed my eyes to try to clear my head.

The blow never landed. When I opened my eyes I saw the big man stagger backward with an arrow in his chest;

dead centre it was. He was dead before he hit the ground. It was a Sarmatian arrow. I stood tottering, shaking my head to clear it.

Drosten had backed away dragging his victim by the halter. I drew my sword but the crowd was becoming uglier by the second, and it was only because my companions on horseback had encircled me they did not attack. They knew Cimbrod for the swordsman he was and at least one of the assembled men had seen him fight at Insi Orc. He dismounted and turned towards Drosten. There was a cold rage expressed in his face.

'Drosten,' he said, dismounting, his voice cold and even, 'you killed my brother, prepare to die.'

'Nechtan will have your head if you touch me,' he said, head up, thrusting his chin forwards. 'He ruled on that matter long ago. It is settled. This has nothing to do with you.'

'Oh, but it does. You took my brother's head and I will take yours.'

He turned to the scowling faces around us, kept at bay for the moment by our drawn weapons.

'Is it not law among you? Do I not have the right to kill this man in return for his murder of my brother? No weregeld was paid. He refused to pay when I asked him for it. I have a right, before the Gods, I have a right.'

Doubt appeared on some of the faces around us and I realised these Britons recognised he spoke truthfully. They backed away and stood a few yards from us as if curious to see what would transpire. I knew what was about to happen. Silence fell. I heard Lucia whimper. I wanted to go to her but Drosten pulled on the thong around her neck and choked off the sound. I wanted him dead. He released his battle-axe from his belt and let go of Lucia's halter. He smiled grimly and approached Cimbrod. There was murder in his eyes. I had to let this happen; this fight was Cimbrod's right of revenge. It angered me all the same. Had he not killed Piso and now I thought he was taking Drosten too. In my jealousy, I felt he had left me nothing but to witness the greatness of his sword skills. There he stood, ready and dangerous; sword against axe, speed against reach and power. In the light of the fluttering flames the two men faced each other in silence. There would be blood soon, I knew it, but whose?

CHAPTER XXII

The crowded warriors were silent as they formed a half-circle to give the two men space. The flickering light from the bonfire cast a golden iridescence on the cobbles of the Roman town square and I hear a faint scream from somewhere off to my right, a woman's voice, though whether it was pain, pleasure or anguish I could not say.

Drosten stood still for a moment then began to circle. His axe had a point at the tip and the blade was double edged. He swung his long-handled weapon above his head and stepped forward with the blade moving horizontally. He brought it down with a diagonal sweep that would have cloven my friend in two had it struck him.

Cimbrod anticipated the blow well. He side-stepped to his right at the last moment. I felt he was lucky for had the blow landed differently it could easily have caught him. He sidled to his right, circling. Drosten followed through and turned with the axe, bringing it round in a circle. Cimbrod seemed to have known that was going to happen too. He side-stepped again.

Drosten was a big man and very strong. He was quick too and I knew that although he was no great swordsman, he had skill with an axe. He stood still looking at his adversary as if puzzled. He was working out how to get close. Drosten was no fool either.

I noticed, like in Insi Orc, my mouth was dry and my heart was beating fast. Sweat trickled down my forehead despite a chill breeze gracing the evening. I willed Cimbrod to strike but he stood for all the world like a statue, sword in hand waiting. He smiled and said something I did not catch. I saw Drosten frown. His face began to redden so deeply we could see it even in the firelight. He charged. He moved his axe with fantastic speed thrusting the steel point at Cimbrod's face. My friend parried with his sword, almost casual. Drosten turned full circle. The axe followed. It was then the fight changed. Cimbrod parried the blow again with his sword. The axe blade struck it with a loud clang. To my horror, it fractured. Cimbrod stepped back. He held the hilt of his sword. He had only six inches of blade remaining. I shook my head. I had to intervene. I was about to step forward but Hengeist drew me back.

He said in a low voice, 'Don't interfere Galdir. It isn't finished yet. Trust him, there are none like him. Even if Cimbrod dies, I will kill Drosten. It is my duty not yours.'

I looked at him and understood. Cimbrod was, as Hengeist said, not finished yet. I was about to throw him my sword but that was when he moved. I had never seen such speed in a fight. He stepped towards Drosten. Before the Caledonian could raise his axe Cimbrod buried the shard of his sword in Drosten's left arm and stepped away. The big man howled. He reached for the hilt projecting from his arm. Cimbrod knew this would happen. He moved fast again and kicked hard at Drosten's right hand. The axe fell to the ground with a clatter. The two faced each other unarmed. Drosten went for the weapon. Cimbrod kicked him full in the face and retrieved the axe as fast as the snapping jaws of a wolf. The balance had changed again and Drosten picked himself up clutching his wounded arm.

He turned, keeping an eye on my friend.

'Give me a weapon, brothers,' he cried, 'give me an axe.'

The onlookers were silent and perhaps because no one had rearmed Cimbrod when his sword broke, or whether it was because Drosten had enemies in the crowd, no one moved.

Cimbrod said, 'You took my brother's head. You sneaked up on him and hewed his head from his neck. Now it is your turn.'

'Please, I'll pay you the weregeld.'

Cimbrod approached slowly. He said, 'Too late. Too little.'

Drosten, who had been backing away, fell to his knees, 'Please. I must live.'

With a speed surprising us all, Cimbrod swung the axe. Drosten's head flew from his shoulders and landed yards away. His headless body remained upright, kneeling before Cimbrod as regular spurts of blood jetted, ever weaker into the night air, shiny and black in the firelight as it ran in rivulets down the dead torso. The body seemed to pause for a moment or two, then slumped forward.

Cimbrod crossed to his horse and mounted. Perhaps he felt safer there. I looked at the crowd and some were still scowling. Crossing to Lucia who had watched the whole thing with wide eyes, I cut her bonds and helped her to her feet. I removed my cloak, wrapped her in it and supported her to Valknir. I had to mount first and Hengeist helped her climb up behind me.

The onlookers were muttering. Presently, a man said, 'Hey, you can't have her. She's not yours.'

There were about thirty of them and they approached with drawn weapons. Their intentions were clear. I heard a voice off to the right.

'What is happening here?'

I looked and saw Nechtan walking fast with his bodyguard around him. He looked down at Drosten's body. I could see the anger and grief appearing. Was it not a familiar feeling to me too?

'Who did this?'

'It was them,' a voice said from the crowd. 'They killed him for that Roman whore.'

Nechtan looked up at us. 'I warned you what would happen if you took vengeance against my friend.'

'It was a fair fight. It was in line with your laws.'

Nechtan turned to his bodyguards.

He drew his great battle sword and said, 'Kill them all.'

We did not wait for the outcome. As the crowd surged forward we turned our horses and rode with what speed we could muster away to the town wall. There was great clamour as we left the enraged Caledonii warriors behind, but there was no pursuit and I assumed it was because there was no one sober enough to mount a horse in Cataractonium. I felt good for the first time in weeks.

We escaped through the gates and rode south, across the battlefield. When we had gained the Roman road, we continued for an hour or so then stopped to rest. Lucia was faint from shock and exhaustion and almost fell from Valknir's back. Hengeist helped her down. She did not speak and I realised it was because of what she must have been through. She had escaped certain rape and probable death, and however resilient she might have been it could not be borne without a price.

Hengeist had some spare leggings and Cimbrod a tunic, so we dressed her in those. She did not object but said nothing. She was shaking and pale and I realised she could not journey far.

'I can't go back now,' Cimbrod said.

'No I suppose not,' I said.

'I told you not to underestimate my brother,' Hengeist said, 'did you see how far that pig's head flew?'

'Hengeist,' I said, 'pigs don't fly.'

'This one did.' He laughed and I realised Drosten's death had released him. He had his honour back and he could get on with his life again.

'It was a good fight,' Lazygis said. 'What will you all do now?'

'I don't know. If I go back, there will be trouble over this. I have been trying to delay that fight for months.'

'Perhaps you could come with Panador and me? You could settle down as a farmer,' Lazygis grinned when he said this. He knew me well enough to anticipate my reply.

'No. Not for me. I have to take Lucia back to the Romans. It will mean travelling to Londinium. They will overrun Eburacum in a day or two. We can't stay there either.'

'Hengeist and I will travel with you,' said Cimbrod. 'We are going home. There is nothing left for us here.'

'How will you get there?' I asked.

'When we came, we had forty men, each boat had twenty. Small crews, but the boats were not big ones. With only two of us, we cannot sail all the way home. If we get to Gaul we can travel by land. It's slower but possible.'

'If you go now, you won't have the gold you wanted to take back,' I said.

'I have gold. Did you not see me acquire it?'

'Where?'

'I picked it up after I took Drosten's head. Lazygis kindly deprived the owner of his life when he was about to expose your brains to the fresh air and I hefted his leather bag.'

He reached up to his saddle and took down the leather bag. He undid the thong closing its neck. Inside was a collection of gold objects, jewellery and some Roman gold coins. Cimbrod gave me a handful of the coins.

'I want you to have this. You never paid me for killing Horsa but I think us sword-brothers should stick together. Don't you?'

'Thanks. I have nothing else and I too have a long journey ahead. I have to get Lucia to Londinium without being caught.'

'No one is looking for you Galdir,' Lazygis said. 'You are not so famous; they even think you were dead. Anyway, the Roman records will show you died in battle. Choose a new name and I'm sure no one will suspect who you are, especially with a Roman general's wife in tow.'

I bade farewell to Lazygis and also Panador, who had said little throughout. I often wondered whether he blamed me for being in Britannia. In a way, he would have been right, for it was my defeat that led to the Sarmatians becoming auxiliaries in the first place. The last thing Lazygis said to me was, 'I hope you awake one night with nail marks on your back my friend, but be careful though that they are not from more incisive weapons.'

They rode silently into the night and I never saw Lazygis again. I did hear he settled in the north-west and his plans of breeding horses were realised. I felt a pang as he disappeared into the dark. I had loved him as a brother for years and he had been the one to teach me how to shoot a bow from horseback. He had taught me more than that. I had learned from him that there are barbarians as noble and intelligent as any Roman. I also learned how shared grief is halved. I recognised he had given me much. His support when we had arrived in Britannia had been the saving of me. The memories of the past we had shared and the laughter we had fostered, brought me through the early part of my time in Britannia. Without it, I would have been driven mad.

'We will have to move on, Galdir,' Hengeist said.

'Yes, we need a horse for Lucia.'

Lucia looked up then and came to my side.

'No, let me ride with you, Galdir,' she said, her voice low and plaintive. It was the first time she had spoken since we had stopped.

'Why?' I said. 'It will slow us down and they may send people after us in the morning.'

'Please,' she said. There were tears in her clear green eyes.

'Maybe for tonight but in a day or so we will have to find you a horse. Valknir is strong but he can't go all the way to Londinium with two people on his back.'

She leaned towards me and I put an arm around her and drew her in. It was not a sexual movement; it was a gesture of comfort. Grief for Oenna was still fresh in me so this was no betrayal. This was a woman with whom I had once been infatuated. Saving her made me feel good. I suspected that after the trauma she had undergone she needed some kind of human contact, as I did. She for her part clung to me as if I was her only source of comfort.

We mounted up, and I said, as Lucia put her arms about my waist, 'Where to, Cimbrod?'

'Eburacum. It is the next Roman town here in the north

and it's the biggest. It is a large port and we can obtain supplies. I need a sword.'

'Yes,' I said. 'Hope it's better than the one you broke against that axe.'

We headed south for another two hours and then made camp, such as it was. We had only a little dried fruit Hengeist produced from his saddlebags and we ate that and drank water from a stream nearby. I slept holding Lucia for she would not leave my side and it was a reunion neither of us would ever have predicted. She never needed me before. When I had made love to her, in the Sarmatian camp, it had been a bit of rough fun for her and I was only a temporary diversion at a time when she used my attraction for her as protection. This night, she cried in her sleep and held tightly on to me whenever she awoke. I cuddled her in and stroked her hair. I must admit I felt like crying too; my heart ached and I kept wishing deep down, it was my Oenna whose body lay so close to mine in the dark. I thought Lucia would recover but it was as if she was some other person, weak and dependant. Where was the Lucia I remembered?

Sleepless for the most part, I thought deeper about it and I knew that in Cataractonium she had lost hope. She had been alone among fierce and violent barbarian people and a woman like her, however strong and independent she was by nature, had come face to face with the inevitability of violation and death. What such treatment would do to her I could not guess even though I knew her character was tough and independent. I only knew she needed me now and perhaps I could help her heal the scars of that night. It was a contradiction in terms for I needed her too; my grief needed some kind of expression. I held her in my arms in the night as one might a child awakened by a nightmare, yet I thought of Oenna and what I had almost had and what I had lost, coming here to this cold miserable land that was no longer as green and pleasant as I had once seen it.

I searched my heart for a glimpse of the future and nothing came into my mind. Where were my dreams? Where were the portents that might help me see the future? There were none. Chlotsuintha did not come to me, Livia did not lace my dreams; all became black before my eyes as sleep came.

CHAPTER XXIII

"The test of any man lies in action"
—Pindar

Most physical hurts heal in time; mental ills are a different matter. There is no accounting for the strength of the human spirit though. Such courage dwells within us all and in some it can only be temporarily subdued even in the face of disasters that would destroy many of us completely. On the journey south, I began to recognise the resilience Lucia had in spirit and mind.

After travelling the whole of the next day, we made camp by a stream, high up where we could see the road below us and any approaching Briton raiding parties. Lucia sat apart looking towards a copse of beech trees, their leaves fresh and green, trembling on a gentle breeze in the failing rays of last light. Hengeist and Cimbrod sat in silence around the little fire and an aura of gloom seemed to have descended upon us all It was as if the violence and its sudden cessation had taken something out of us all and left us empty and grief-struck.

I approached Lucia and sat beside her. She was weeping, and she looked up at me as I sat down. Neither of us spoke, words unnecessary in the approaching gloom, both of us in pain. We saw a scene unfold before us then that turned her around and I have often thought of it since, for it changed me too, at least Lucia's interpretation changed me.

We heard the sudden sounds of a chase and the scream of a hare attacked in the field below us. A fox was after it. We both stood, perhaps out of curiosity. It was a small fox, perhaps a yearling, and its russet fur and white tail bobbed in the long grass as it chased its prey. The hare, all brown leaps and bounds, fled towards us. It moved fast, zigzagging as it ran, but the fox was quick too and its blood was up. It intercepted the hare and turned its head with snarling, ravening fangs. It bit. The hare rolled and tried to stand. The fox was on top in a flash of red fur. The bestial violence of it teeth and quivering muzzle spelled certain death. I wished him a good feast, but with a suddenness that surprised, the hare fought back. It was unnatural, but I swear it was so. That brown runner bent its hind legs and scrabbled with them hard and furious. Its front legs boxed and struck. The claws bit into the predator. The fox tried to get a hold on its victim, but without success. It stopped with a loud abrupt yelp and leapt away. The hare for its part struggled to its feet and stood looking at the fox. I realised it was a small fox and a large hare, but all the same it was a surprising outcome for it should have spelled certain death for the hare.

It was probably a male fox and the hare's scouring claws must have found its genitals, a sensitive area for us all. The pain of the fox would have been considerable for it turned and slunk away as if it had learned a lesson and the victorious hare turned its gaze towards us, erect, swivelling on its hind legs. It stared. It remained thus for a minute at least, then turned and limping, made its way towards the wooded slopes below us.

'Oh Galdir,' Lucia said, 'it is a sign from Ceres.'

'How do you know that?'

'Ceres is the Goddess of the earth and growing and living

425

things. She has sent me this sign. What we witnessed was a message.'

'What do you mean?'

'That rabbit was attacked and going to die. It fought for its life and lived. It carried on with life. It is a sign I should too.'

'Poor Lucia,' I said, 'it was a hare not a rabbit, but it may well have been a sign. I'm not very good at interpreting these things myself, but if you choose to see it that way perhaps it tells you to fight. Of course it might just mean men's genitals are sensitive.'

'Yes,' she said, suddenly thoughtful with no trace of a smile upon her full, red, bruised lips.

'You know he's dead, don't you?'

'Who?'

'Your husband. I saw his body.'

'The Britons made sure I knew that. The one with the red hair, who Cimbrod killed, kept telling me how he had killed him himself, when he raped me.'

'He didn't...' I stopped myself then for there was no need for her to know who had killed Piso.

'He did. When he had done that, he wanted to sell me to those other brutes.'

Tears appeared in her eyes. And I put my arm around her for comfort. She began to sob.

'I tried to fight him off. I scratched and bit but he took me anyway. I am glad he died.'

'Lucia, don't think about it.'

'I must. I will fight like that rab... hare. I will survive. Say you will take me home Galdir. Take me home.'

'I... I will consider it,' I said. I would have said anything to comfort her then but I had no real intention of returning to Rome, I had always hated the place.

I looked at her. The tears ran down her bruised and cut face leaving long marks in the grime, like spears pointing at her throat, and I marvelled at her self-possession. Her eyes had become set and I knew she meant it. It was only a scene of a hare and a fox, yet it had given her something material to hang on to. I decided not to discourage her. It was as if her spirit needed something to use, something that would give her back her strength. Perhaps it was indeed a sign from the Gods, but which Gods? There seemed to be three groups of deities to choose from: mine, Lucia's and Oenna's. The triangle of beliefs seemed incongruous and I wondered then whether all religions might be the same in their basis and the spirit world the same for us all.

We sat thus for a long time in the gloaming. Darkness descended and Hengeist lit a fire although he had nothing left to eat. There was little we could do apart from try to keep warm around the little blaze. Lucia went to the stream. I could hear the sound of her bathing. The water must have been icy but I understood it was symbolic to her after what she had been through at Drosten's hands. I spat at the fire when I thought of him and a picture of Adelmar's smiling face came into my head. I thought with regret how I could have been a better friend to him. I should have known Drosten meant his threats in his jealousy over Ancamma. I knew Drosten had not loved her, and that made killing Adelmar doubly senseless, for Drosten was involved with Nechtan. I concluded in the end it was only the fierce honour of these strange Caledonii that had driven him to it. Whether he had a taste for men or not, he had regarded Ancamma as his chattel and our arrival spoiled his plans. It all seemed so meaningless in the scheme of things but I was glad he died without a sword in his hand. It meant I would never see him again.

'Galdir?' Cimbrod said.

'What?'

'What do we do when we reach Eburacum tomorrow?'

'I thought you were going to either find a boat there or travel south with me.'

'I can't go home feeling like this. I feel as if I have lost everything that mattered to me. There is nothing for a man to do in Cimbria; it was what drove me to come here. I had no idea then, that all I would find was pain.'

'You've changed since that day when I killed Horsa. You were only a boy then. Perhaps the pain you feel will make you stronger since you have survived it all in the end.'

'I... I'm not sure I want to have survived it. I have lost my brothers and now Ancamma. There is nothing left for me.'

'Cimbrod,' Hengeist said, 'I am here with you.'

Cimbrod smiled, 'Yes my brother, you are all that survives of us now. Two out of seven. How can we face our father now?'

Hengeist said, 'Our father is not the sensitive individual you seem to think he is. There is his daughter Birgit for a start. She always was the apple of his eye and our two younger brothers always had his attention more than we did. He has not been left without issue. He knew we could all have died but he did not wish to stop us. I don't think he will blame you. He is more likely to blame the Gods and he will honour our brothers' memory. The bards will sing songs of your battles and I will join them in that, Cimbrod. You always were the best of us, my brother.'

'You have other brothers?' I said.

'Yes, they are twins. Our father favours them for he loves

his new wife and they resemble their mother. He always says it is because they are young and need more from him but we know he loves them more than he does us. It was another of the reasons we came here.'

'So you thought you would rise in his affections if you returned with gold and stories of heroic battles, did you?'

'Something like that,' Cimbrod said, looking down at the ground.

Lucia Interrupted us. She had cleaned the blood and grime from her face and the swelling was receding. Her eyes glinted in the firelight for it was dark now and a canopy of stars looked down upon our sad little group.

'When we get to Eburacum, I have friends there,' she said. 'If you will protect me on the way home I can reward you well for what you did. I am very wealthy now. Half my husband's estate will pass to me and I can easily repay you all in gold. I want Galdir to come because I would not feel safe with anyone else beside me. I owe you two my life also. If you had not slain that animal with the red hair I dare not think of what would have become of me. All Rome will honour the three of you.'

'They would kill us for the rebels we are,' Hengeist said.

'How would they know?' she said.

'Isn't it obvious?'

'You look no different from Galdir. Who could say you were not riding with the Sarmatians?'

'She is right,' I said. 'The Romans only recorded our numbers, they couldn't record our names. There were no Romans who could even say the Sarmatian's names, let alone write them down, so they simply had a head count when we came. I'm sure you will both be safe posing as Sarmatian cavalrymen.'

'But we don't have their gear, and our horses have no armour,' Hengeist said.

'Mine does and for all anyone knows you had to change mounts after the battle. Besides, no one will talk to you since you don't speak Latin. Let me do the talking and we will be fine,' I said.

Lucia sat down. She had changed. Only one day before, she had been tied and haltered in Cataractonium's market square. Tonight, she seemed determined to hide her pain. It seemed as if she had buried her feelings deep within but I wondered if they would emerge somehow in some other form.

'After I return you to Rome, I must go home,' I said.

'And what will you do there? Become a farmer?'

'No I am still Warlord.'

'Warlord of what?' she said.

'The Franks of course. They need me.'

'Did you really think that when Marcus Aurelius died all would be forgotten? You are so naive it amazes me. The state of your people is recorded and sanctioned by the Senate. Your home has been annexed, Galdir. Only an Emperor can change their situation and the Senate has to ratify that declaration. You are playing a dangerous game with the lives of your people. If you are discovered trying to set yourself up a as a returning leader your nation will go the way of the Sarmatians and the Chatti. You can't go home.'

'So it was all a waste of time?'

'No, I know the Emperor well, we grew up together. He is a wastrel but eventually he may listen if I put it to him in the right way at the right time. He cares more for sport and fighting than he does for politics, believe me. It was one reason why my husband was never brought back to Rome when Aurelius died.'

Cimbrod said, 'I don't understand you. Only hours ago you were like some whimpering damaged maiden. Now you talk of power and wealth as if it were your daily bread.'

Her eyes flashed in the firelight. She cast Cimbrod a withering glance and said, 'I am a Roman woman. Throughout the foundation of the Empire they brought us up to be strong. Our men have died for the glory that is Rome and we have stood behind them and fought our battles too. Not with weapons, but with mental strife, with determination. Our Gods stand behind us in their turn and make us what we are today, a proud nation. The power of Rome is not concentrated in the men. They lack the subtlety of women. We survive and we drive the men-folk. We give them the ideas that have made Rome great even though they think women are poor creatures who have no rights. We don't need to vote, we influence our men to vote correctly. We make things happen, but quietly, unrecognised and unsung.'

Cimbrod regarded her with disbelief in his eyes. I could see a smile begin to appear, but it vanished almost as soon as it had begun and he said, 'You may be right about Roman women. I do not know. I can see a strength in you I had underestimated. If Hengeist is willing we could modify our plans and accompany you some of the way. We are in no particular hurry to return to the boredom of home. What say you Hengeist?'

Hengeist did not reply at first, he looked long and deep into the fire and seemed to weigh his words carefully.

He said, 'It seems to me we are at a fork in the road of our destinies. Returning home without Adelmar and the others holds nothing for me but shame. Boior always said I should have protected Adelmar, but I was not there for him when Drosten killed him. I would rather it had been me that had died, to be honest. To travel on to an unknown future will take more courage perhaps than I can muster at this time but seems to me to be the right road. I will sleep on this and tell you my answer in the morning.'

'You would go home alone?' Cimbrod said.

'Returning home was the plan yesterday, but you seem to change your mind so often I can hardly follow your thoughts in this.'

'Look my friends, I may have to go to Rome now. If what Lucia says is true then I have little other option.' I turned to Lucia and said, 'I do not doubt your words, but returning to Rome is the last thing I would have wanted. It was where I grew up, but my upbringing was not like yours, with privilege and wealth. I was a slave. You didn't know that did you?'

'I had guessed that long ago from what you said when we were together with the Sarmatians. You think I am so stupid I didn't read between the lines of your explanations?'

'You knew?'

'Yes, I also surmised you might be the same man who escaped after Marcus' father was murdered. You must think I'm stupid.'

'I didn't realise. You don't seem perturbed by that possibility then?' I said.

'Marcus is dead. His only surviving relative is his brother Lucius. Lucius will only inherit part of the estate, and as far as I know he is in complete ignorance of the whole matter. He is such a dull boy he will never make the connection even if you call yourself by the same Roman name. No one would know apart from me and I have no reason to tell. You saved my life and I will never forget that.'

'So we go to Londinium?' I said.

'No, she said, 'To Eburacum. As I said, I have friends there. You can hardly expect me to travel dressed like this? I need food and clothes and a horse. If you stay as my body-guards until Rome you will be rewarded.'

'You are a strange woman,' Cimbrod said. 'One minute you are helpless and a victim and in a few hours you become the leader, telling us where to go and what to do.'

'She's Roman. Aren't all Romans like that?' Hengeist said.

She said, 'Perhaps, but I know now what I must do. Galdir stays with me anyway, don't you?'

'I promised I would see you safely on the road home and I have nothing now to stay for. I believed in the Britons' cause at one time but after Oenna's death there is little for me here.'

We were all silent, deep in thought. A new road had opened up before me. I began to think it might be possible to do as Lucia had determined. It was true what she said about the Romans and their laws. She knew all about how to turn things around for my people. If I returned home and fought the armies of Rome, I knew there was little chance of success. She was right, of course, and I came to a realisation that all that had occurred in Britannia was only the Gods' way of making things happen for the Franks and for me. Chlotsuintha had always been right. Oenna, giving me the courage and will to fight, Piso's death, my grief - it was all a means to an end. Finding and saving Lucia was clearly as strong evidence of the Gods' machinations as the little scene with the rabbit and the fox; it was evidence of my destiny too. Chlotsuintha had told me about that so often, it re-quired little on my part now to see it.

If I was to fulfil the destiny that had been revealed to me all those years before, it was clear I had to return to Rome and somehow use Lucia to bring about a change in policy towards my people. Had I not said it myself when I had addressed Marcus Aurelius? The words had come from nowhere at the time, as if the land itself spoke through me. I had puzzled often on how that had come about, for I have never been an eloquent man despite my Roman education. Had I not said that one day the Romans would need us as allies? I had even promised that if he spared my people we would be friends and defenders of Rome. For all those things to come about I had to master my grief; I had to become the man who had spoken so fluently and eruditely to the Roman Emperor after the battle of Sicambra. I knew Lucia would be a formidable ally; after all, she acknowledged she owed me her life, but she seemed to change by the minute as Cimbrod had said and I wondered how long I could rely on her feelings of indebtedness to me.

I could return to the victorious Britons in the north and no doubt would be able to live there despite the death of Nechtan's 'friend' Drosten. I also knew there would be war between Drest and the Caledonii if I did return and it all seemed pointless. Nechtan would never forgive me for the death of his friend. It seemed there was only one road for me now, but I gained great comfort from my companions' willingness to follow me. Cimbrod would in time feel less pain. Grief never goes, it only attenuates. I had found that with the passage of time, I thought less about Livia's death, but when I did, it was acute and rubbed me as raw as the day Sartorius killed her. I knew also my grief for Medana's death and that of Cornelius, had assuaged itself and I hoped losing Oenna would also hurt less often.

I could not escape the feeling it meant I was shallow and had no capacity for true and lasting emotional attachment, but I excused myself, for I had never had the chance of forming such lasting bonds with another human being in my life. Ripped away from my murdered mother, I had lost everyone I loved in such a short time, yet I knew I had truly loved these people who had made me into the person I had become. I had no inclination to end my life. I had not reached such a low ebb and perhaps it was the hope of a future, saving and leading my people, that kept me going. Whether this was so or not, only the Norns, who weave men's futures could have said, but I recognised how all that had gone before had been there to strengthen me and not to reduce me.

I would go to Rome. I would continue the fight, but it had now to be a fight without weapons. It would be a fight with words and the arts and science of politics for which I was untrained and unprepared. I had the will to win and Lucia was my ally. Could I do it? Although doubt whispered at my shoulder, it was a call I had no choice but to answer.

AUTHOR'S NOTE

Of course the characters in this story are fictitious but some of the details are historically correct. Historians acknowledge that around the year 180 AD the Northern Scots tribes did overrun Hadrian's Wall and no details of what went on afterwards appear in recorded history. It is equally true that the Scots held their position for almost twenty years before being bought off and The Wall returned to Roman hands.

The references to the Celtic customs, religion and culture are, as far as my research went, accurate though I must confess to having made up characters' names, because it is not clear in these pre-Pictish times whether male or female names ended in 'a' or any other syllable. There were no Celtic written records at that time, after all. The Picts, so often described in historical fiction, did not appear at this time as they only became a real entity much later. Many of the place names are accurate as far as I can ascertain.

The Cimbrii were a real nation who came from northern Denmark. They were seafaring folk and were doughty warriors. References to the Scots using the type of military tactics referred to in this book are made up. It was the Saxons who developed short swords (seax) and that was much later. Some tribes in Germania (Chatti) did however style themselves along Roman military lines but that is mentioned in another book, not this one.

I hope you enjoyed Galdir's sojourn in Scotland. The premise is that a determined man will succeed whatever calamities are set in his path by fate.

In Galdir III you will find out what he manages to achieve in Rome. Will he win through?

I'm not telling!

ALSO BY FREDRIK NATH FROM
FINGERPRESS:

THE CYCLIST

A World War II Drama

"Brilliantly executed... Nath's biggest success is the sustained
atmospheric tension that he creates somewhat effortlessly."
-LittleInterpretations.com

"A haunting and bittersweet novel that stays with you long
after the final chapter—always the sign of a really well-
written and praiseworthy story. It would also make an
excellent screenplay."
-Historical Novels Review—Editor's Choice, Feb 2011

www.fingerpress.co.uk/the-cyclist

FAREWELL BERGERAC

A Wartime Tale of Love, Loss and Redemption

François Dufy, alcoholic and alone, is dragged into the war effort when he rescues a young Jewish girl from the Nazi Security Police.

Then the British drop supplies and a beautiful SOE agent whom Dufy falls in love with. But as the invaders hunt down the partisans in the deep, crisp woodland, nothing works out as Dufy had hoped.

www.fingerpress.co.uk/farewell-bergerac

GALDIR: REBEL OF THE NORTH

Barbarian Warlord Saga, Volume II

A dark tale of Celtic mysticism, grief and battle.

Forced to serve the Roman Emperor as an auxiliary
commander of cavalry on Hadrian's Wall, Galdir faces
increasingly fierce attacks from hostile Celtic tribes north of
the Wall.

www.fingerpress.co.uk/galdir-rebel-north